THE MAGIC PORTAL #1
THE DAWN OF TIME

AN UNOFFICIAL GRAPHIC NOVEL FOR MINECRAFTERS

CARA J. STEVENS

ILLUSTRATED BY SAM NEEDHAM

SKY PONY PRESS
New York

Sky Pony Press books may be purchased in bulk at special discounts for sales promotion, corporate gifts, fund-raising, or educational purposes. Special editions can also be created to specifications. For details, contact the Special Sales Department, Sky Pony Press, 307 West 36th Street, 11th Floor, New York, NY 10018 or info@skyhorsepublishing.com.

Sky Pony® is a registered trademark of Skyhorse Publishing, Inc.®, a Delaware corporation.

Visit our website at www.skyponypress.com.

10 9 8 7 6 5 4 3 2 1

Library of Congress Cataloging-in-Publication Data is available on file.

Cover design by Brian Peterson
Cover and interior art by Sam Needham

Print ISBN: 978-1-5107-6660-0
Ebook ISBN: 978-1-5107-7081-2

Printed in China

#1

THE MAGIC PORTAL
THE DAWN OF TIME

INTRODUCTION

Long, long ago, the realms were created and creatures (called mobs) began to roam the land, sea, air, and dark spaces. It was a developing world full of new challenges for innocent creatures discovering their place in the realm.

Time passed, and eventually people arrived. Villagers and miners became the rulers of all the realms and used many of the creatures for their own purposes. Mobs who could be tamed became pets or food. Mobs who could not became enemies.

Our story begins in a realm where teams have formed and games take up young miners' every waking hour and replay in their dreams each night. While the miners all play against each other, they also have a common enemy: hostile mobs. Creatures are always getting in the way of the games, destroying the playing fields, interrupting Capture the Flag, and putting their lives in danger.

As our story begins, one girl at the bottom of her squad has set out to prove her value to her team. She has made a deal with a village of mysterious traders to help her get rid of the peskiest mobs once and for all.

CHAPTER 1
THE GAME

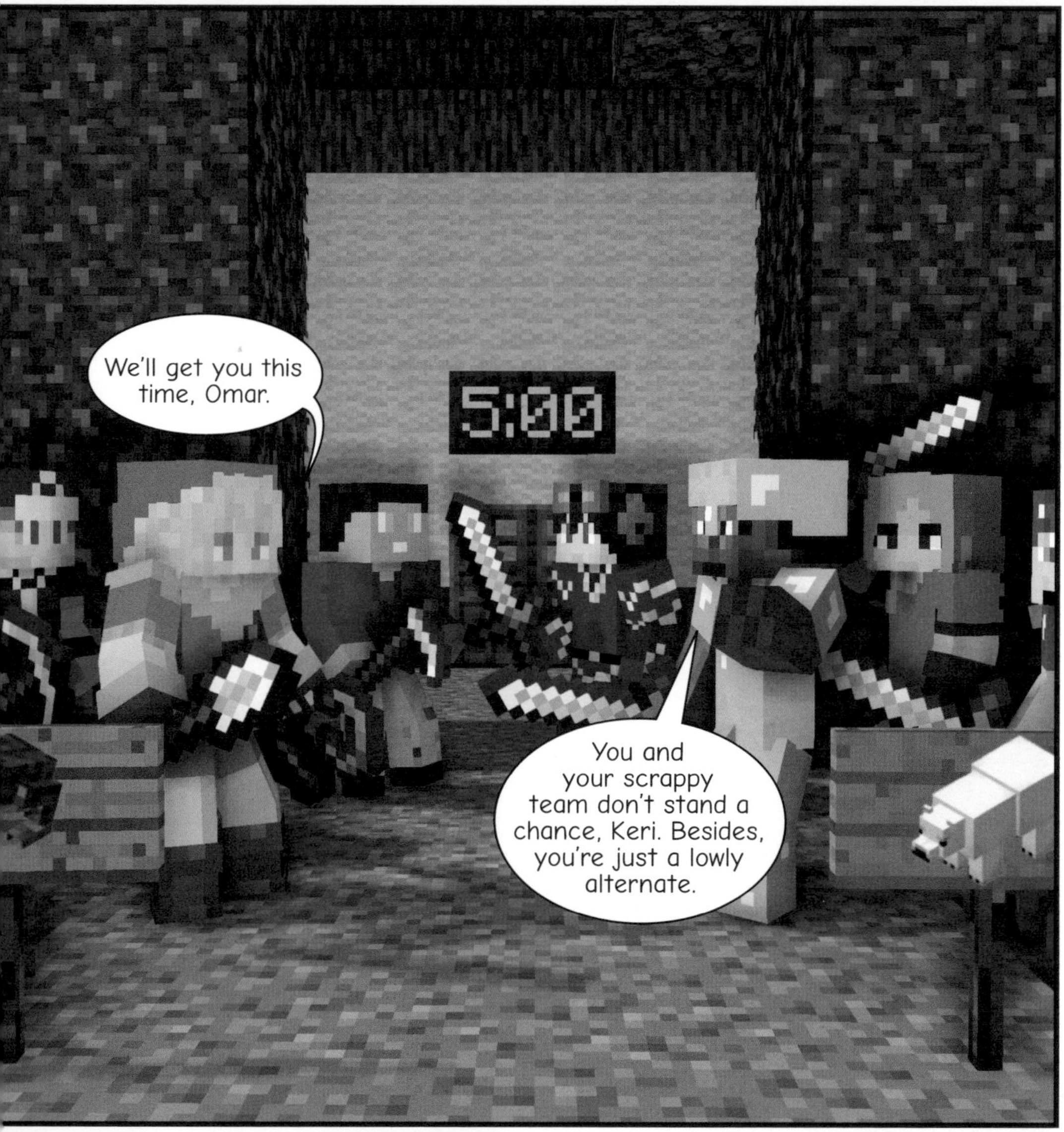
We'll get you this time, Omar.
5:00
You and your scrappy team don't stand a chance, Keri. Besides, you're just a lowly alternate.

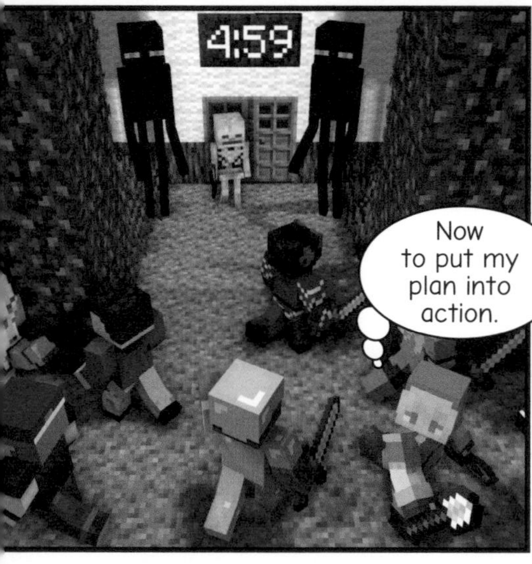
4:59
Now to put my plan into action.

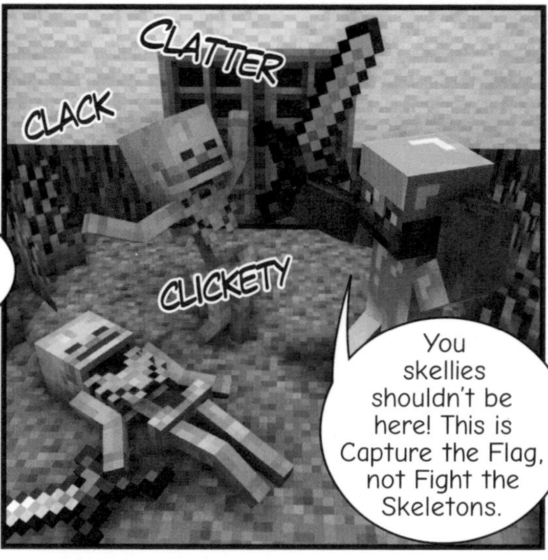
CLATTER
CLACK
CLICKETY
You skellies shouldn't be here! This is Capture the Flag, not Fight the Skeletons.

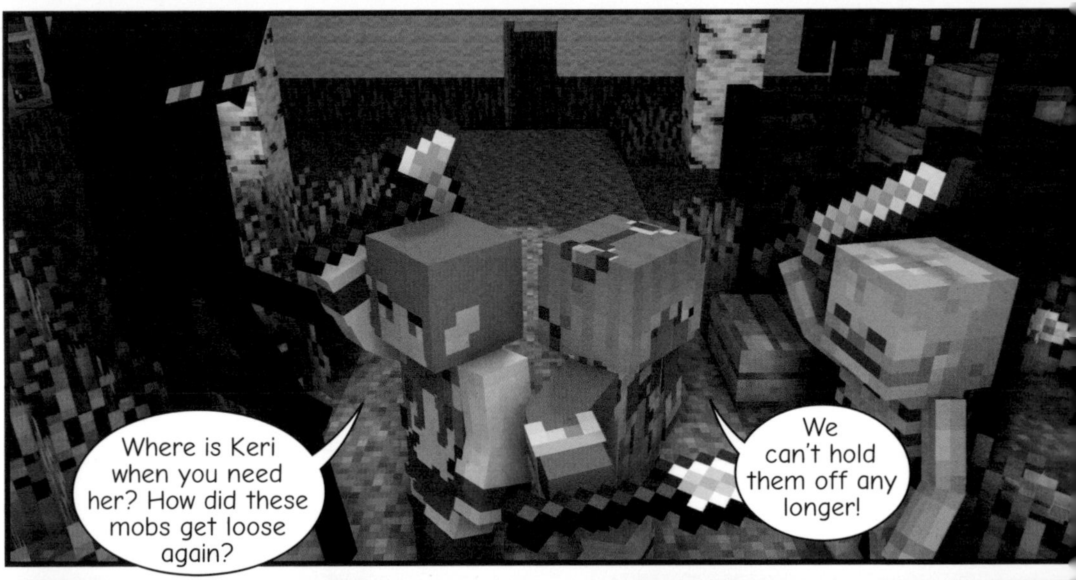
Where is Keri when you need her? How did these mobs get loose again?
We can't hold them off any longer!
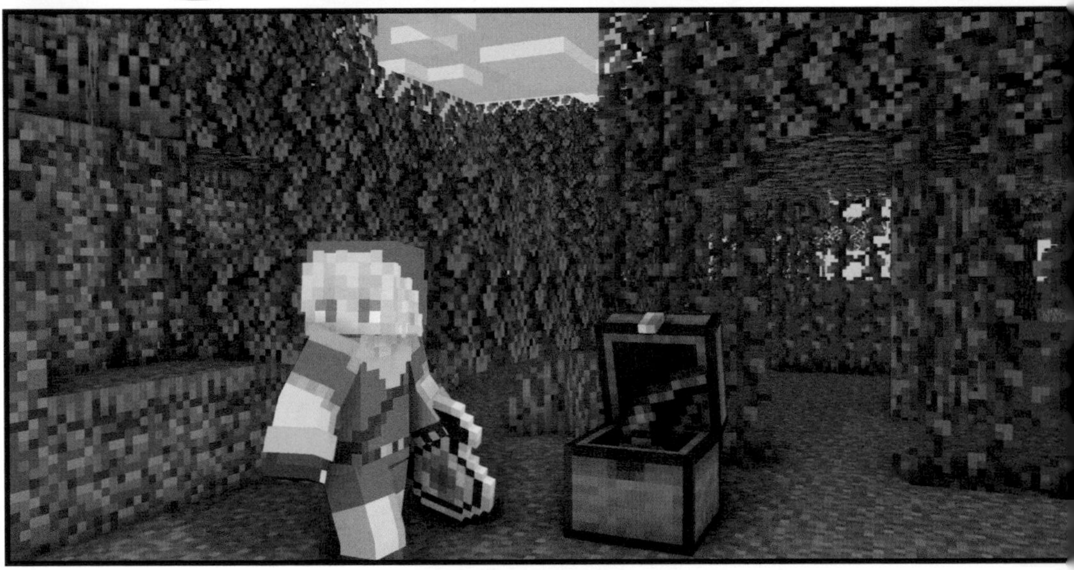
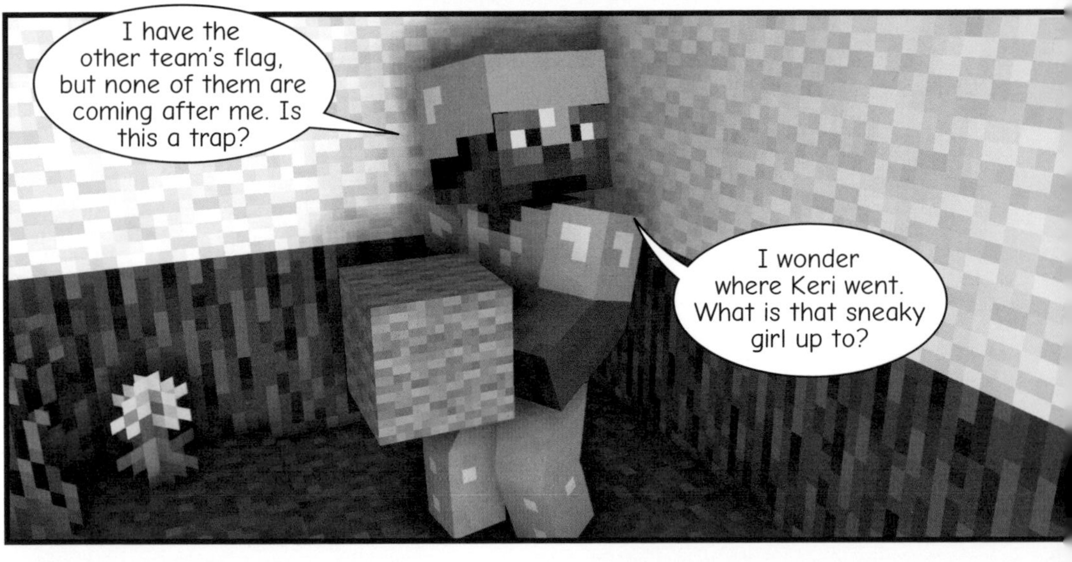
I have the other team's flag, but none of them are coming after me. Is this a trap?
I wonder where Keri went. What is that sneaky girl up to?

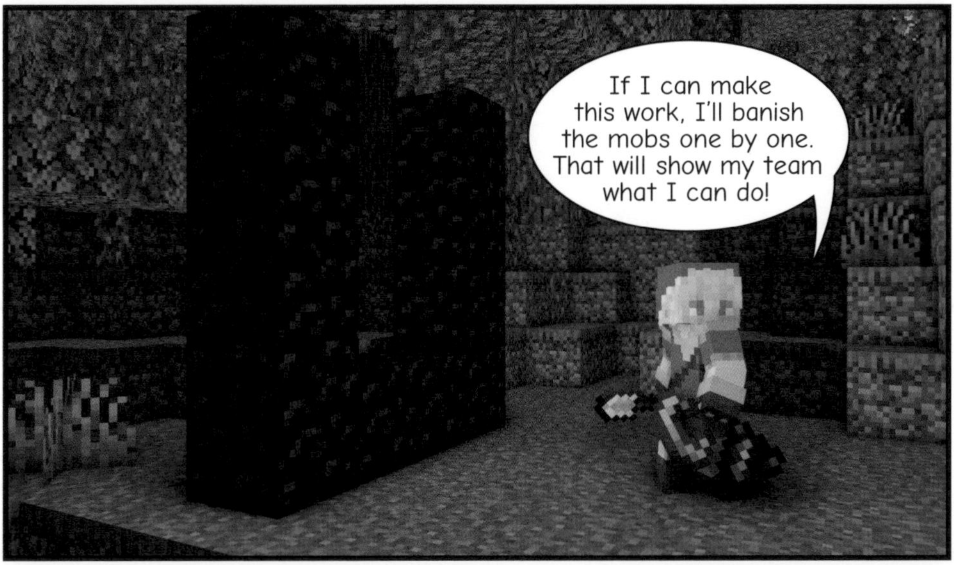
If I can make this work, I'll banish the mobs one by one. That will show my team what I can do!

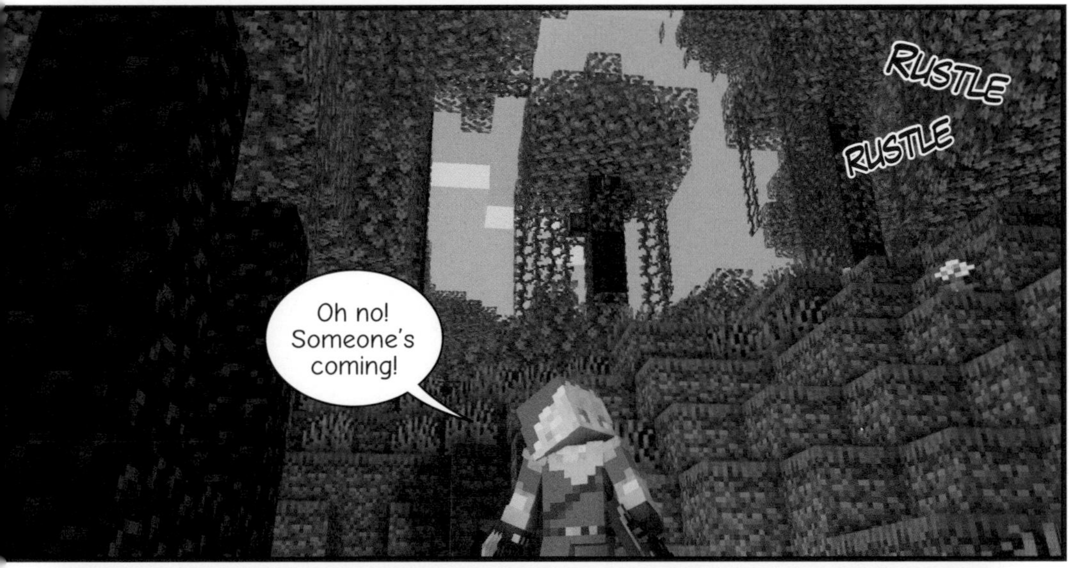
RUSTLE
RUSTLE
Oh no! Someone's coming!

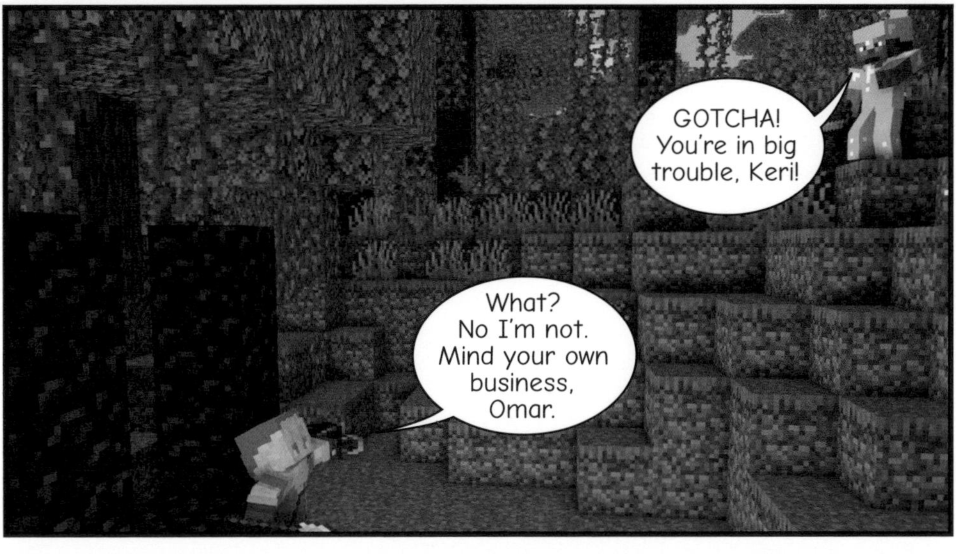
GOTCHA! You're in big trouble, Keri!
What? No I'm not. Mind your own business, Omar.

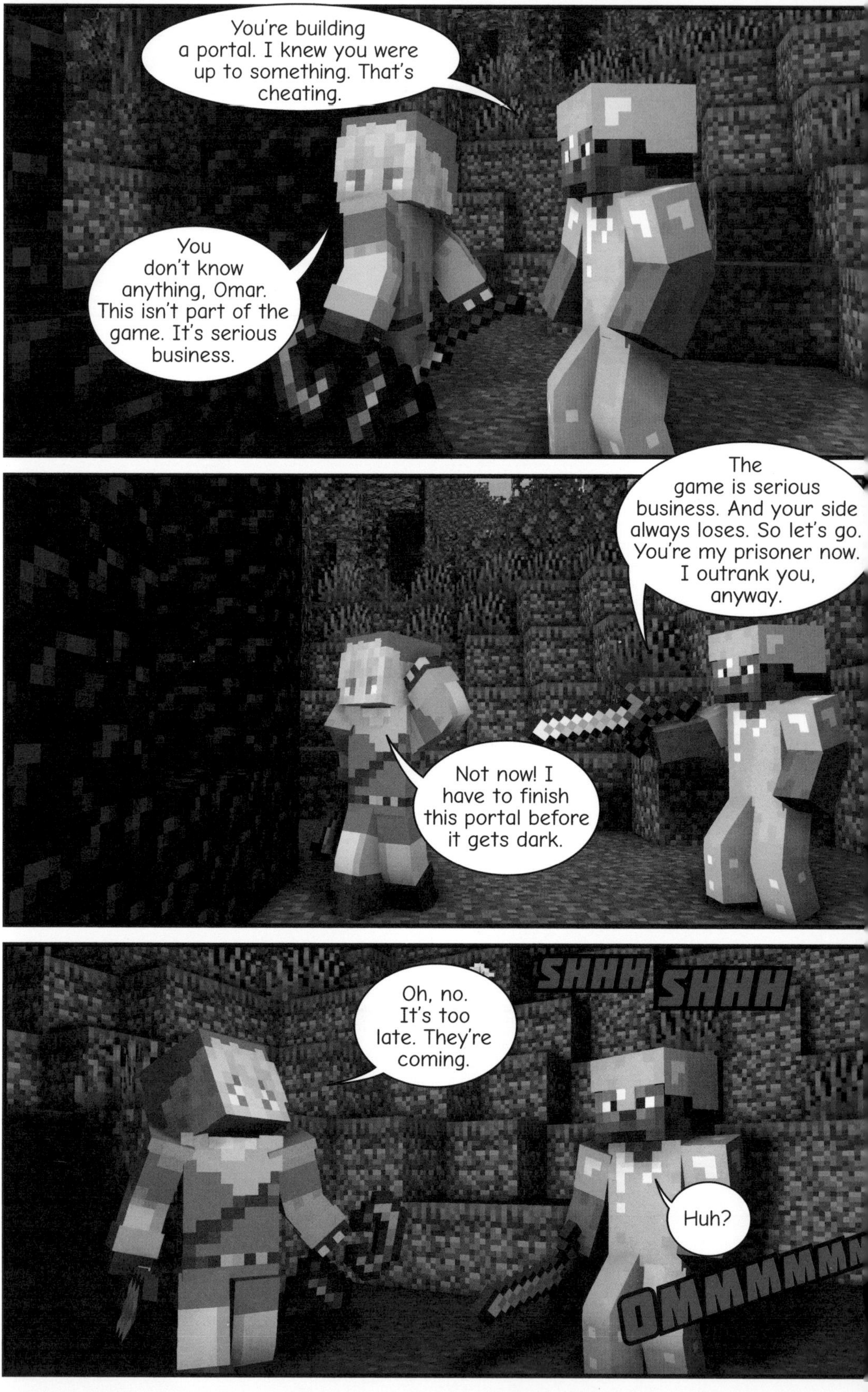
You're building a portal. I knew you were up to something. That's cheating.
You don't know anything, Omar. This isn't part of the game. It's serious business.
The game is serious business. And your side always loses. So let's go. You're my prisoner now. I outrank you, anyway.
Not now! I have to finish this portal before it gets dark.
SHHH SHHH
Oh, no. It's too late. They're coming.
Huh?
OMMMMM

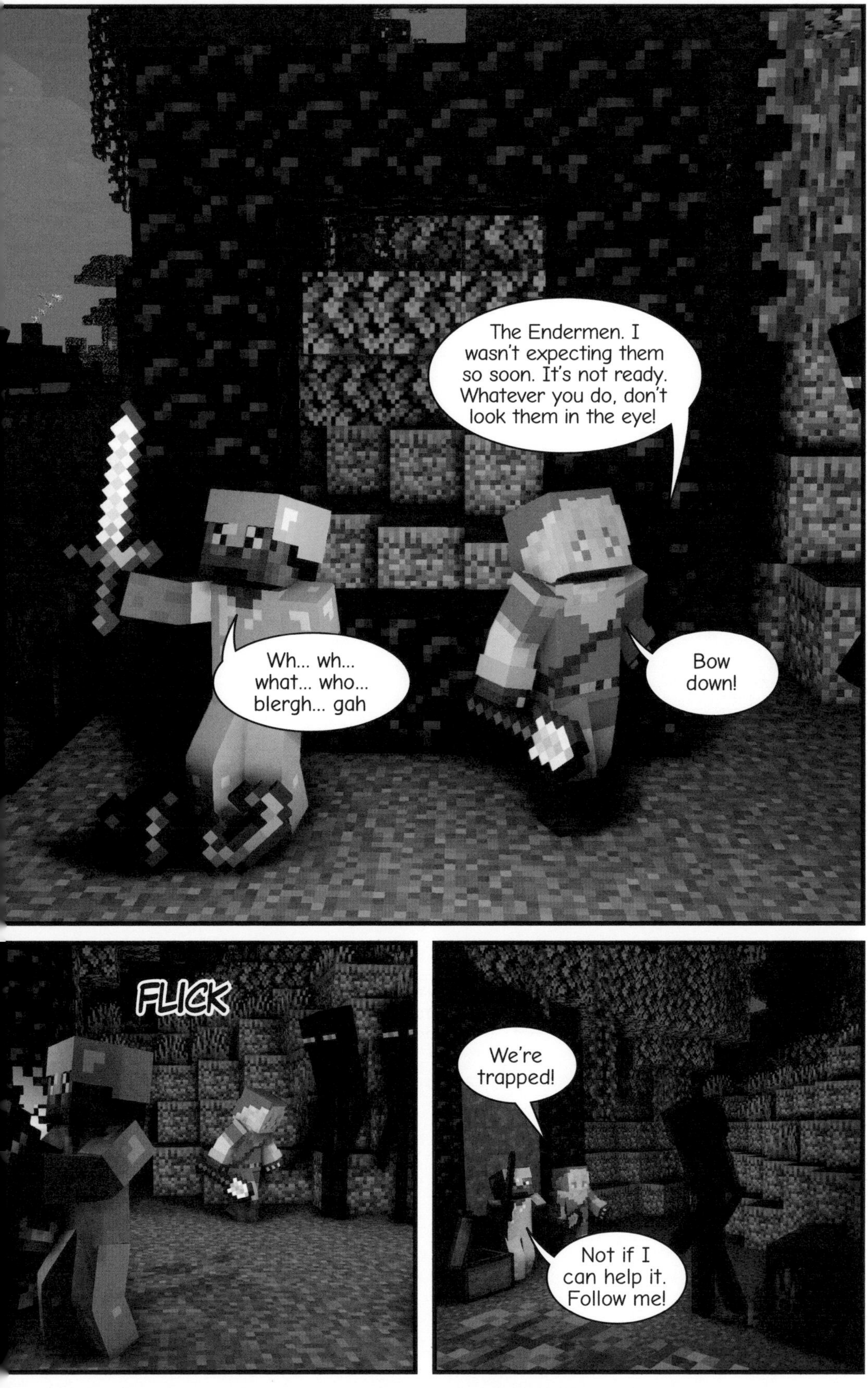
The Endermen. I wasn't expecting them so soon. It's not ready. Whatever you do, don't look them in the eye!
Wh... wh... what... who... blergh... gah
Bow down!
FLICK
We're trapped!
Not if I can help it. Follow me!

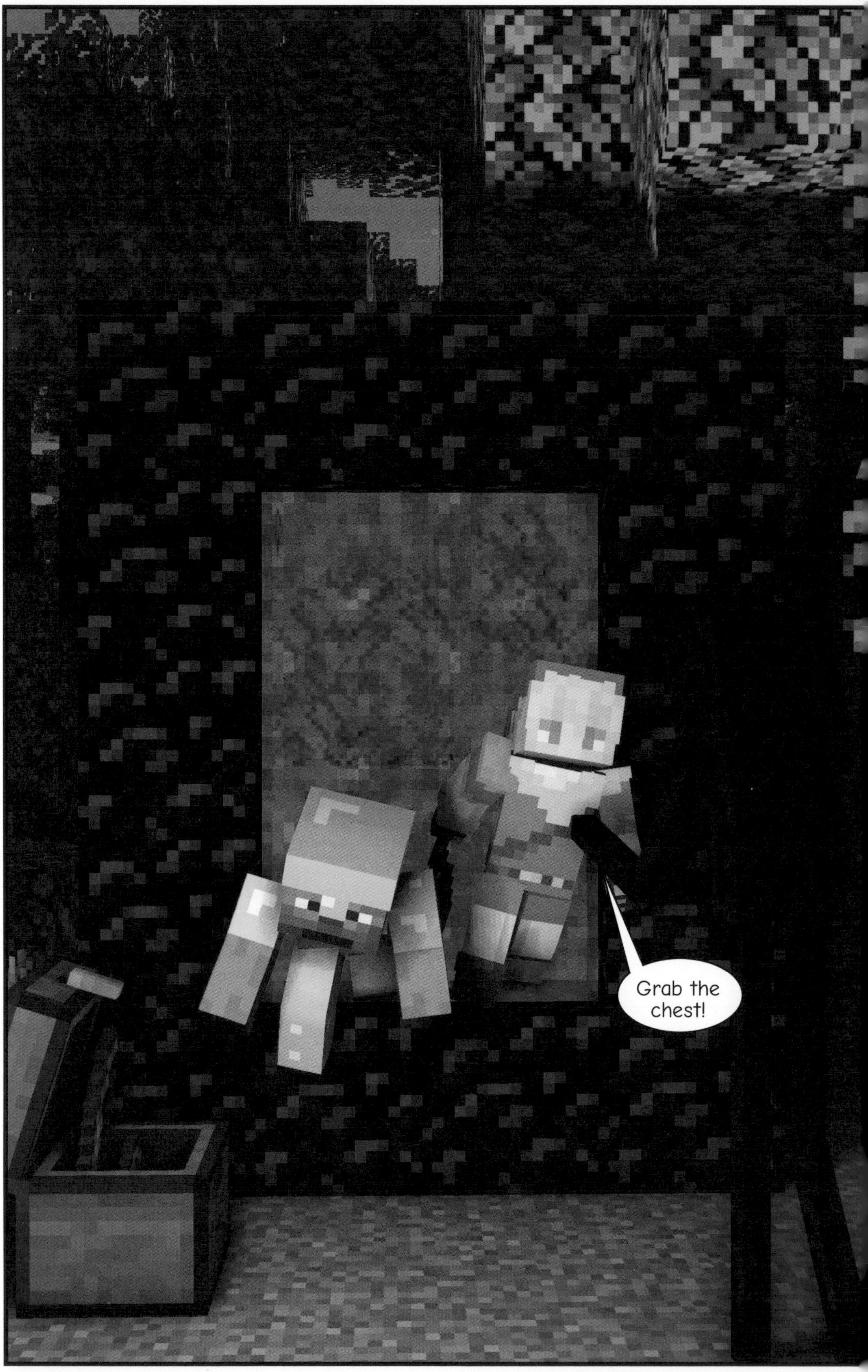
Grab the chest!

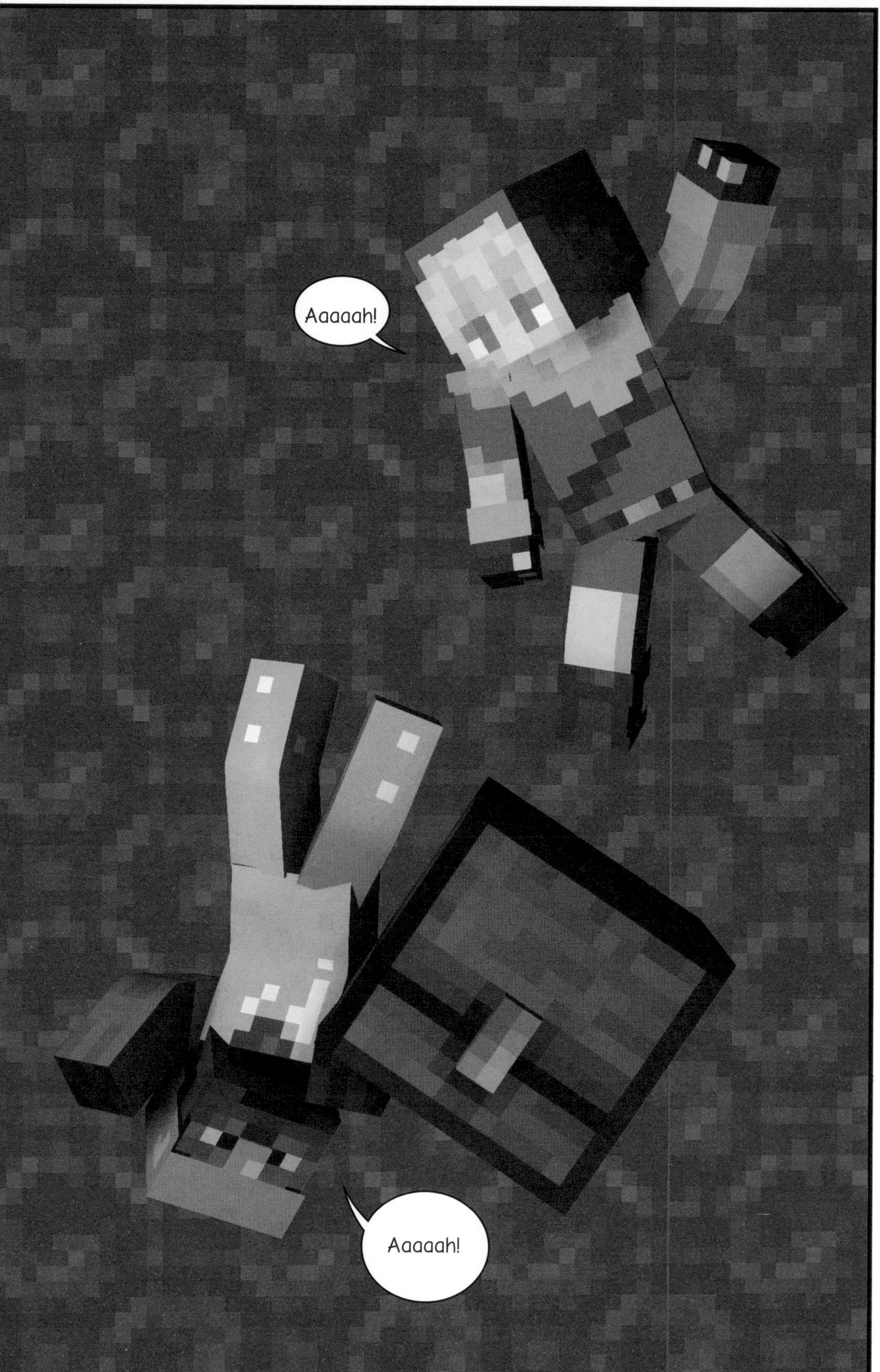
Aaaaah!
Aaaaah!

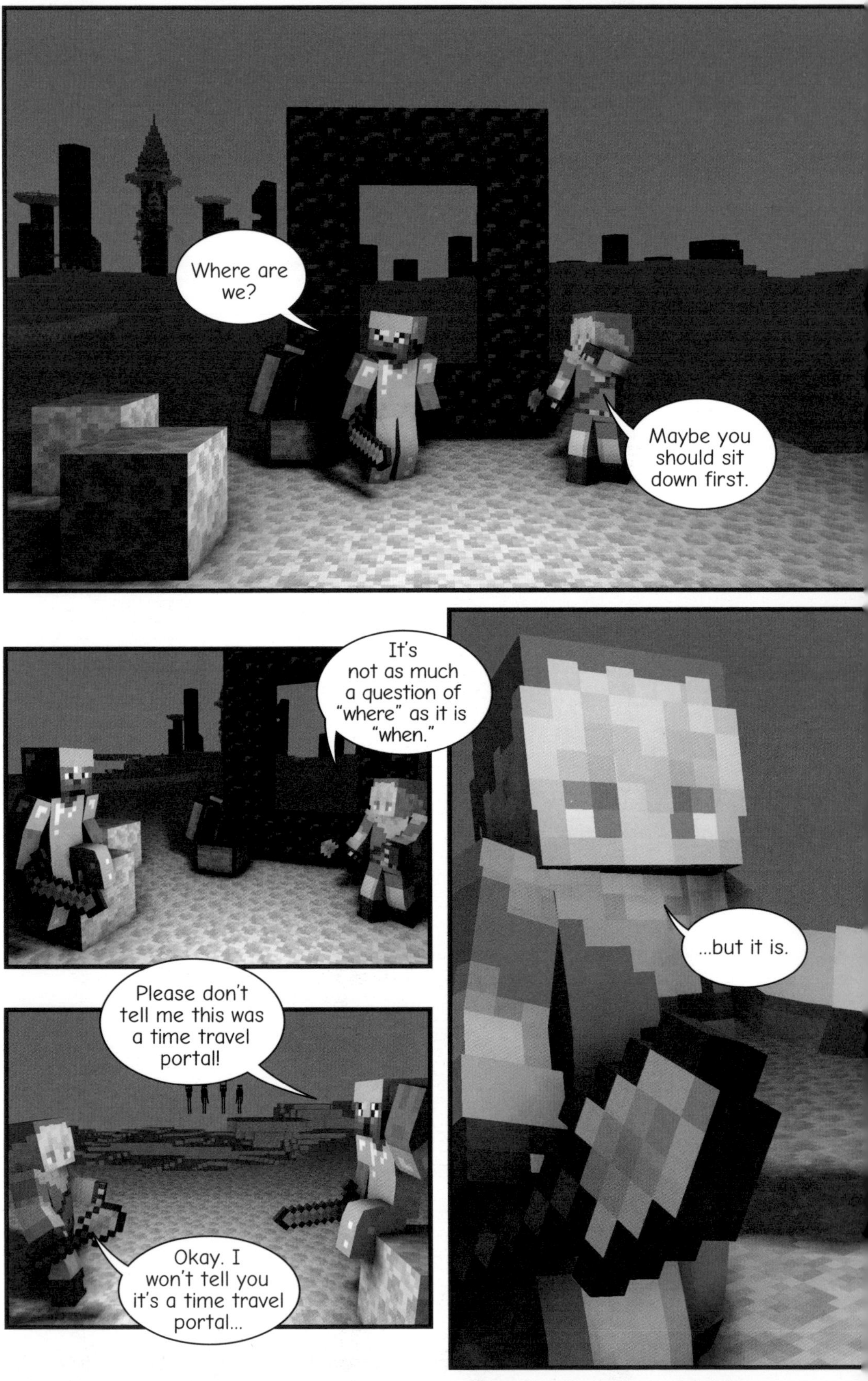
Where are we?
Maybe you should sit down first.
It's not as much a question of "where" as it is "when."
...but it is.
Please don't tell me this was a time travel portal!
Okay. I won't tell you it's a time travel portal...

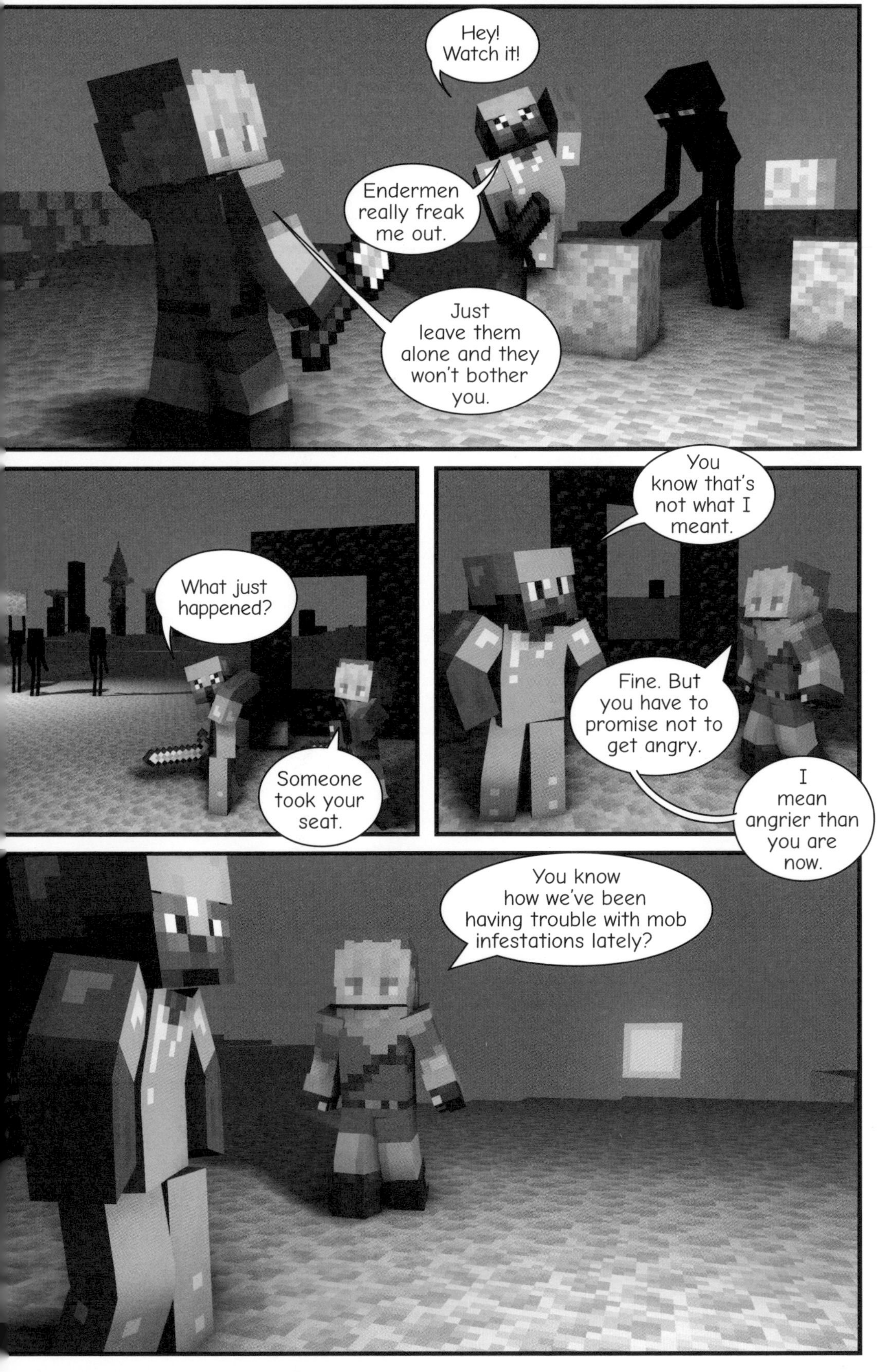
Hey! Watch it!
Endermen really freak me out.
Just leave them alone and they won't bother you.
What just happened?
Someone took your seat.
You know that's not what I meant.
Fine. But you have to promise not to get angry.
I mean angrier than you are now.
You know how we've been having trouble with mob infestations lately?

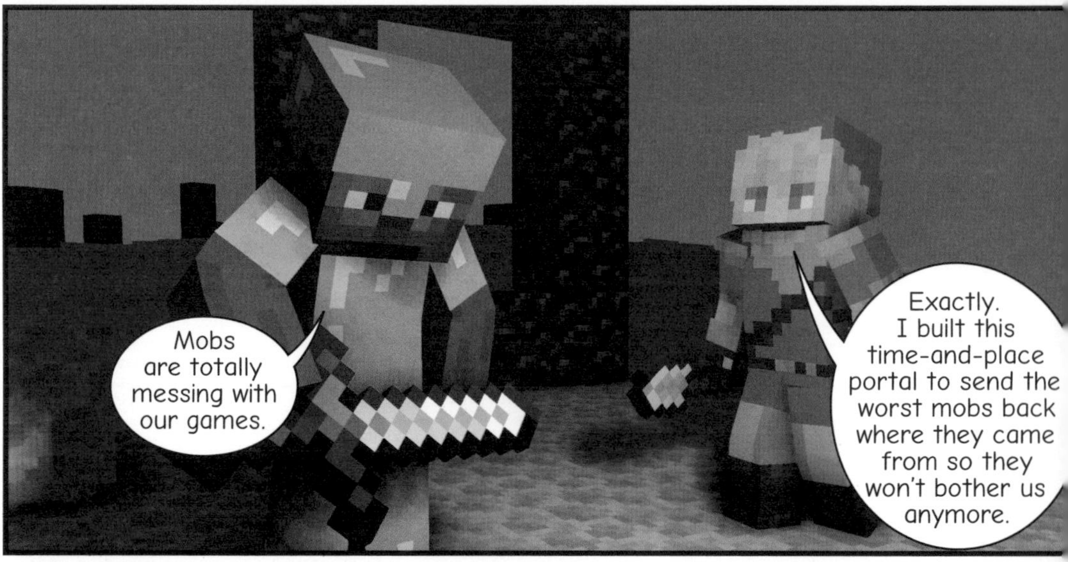
Mobs are totally messing with our games.
Exactly. I built this time-and-place portal to send the worst mobs back where they came from so they won't bother us anymore.

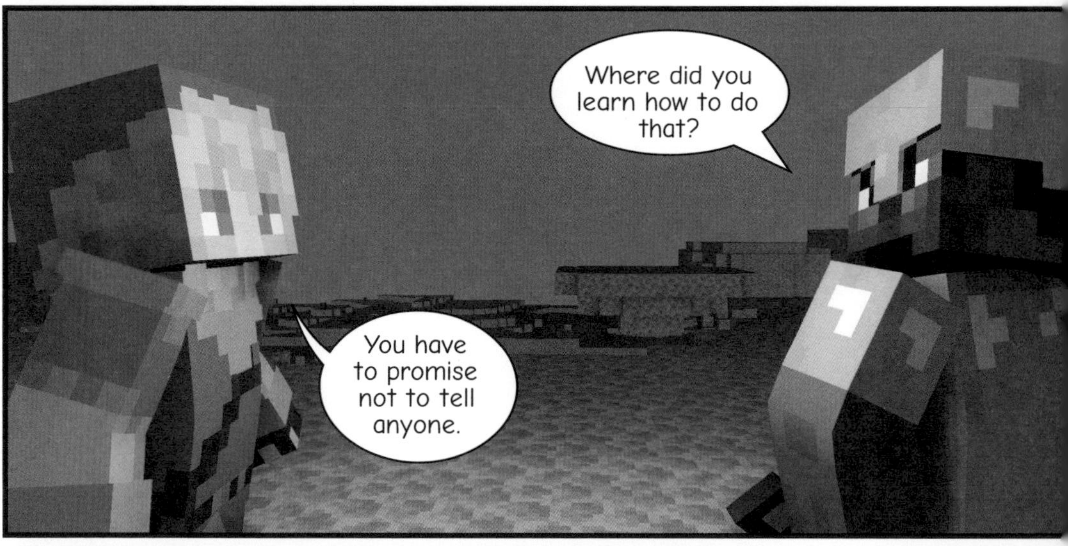
Where did you learn how to do that?
You have to promise not to tell anyone.

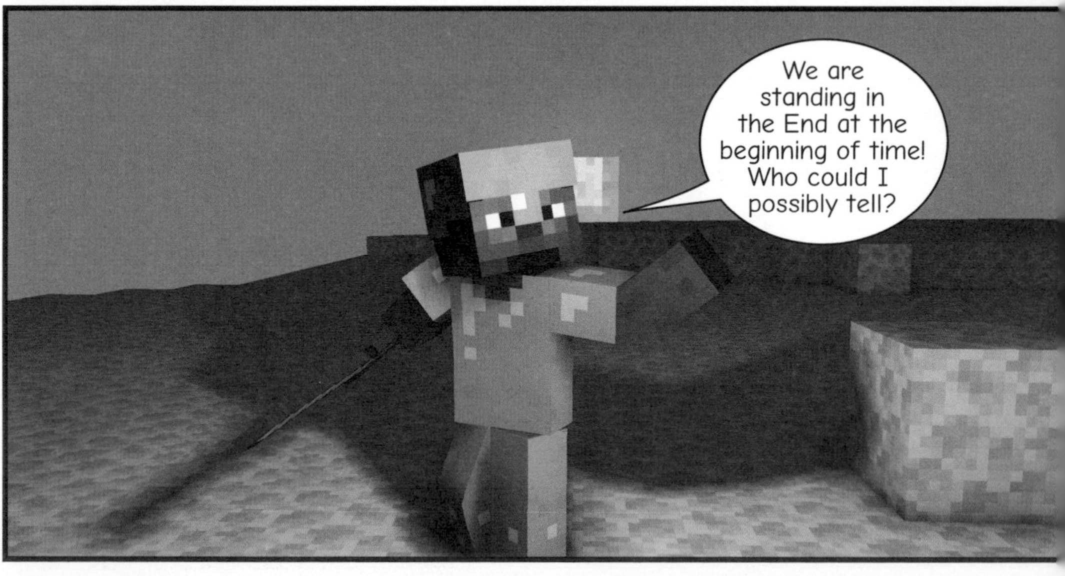
We are standing in the End at the beginning of time! Who could I possibly tell?

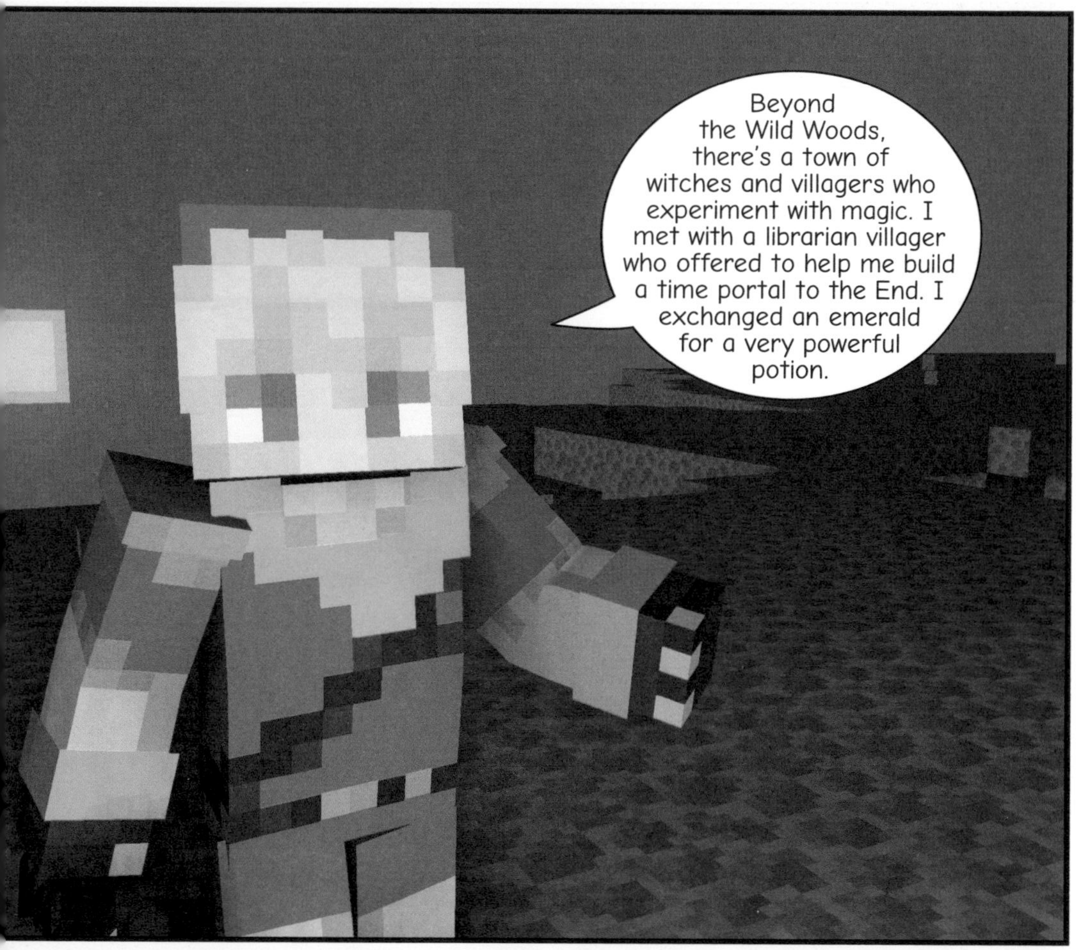
Beyond the Wild Woods, there's a town of witches and villagers who experiment with magic. I met with a librarian villager who offered to help me build a time portal to the End. I exchanged an emerald for a very powerful potion.

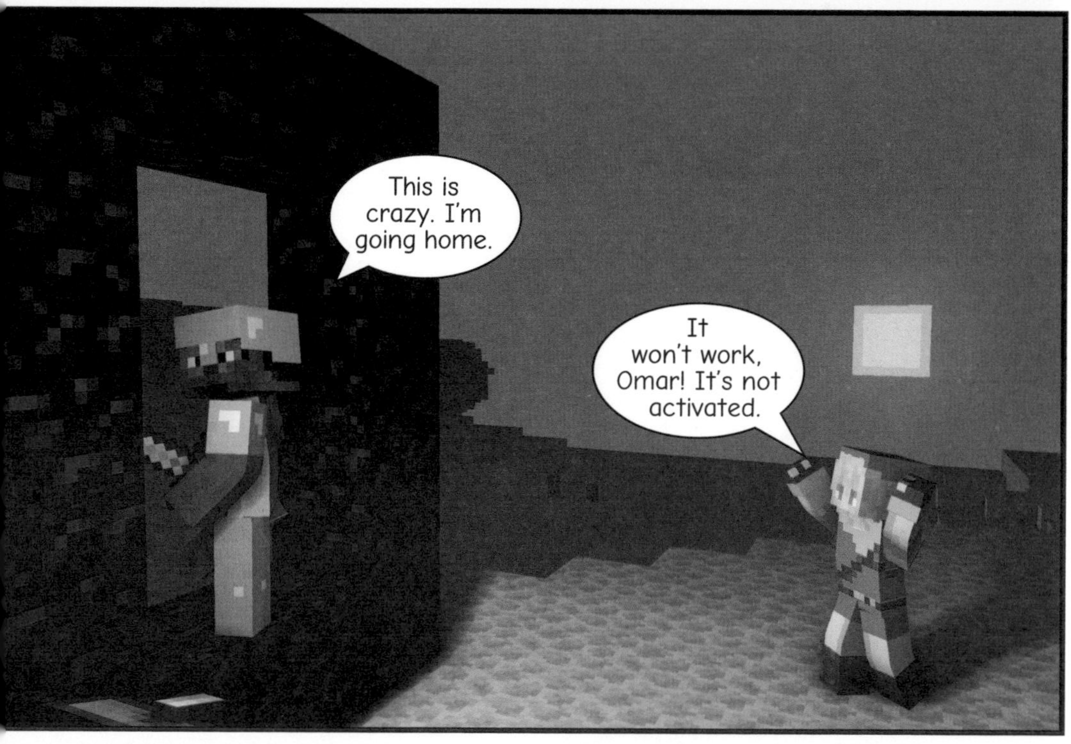
This is crazy. I'm going home.
It won't work, Omar! It's not activated.

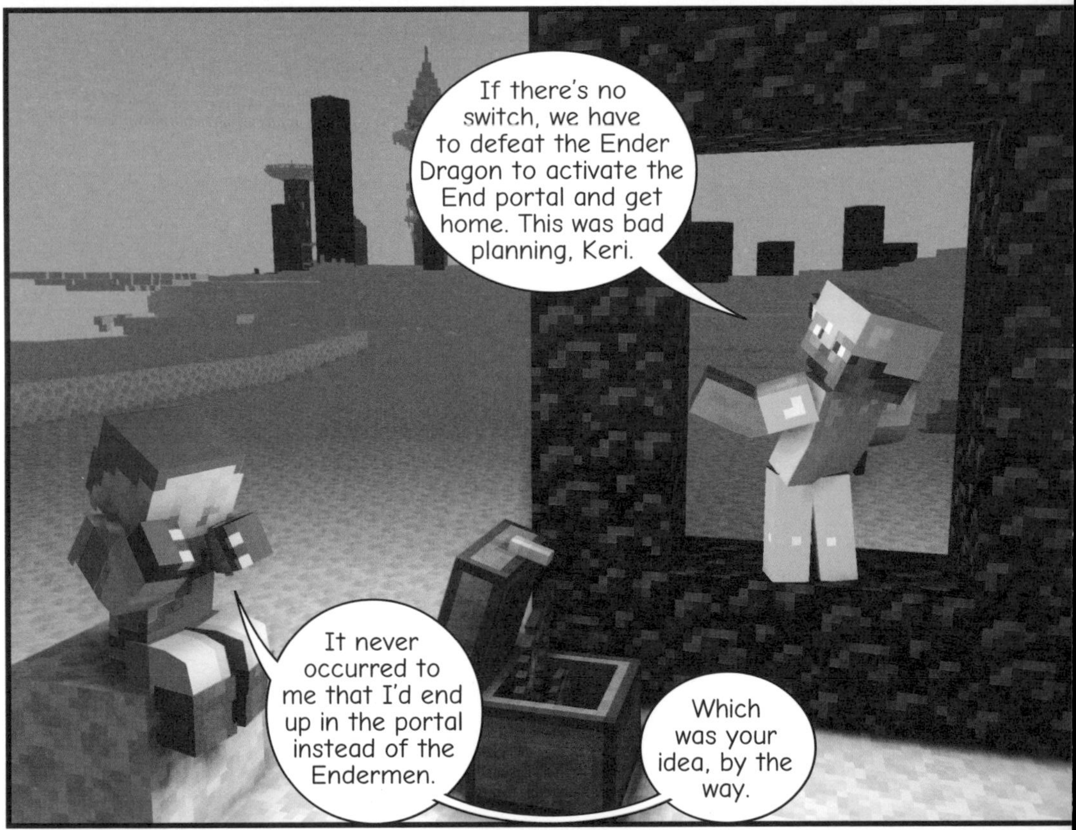
If there's no switch, we have to defeat the Ender Dragon to activate the End portal and get home. This was bad planning, Keri.
It never occurred to me that I'd end up in the portal instead of the Endermen.
Which was your idea, by the way.

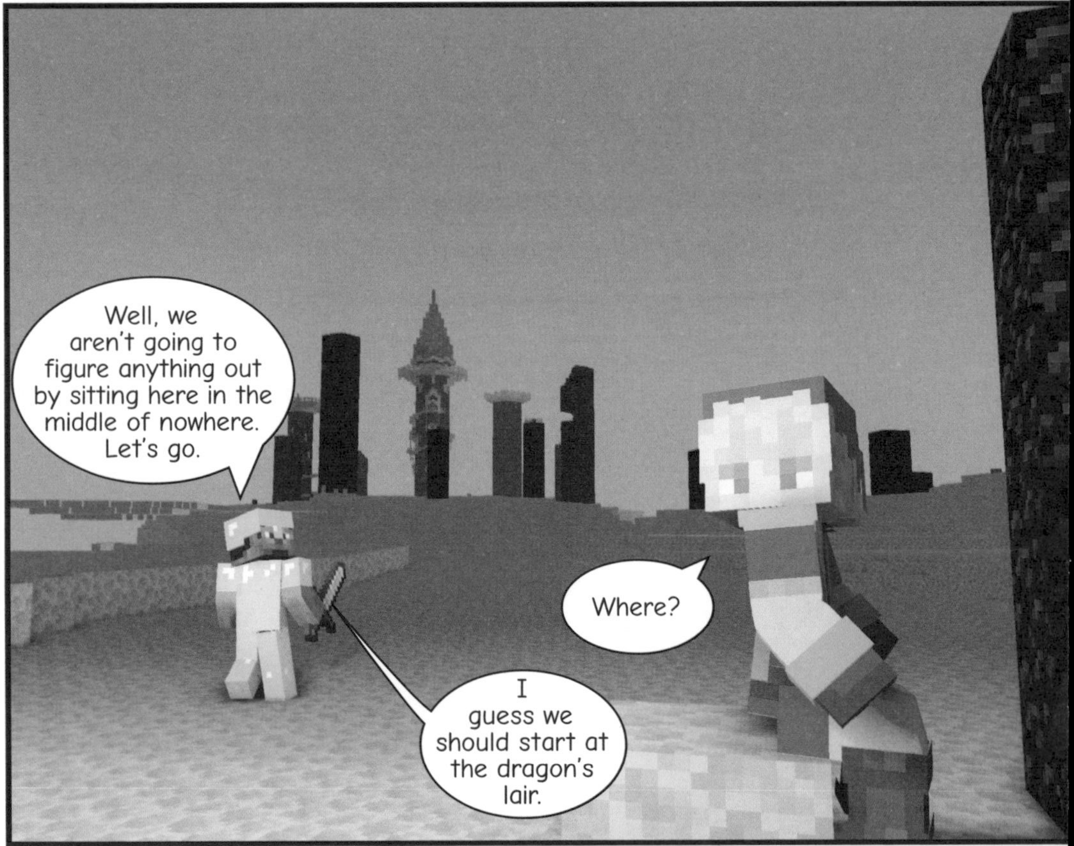
Well, we aren't going to figure anything out by sitting here in the middle of nowhere. Let's go.
Where?
I guess we should start at the dragon's lair.

CHAPTER 2
GORGAR AND THE ENDERMEN

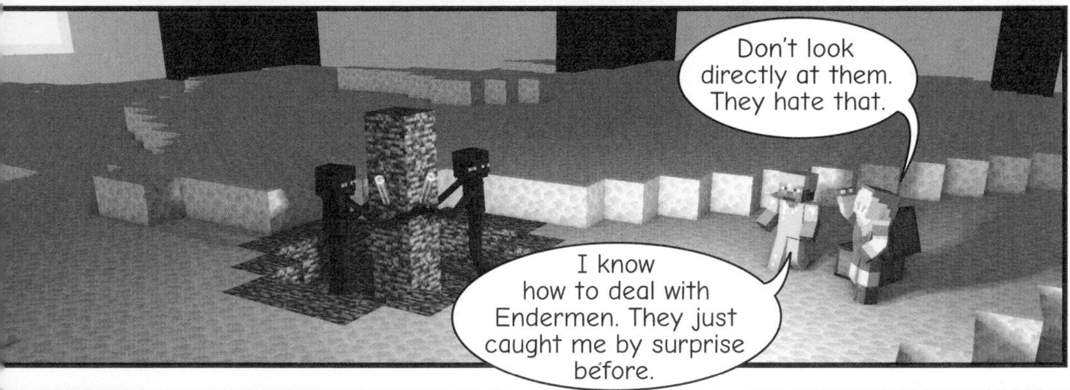
Don't look directly at them. They hate that.
I know how to deal with Endermen. They just caught me by surprise before.

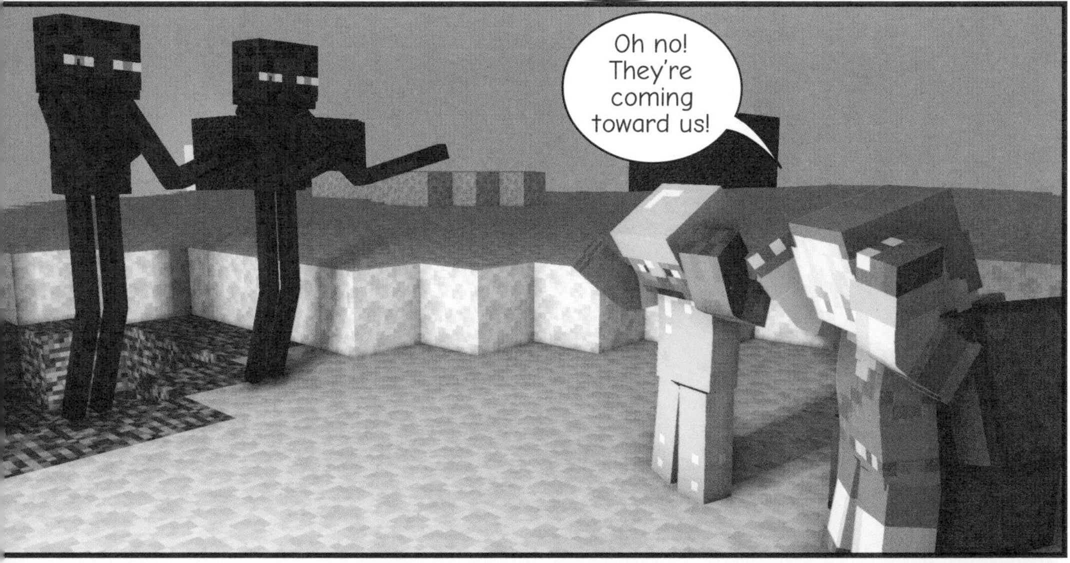
Oh no! They're coming toward us!

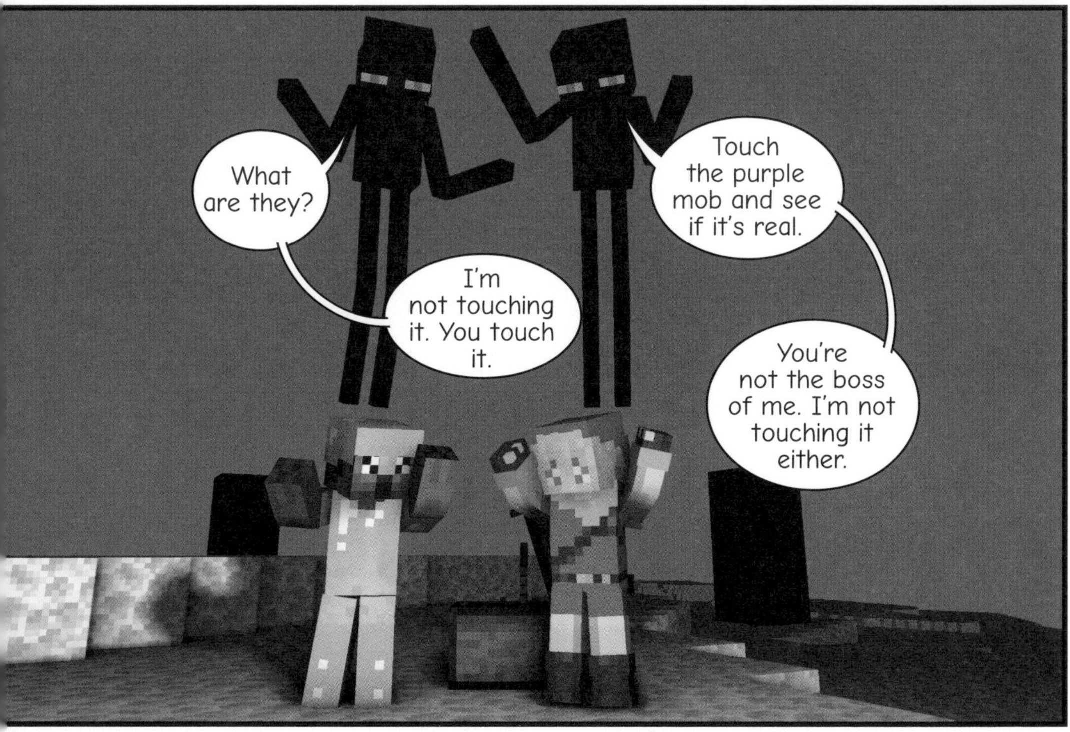
What are they?
Touch the purple mob and see if it's real.
I'm not touching it. You touch it.
You're not the boss of me. I'm not touching it either.

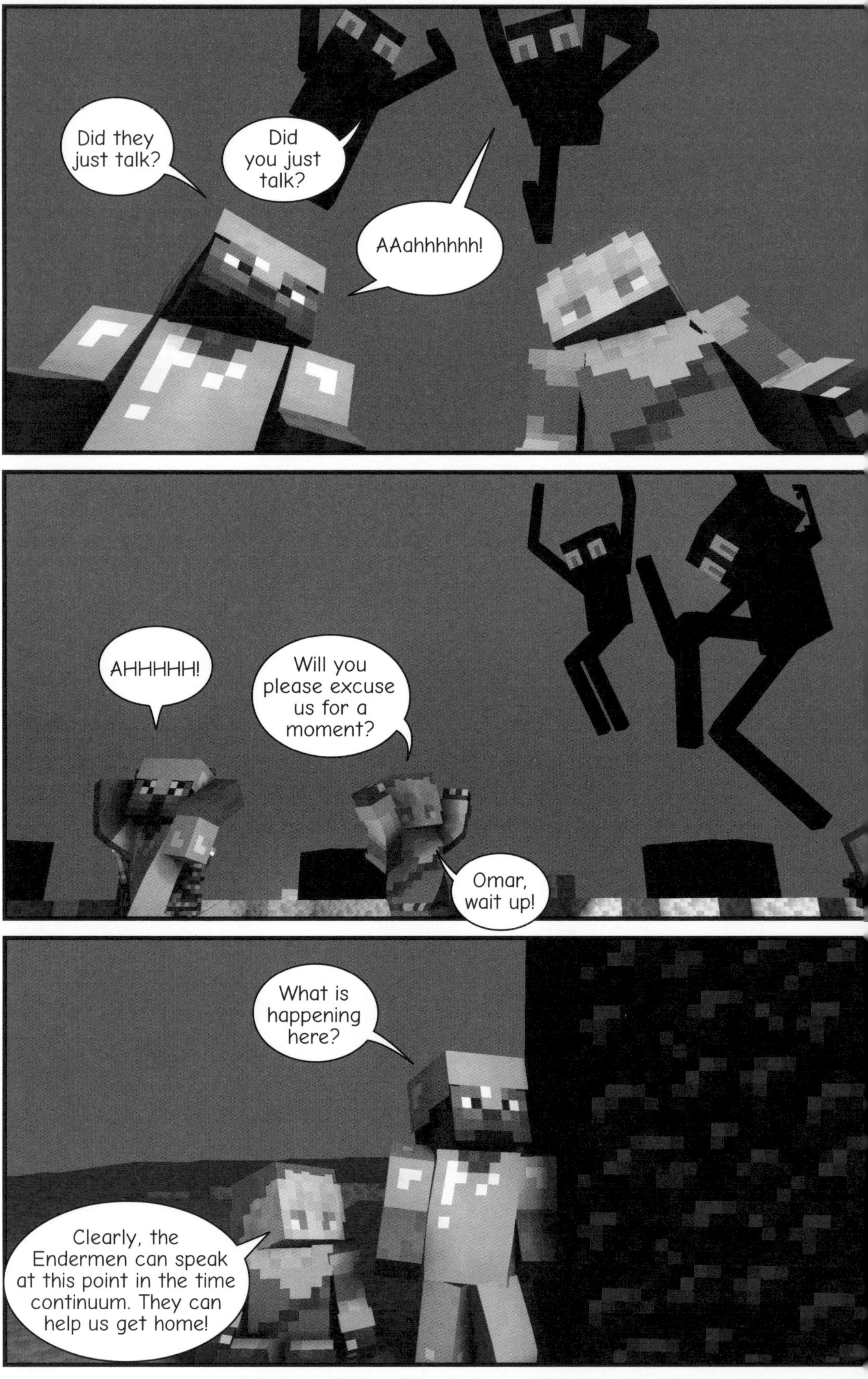
Did they just talk?
Did you just talk?
AAahhhhhh!
AHHHHH!
Will you please excuse us for a moment?
Omar, wait up!
What is happening here?
Clearly, the Endermen can speak at this point in the time continuum. They can help us get home!

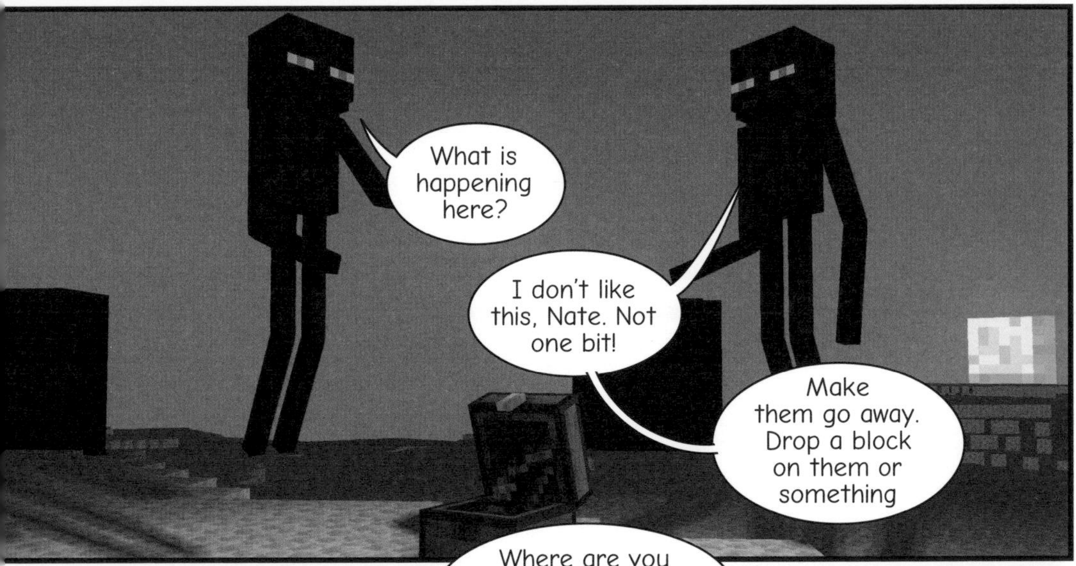
What is happening here?
I don't like this, Nate. Not one bit!
Make them go away. Drop a block on them or something

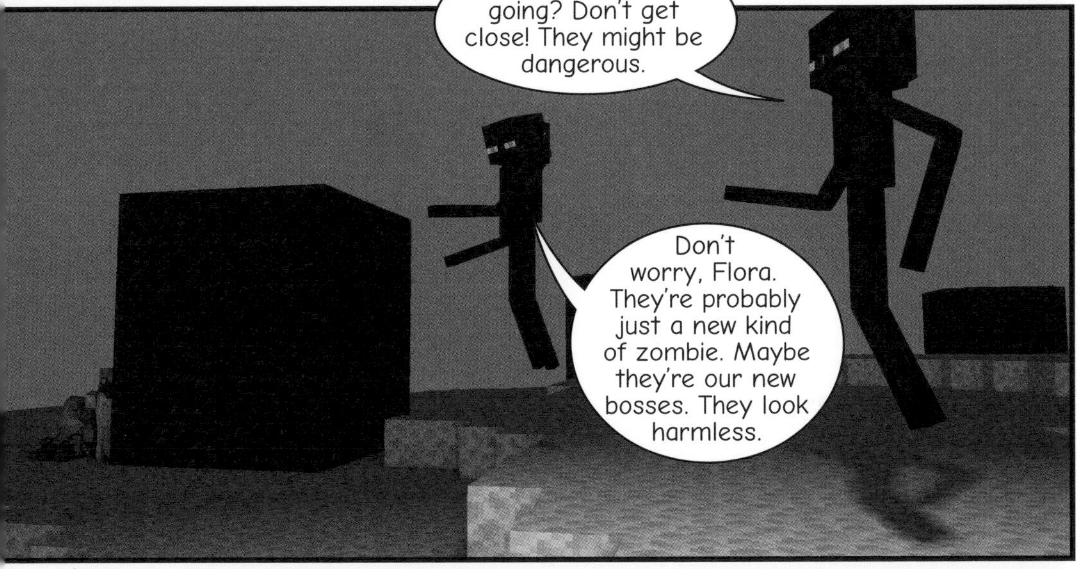
Where are you going? Don't get close! They might be dangerous.
Don't worry, Flora. They're probably just a new kind of zombie. Maybe they're our new bosses. They look harmless.

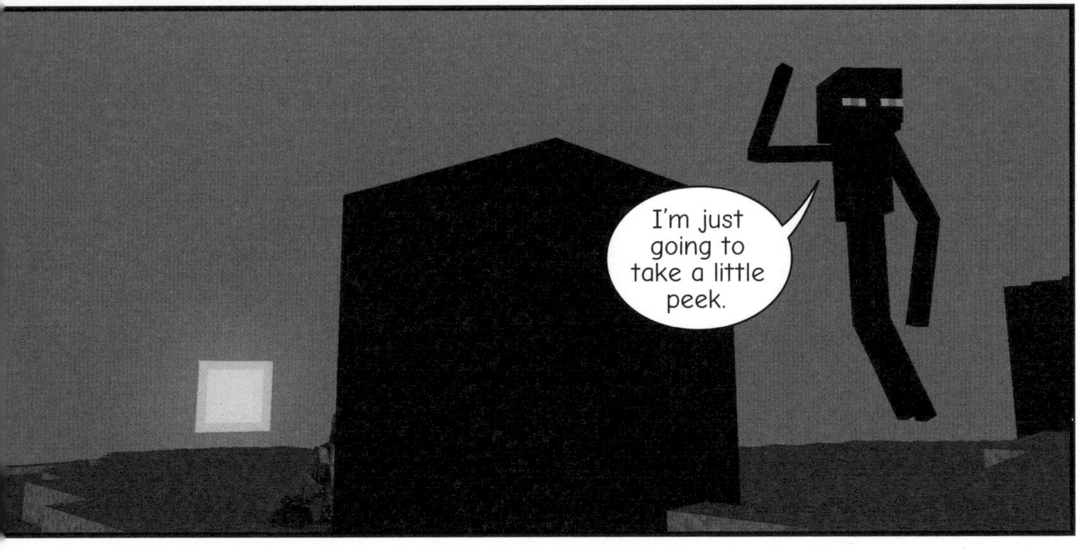
I'm just going to take a little peek.

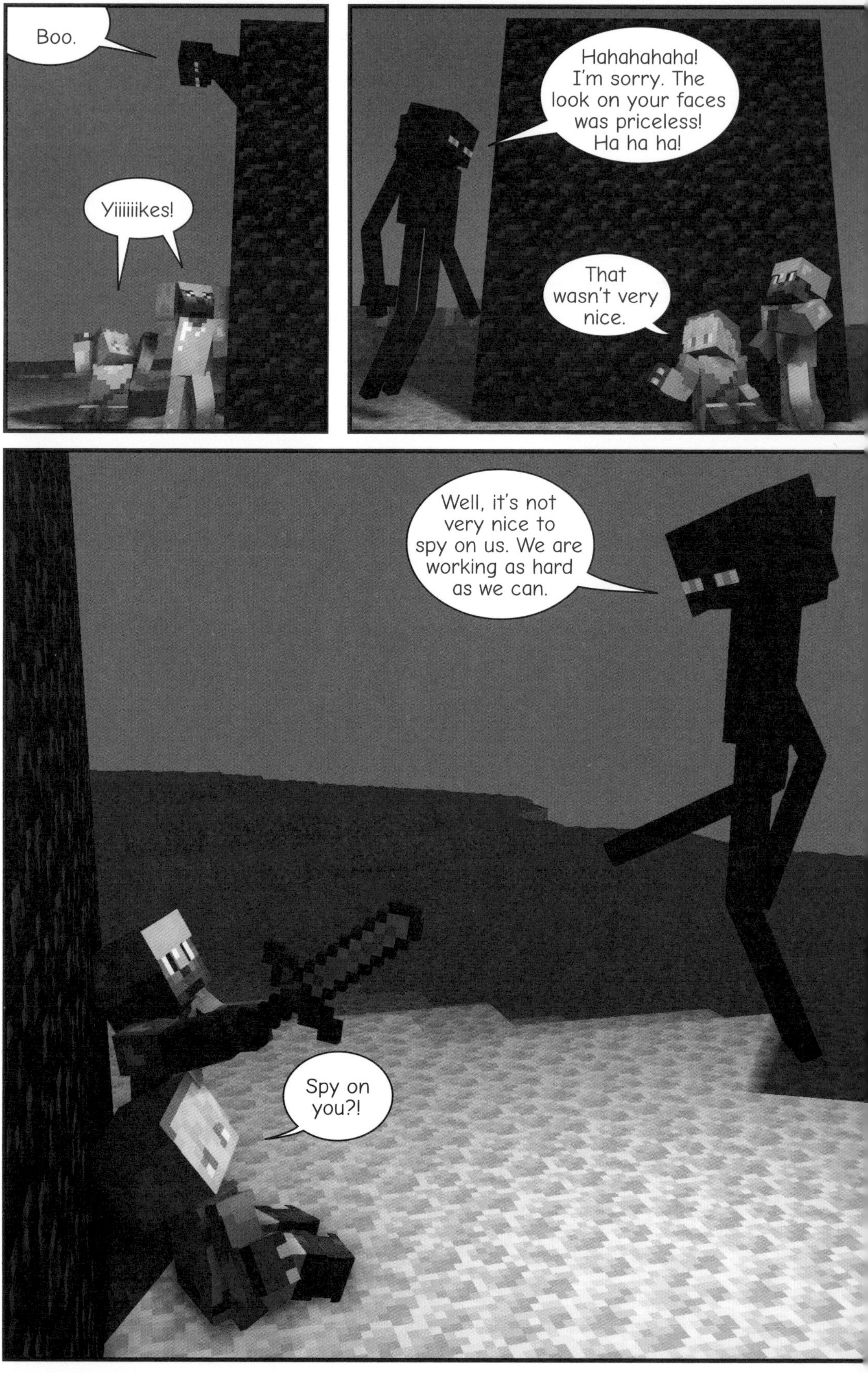
Boo.
Yiiiiiikes!
Hahahahaha! I'm sorry. The look on your faces was priceless! Ha ha ha!
That wasn't very nice.
Well, it's not very nice to spy on us. We are working as hard as we can.
Spy on you?!

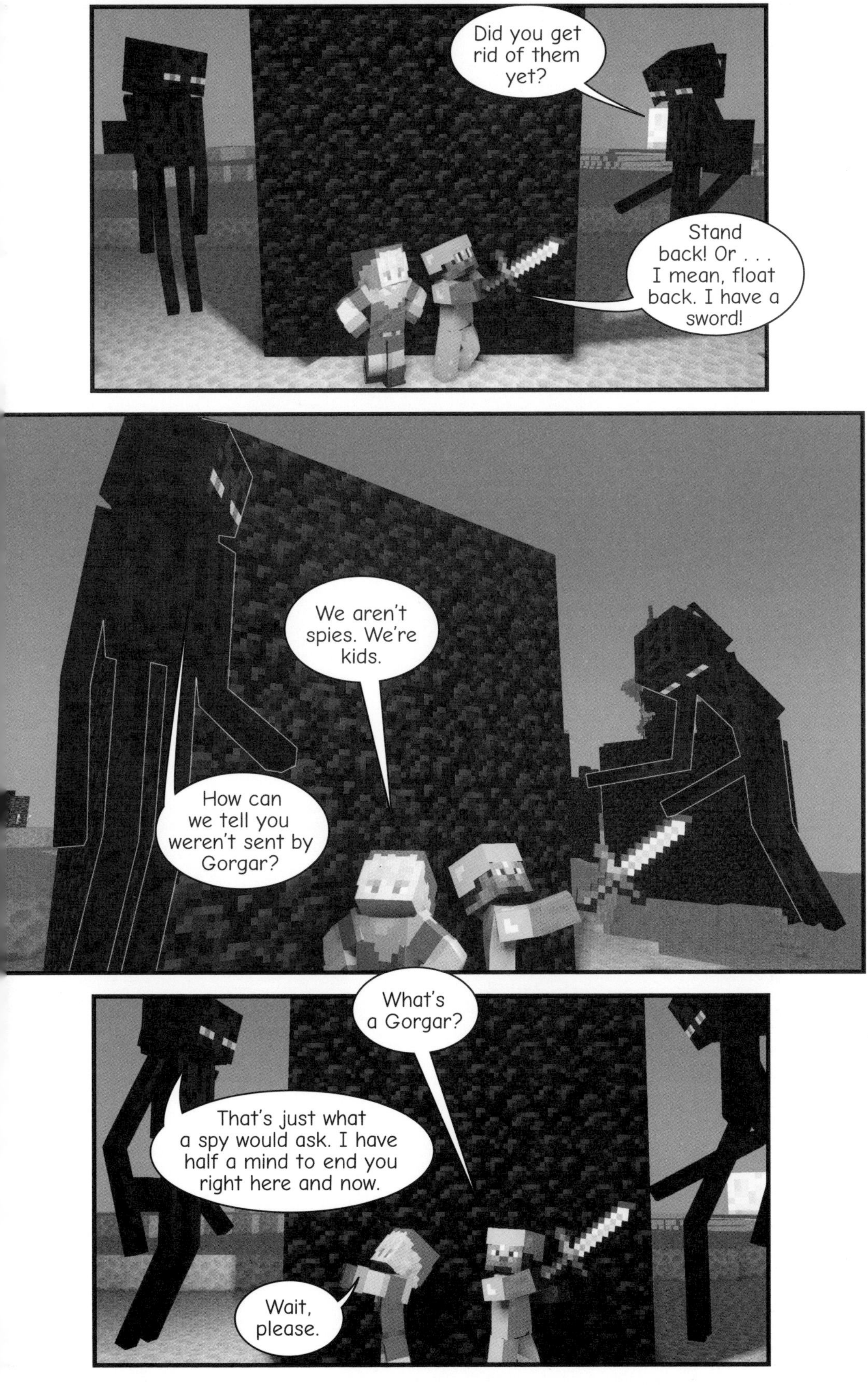
Did you get rid of them yet?
Stand back! Or . . . I mean, float back. I have a sword!
We aren't spies. We're kids.
How can we tell you weren't sent by Gorgar?
What's a Gorgar?
That's just what a spy would ask. I have half a mind to end you right here and now.
Wait, please.

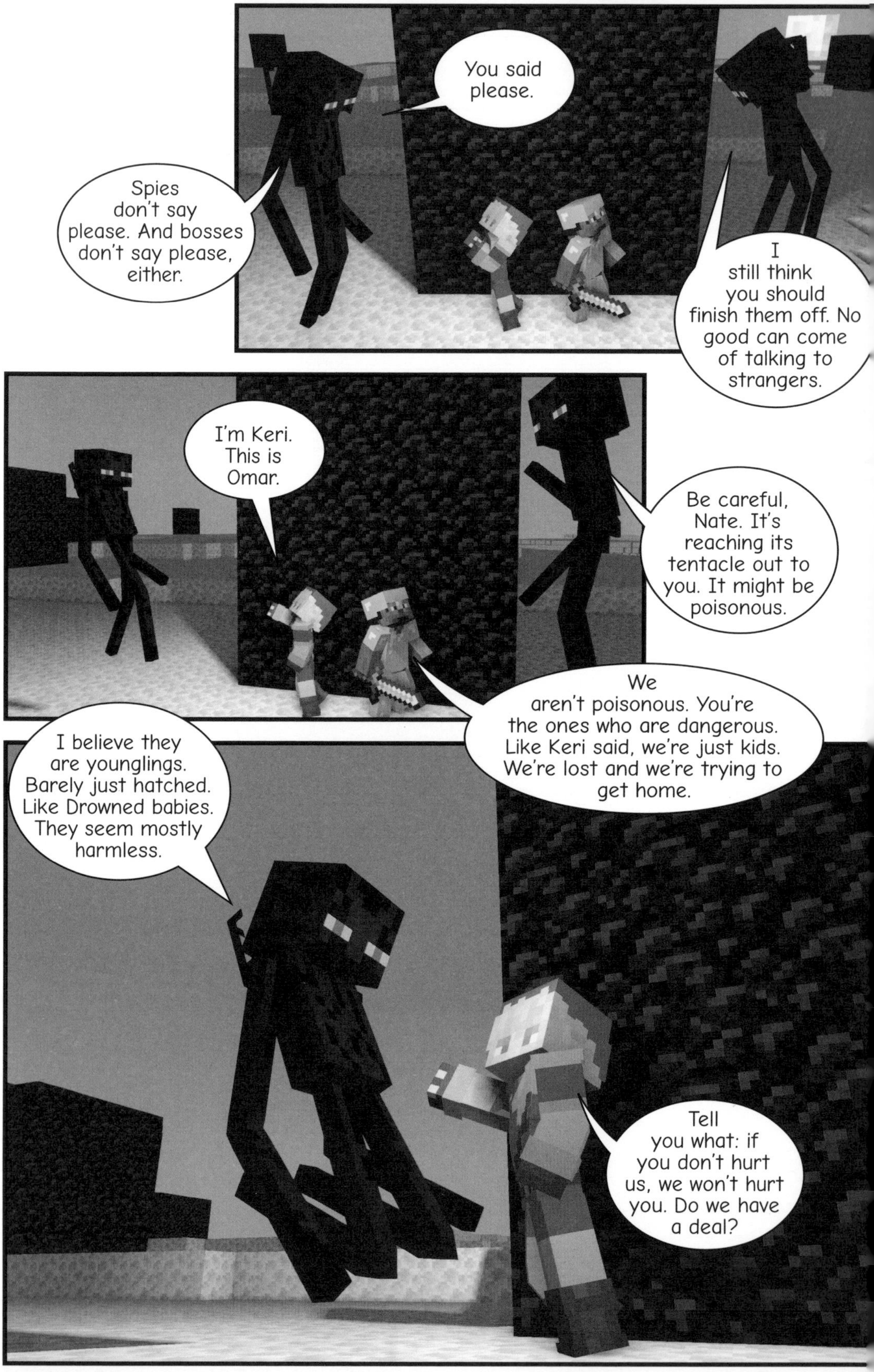
You said please.
Spies don't say please. And bosses don't say please, either.
I still think you should finish them off. No good can come of talking to strangers.
I'm Keri. This is Omar.
Be careful, Nate. It's reaching its tentacle out to you. It might be poisonous.
We aren't poisonous. You're the ones who are dangerous. Like Keri said, we're just kids. We're lost and we're trying to get home.
I believe they are younglings. Barely just hatched. Like Drowned babies. They seem mostly harmless.
Tell you what: if you don't hurt us, we won't hurt you. Do we have a deal?

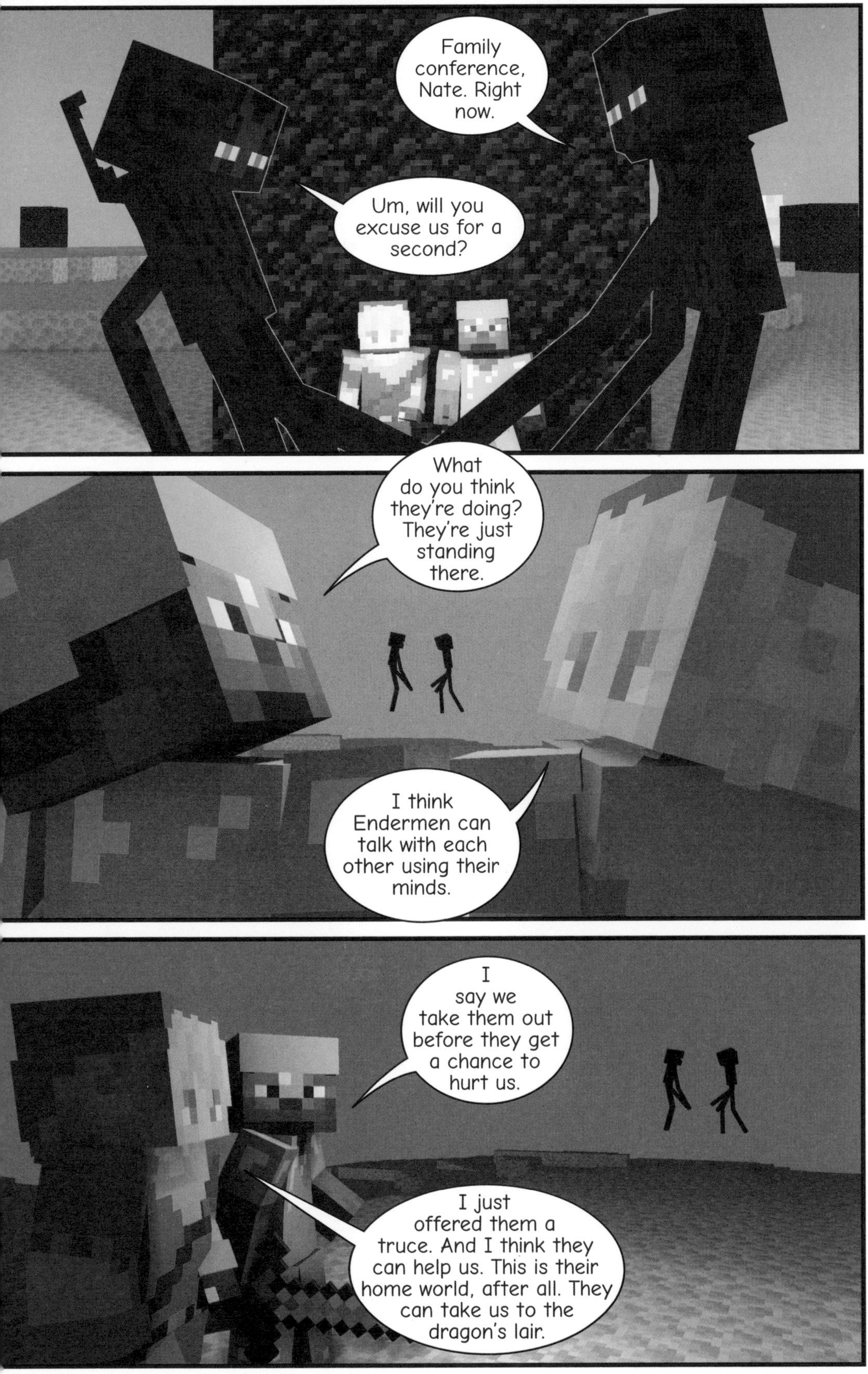
Family conference, Nate. Right now.
Um, will you excuse us for a second?
What do you think they're doing? They're just standing there.
I think Endermen can talk with each other using their minds.
I say we take them out before they get a chance to hurt us.
I just offered them a truce. And I think they can help us. This is their home world, after all. They can take us to the dragon's lair.

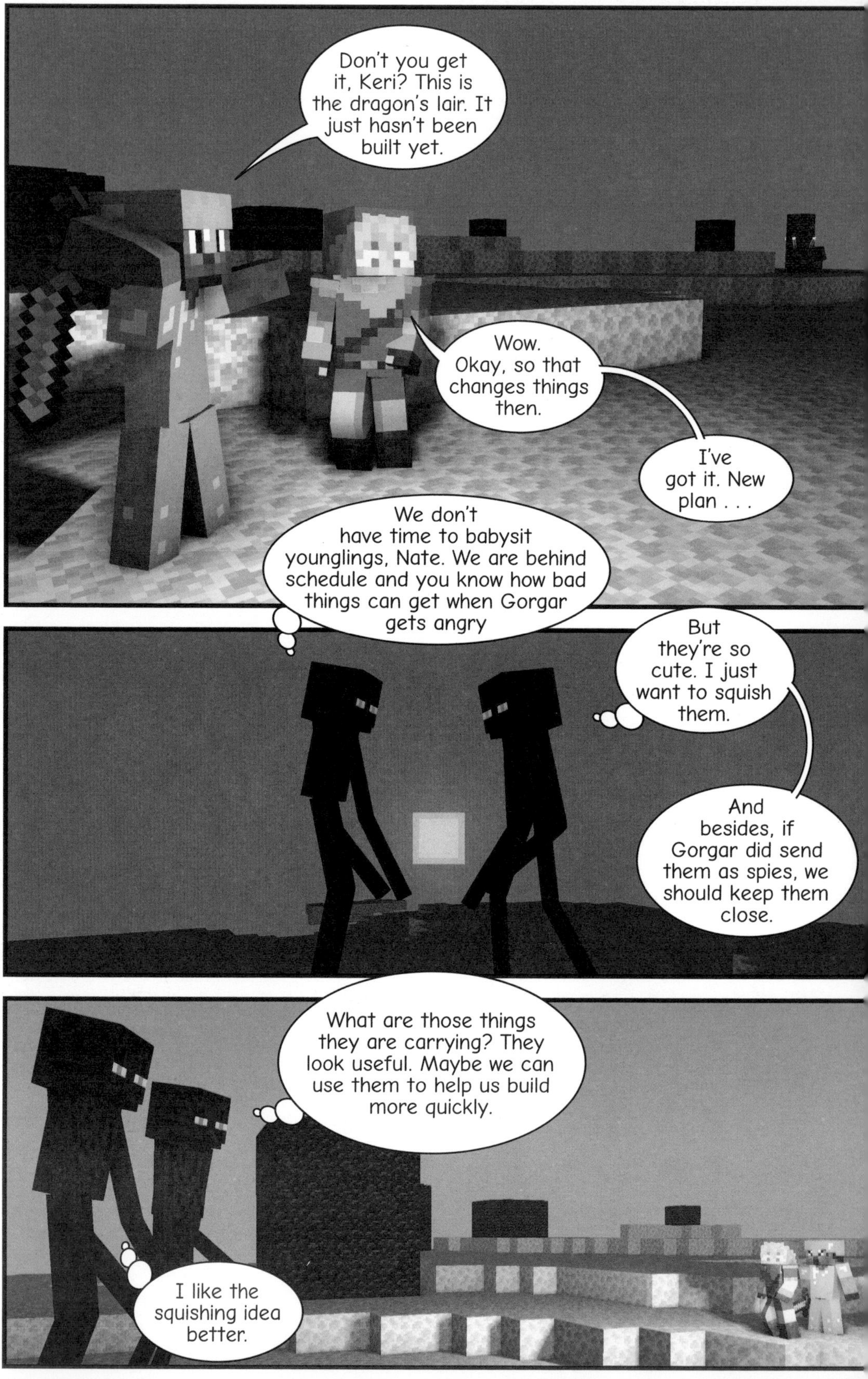
Don't you get it, Keri? This is the dragon's lair. It just hasn't been built yet.
Wow. Okay, so that changes things then.
I've got it. New plan . . .
We don't have time to babysit younglings, Nate. We are behind schedule and you know how bad things can get when Gorgar gets angry
But they're so cute. I just want to squish them.
And besides, if Gorgar did send them as spies, we should keep them close.
What are those things they are carrying? They look useful. Maybe we can use them to help us build more quickly.
I like the squishing idea better.

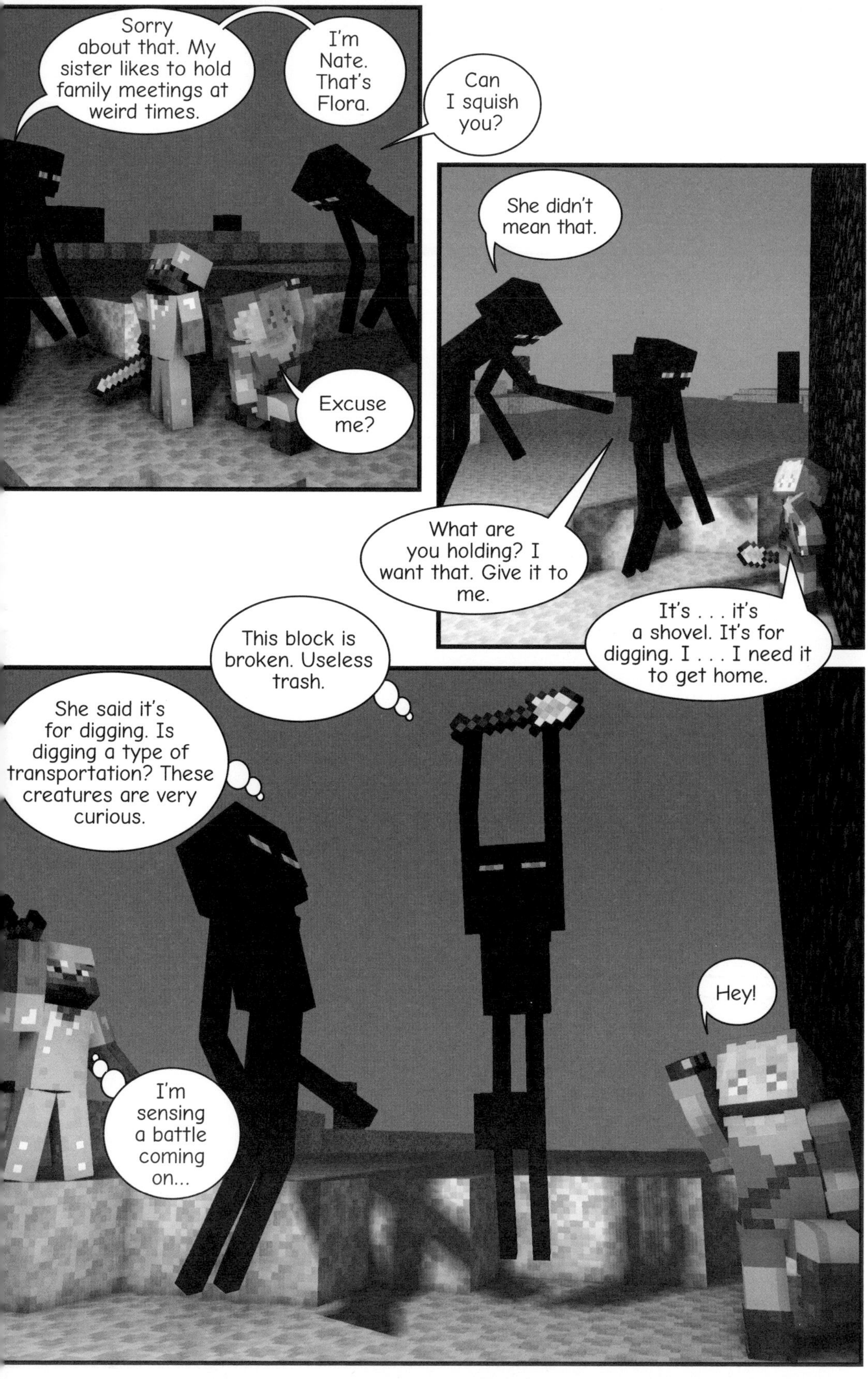
Sorry about that. My sister likes to hold family meetings at weird times.
I'm Nate. That's Flora.
Can I squish you?
Excuse me?
She didn't mean that.
What are you holding? I want that. Give it to me.
It's . . . it's a shovel. It's for digging. I . . . I need it to get home.
This block is broken. Useless trash.
She said it's for digging. Is digging a type of transportation? These creatures are very curious.
Hey!
I'm sensing a battle coming on...

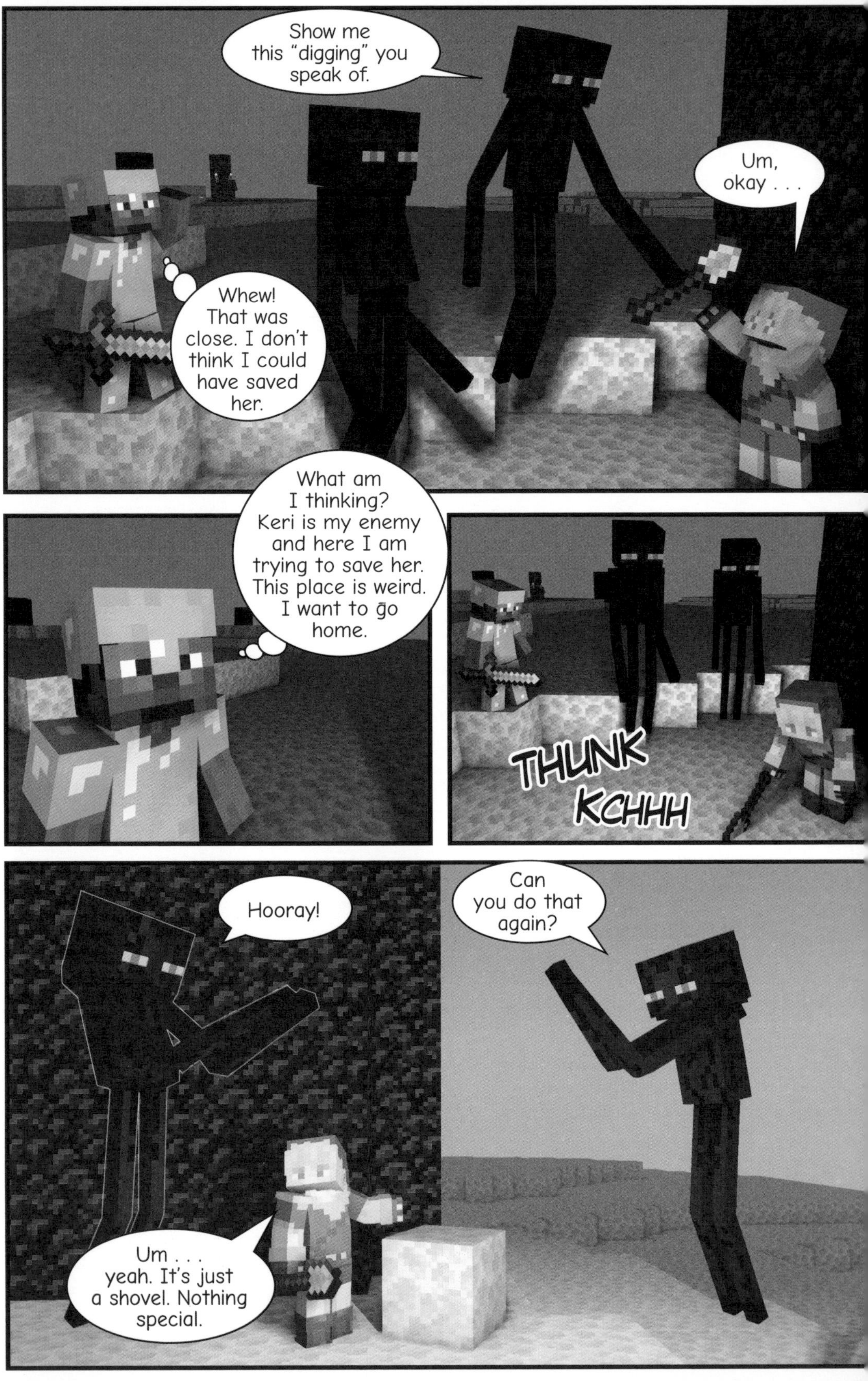
Show me this "digging" you speak of.
Um, okay . . .
Whew! That was close. I don't think I could have saved her.
What am I thinking? Keri is my enemy and here I am trying to save her. This place is weird. I want to go home.
THUNK
KCHHH
Hooray!
Can you do that again?
Um . . . yeah. It's just a shovel. Nothing special.

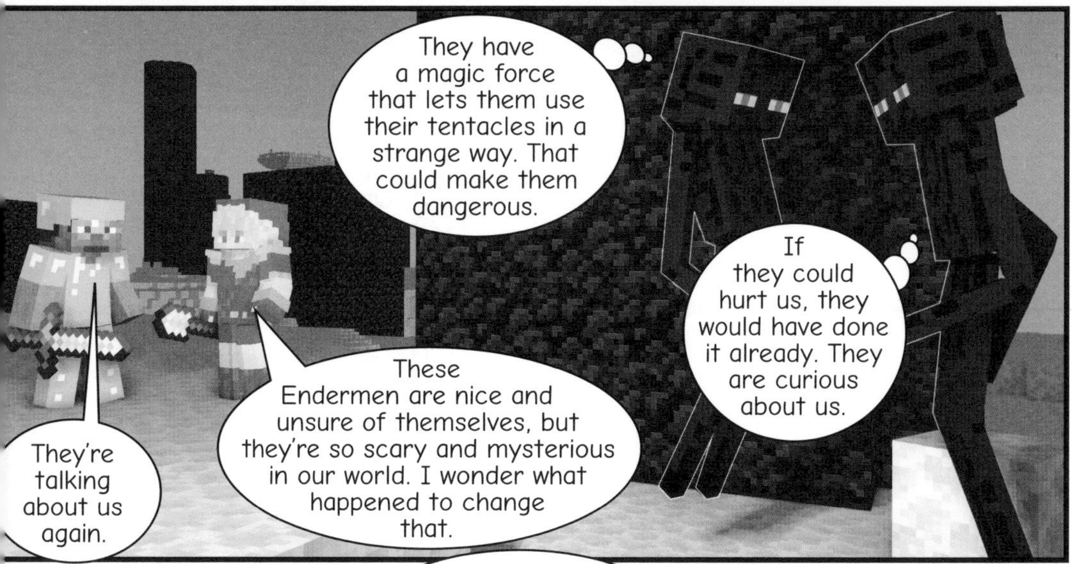
They have a magic force that lets them use their tentacles in a strange way. That could make them dangerous.
If they could hurt us, they would have done it already. They are curious about us.
These Endermen are nice and unsure of themselves, but they're so scary and mysterious in our world. I wonder what happened to change that.
They're talking about us again.

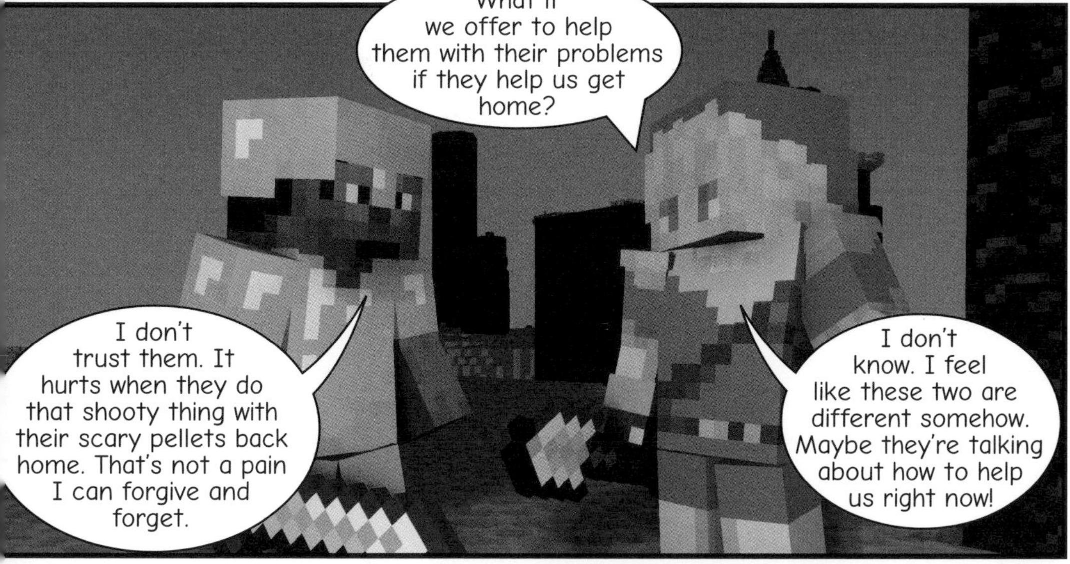
What if we offer to help them with their problems if they help us get home?
I don't trust them. It hurts when they do that shooty thing with their scary pellets back home. That's not a pain I can forgive and forget.
I don't know. I feel like these two are different somehow. Maybe they're talking about how to help us right now!

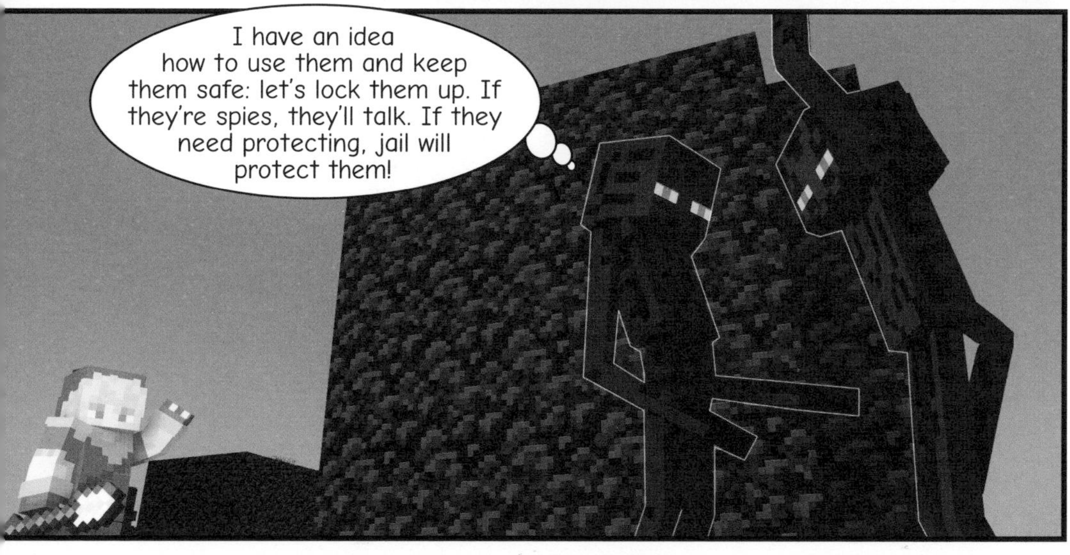
I have an idea how to use them and keep them safe: let's lock them up. If they're spies, they'll talk. If they need protecting, jail will protect them!

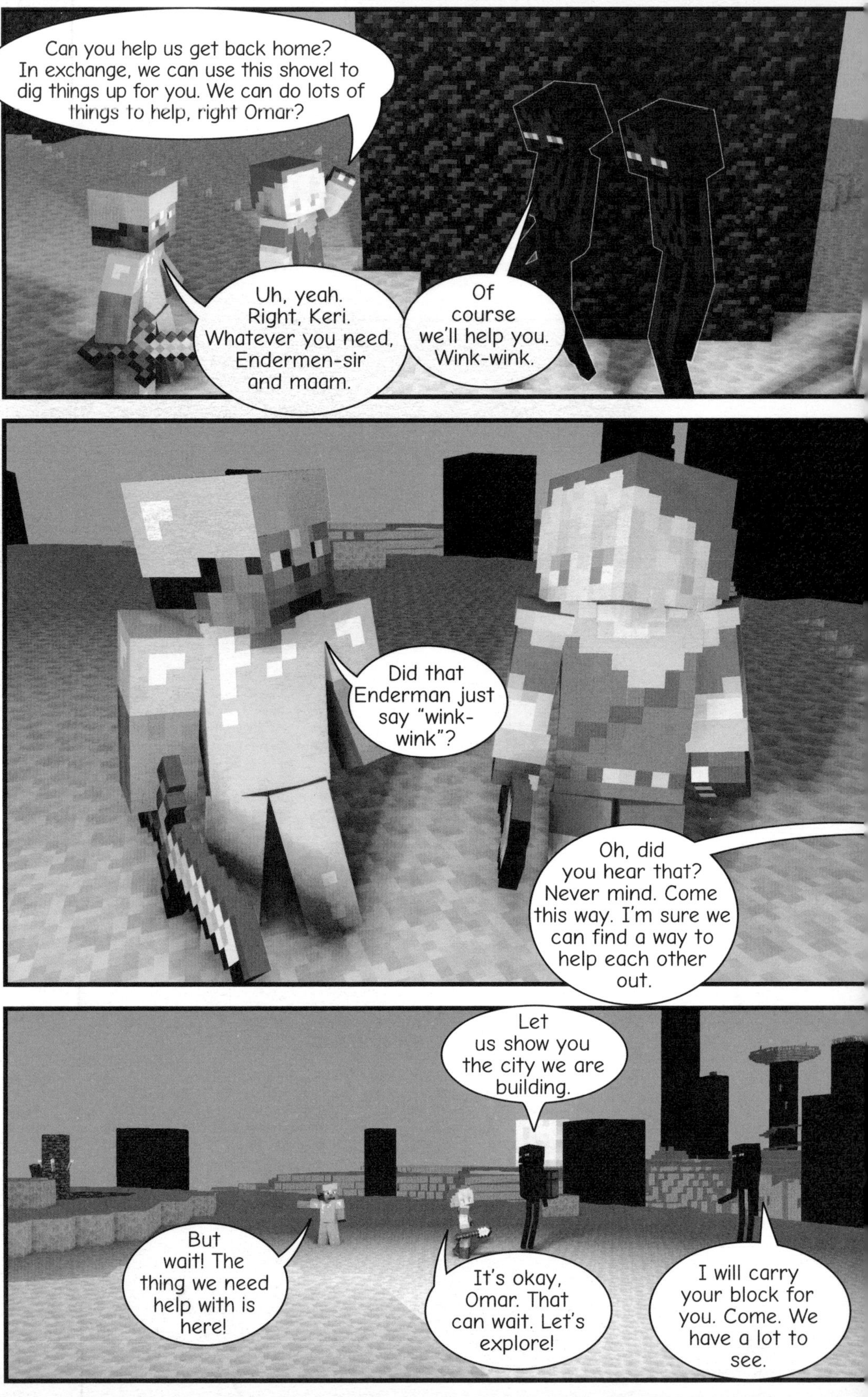

Can you help us get back home? In exchange, we can use this shovel to dig things up for you. We can do lots of things to help, right Omar?
Uh, yeah. Right, Keri. Whatever you need, Endermen-sir and maam.
Of course we'll help you. Wink-wink.
Did that Enderman just say "wink-wink"?
Oh, did you hear that? Never mind. Come this way. I'm sure we can find a way to help each other out.
Let us show you the city we are building.
But wait! The thing we need help with is here!
It's okay, Omar. That can wait. Let's explore!
I will carry your block for you. Come. We have a lot to see.

CHAPTER 3
TRAPPED

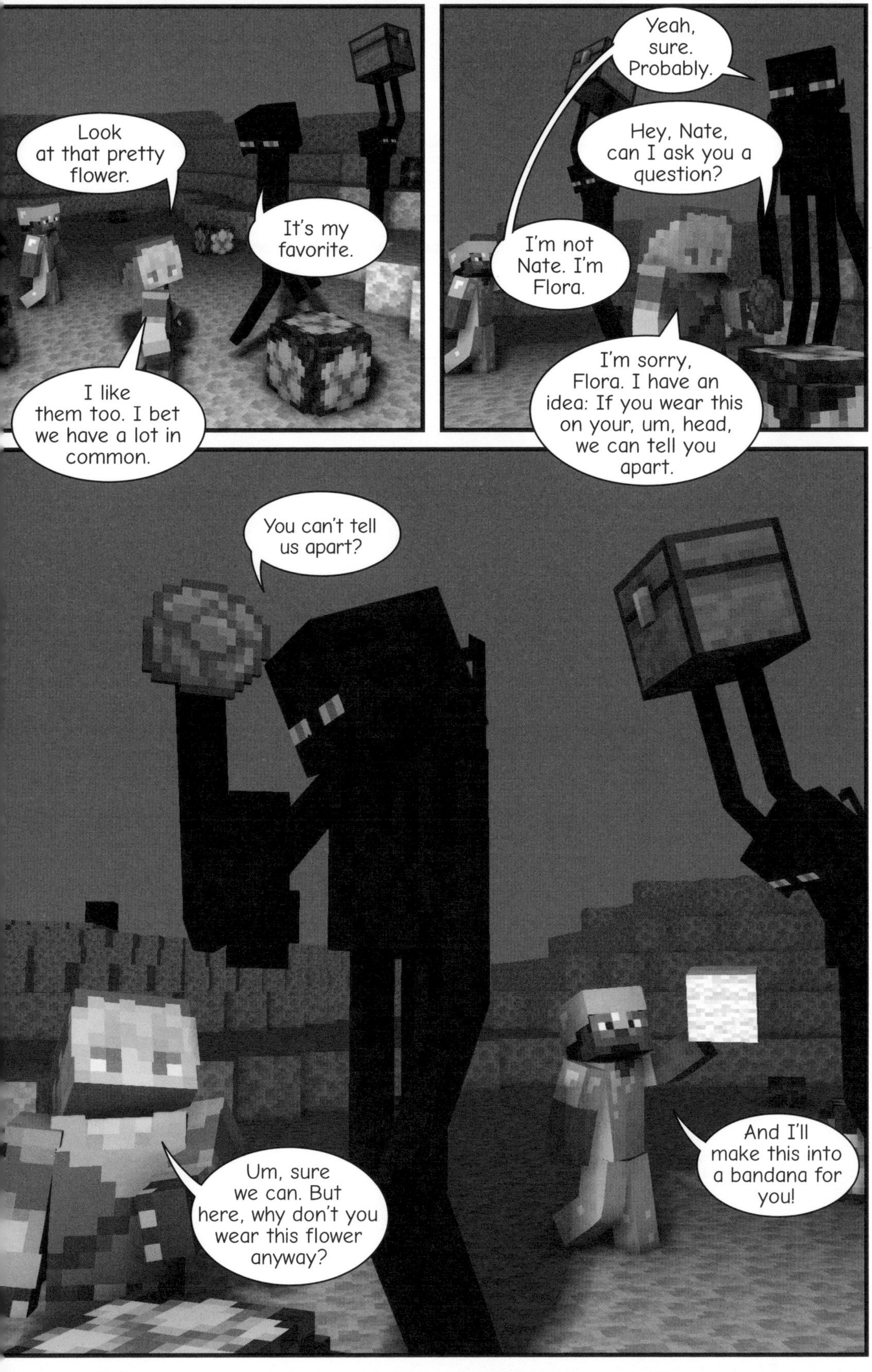

Look at that pretty flower.
It's my favorite.
I like them too. I bet we have a lot in common.
Yeah, sure. Probably.
Hey, Nate, can I ask you a question?
I'm not Nate. I'm Flora.
I'm sorry, Flora. I have an idea: If you wear this on your, um, head, we can tell you apart.
You can't tell us apart?
Um, sure we can. But here, why don't you wear this flower anyway?
And I'll make this into a bandana for you!

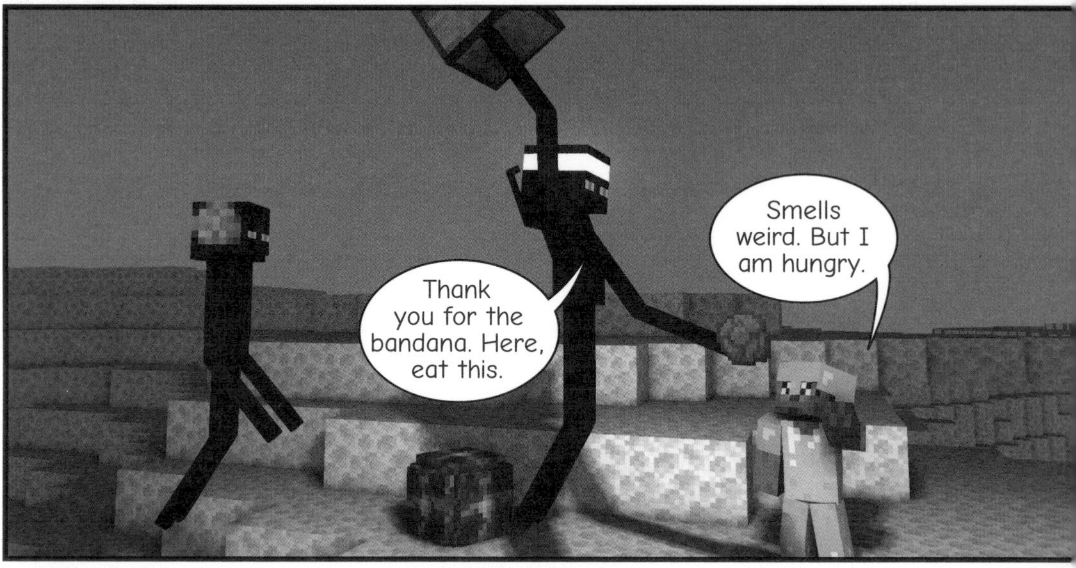
Thank you for the bandana. Here, eat this.
Smells weird. But I am hungry.

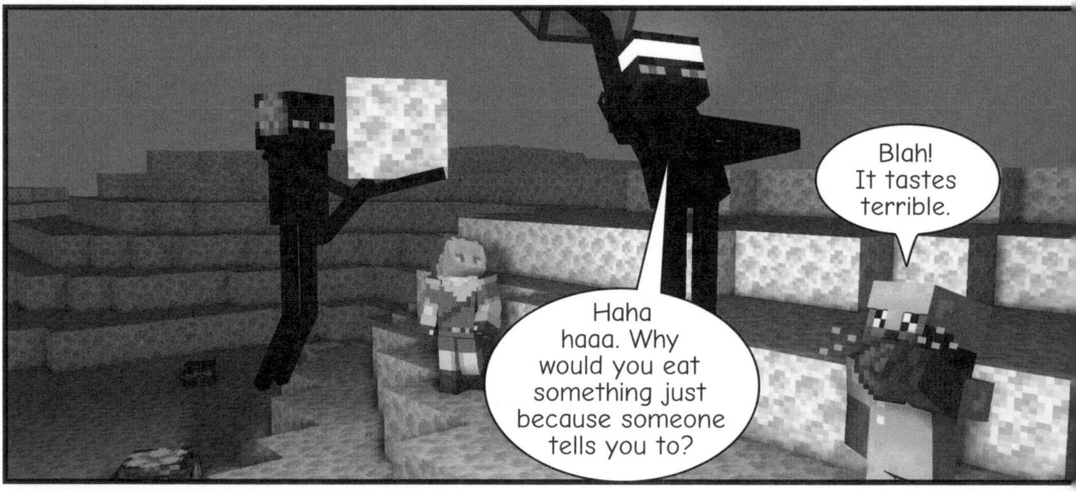
Blah! It tastes terrible.
Haha haaa. Why would you eat something just because someone tells you to?

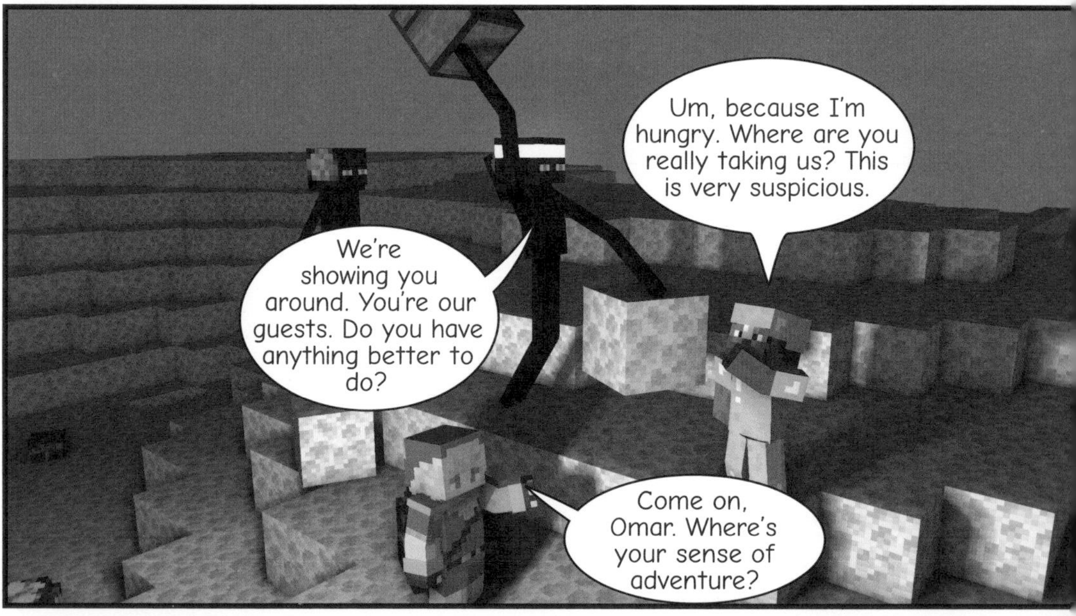
Um, because I'm hungry. Where are you really taking us? This is very suspicious.
We're showing you around. You're our guests. Do you have anything better to do?
Come on, Omar. Where's your sense of adventure?

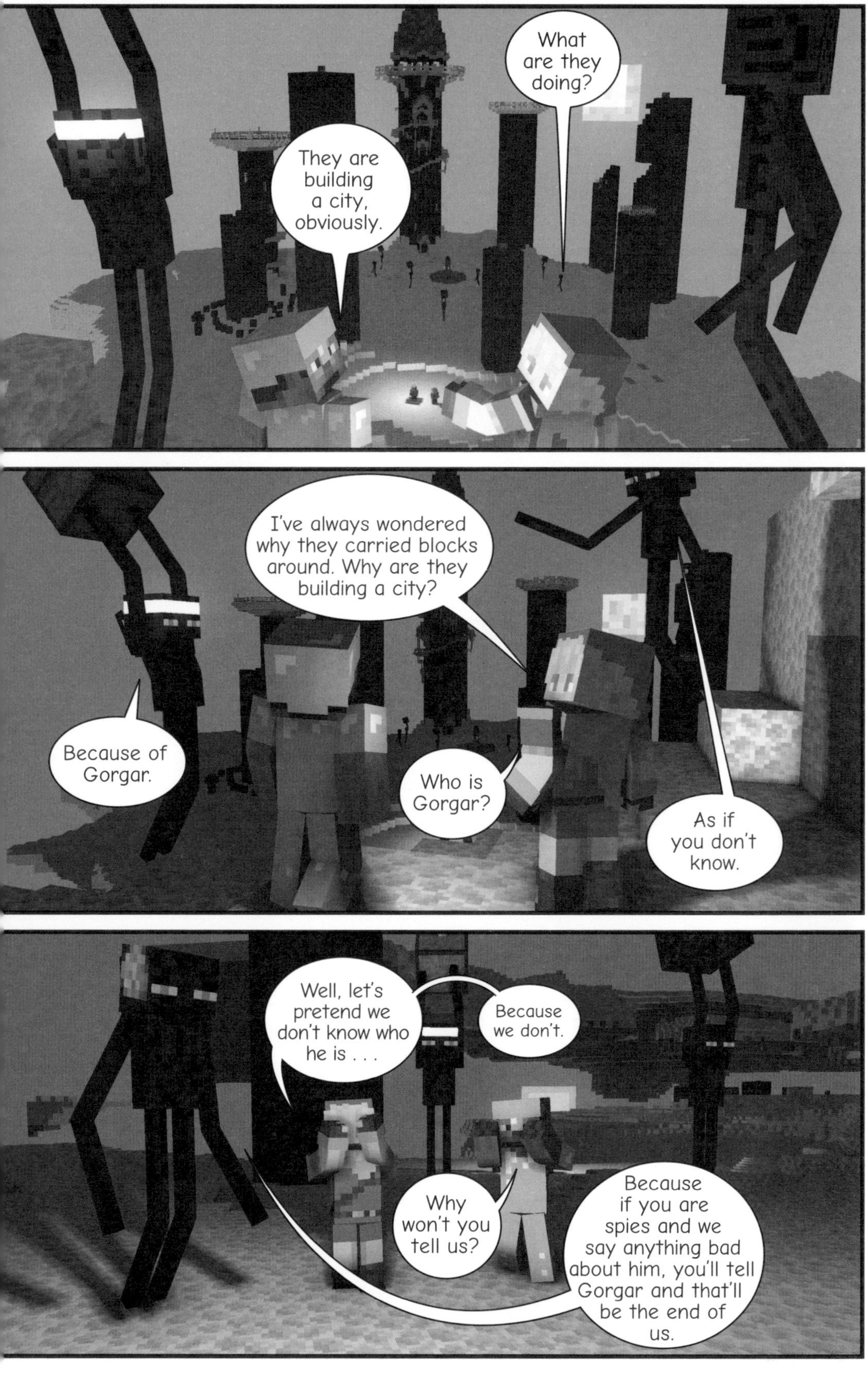
What are they doing?
They are building a city, obviously.
I've always wondered why they carried blocks around. Why are they building a city?
Because of Gorgar.
Who is Gorgar?
As if you don't know.
Well, let's pretend we don't know who he is . . .
Because we don't.
Why won't you tell us?
Because if you are spies and we say anything bad about him, you'll tell Gorgar and that'll be the end of us.

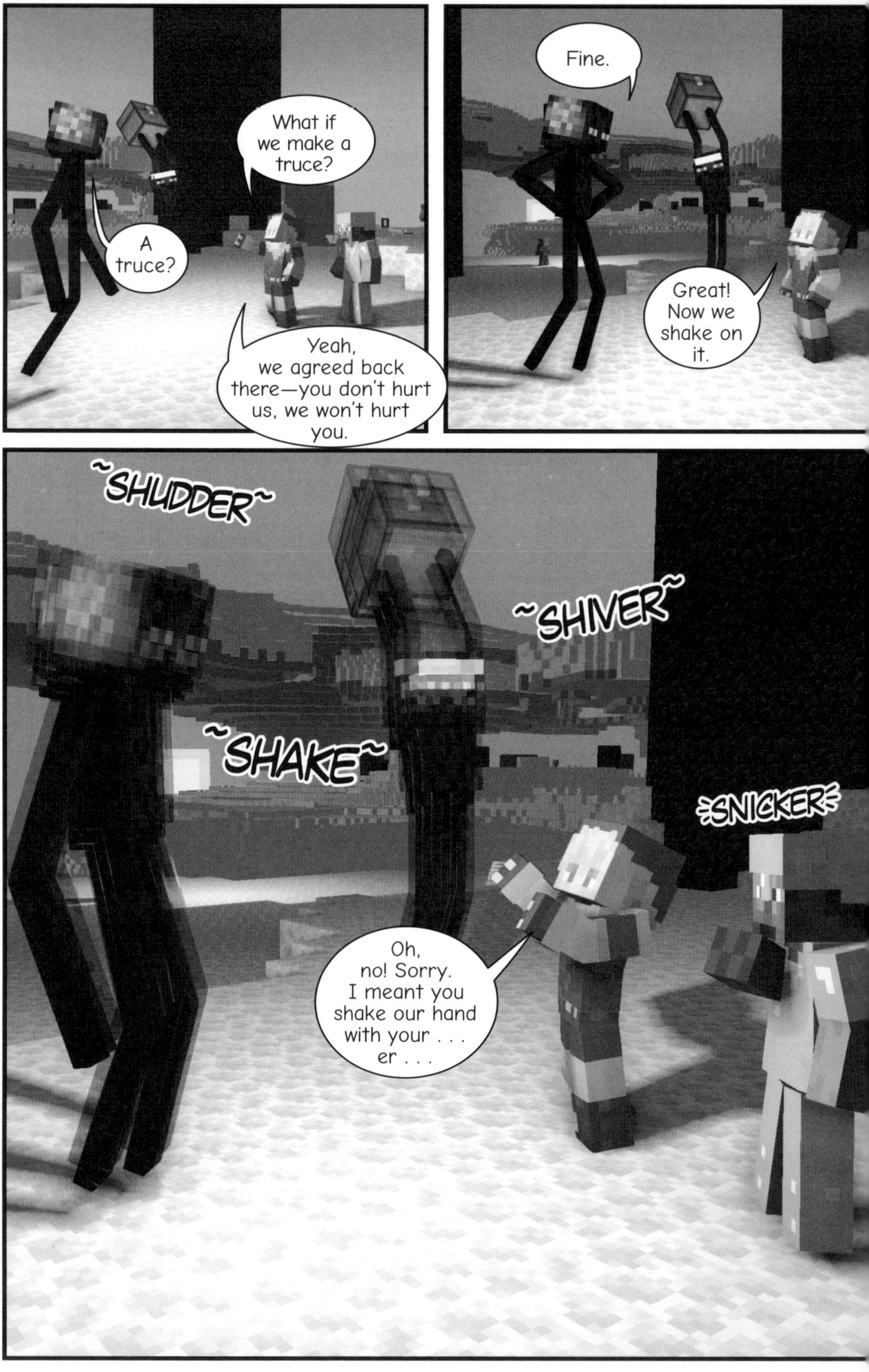
What if we make a truce?
A truce?
Yeah, we agreed back there—you don't hurt us, we won't hurt you.
Fine.
Great! Now we shake on it.
~SHUDDER~
~SHIVER~
~SHAKE~
≈SNICKER≈
Oh, no! Sorry. I meant you shake our hand with your . . . er . . .

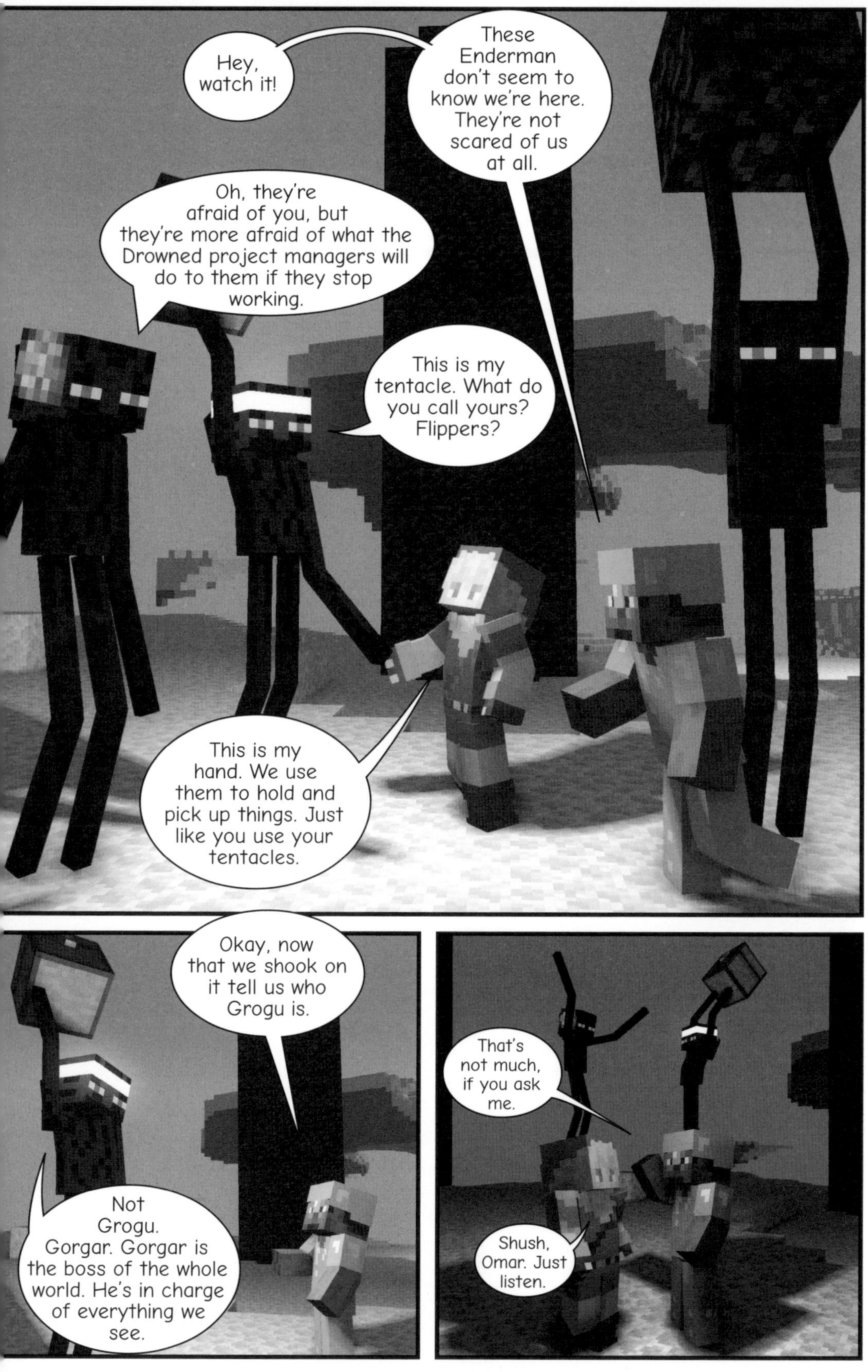
Hey, watch it!
These Enderman don't seem to know we're here. They're not scared of us at all.
Oh, they're afraid of you, but they're more afraid of what the Drowned project managers will do to them if they stop working.
This is my tentacle. What do you call yours? Flippers?
This is my hand. We use them to hold and pick up things. Just like you use your tentacles.
Okay, now that we shook on it tell us who Grogu is.
Not Grogu. Gorgar. Gorgar is the boss of the whole world. He's in charge of everything we see.
That's not much, if you ask me.
Shush, Omar. Just listen.

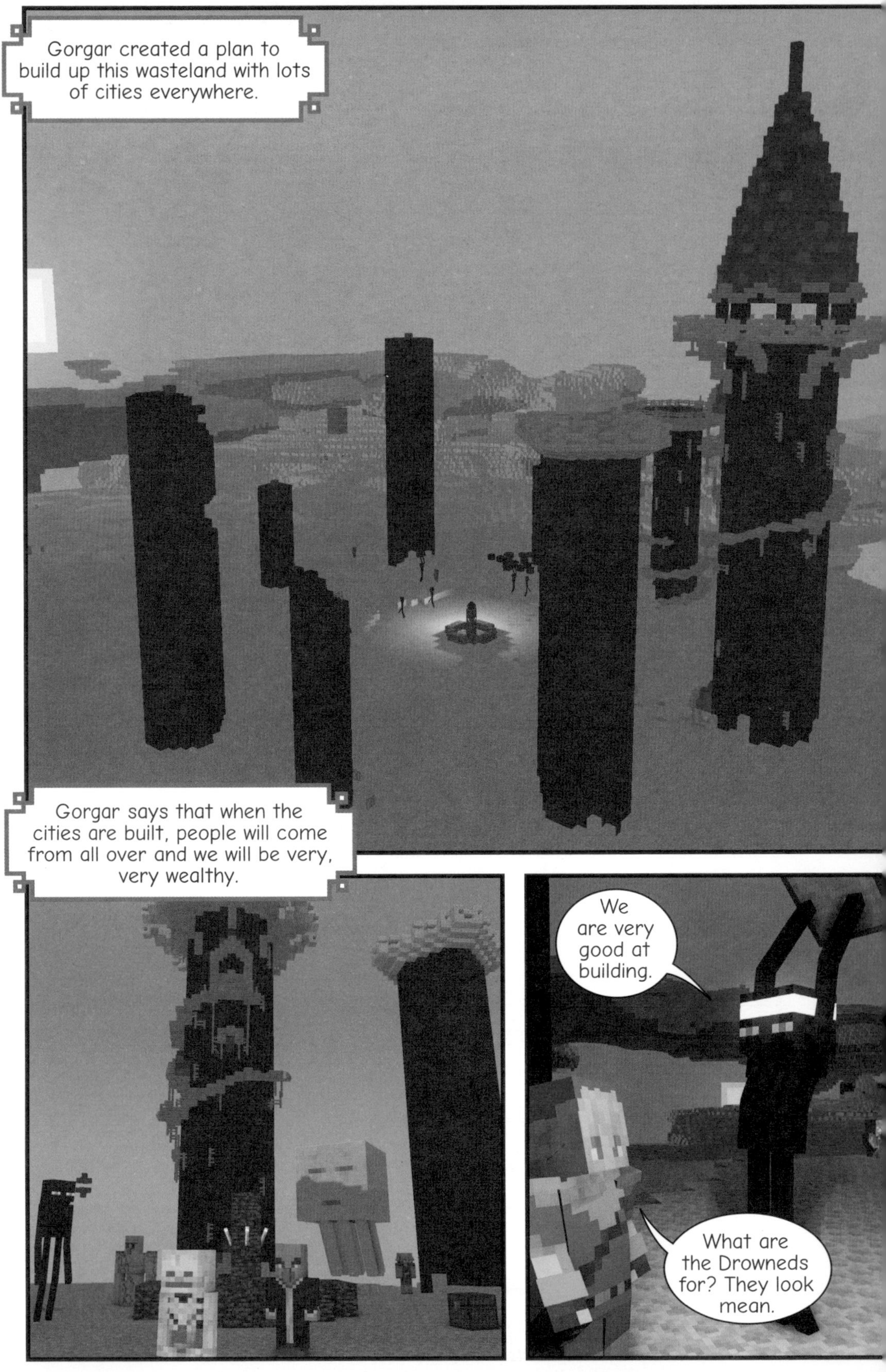
Gorgar created a plan to build up this wasteland with lots of cities everywhere.
Gorgar says that when the cities are built, people will come from all over and we will be very, very wealthy.
We are very good at building.
What are the Drowneds for? They look mean.

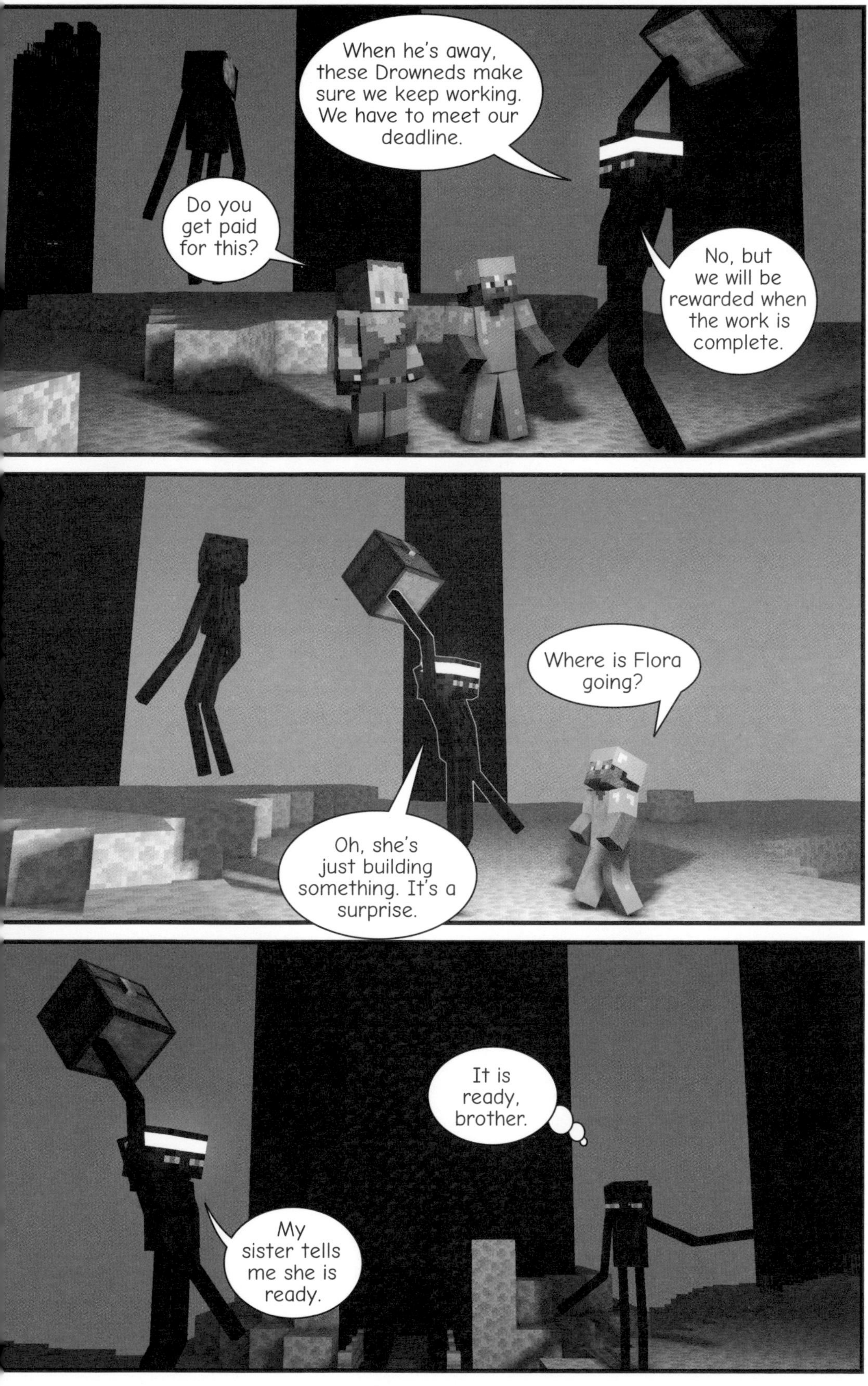
When he's away, these Drowneds make sure we keep working. We have to meet our deadline.
Do you get paid for this?
No, but we will be rewarded when the work is complete.
Where is Flora going?
Oh, she's just building something. It's a surprise.
It is ready, brother.
My sister tells me she is ready.

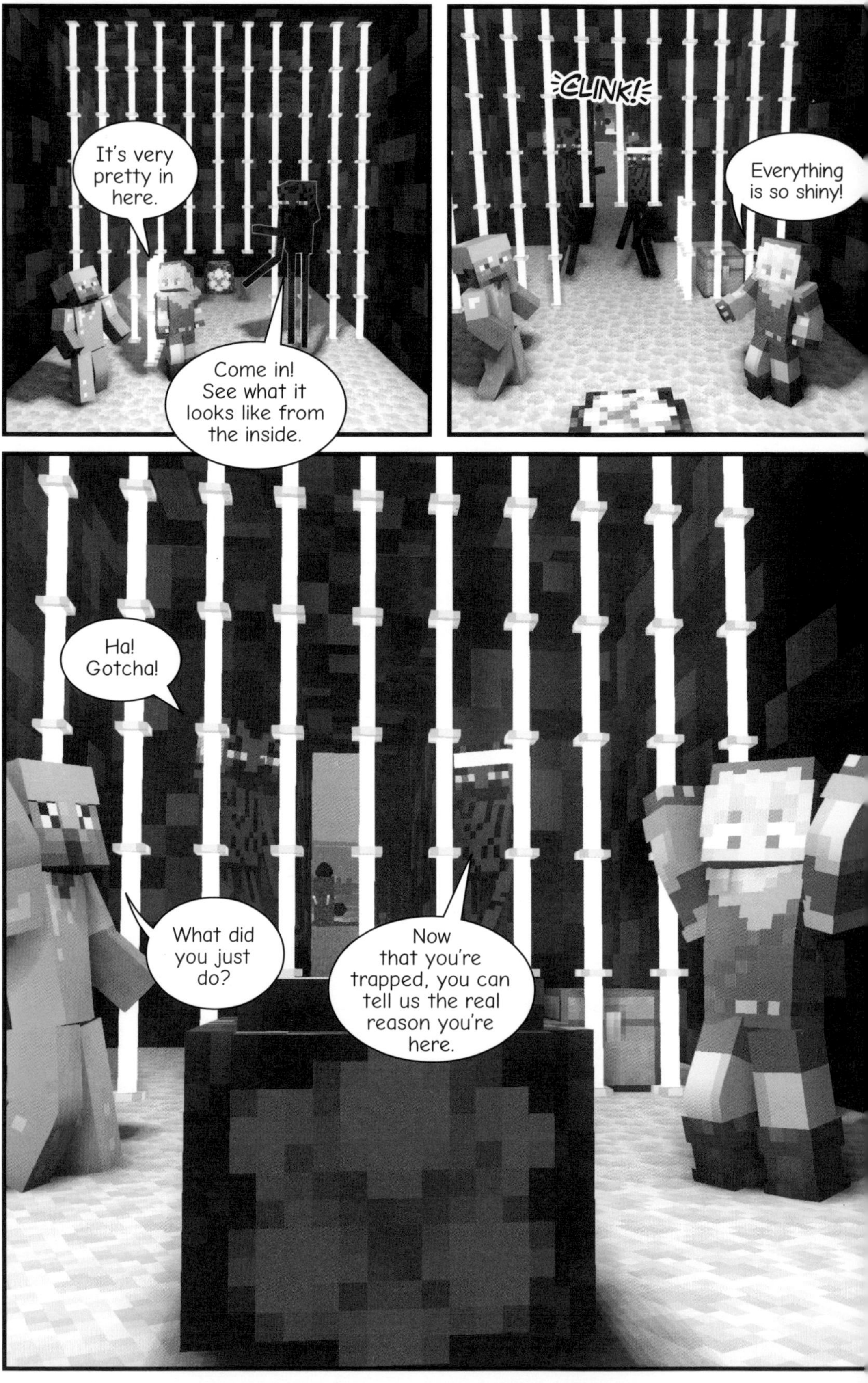
It's very pretty in here.
Come in! See what it looks like from the inside.
CLINK!
Everything is so shiny!
Ha! Gotcha!
What did you just do?
Now that you're trapped, you can tell us the real reason you're here.

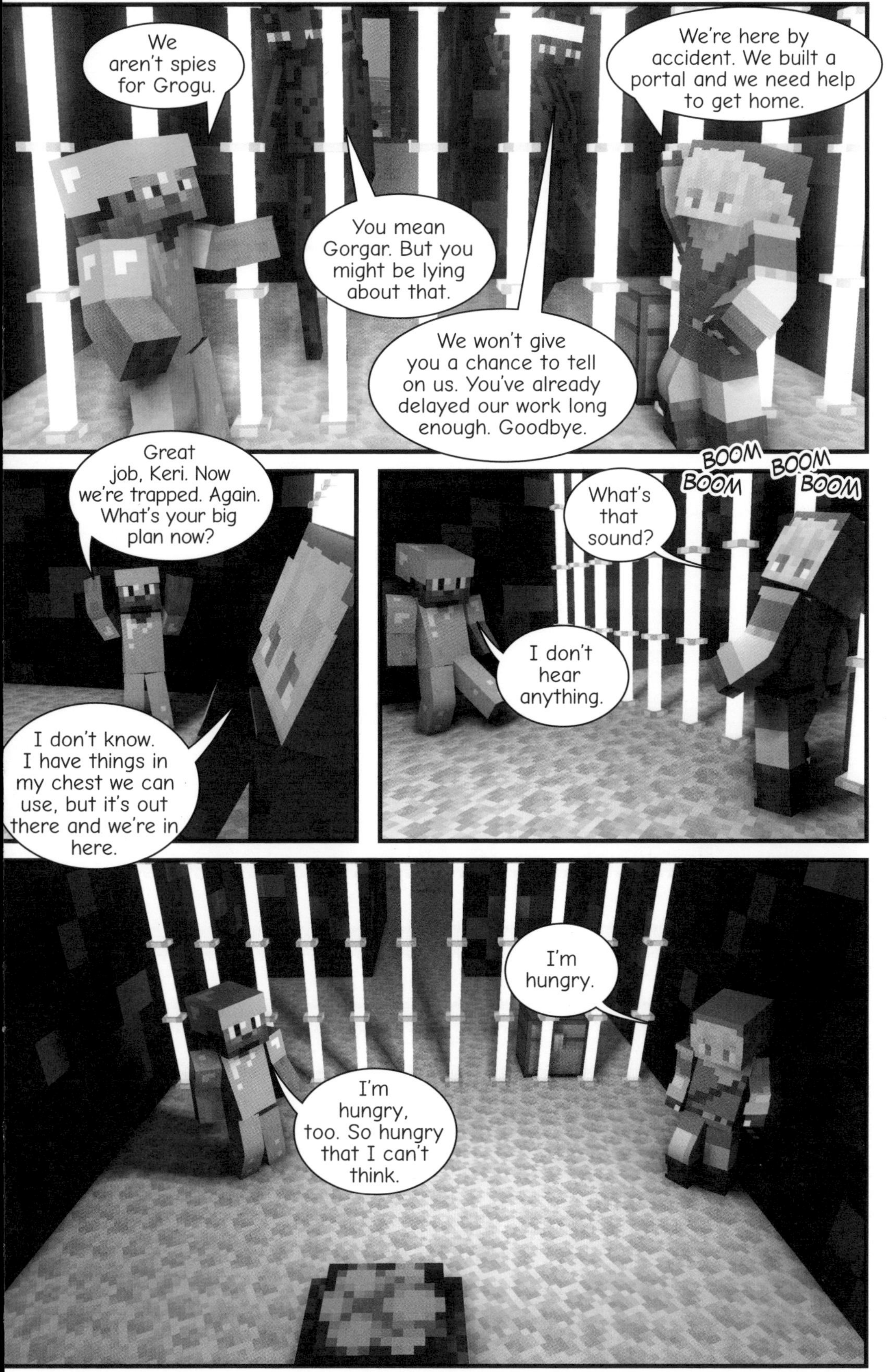

We aren't spies for Grogu.
We're here by accident. We built a portal and we need help to get home.
You mean Gorgar. But you might be lying about that.
We won't give you a chance to tell on us. You've already delayed our work long enough. Goodbye.
Great job, Keri. Now we're trapped. Again. What's your big plan now?
I don't know. I have things in my chest we can use, but it's out there and we're in here.
BOOM BOOM BOOM BOOM
What's that sound?
I don't hear anything.
I'm hungry.
I'm hungry, too. So hungry that I can't think.

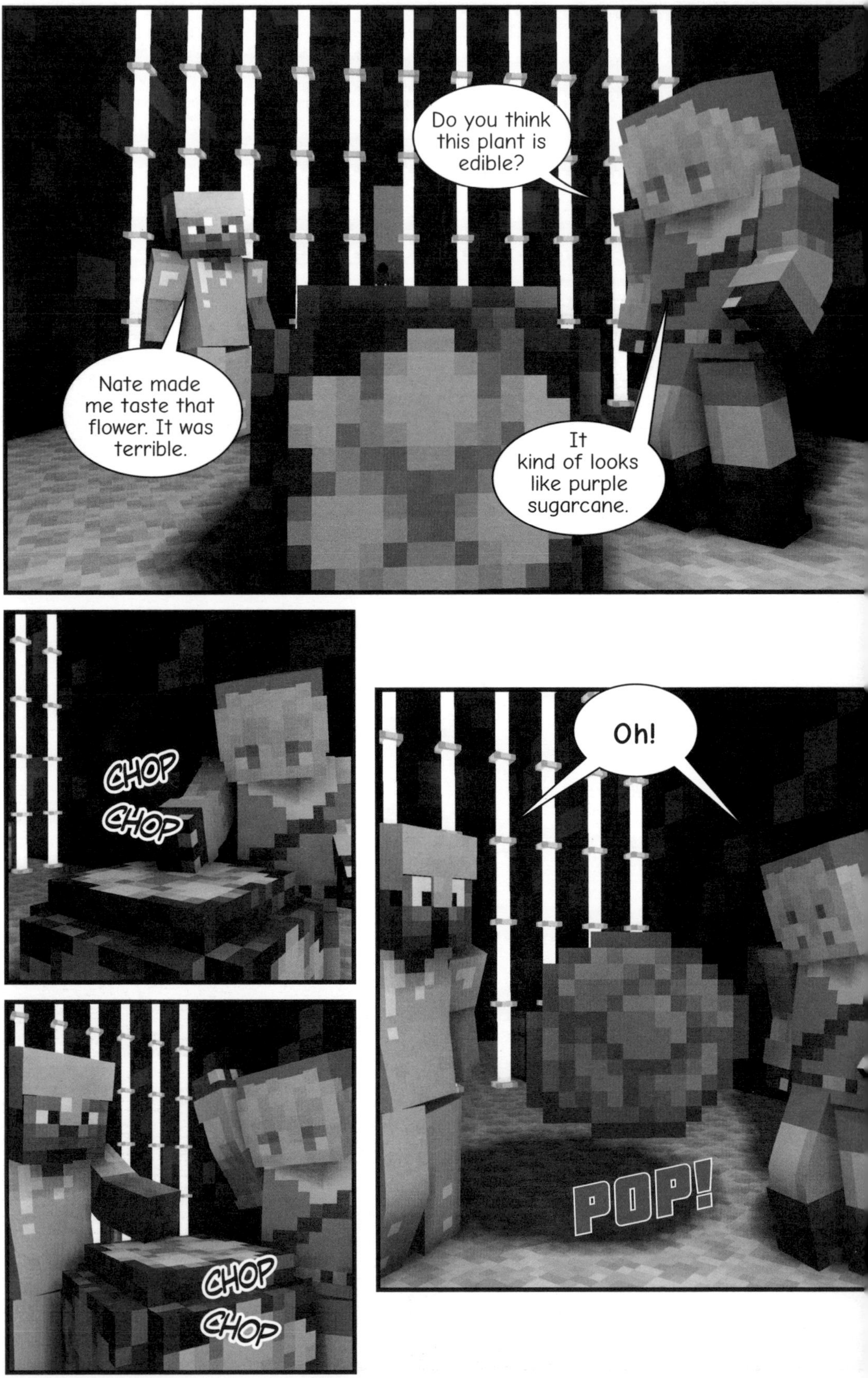
Do you think this plant is edible?
Nate made me taste that flower. It was terrible.
It kind of looks like purple sugarcane.
CHOP CHOP
CHOP CHOP
Oh!
POP!

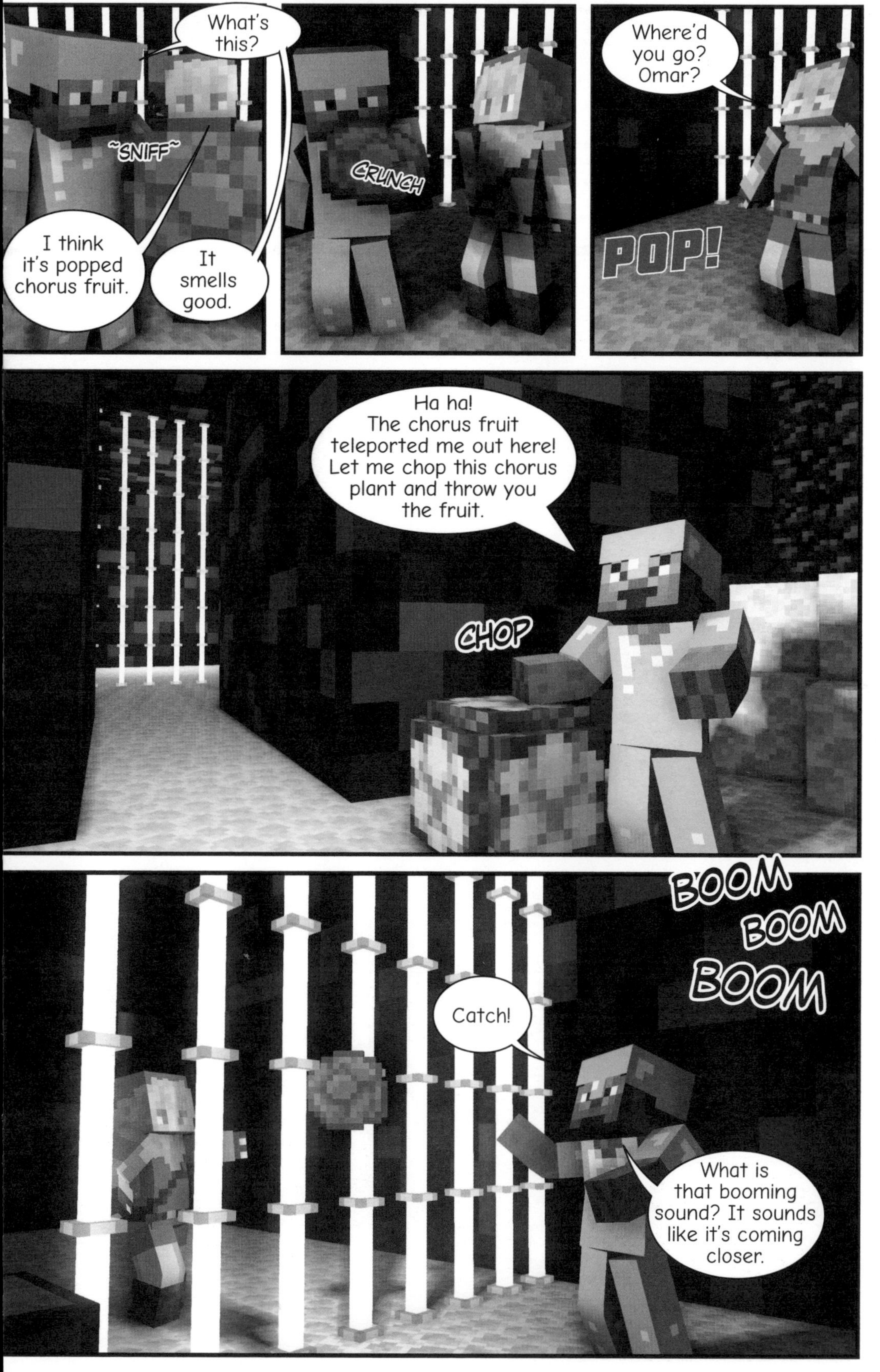
What's this?
~SNIFF~
I think it's popped chorus fruit.
It smells good.
CRUNCH
Where'd you go? Omar?
POP!
Ha ha! The chorus fruit teleported me out here! Let me chop this chorus plant and throw you the fruit.
CHOP
BOOM BOOM BOOM
Catch!
What is that booming sound? It sounds like it's coming closer.

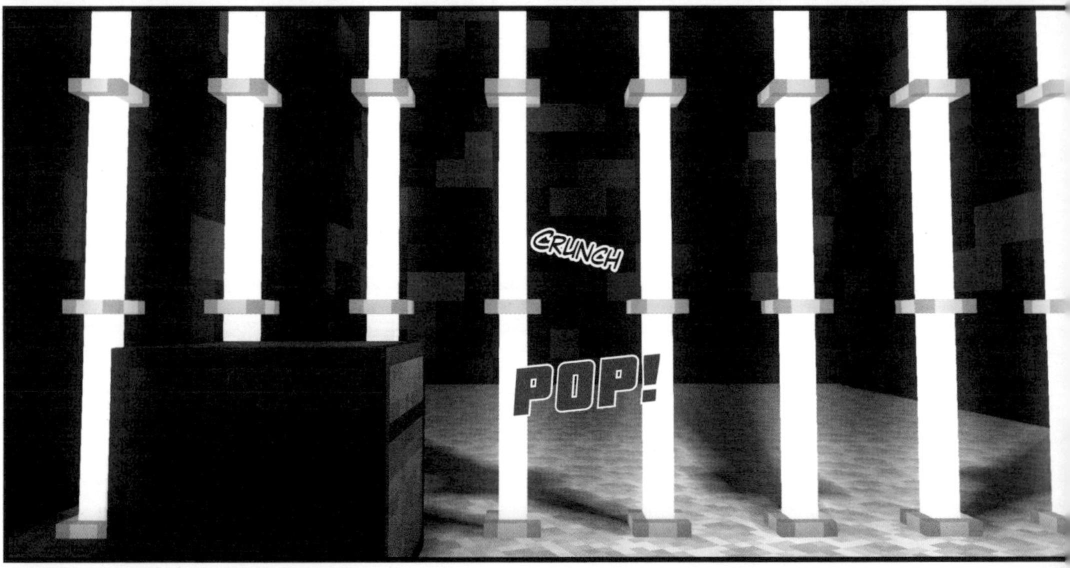
CRUNCH
POP!

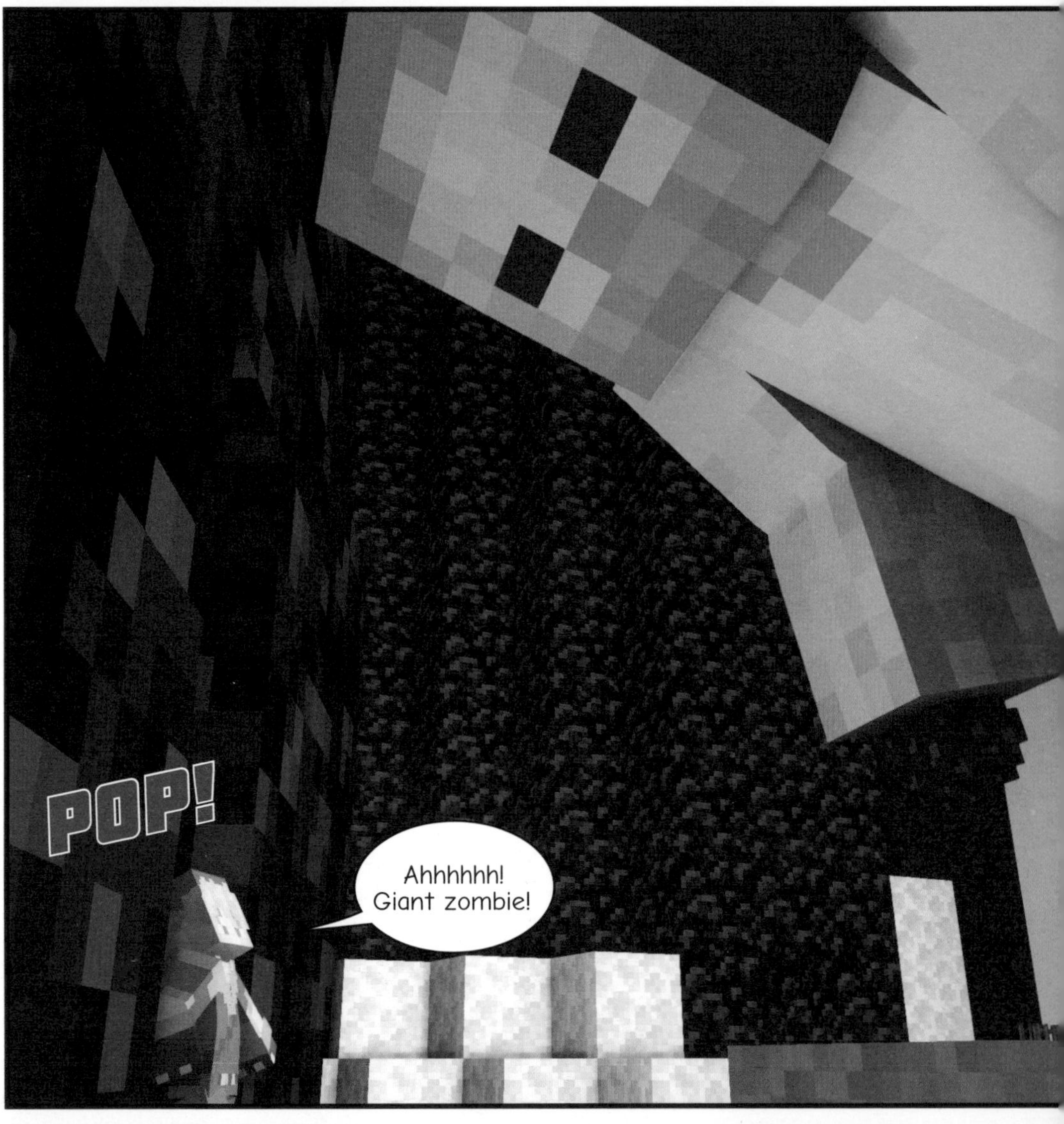
POP!
Ahhhhhh!
Giant zombie!

CHAPTER 4
MOBBED

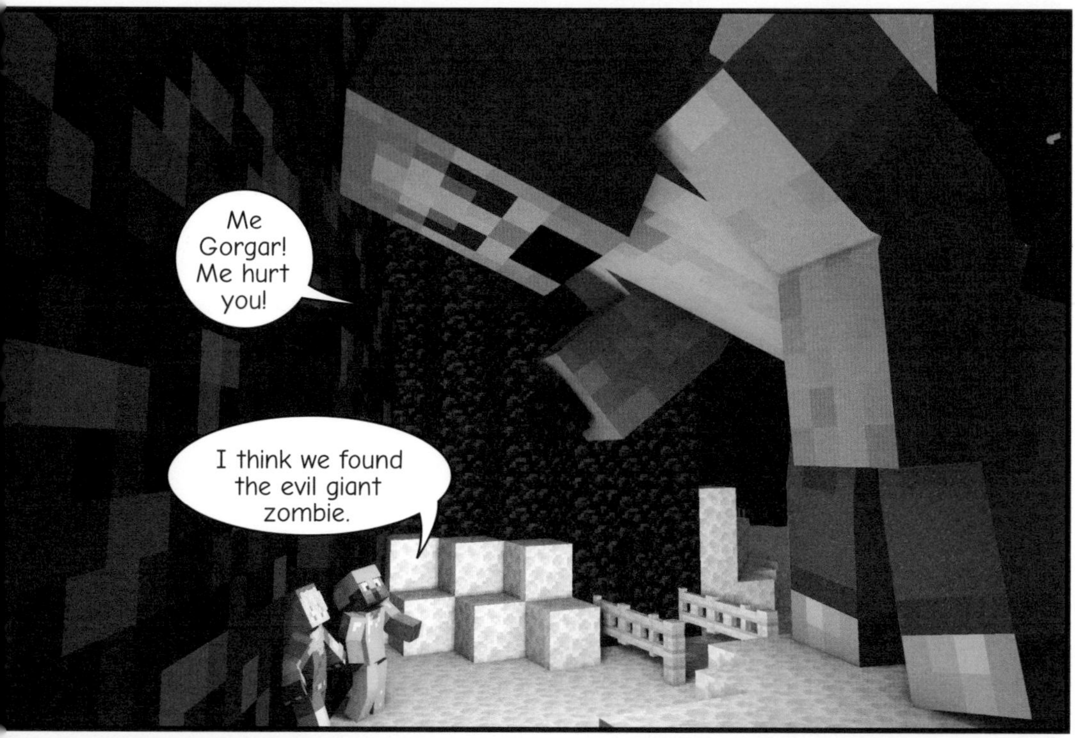
Me Gorgar! Me hurt you!
I think we found the evil giant zombie.

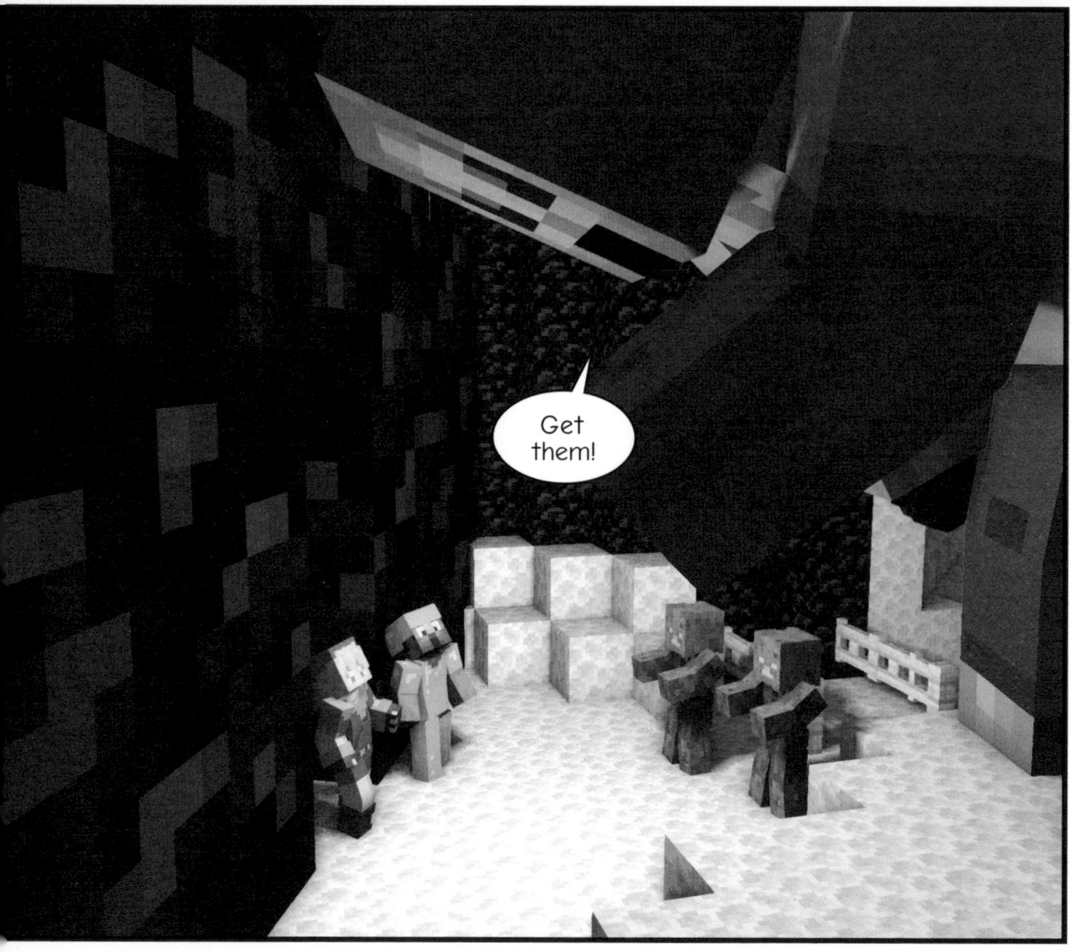
Get them!

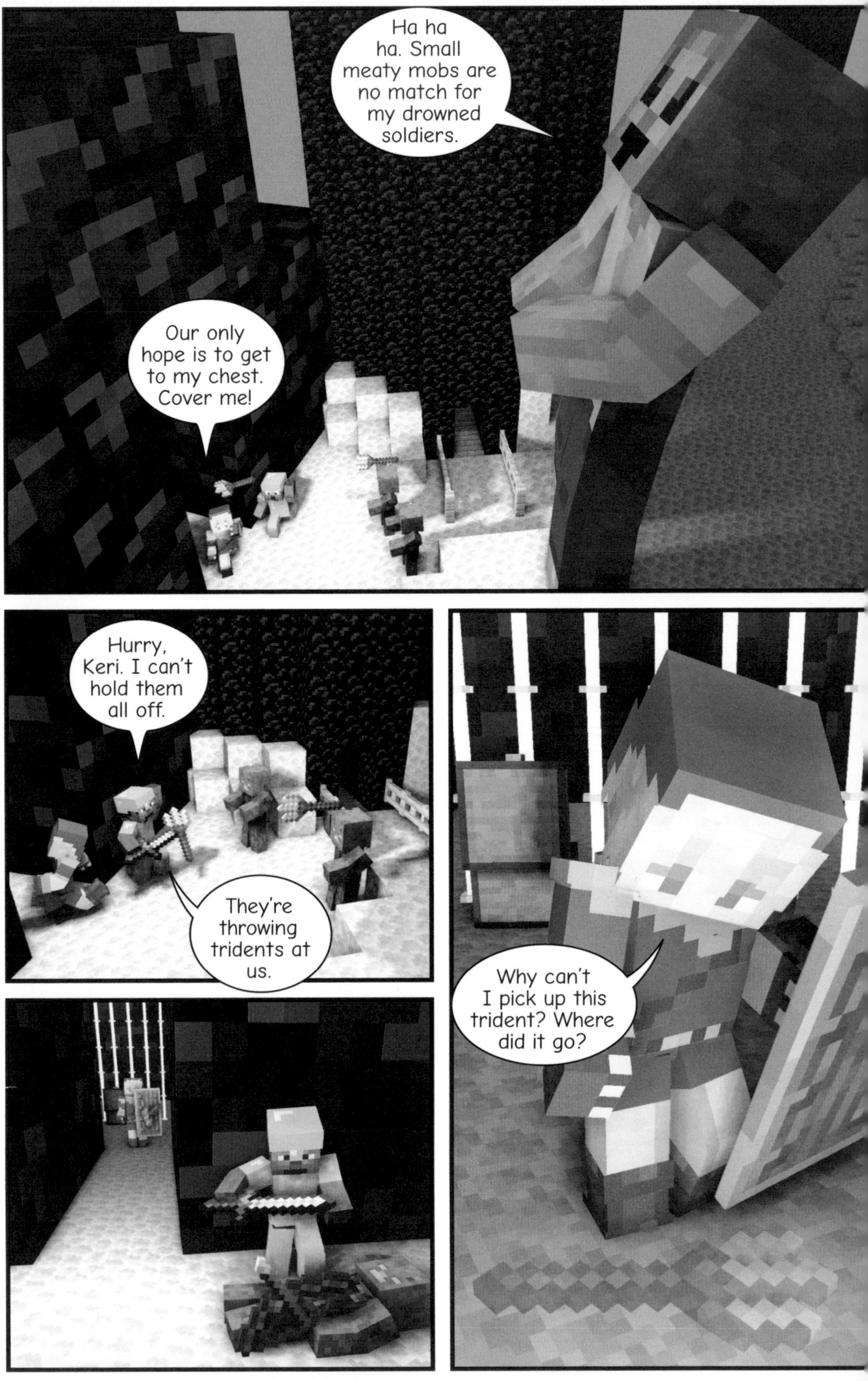
Ha ha ha. Small meaty mobs are no match for my drowned soldiers.
Our only hope is to get to my chest. Cover me!
Hurry, Keri. I can't hold them all off.
They're throwing tridents at us.
Why can't I pick up this trident? Where did it go?

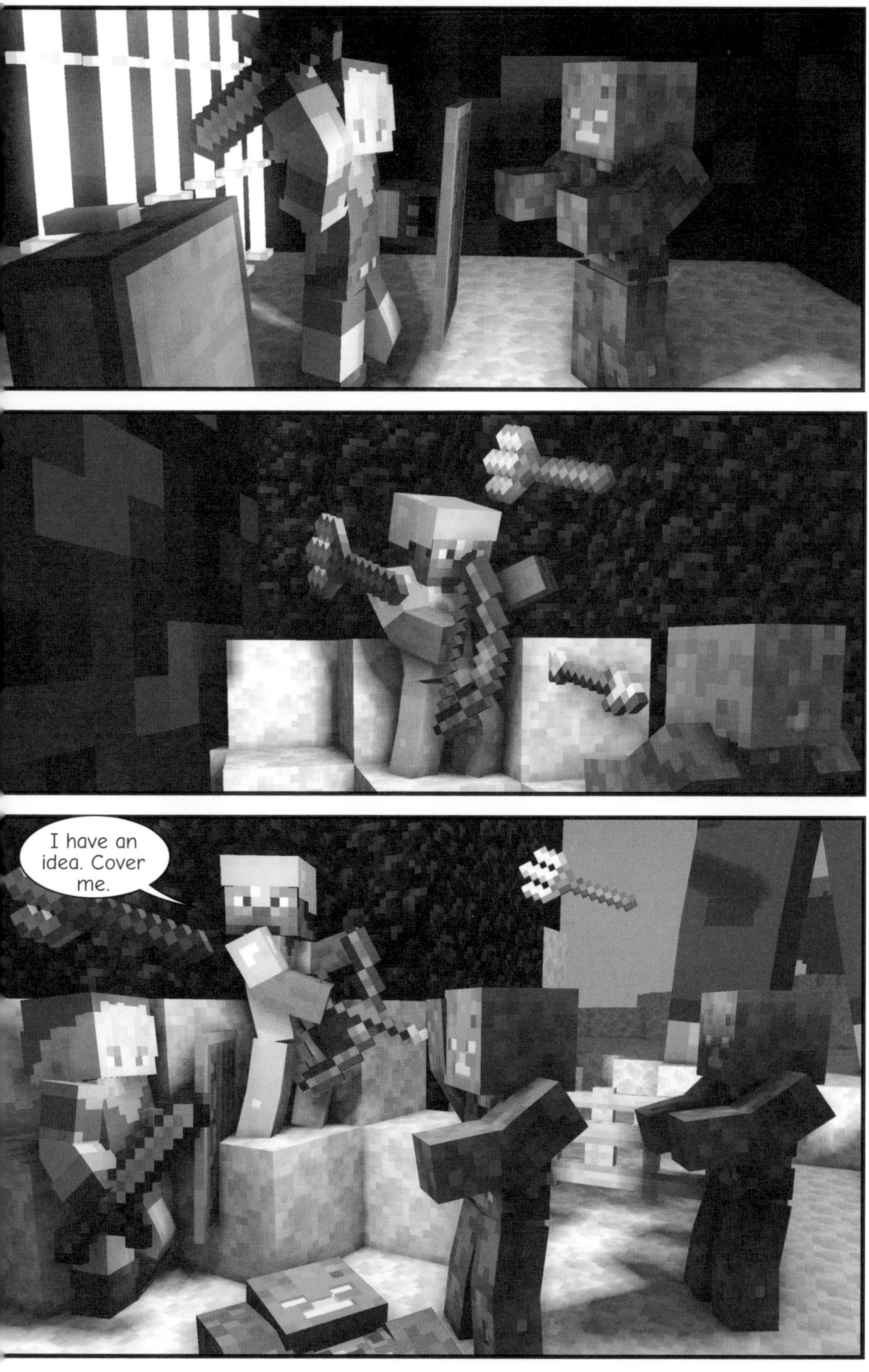
I have an idea. Cover me.

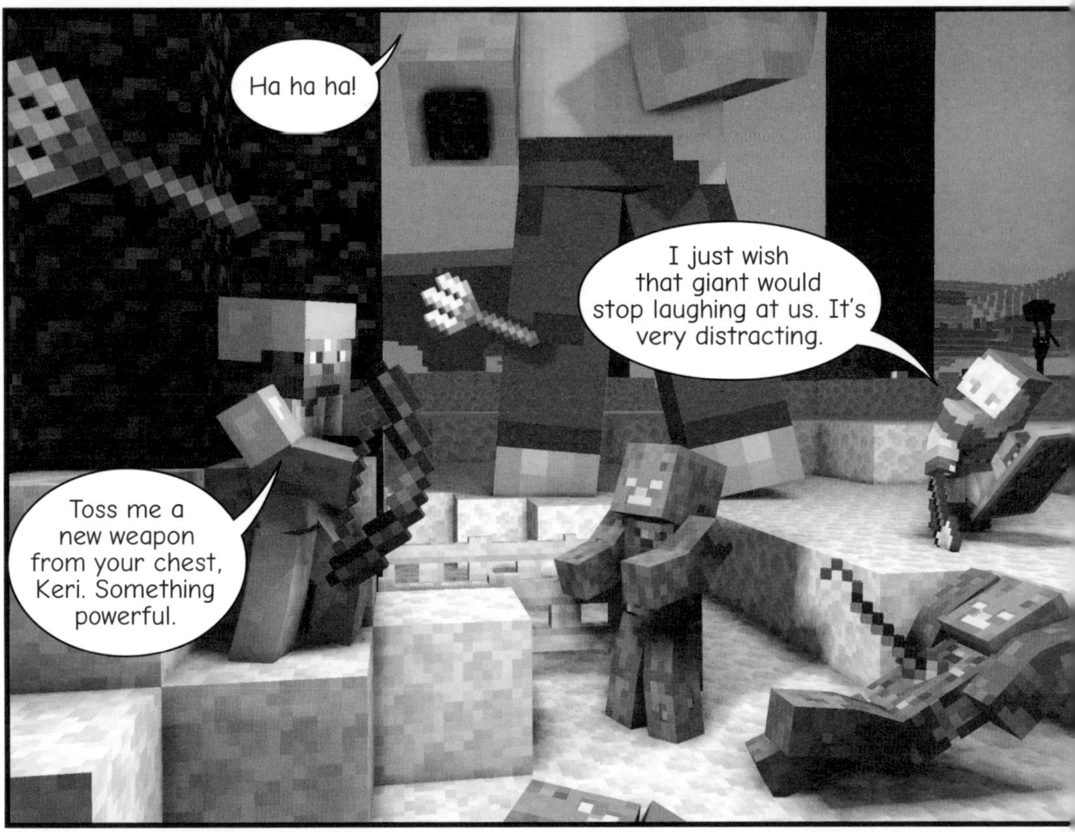
Ha ha ha!
I just wish that giant would stop laughing at us. It's very distracting.
Toss me a new weapon from your chest, Keri. Something powerful.

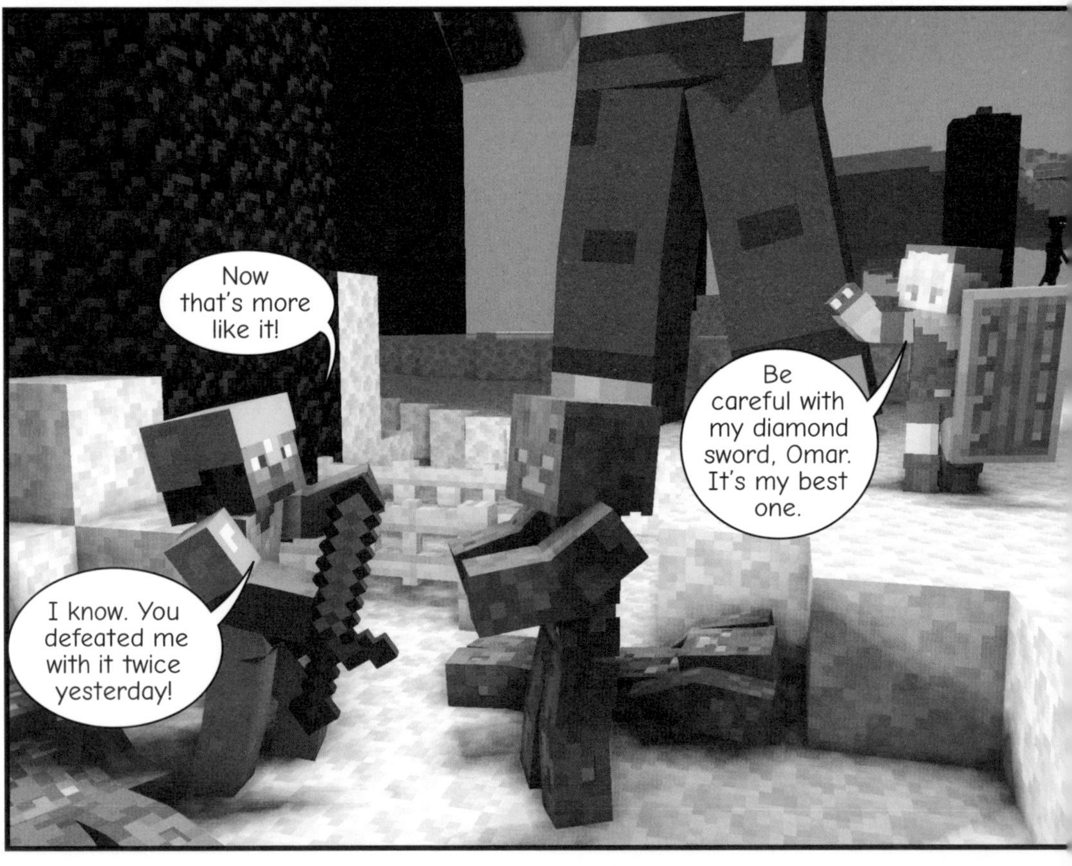
Now that's more like it!
Be careful with my diamond sword, Omar. It's my best one.
I know. You defeated me with it twice yesterday!

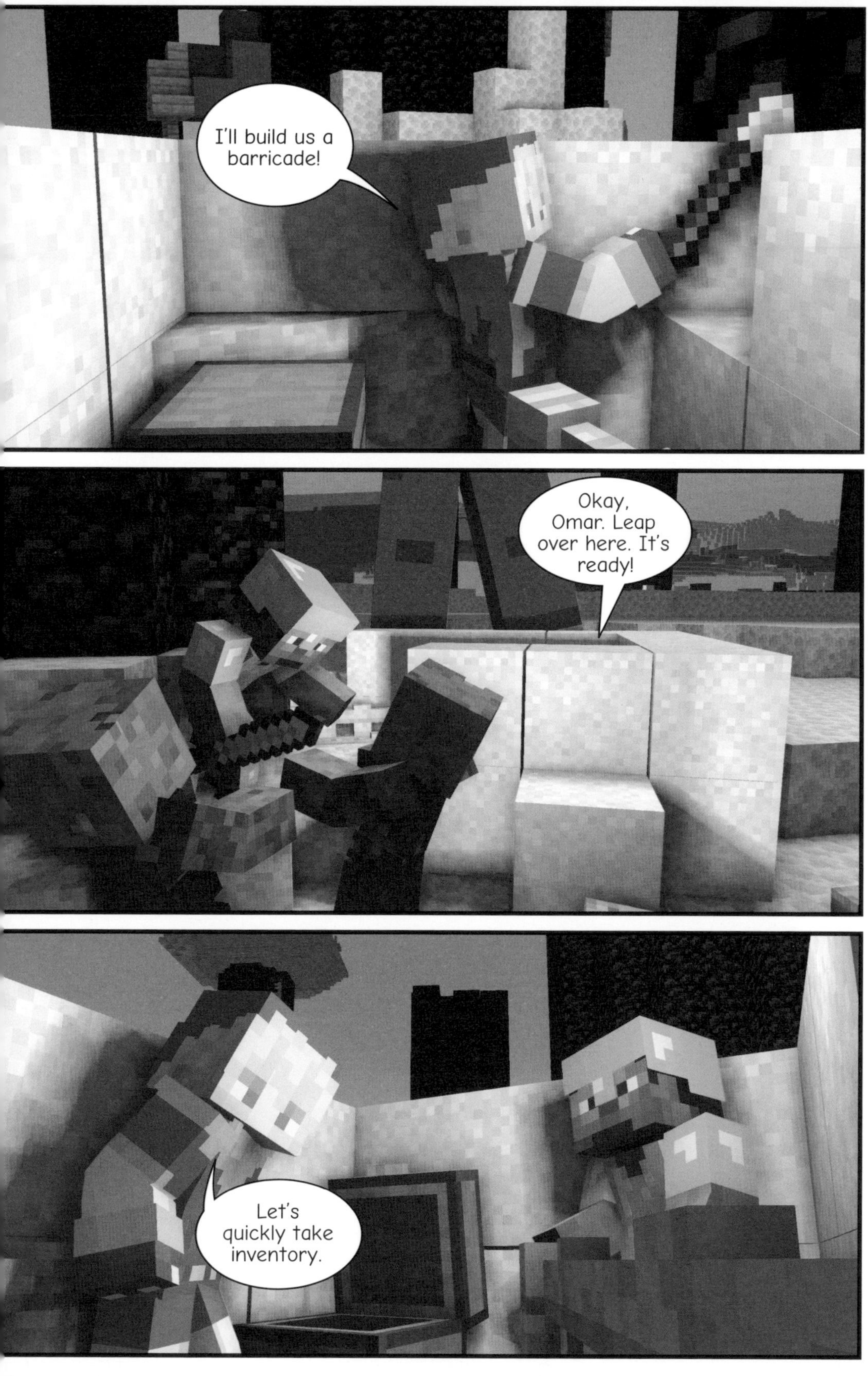
I'll build us a barricade!
Okay, Omar. Leap over here. It's ready!
Let's quickly take inventory.

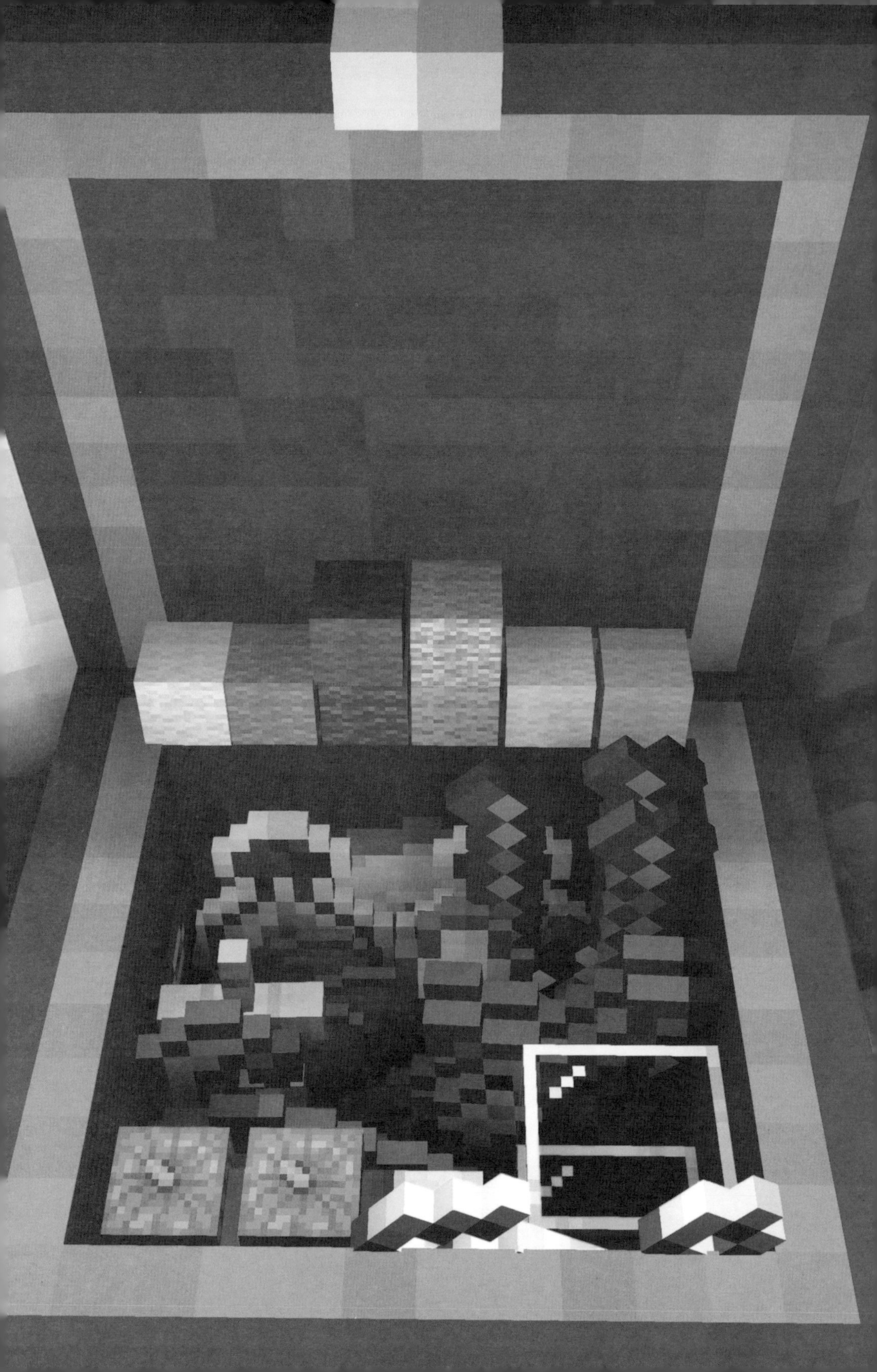

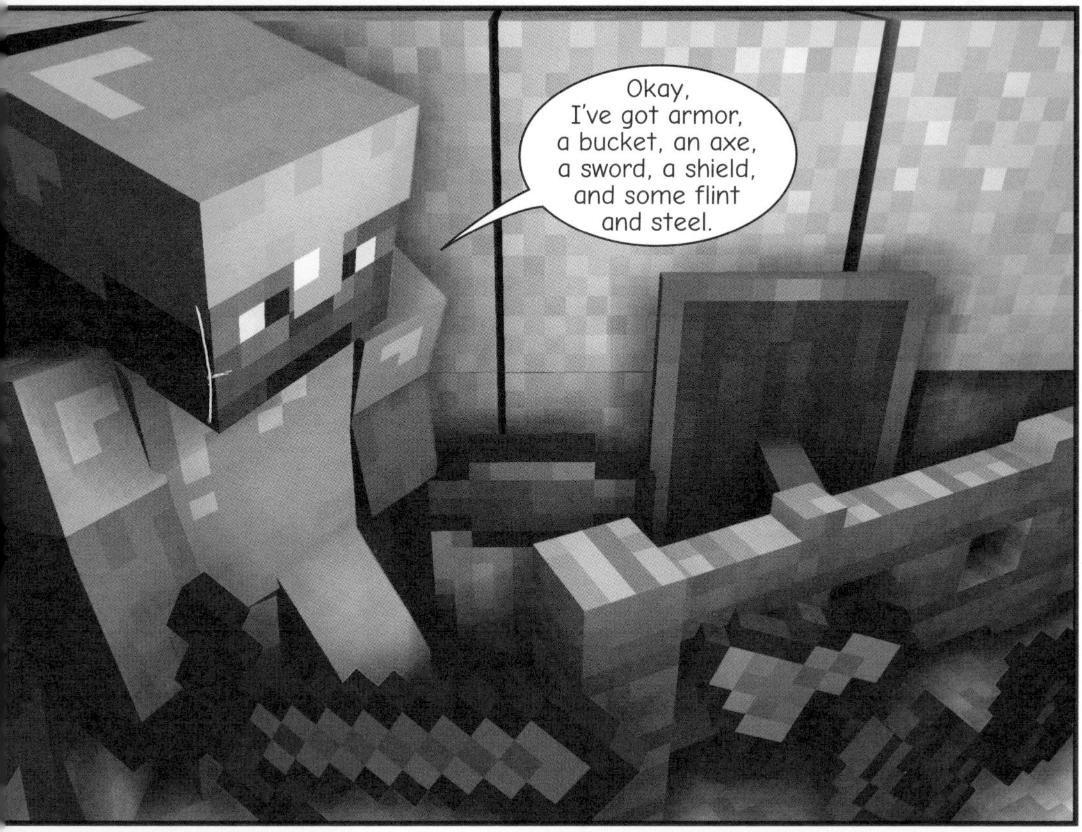
Okay, I've got armor, a bucket, an axe, a sword, a shield, and some flint and steel.

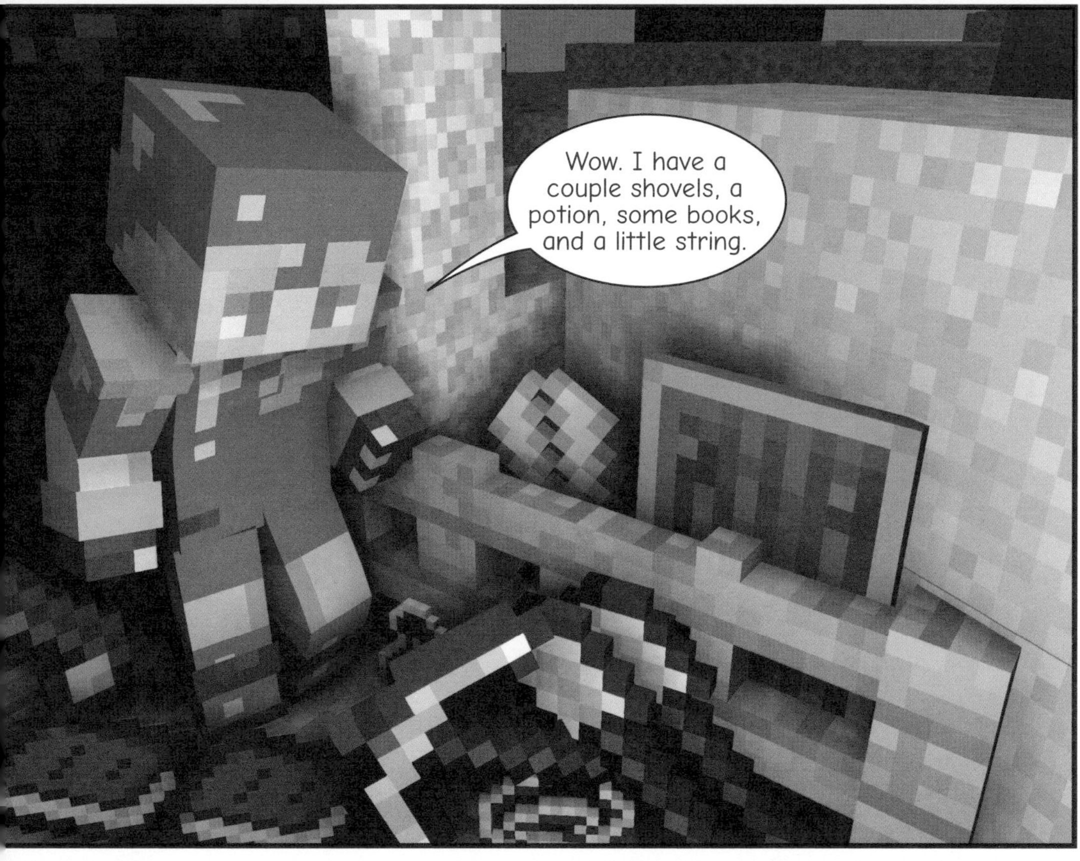
Wow. I have a couple shovels, a potion, some books, and a little string.

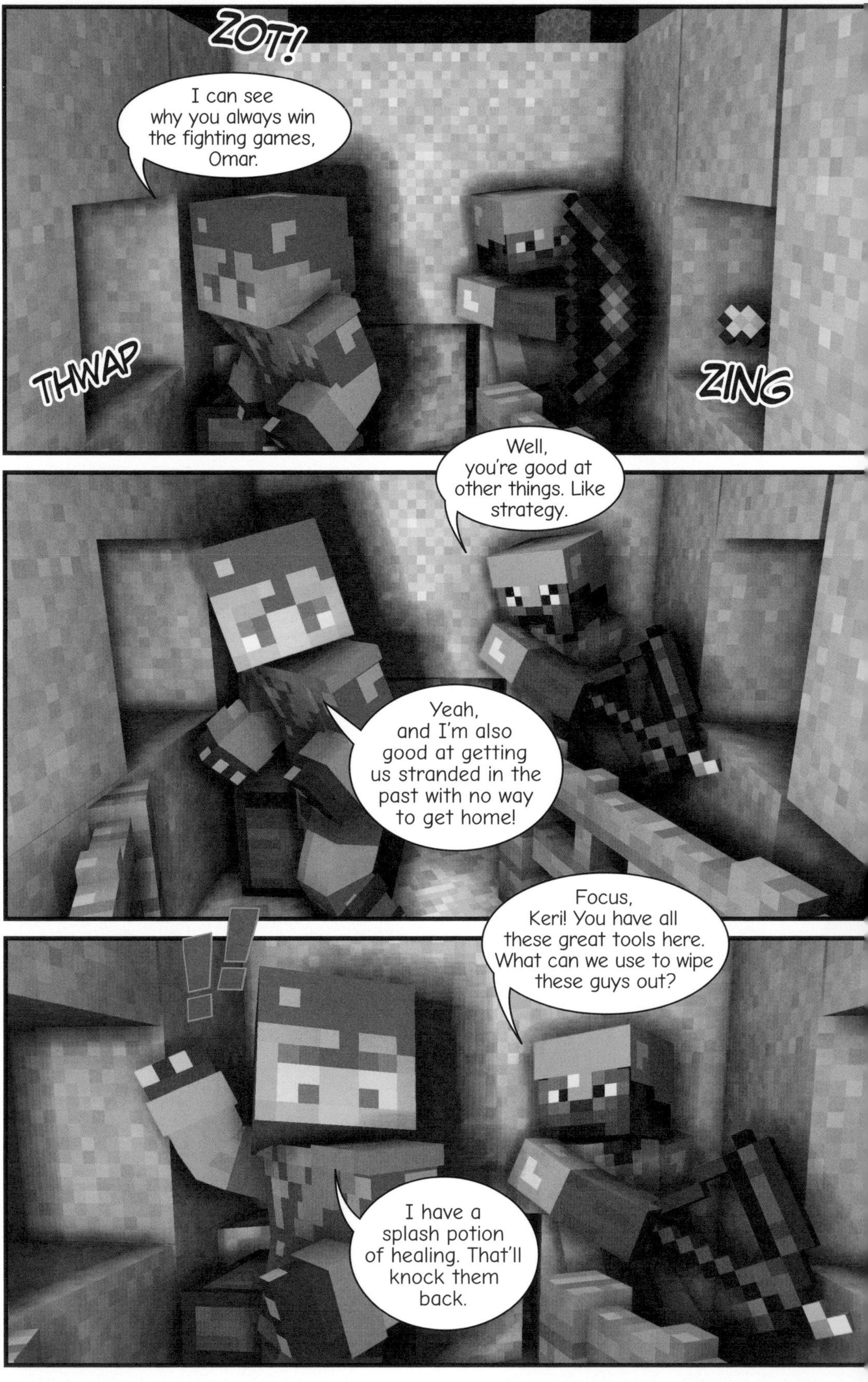
ZOT!
I can see why you always win the fighting games, Omar.
THWAP
ZING
Well, you're good at other things. Like strategy.
Yeah, and I'm also good at getting us stranded in the past with no way to get home!
Focus, Keri! You have all these great tools here. What can we use to wipe these guys out?
I have a splash potion of healing. That'll knock them back.

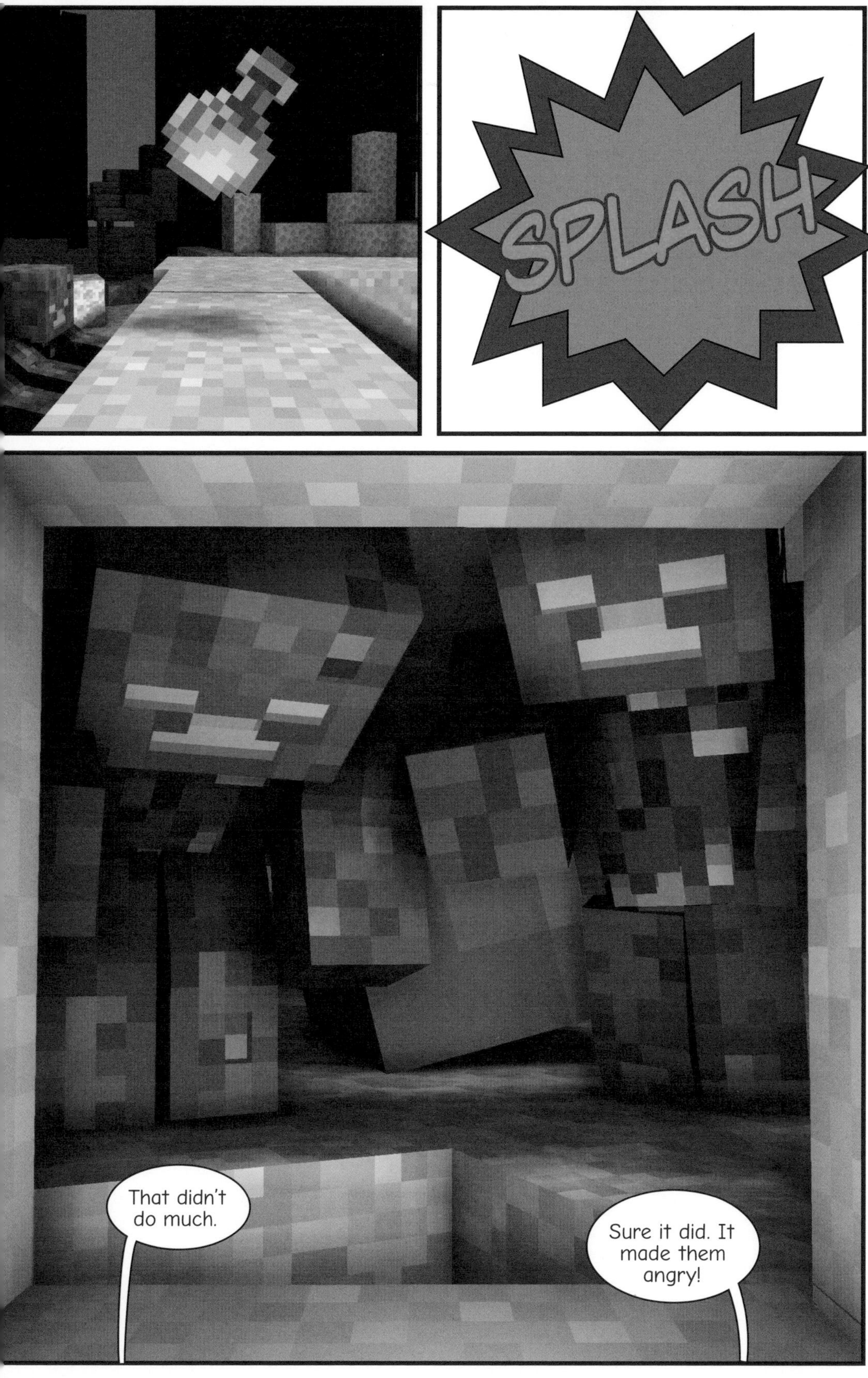
SPLASH
That didn't do much.
Sure it did. It made them angry!

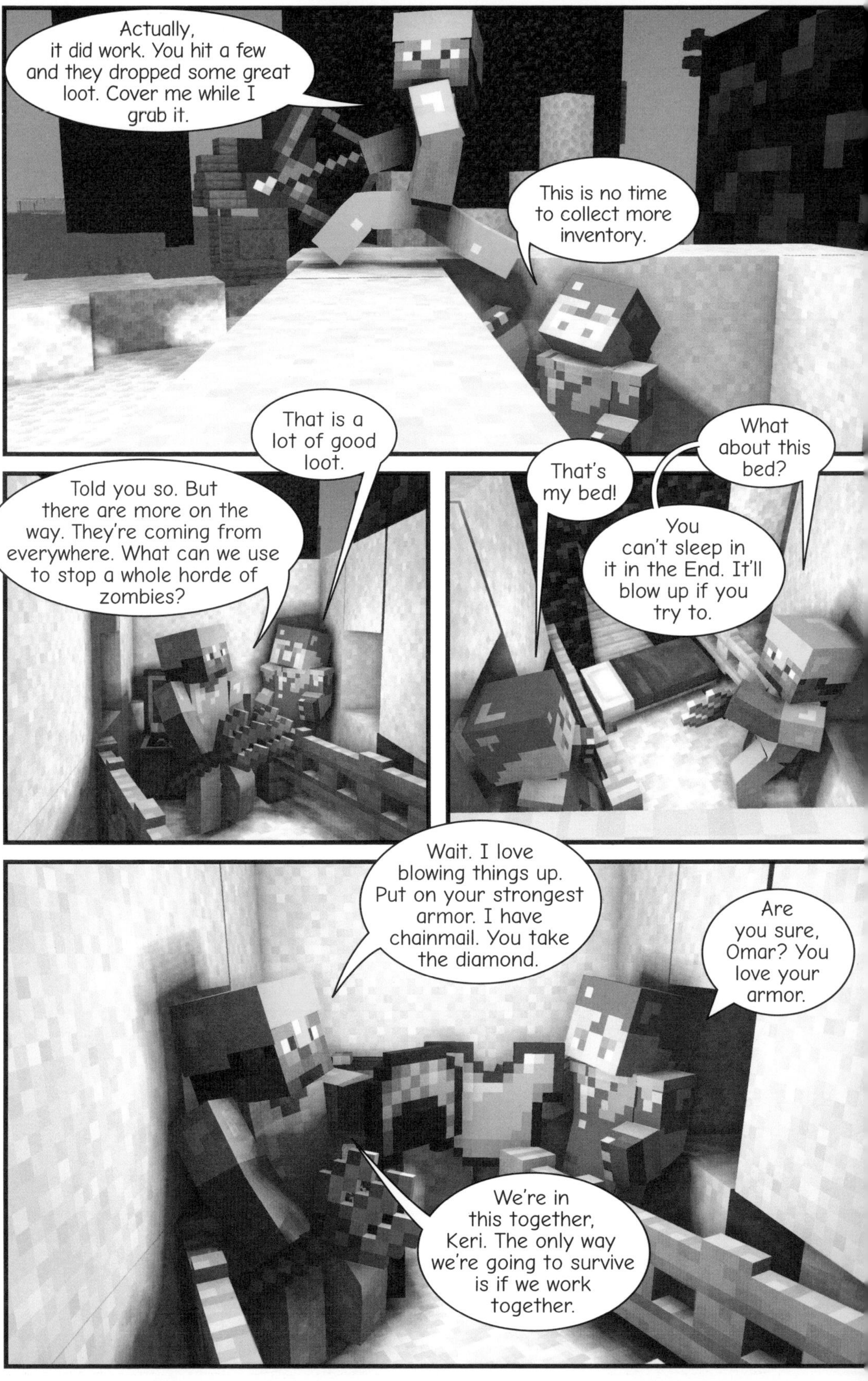
Actually, it did work. You hit a few and they dropped some great loot. Cover me while I grab it.
This is no time to collect more inventory.
Told you so. But there are more on the way. They're coming from everywhere. What can we use to stop a whole horde of zombies?
That is a lot of good loot.
That's my bed!
What about this bed?
You can't sleep in it in the End. It'll blow up if you try to.
Wait. I love blowing things up. Put on your strongest armor. I have chainmail. You take the diamond.
Are you sure, Omar? You love your armor.
We're in this together, Keri. The only way we're going to survive is if we work together.

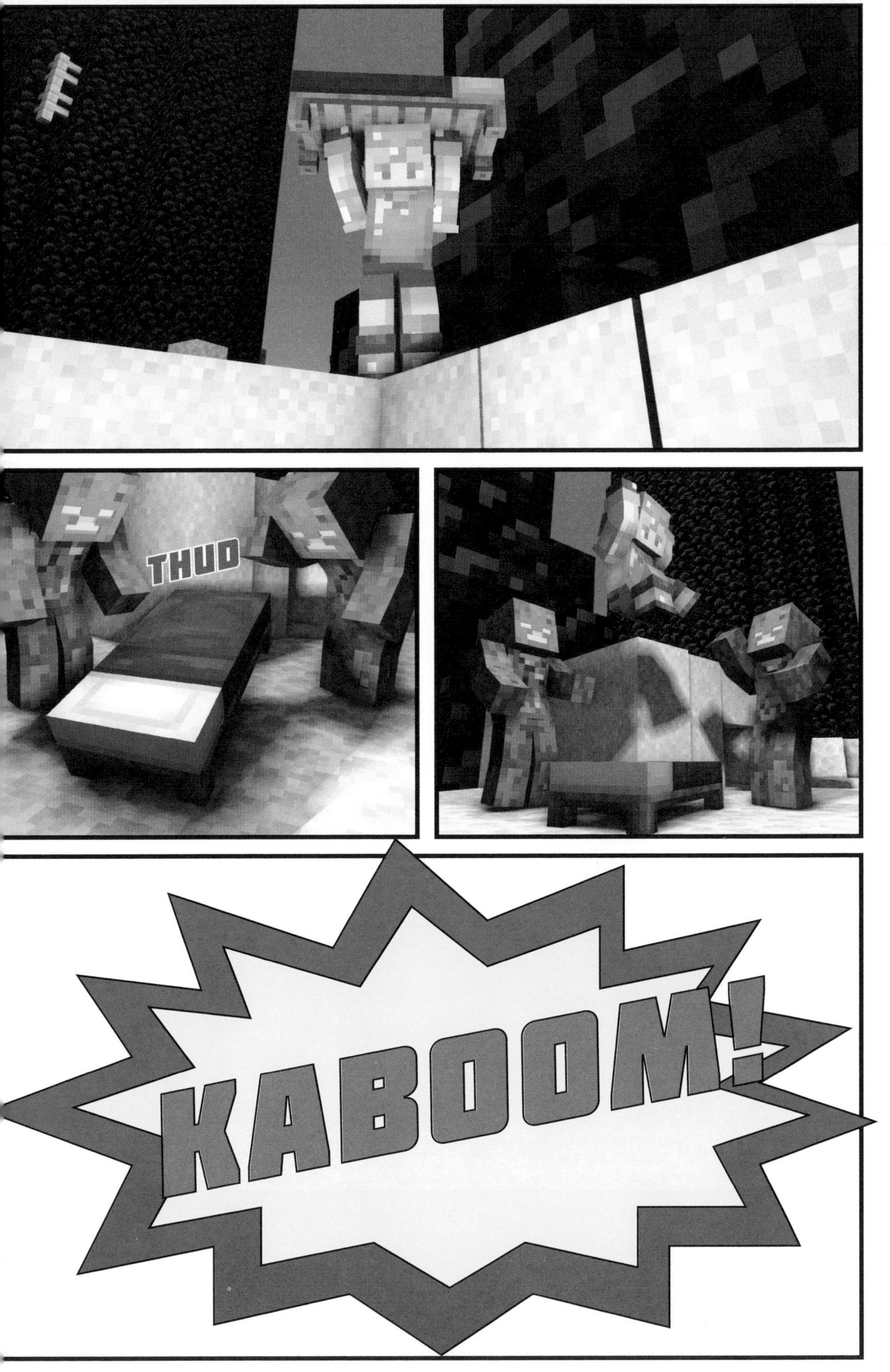
THUD
KABOOM!

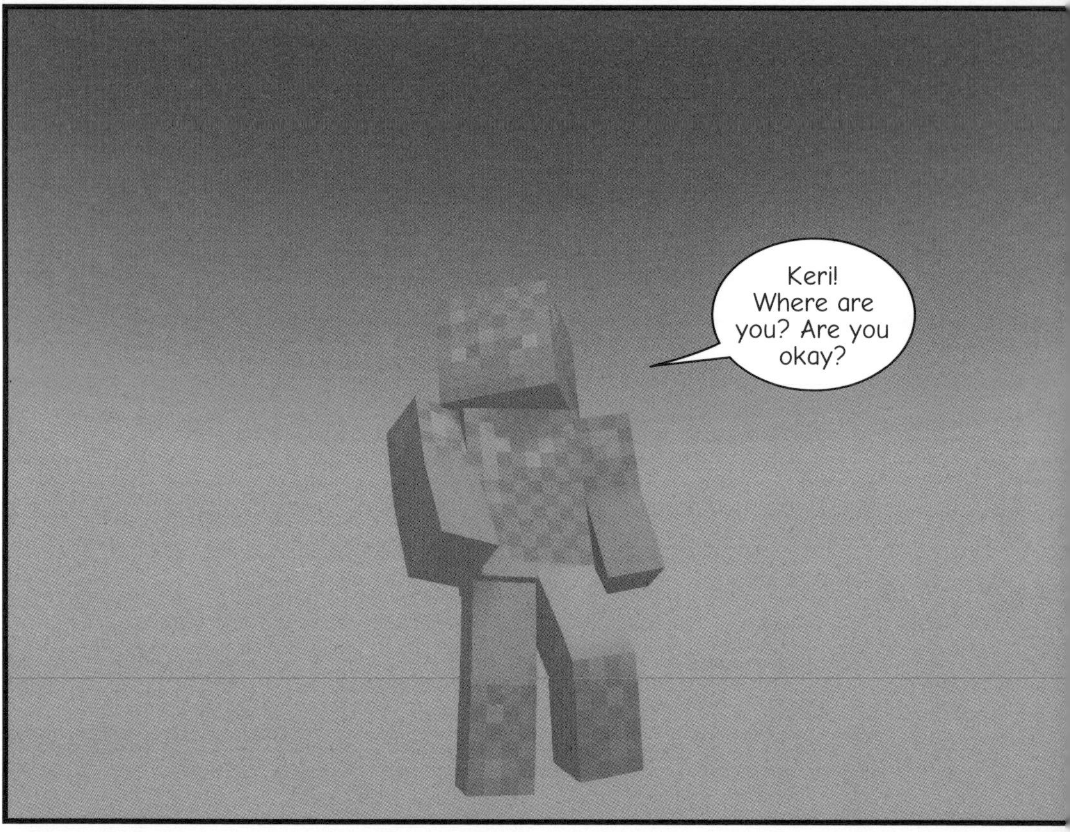
Keri! Where are you? Are you okay?

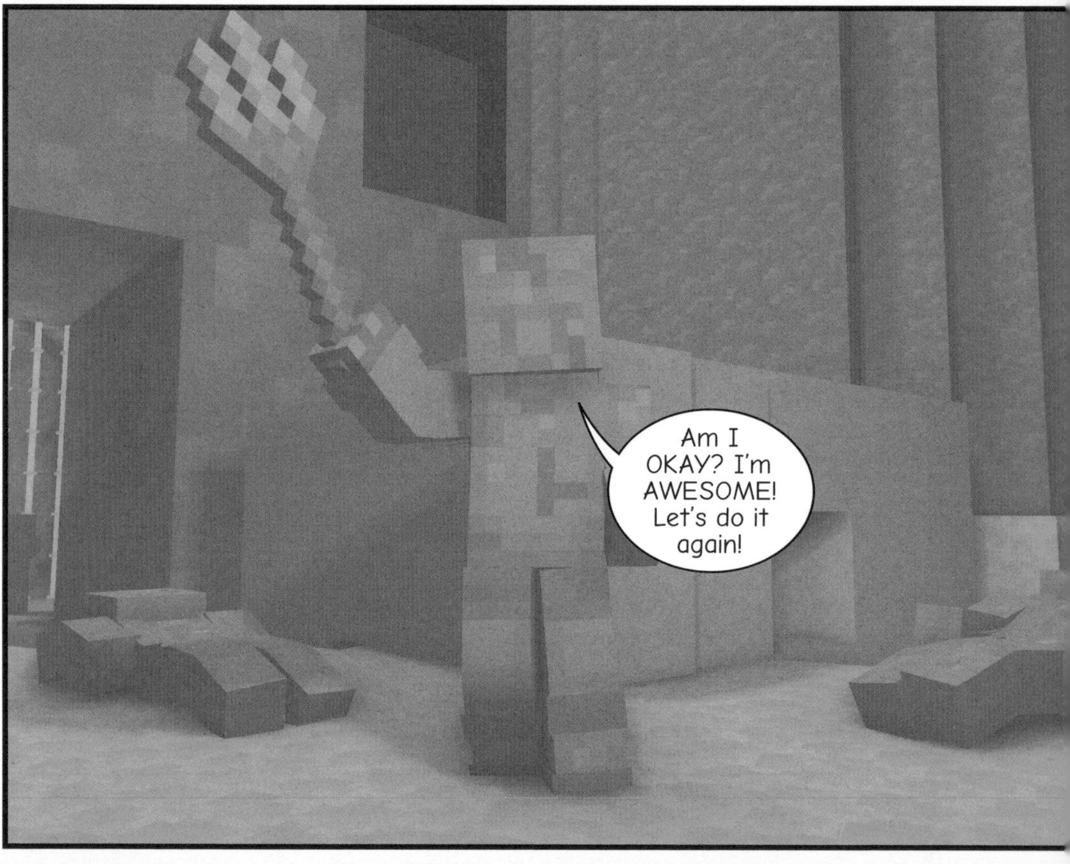
Am I OKAY? I'm AWESOME! Let's do it again!

CHAPTER 5
BACK ON
TRACK

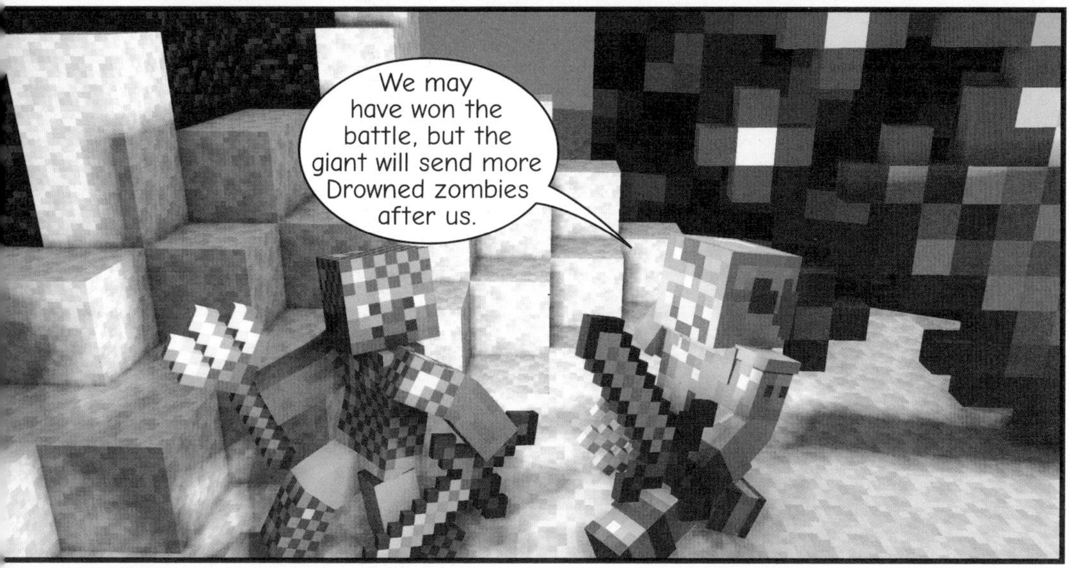
We may have won the battle, but the giant will send more Drowned zombies after us.

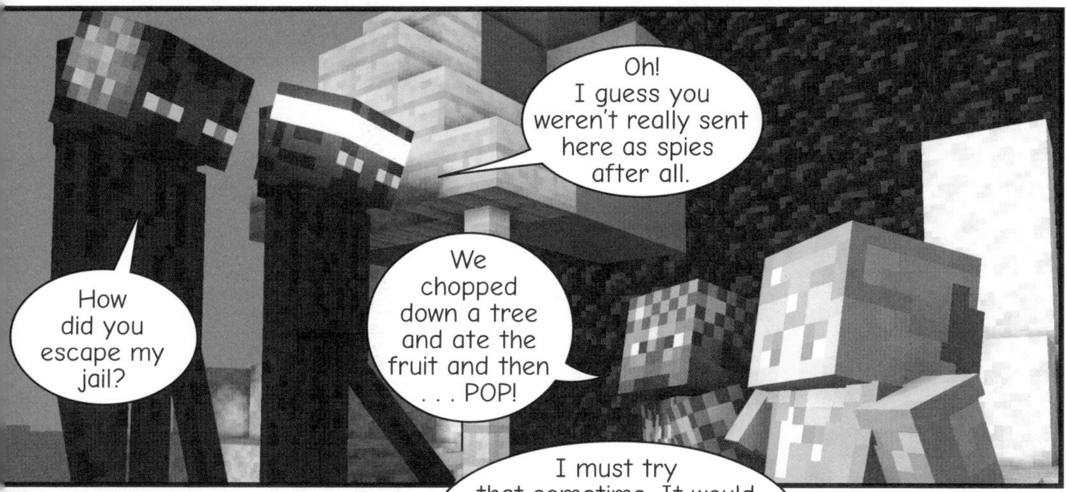
Oh! I guess you weren't really sent here as spies after all.
How did you escape my jail?
We chopped down a tree and ate the fruit and then . . . POP!

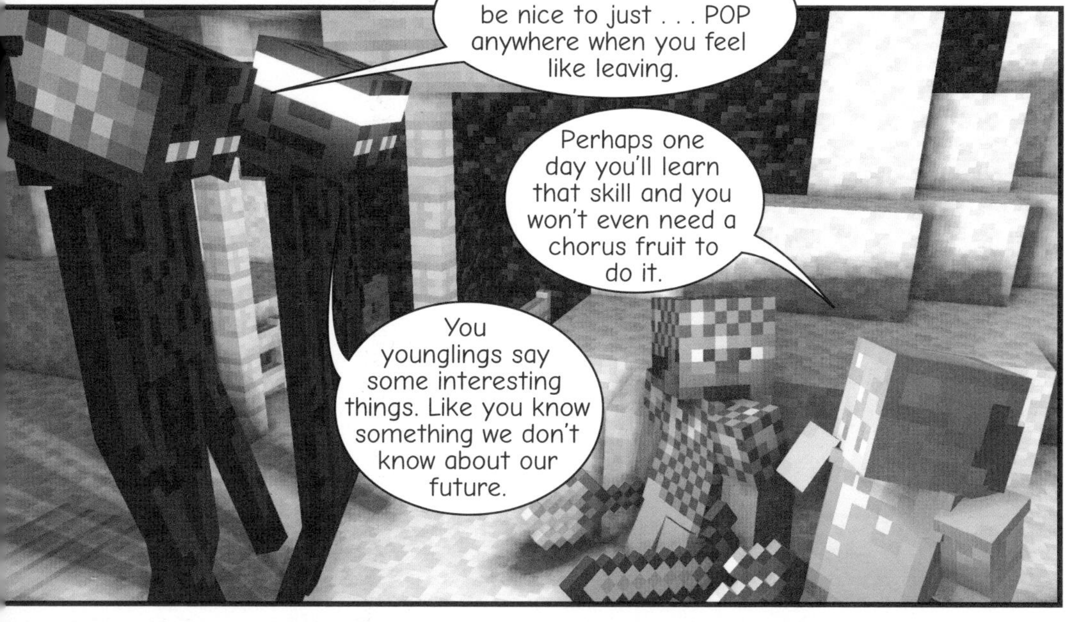
I must try that sometime. It would be nice to just . . . POP anywhere when you feel like leaving.
Perhaps one day you'll learn that skill and you won't even need a chorus fruit to do it.
You younglings say some interesting things. Like you know something we don't know about our future.

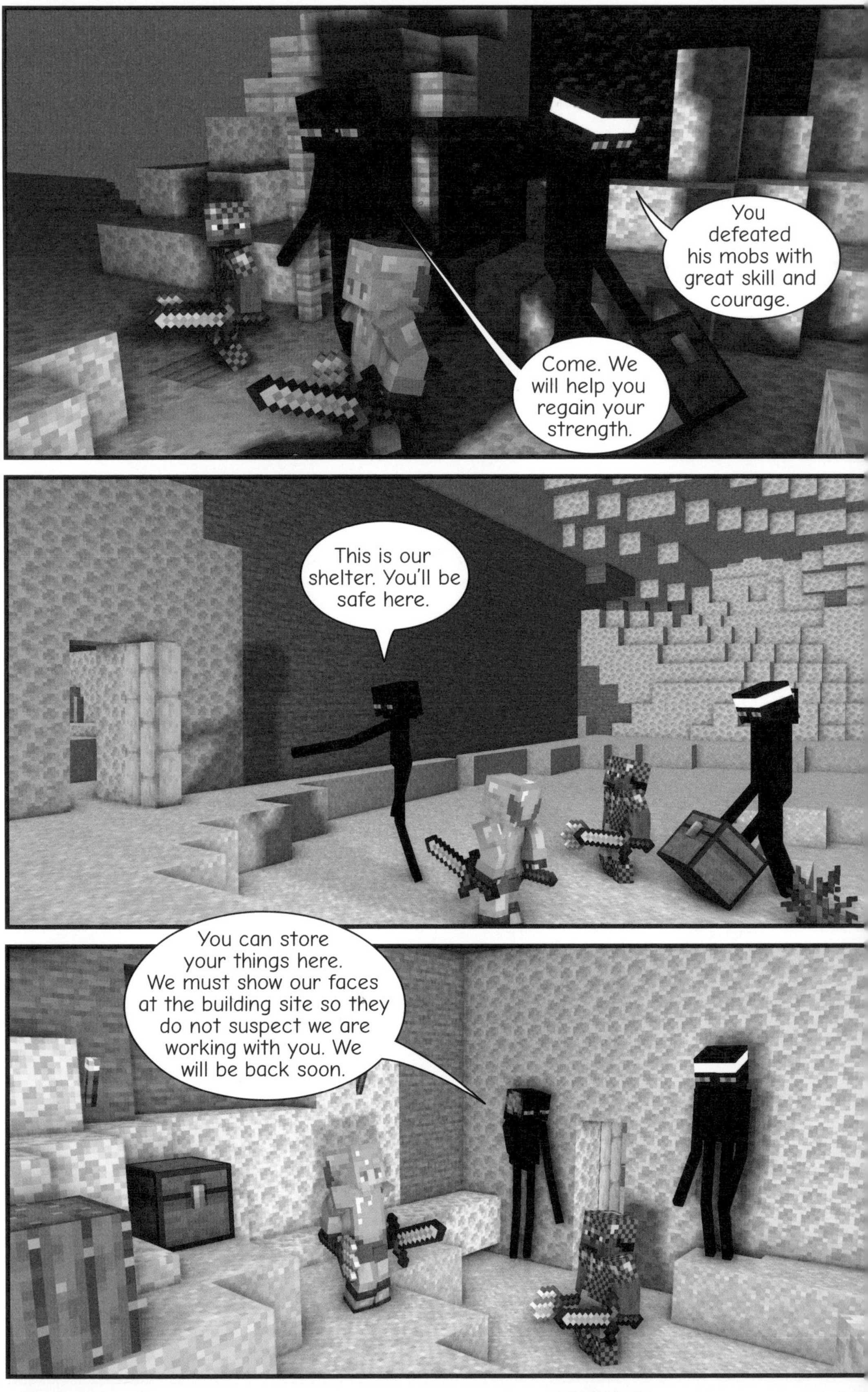
You defeated his mobs with great skill and courage.
Come. We will help you regain your strength.
This is our shelter. You'll be safe here.
You can store your things here. We must show our faces at the building site so they do not suspect we are working with you. We will be back soon.

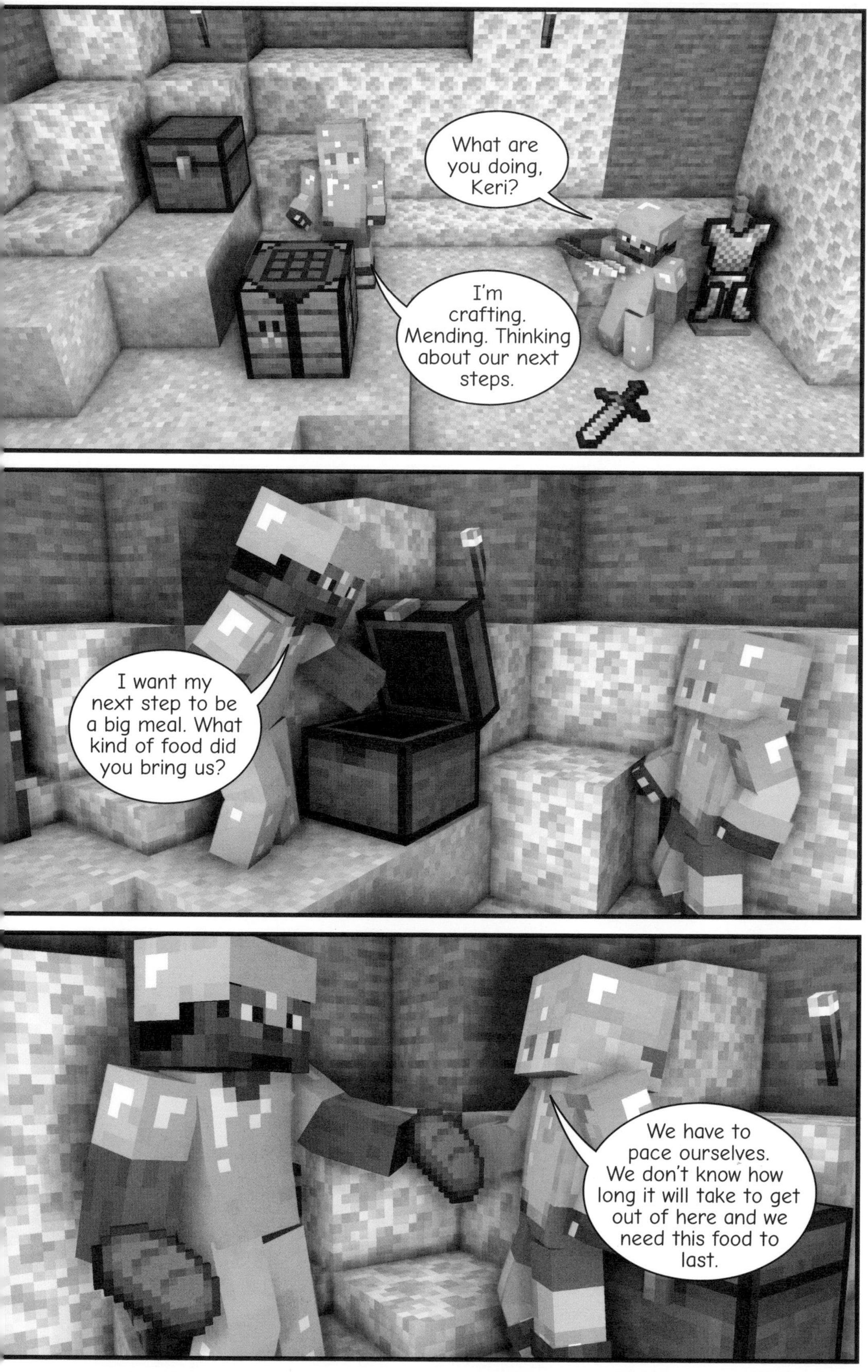
What are you doing, Keri?
I'm crafting. Mending. Thinking about our next steps.
I want my next step to be a big meal. What kind of food did you bring us?
We have to pace ourselves. We don't know how long it will take to get out of here and we need this food to last.

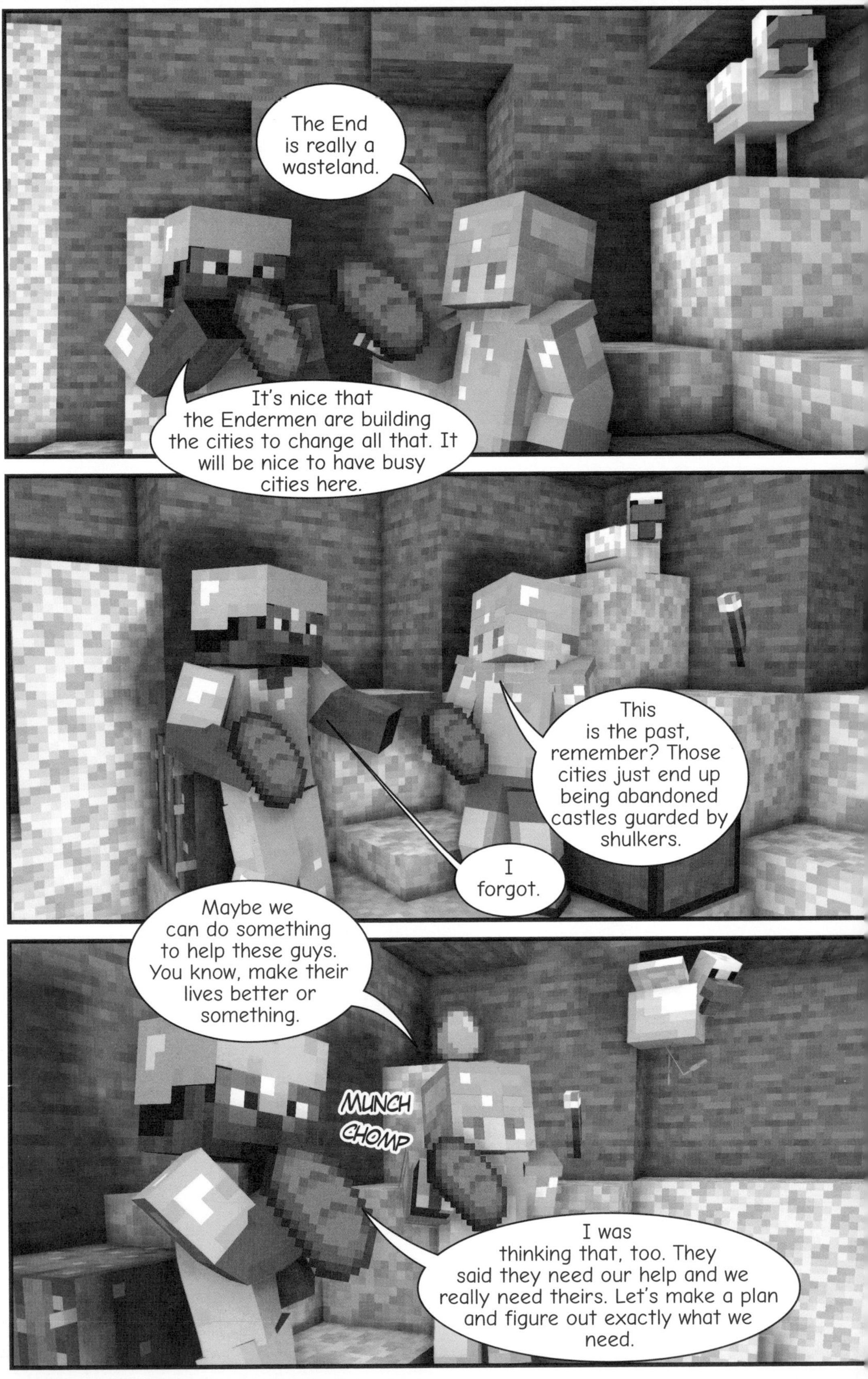
The End is really a wasteland.
It's nice that the Endermen are building the cities to change all that. It will be nice to have busy cities here.
This is the past, remember? Those cities just end up being abandoned castles guarded by shulkers.
I forgot.
Maybe we can do something to help these guys. You know, make their lives better or something.
MUNCH
CHOMP
I was thinking that, too. They said they need our help and we really need theirs. Let's make a plan and figure out exactly what we need.

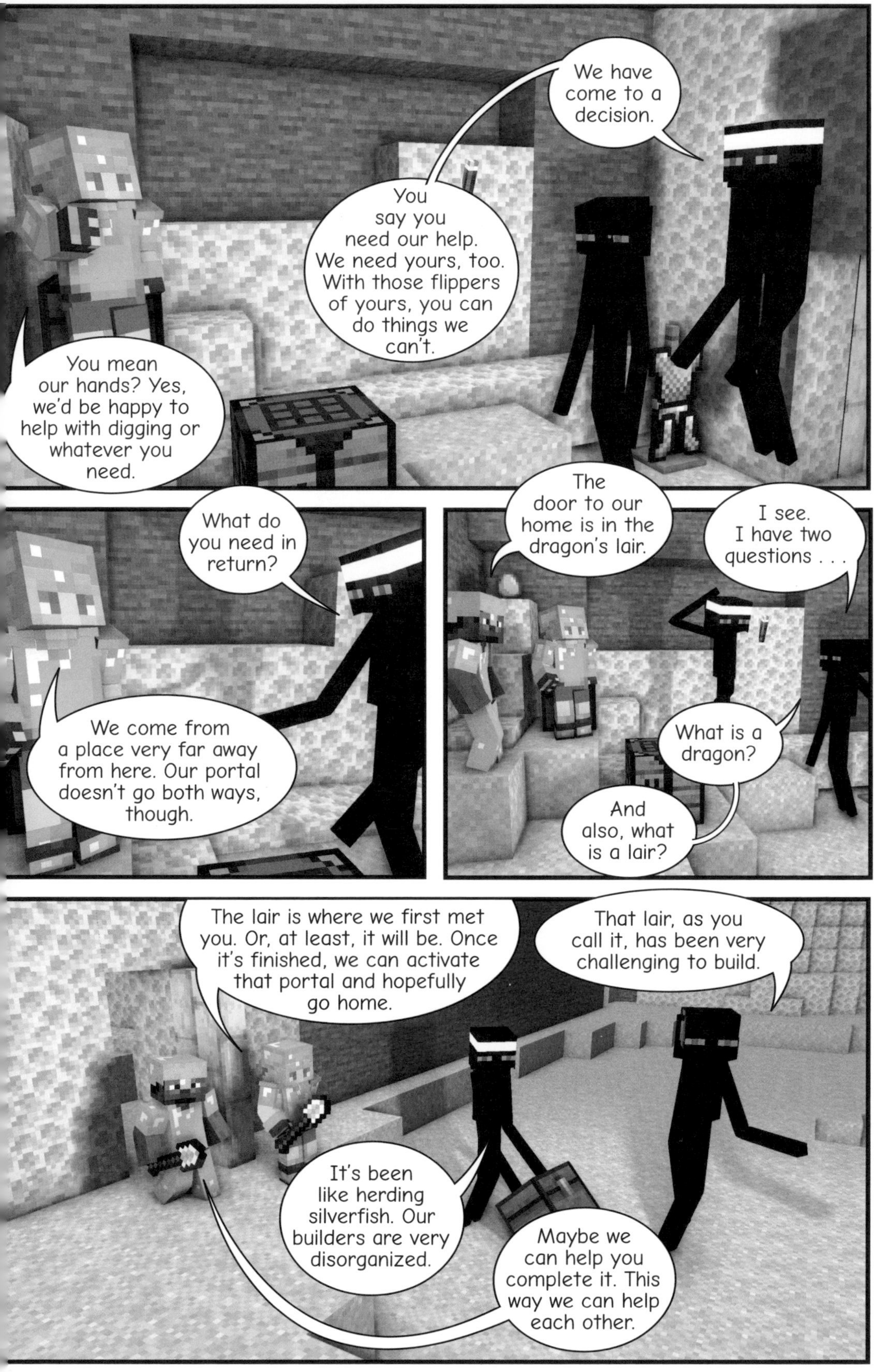
We have come to a decision.
You say you need our help. We need yours, too. With those flippers of yours, you can do things we can't.
You mean our hands? Yes, we'd be happy to help with digging or whatever you need.
What do you need in return?
We come from a place very far away from here. Our portal doesn't go both ways, though.
The door to our home is in the dragon's lair.
I see. I have two questions . . .
What is a dragon?
And also, what is a lair?
The lair is where we first met you. Or, at least, it will be. Once it's finished, we can activate that portal and hopefully go home.
That lair, as you call it, has been very challenging to build.
It's been like herding silverfish. Our builders are very disorganized.
Maybe we can help you complete it. This way we can help each other.

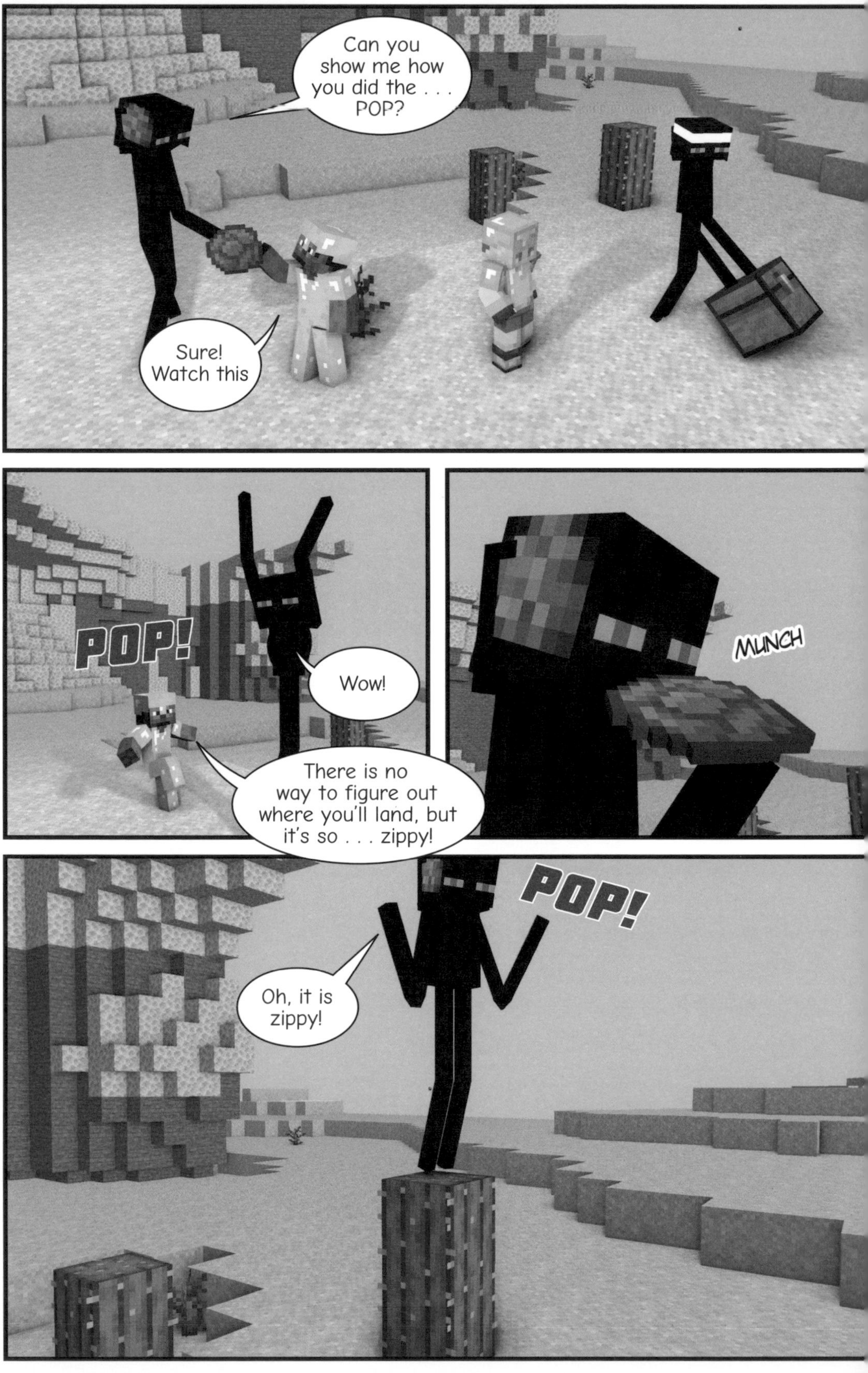

Can you show me how you did the . . . POP?
Sure! Watch this
POP!
Wow!
There is no way to figure out where you'll land, but it's so . . . zippy!
MUNCH
POP!
Oh, it is zippy!

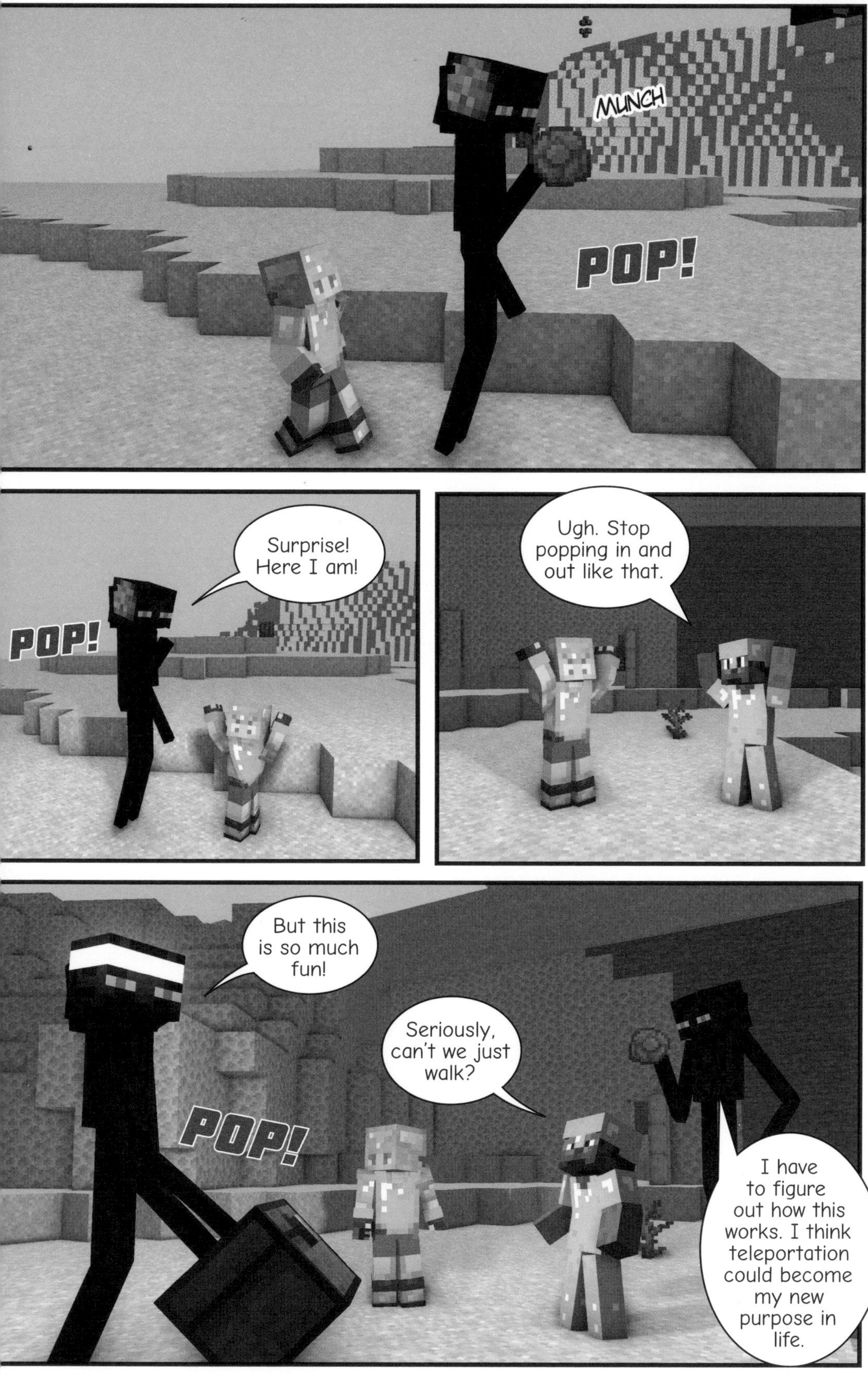
MUNCH
POP!
POP!
Surprise! Here I am!
Ugh. Stop popping in and out like that.
But this is so much fun!
POP!
Seriously, can't we just walk?
I have to figure out how this works. I think teleportation could become my new purpose in life.

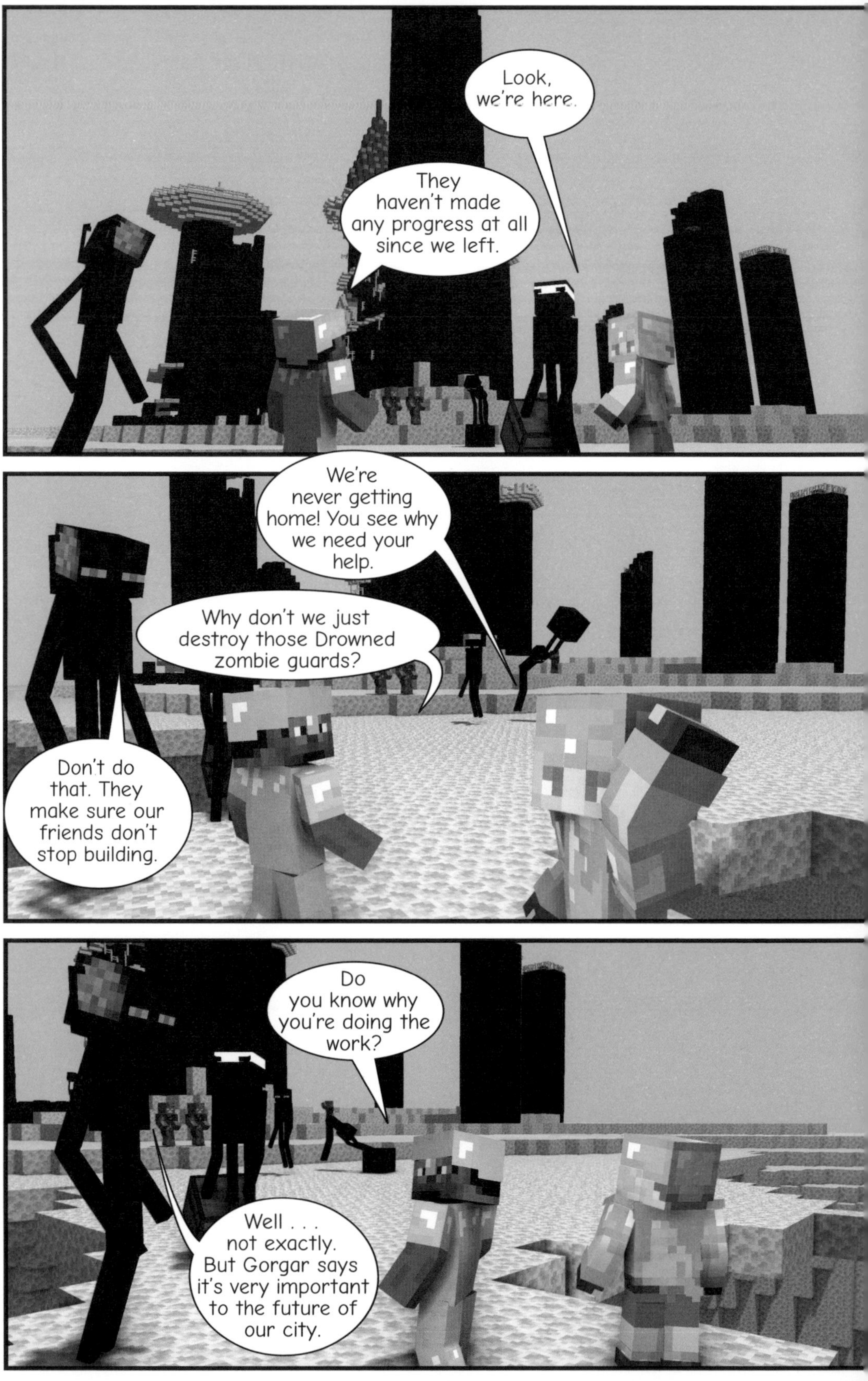
Look, we're here.
They haven't made any progress at all since we left.
We're never getting home! You see why we need your help.
Why don't we just destroy those Drowned zombie guards?
Don't do that. They make sure our friends don't stop building.
Do you know why you're doing the work?
Well . . . not exactly. But Gorgar says it's very important to the future of our city.

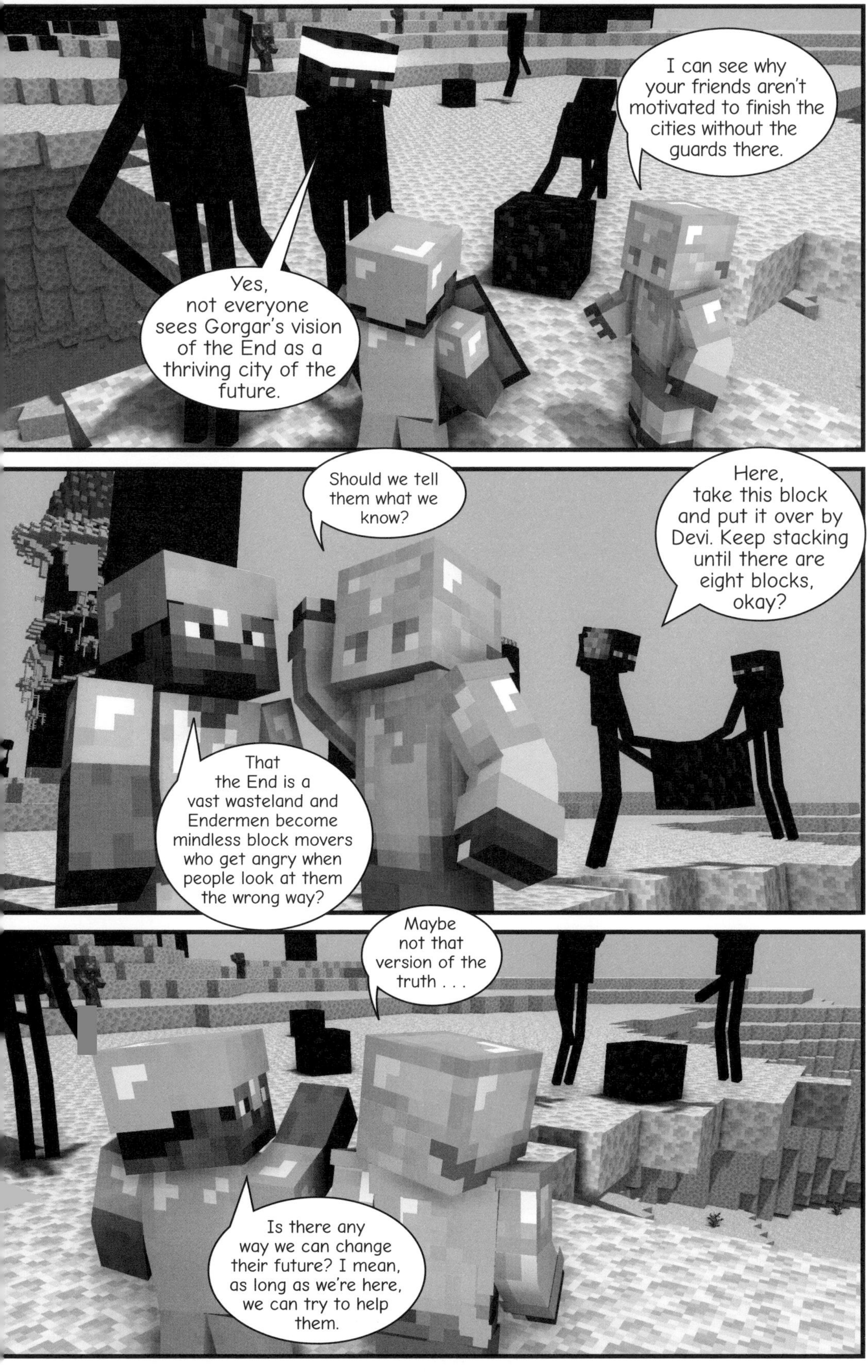
I can see why your friends aren't motivated to finish the cities without the guards there.
Yes, not everyone sees Gorgar's vision of the End as a thriving city of the future.
Should we tell them what we know?
Here, take this block and put it over by Devi. Keep stacking until there are eight blocks, okay?
That the End is a vast wasteland and Endermen become mindless block movers who get angry when people look at them the wrong way?
Maybe not that version of the truth . . .
Is there any way we can change their future? I mean, as long as we're here, we can try to help them.

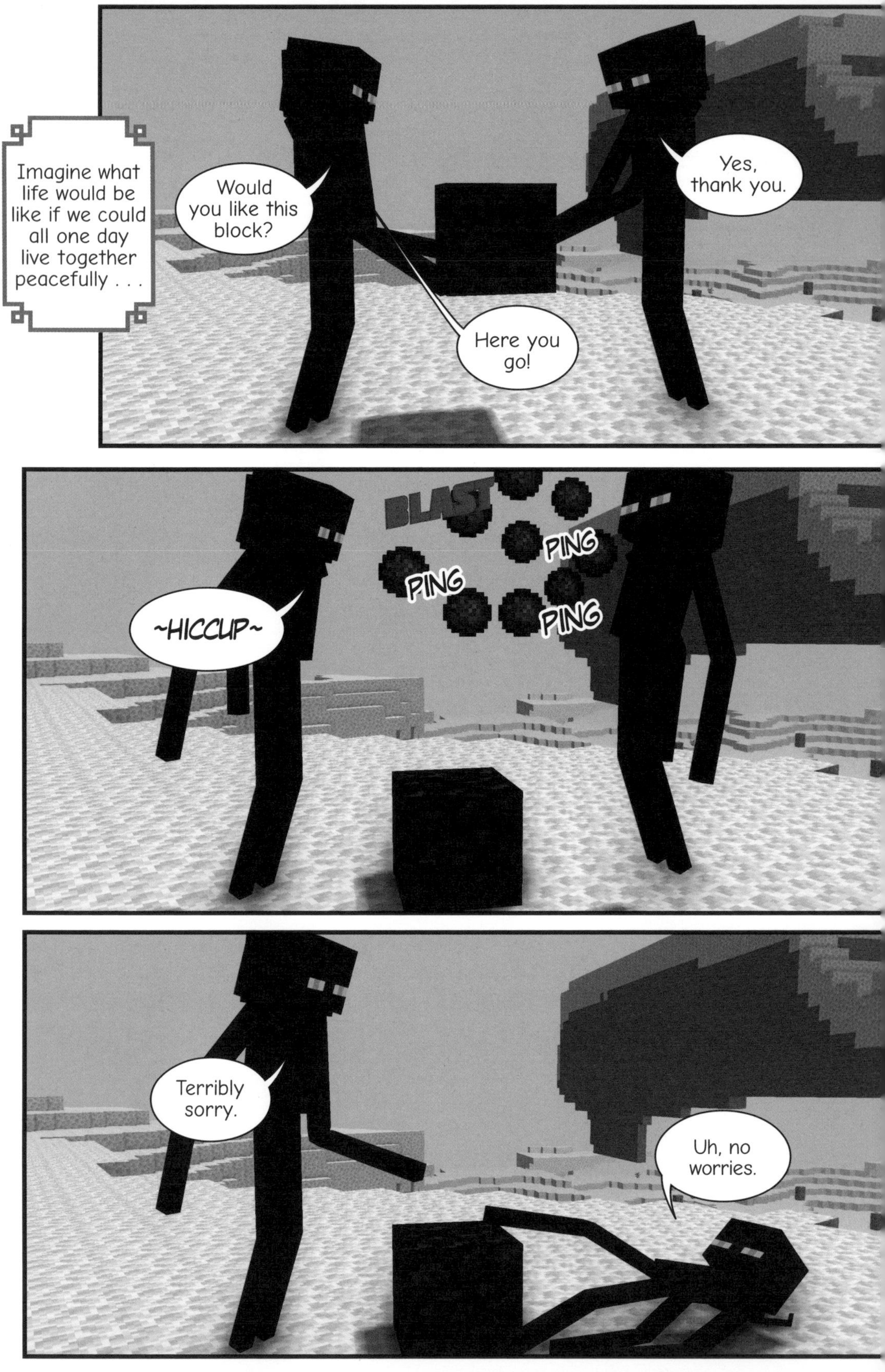
Imagine what life would be like if we could all one day live together peacefully . . .
Would you like this block?
Yes, thank you.
Here you go!
BLAST
PING
PING
~HICCUP~
PING
Terribly sorry.
Uh, no worries.

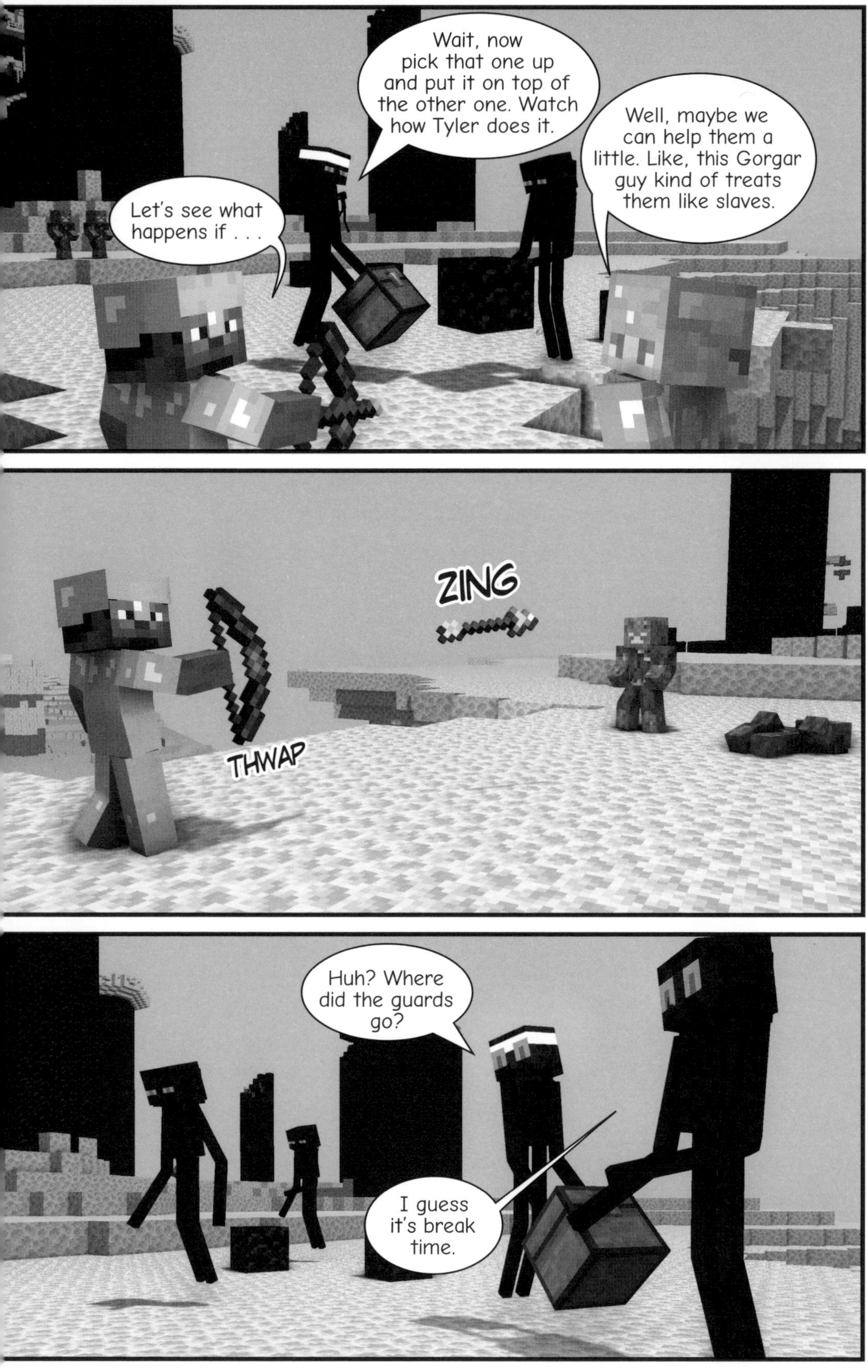
Let's see what happens if . . .
Wait, now pick that one up and put it on top of the other one. Watch how Tyler does it.
Well, maybe we can help them a little. Like, this Gorgar guy kind of treats them like slaves.
ZING
THWAP
Huh? Where did the guards go?
I guess it's break time.

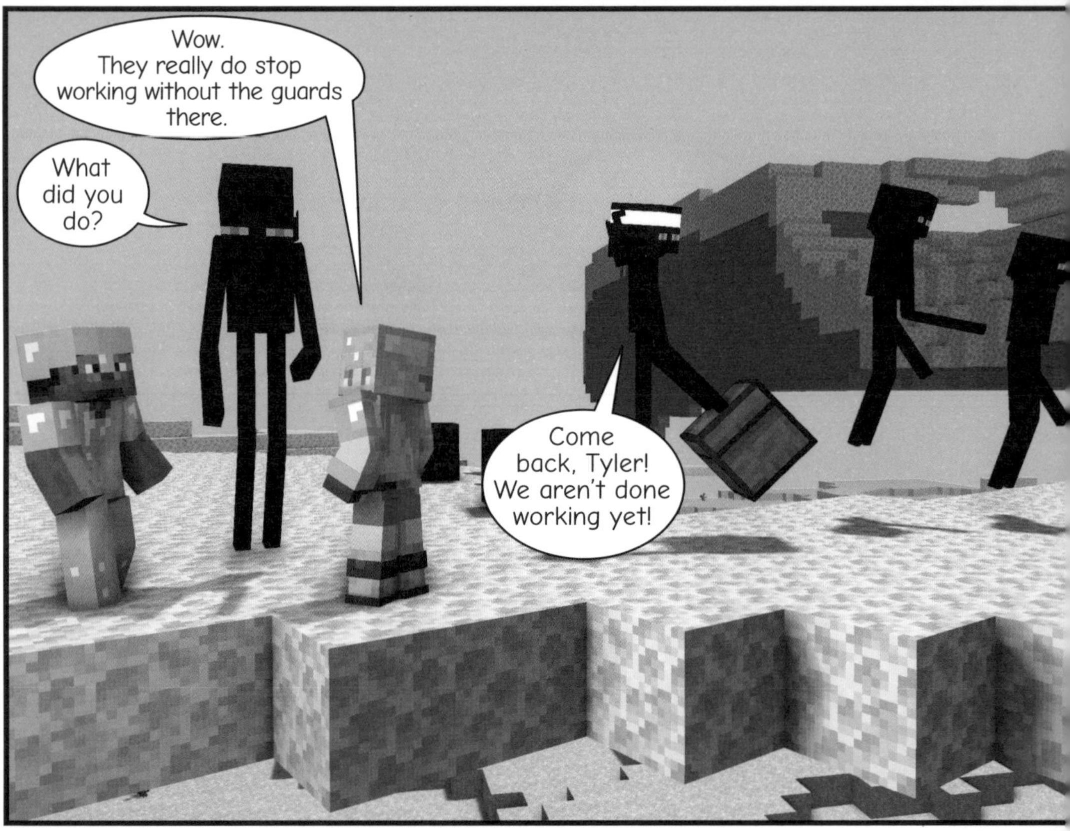
Wow. They really do stop working without the guards there.
What did you do?
Come back, Tyler! We aren't done working yet!

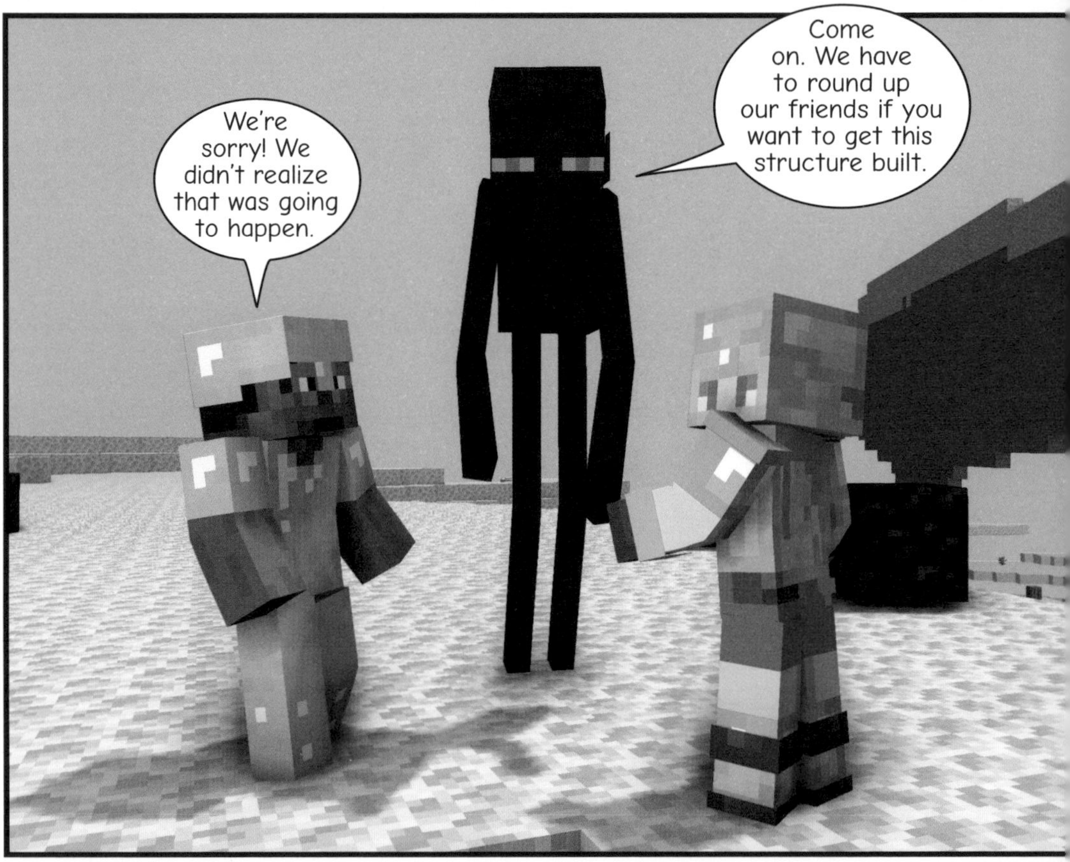
We're sorry! We didn't realize that was going to happen.
Come on. We have to round up our friends if you want to get this structure built.

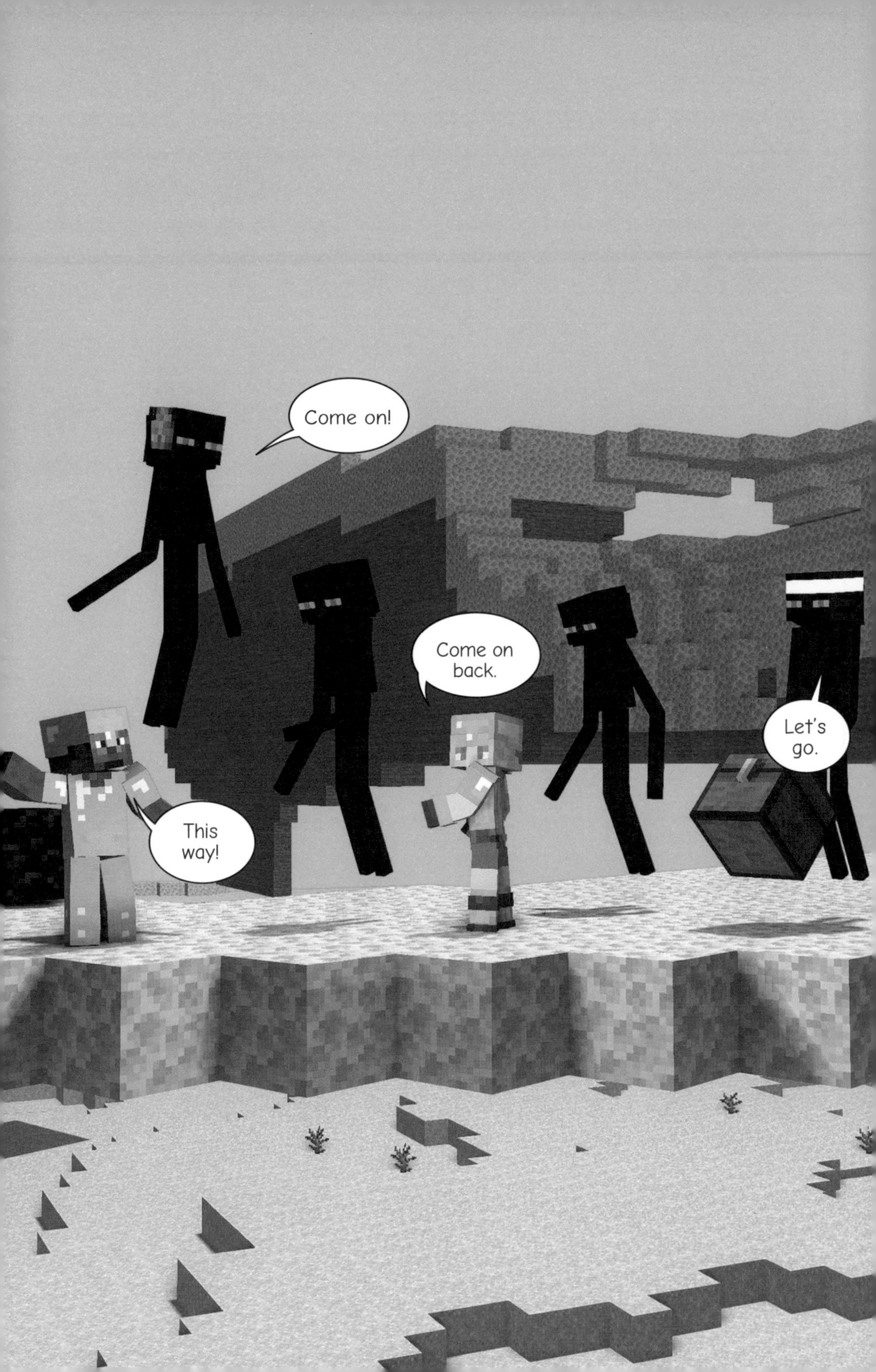
Come on!
This way!
Come on back.
Let's go.

CHAPTER 6
DANCE PARTY

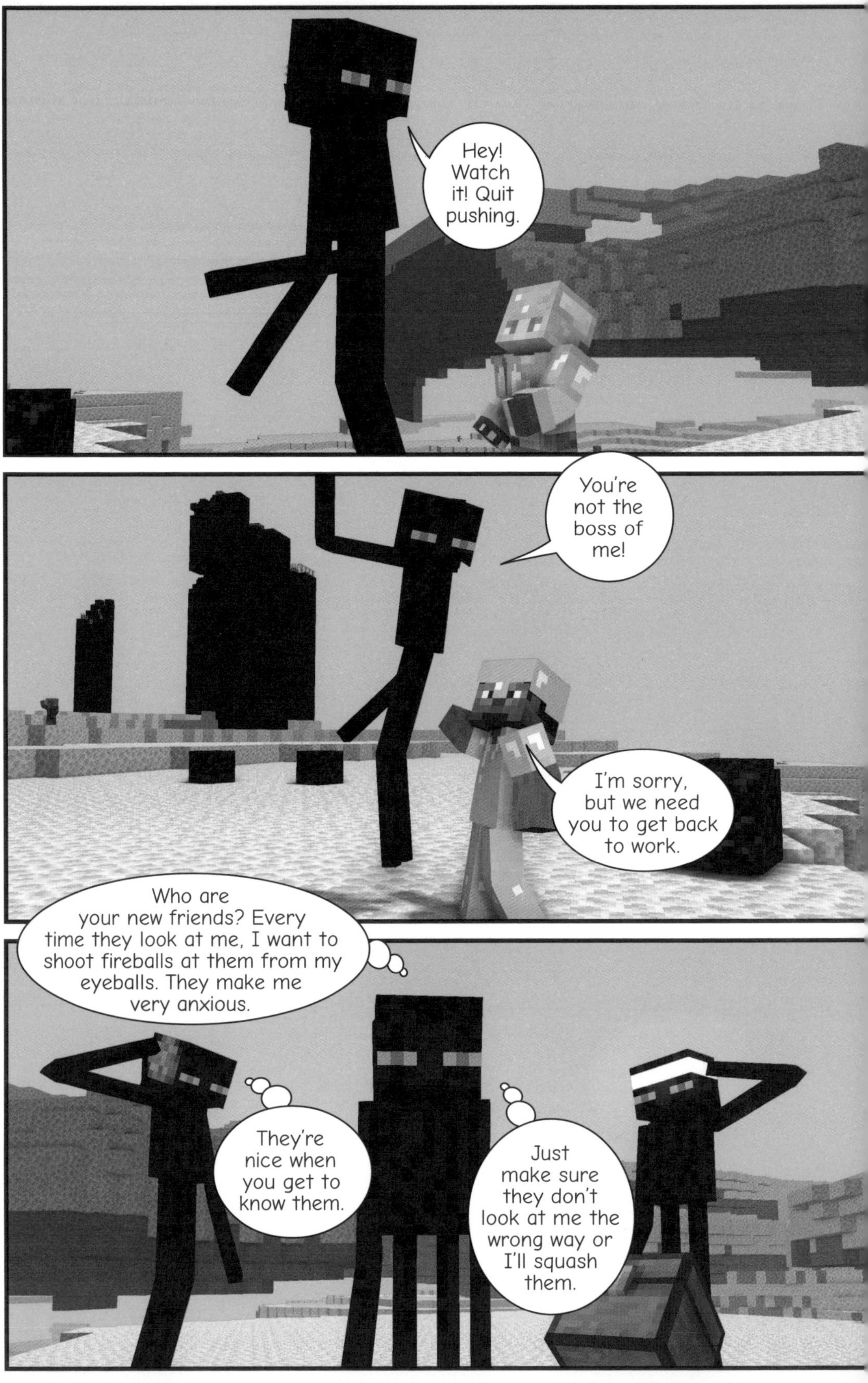
Hey! Watch it! Quit pushing.
You're not the boss of me!
I'm sorry, but we need you to get back to work.
Who are your new friends? Every time they look at me, I want to shoot fireballs at them from my eyeballs. They make me very anxious.
They're nice when you get to know them.
Just make sure they don't look at me the wrong way or I'll squash them.

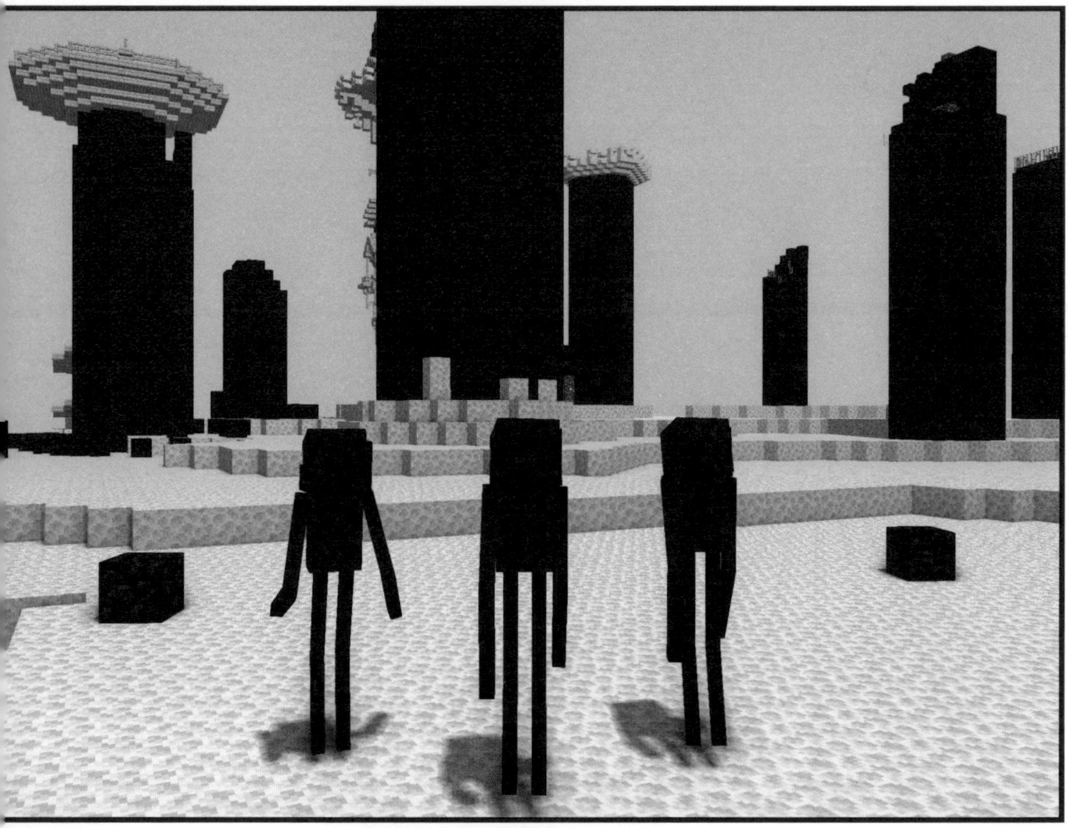

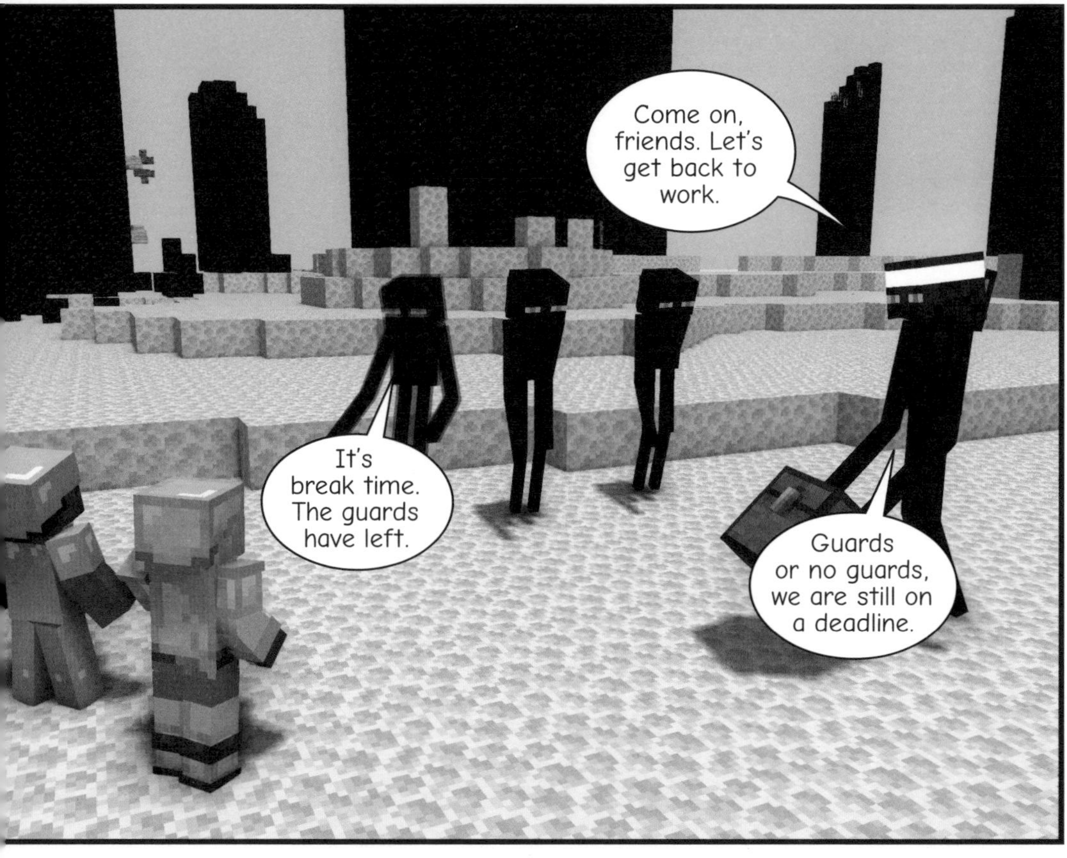
Come on, friends. Let's get back to work.
It's break time. The guards have left.
Guards or no guards, we are still on a deadline.

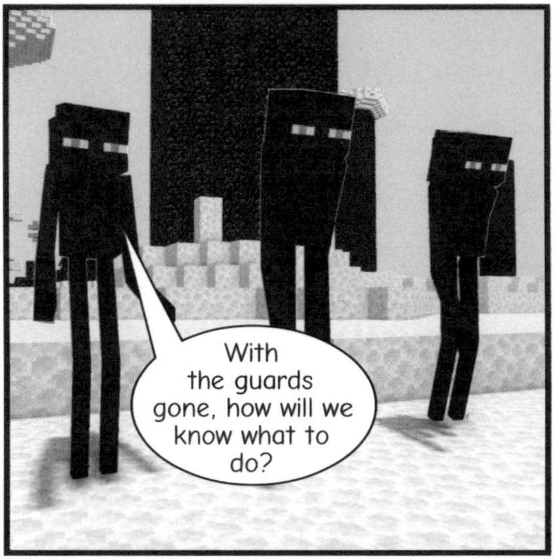
With the guards gone, how will we know what to do?

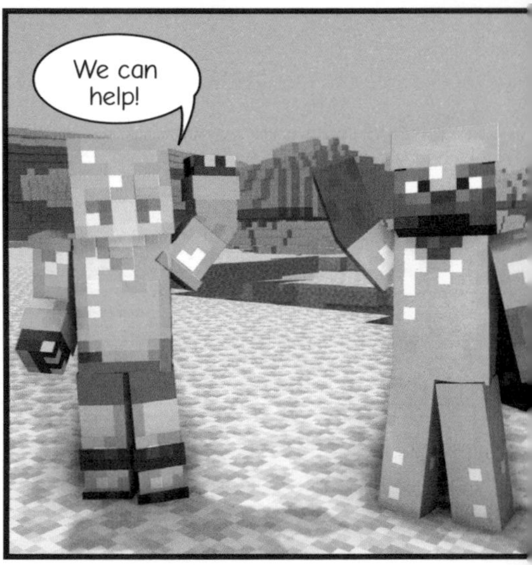
We can help!

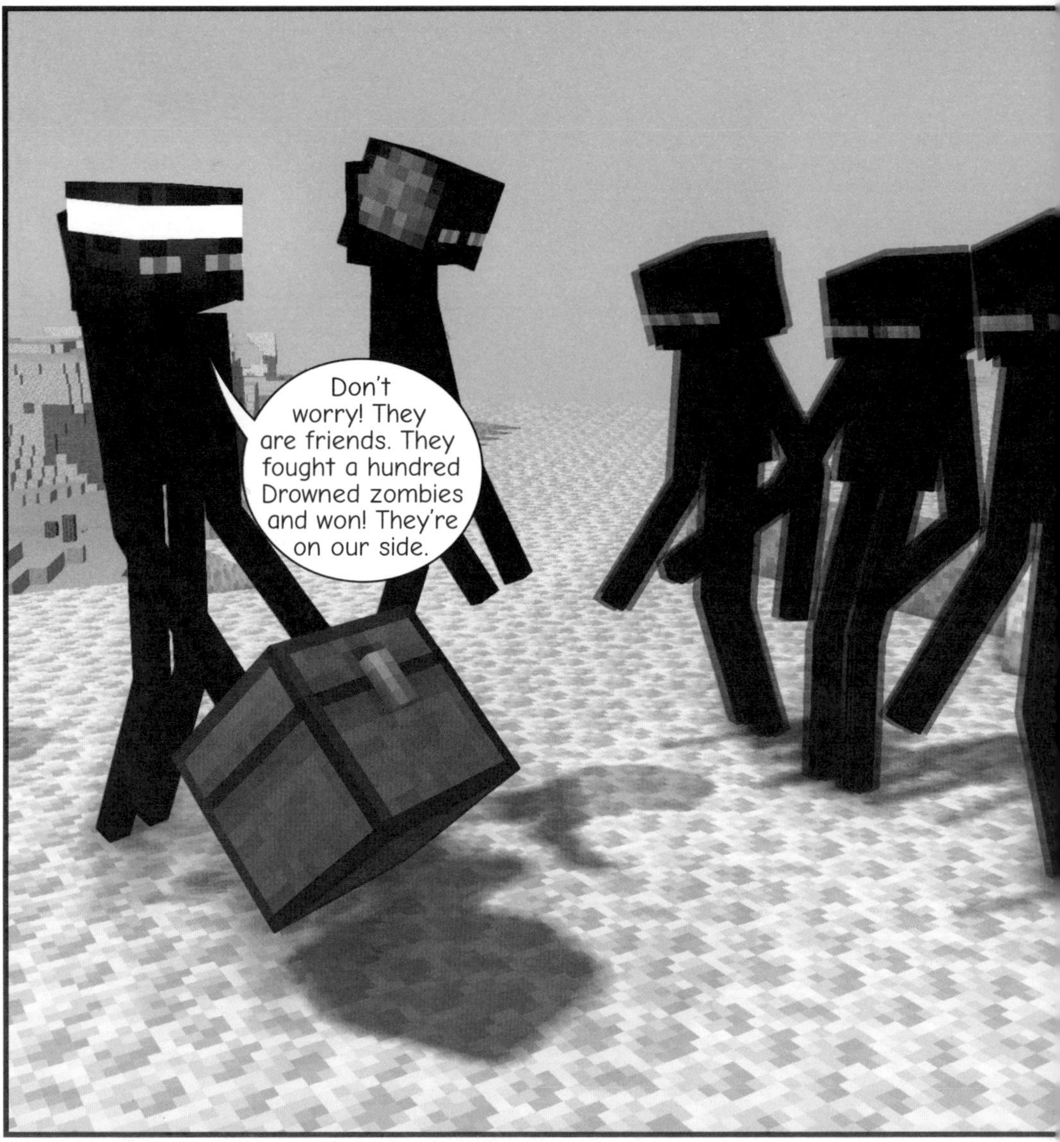
Don't worry! They are friends. They fought a hundred Drowned zombies and won! They're on our side.

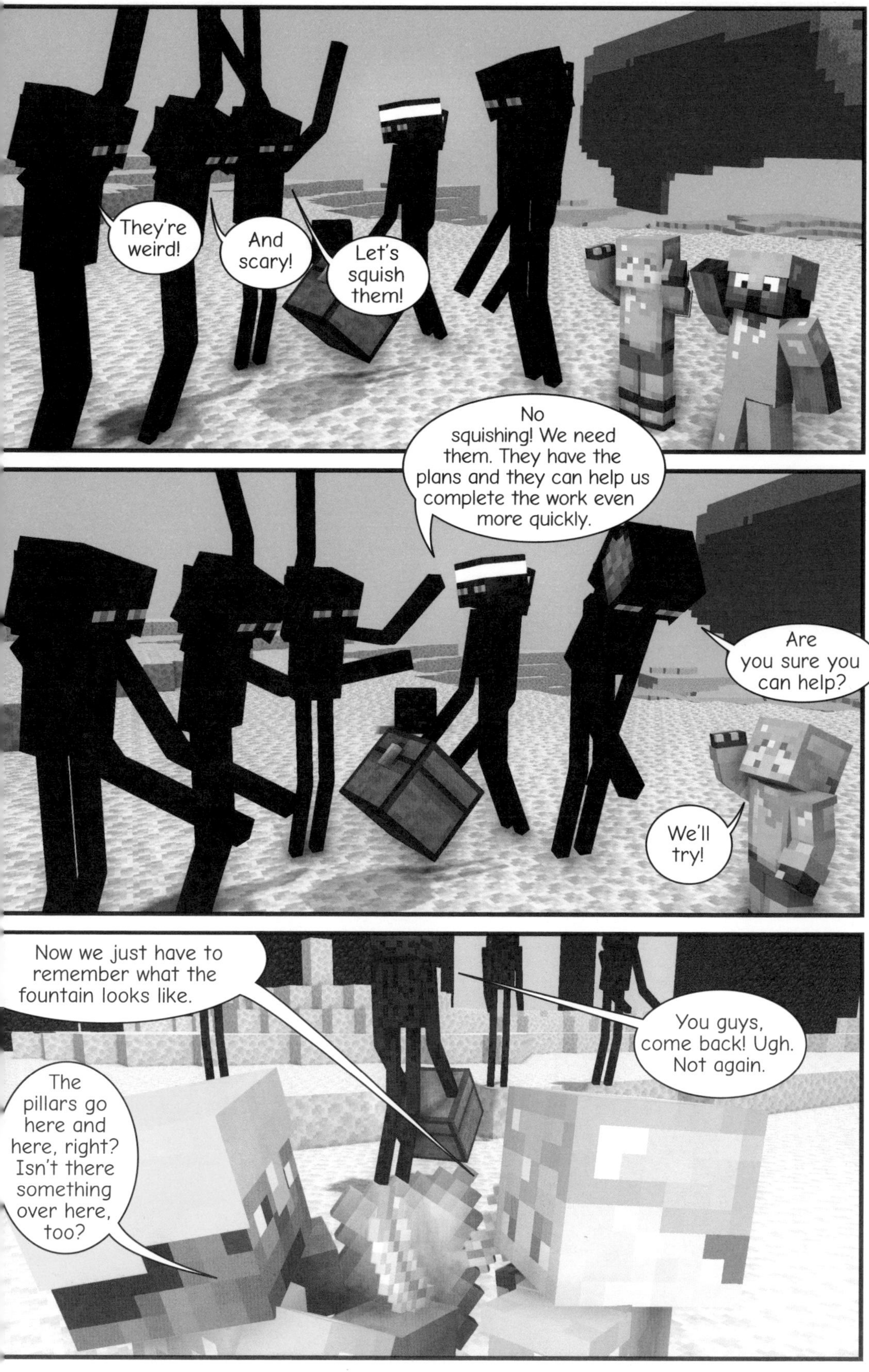
They're weird!
And scary!
Let's squish them!
No squishing! We need them. They have the plans and they can help us complete the work even more quickly.
Are you sure you can help?
We'll try!
Now we just have to remember what the fountain looks like.
You guys, come back! Ugh. Not again.
The pillars go here and here, right? Isn't there something over here, too?

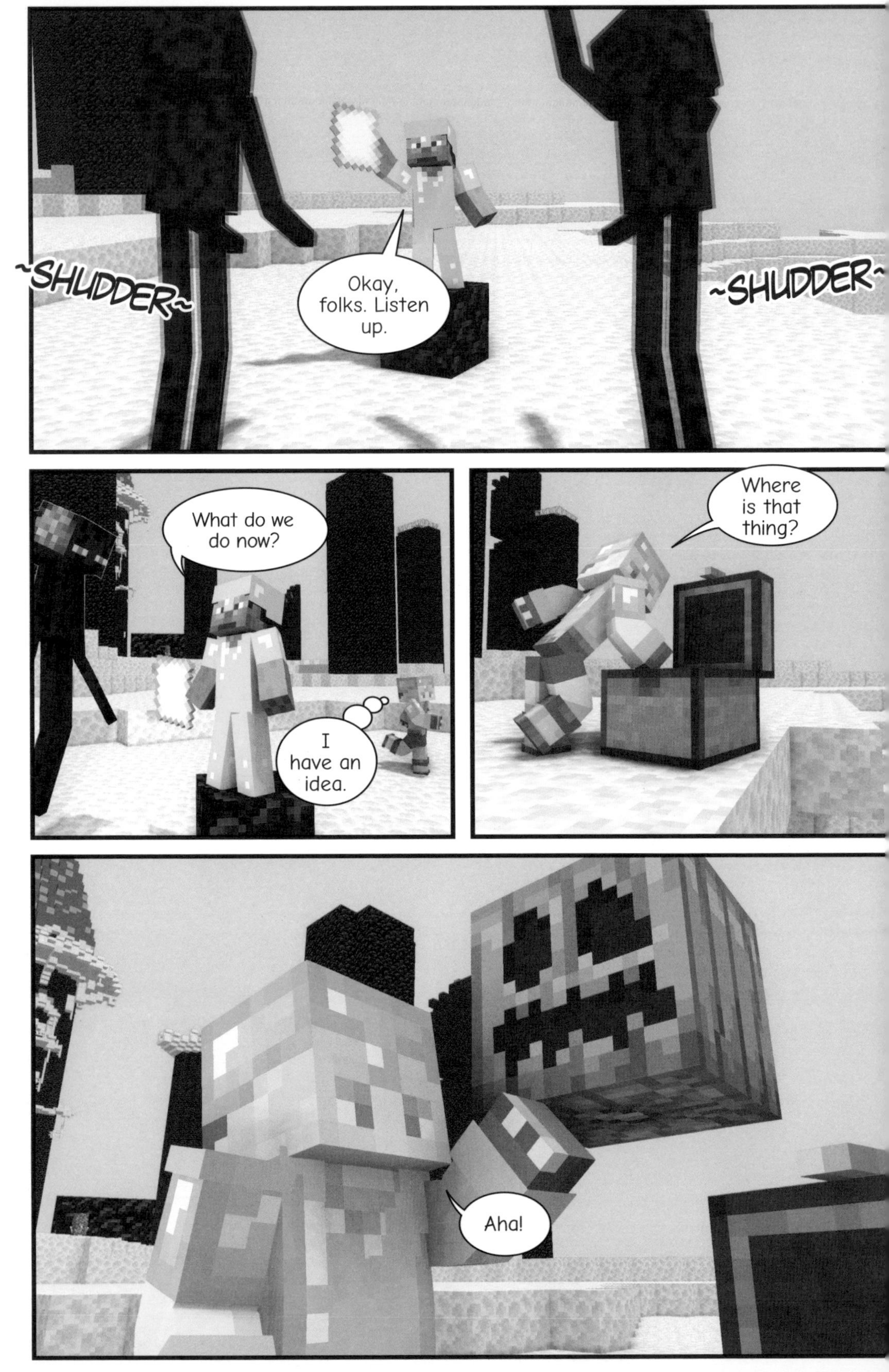
~SHUDDER~
Okay, folks. Listen up.
~SHUDDER~
What do we do now?
I have an idea.
Where is that thing?
Aha!

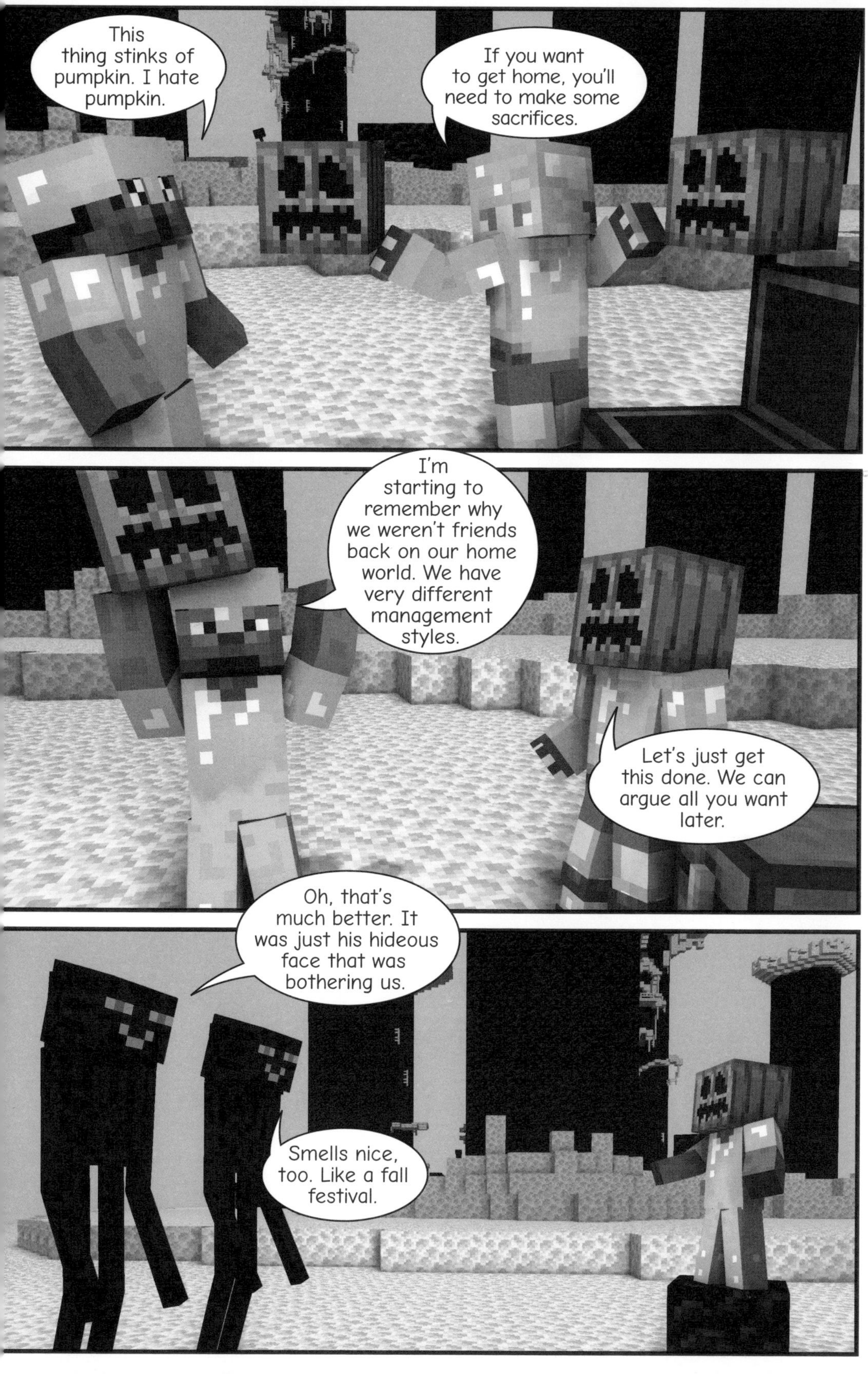
This thing stinks of pumpkin. I hate pumpkin.
If you want to get home, you'll need to make some sacrifices.
I'm starting to remember why we weren't friends back on our home world. We have very different management styles.
Let's just get this done. We can argue all you want later.
Oh, that's much better. It was just his hideous face that was bothering us.
Smells nice, too. Like a fall festival.

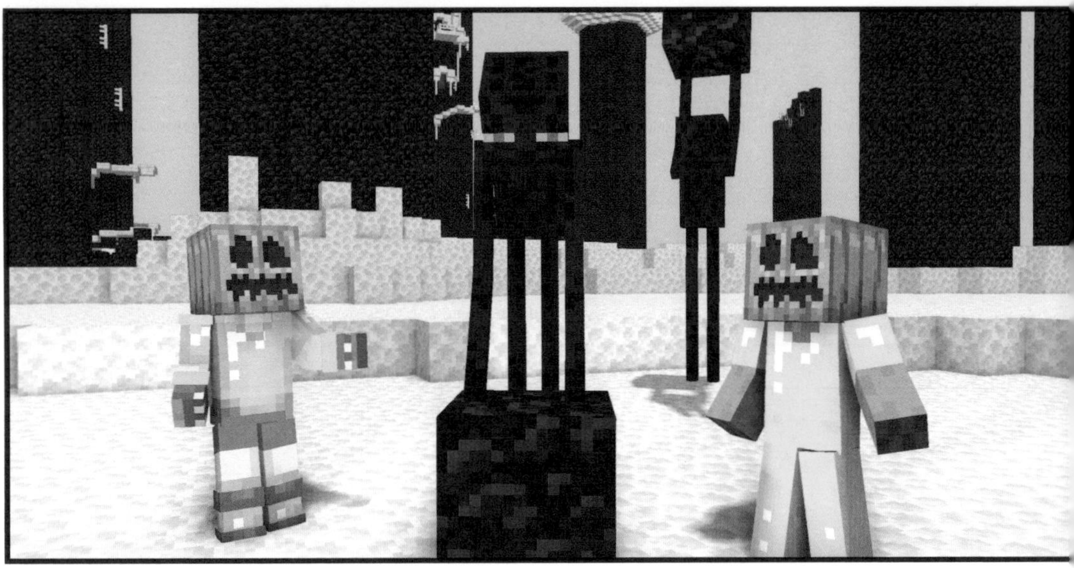

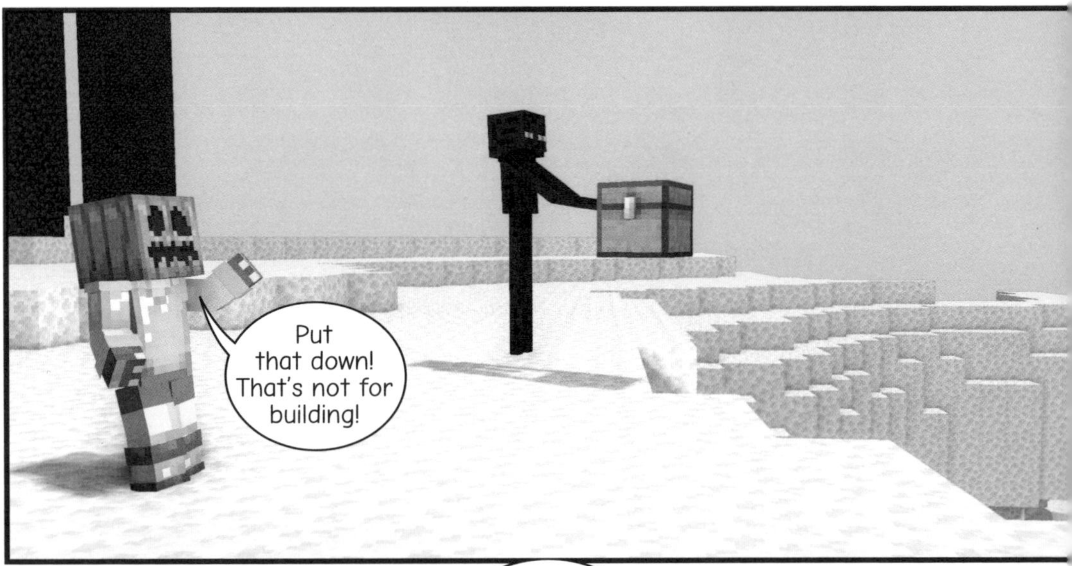
Put that down! That's not for building!

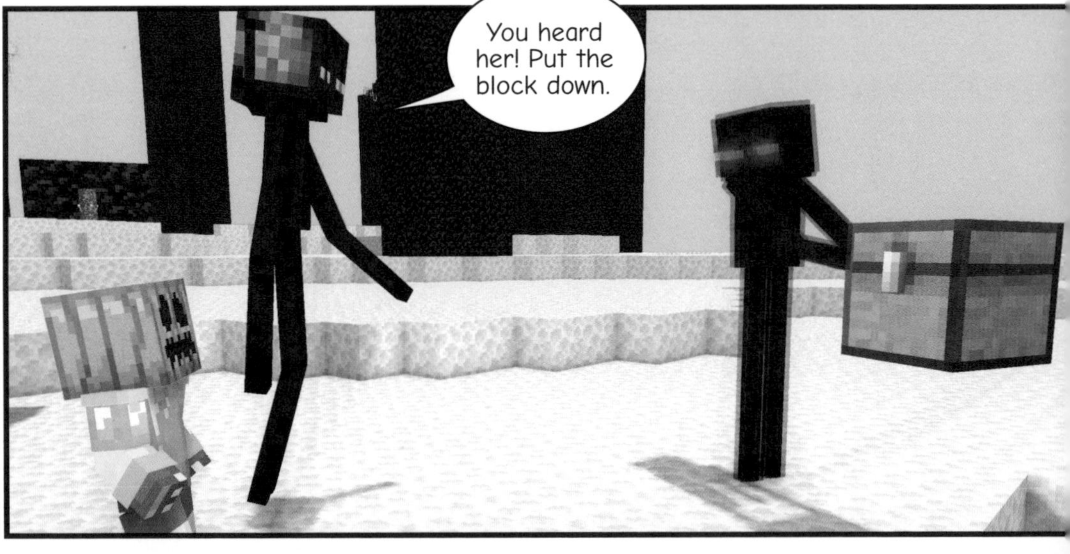
You heard her! Put the block down.

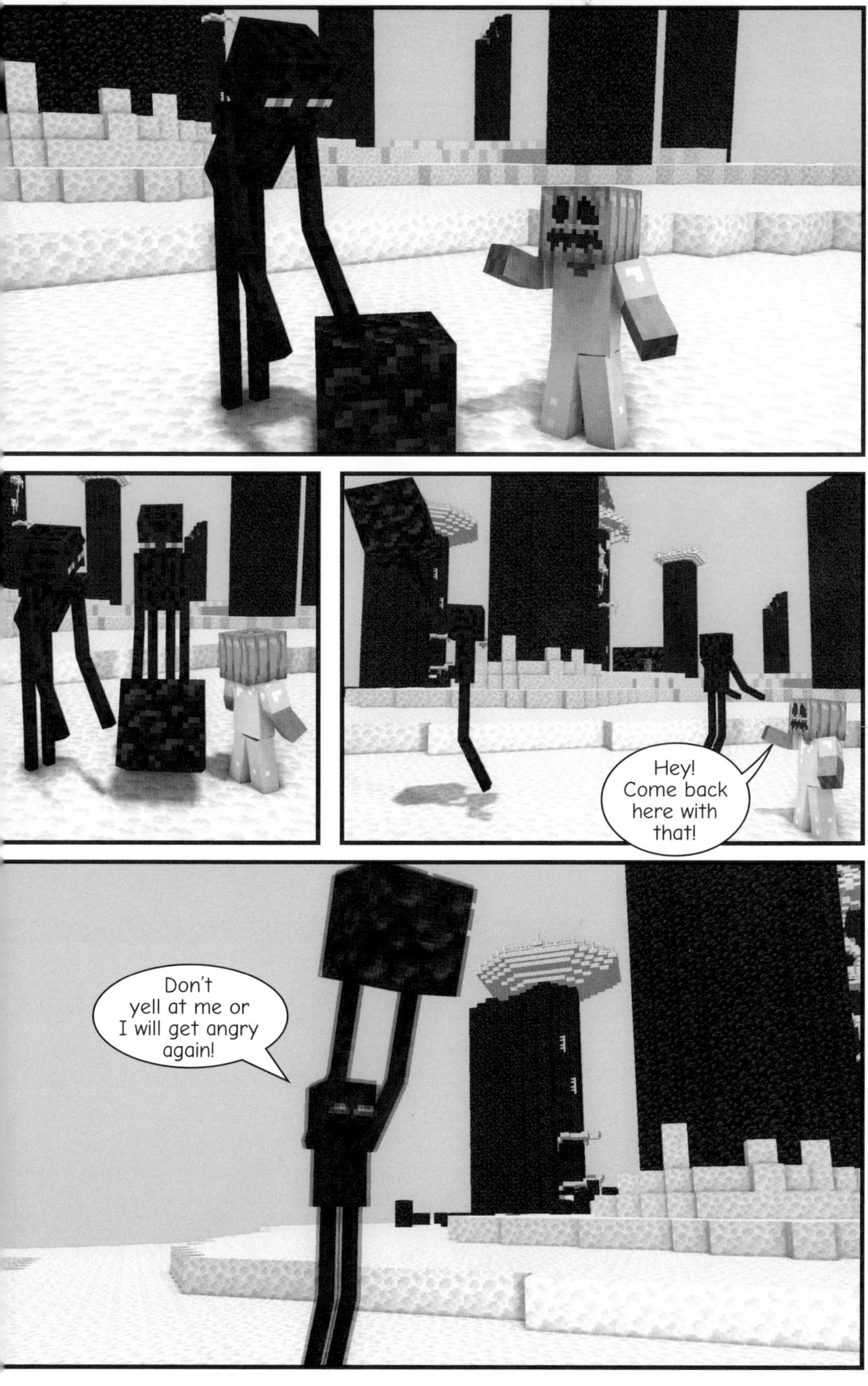
Hey! Come back here with that!
Don't yell at me or I will get angry again!

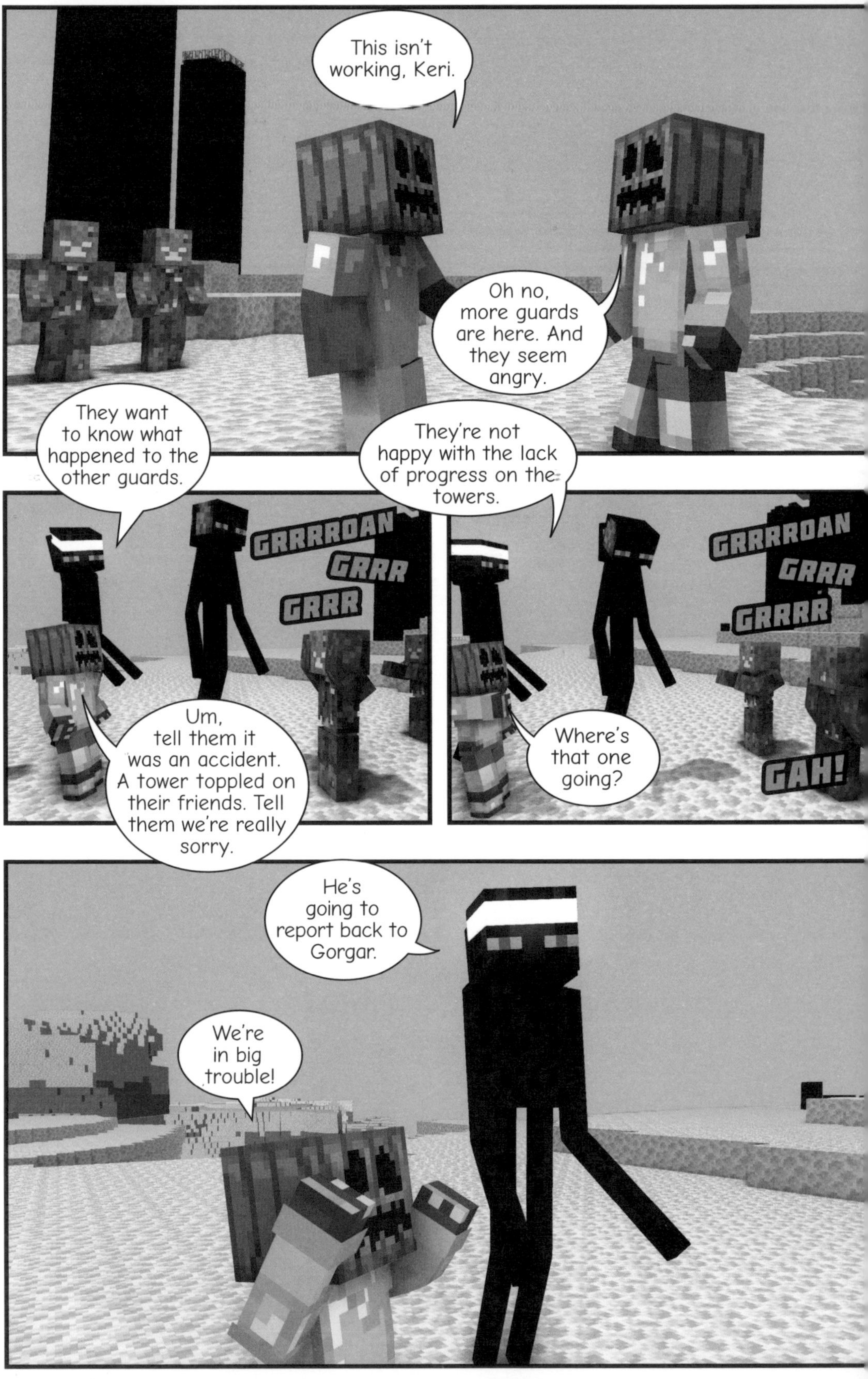
This isn't working, Keri.
Oh no, more guards are here. And they seem angry.
They want to know what happened to the other guards.
GRRRROAN
GRRR
GRRR
Um, tell them it was an accident. A tower toppled on their friends. Tell them we're really sorry.
They're not happy with the lack of progress on the towers.
GRRRROAN
GRRR
GRRRR
Where's that one going?
GAH!
He's going to report back to Gorgar.
We're in big trouble!

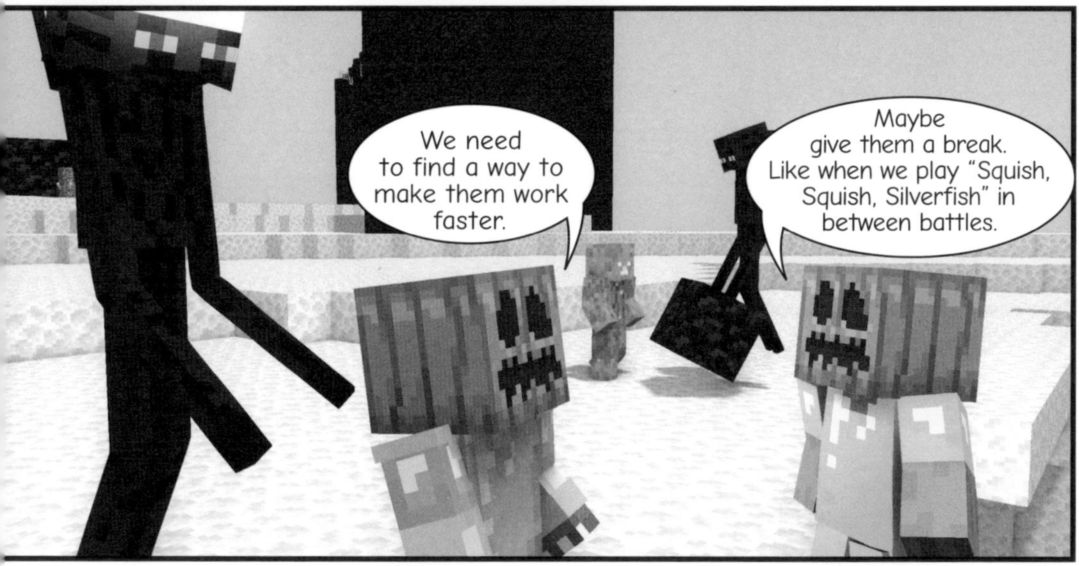
We need to find a way to make them work faster.
Maybe give them a break. Like when we play "Squish, Squish, Silverfish" in between battles.

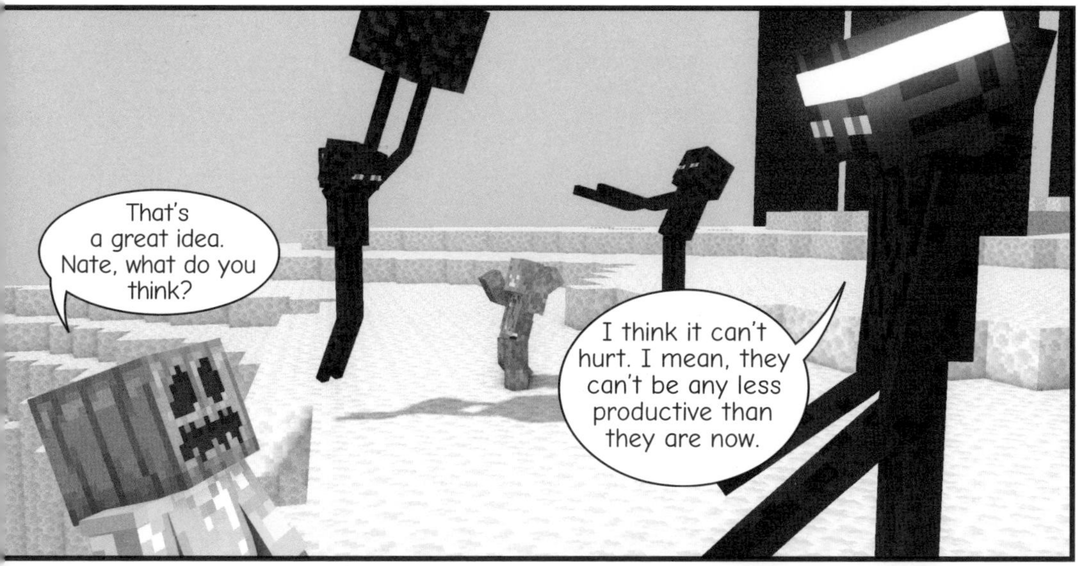
That's a great idea. Nate, what do you think?
I think it can't hurt. I mean, they can't be any less productive than they are now.

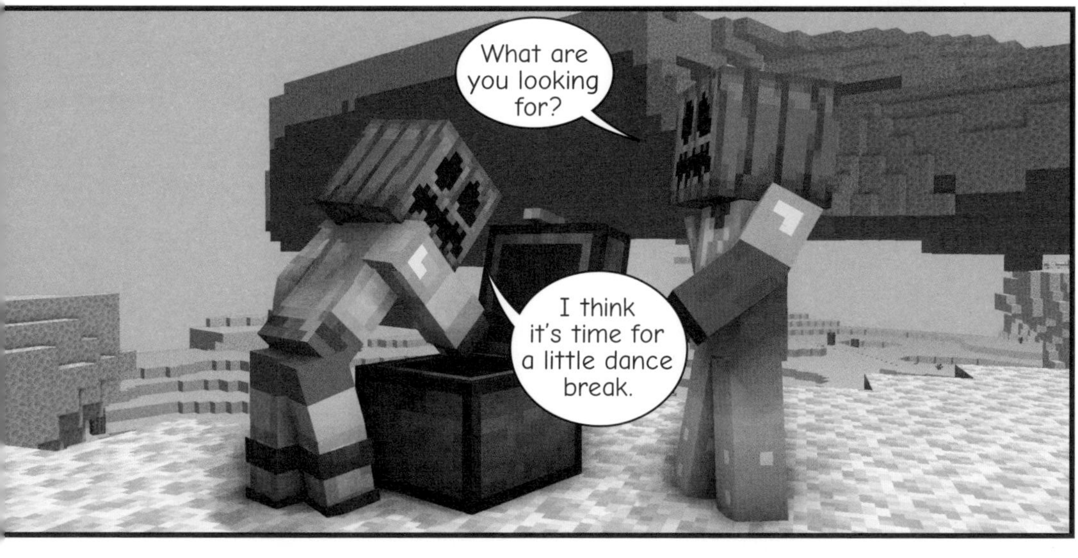
What are you looking for?
I think it's time for a little dance break.

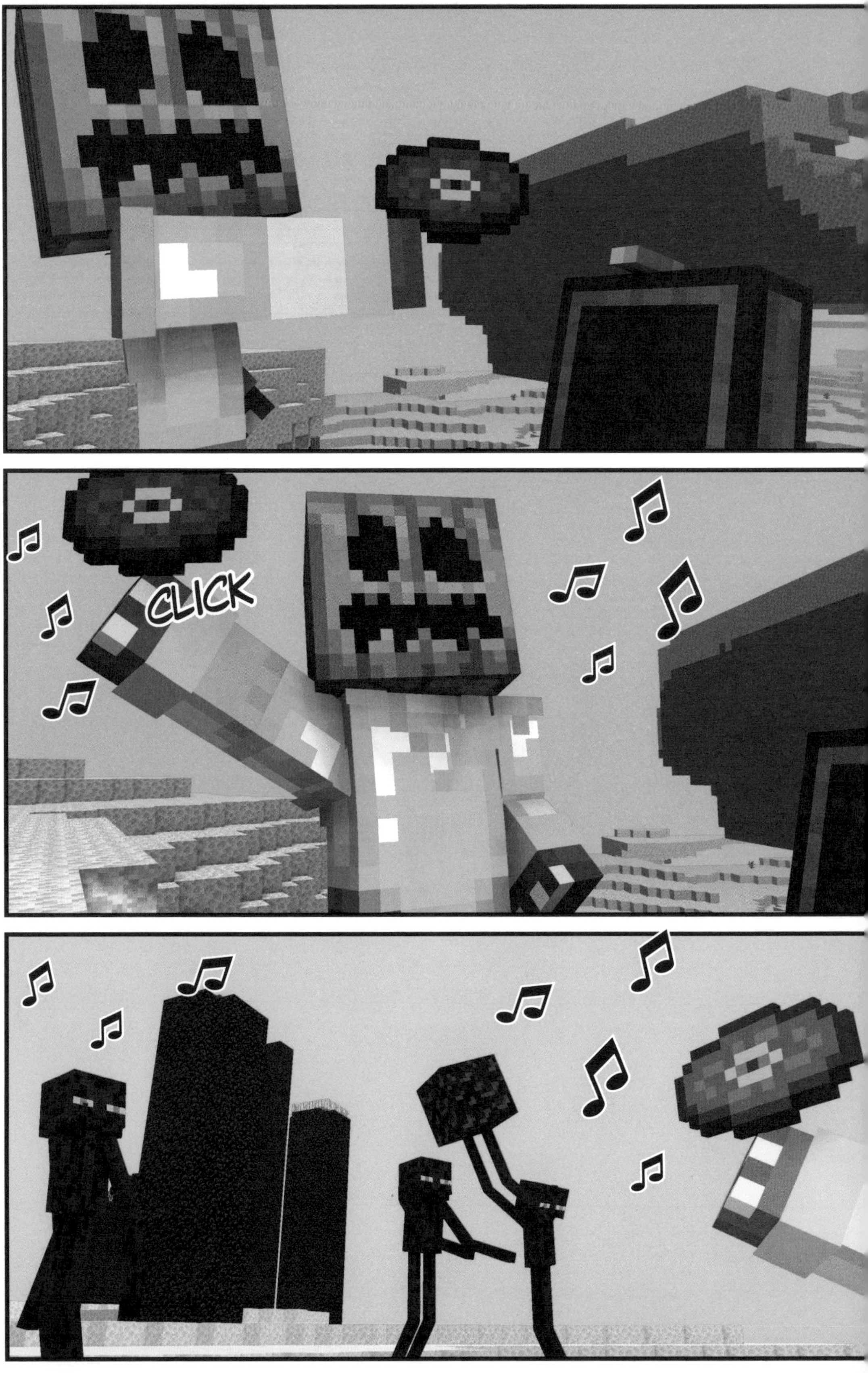
CLICK

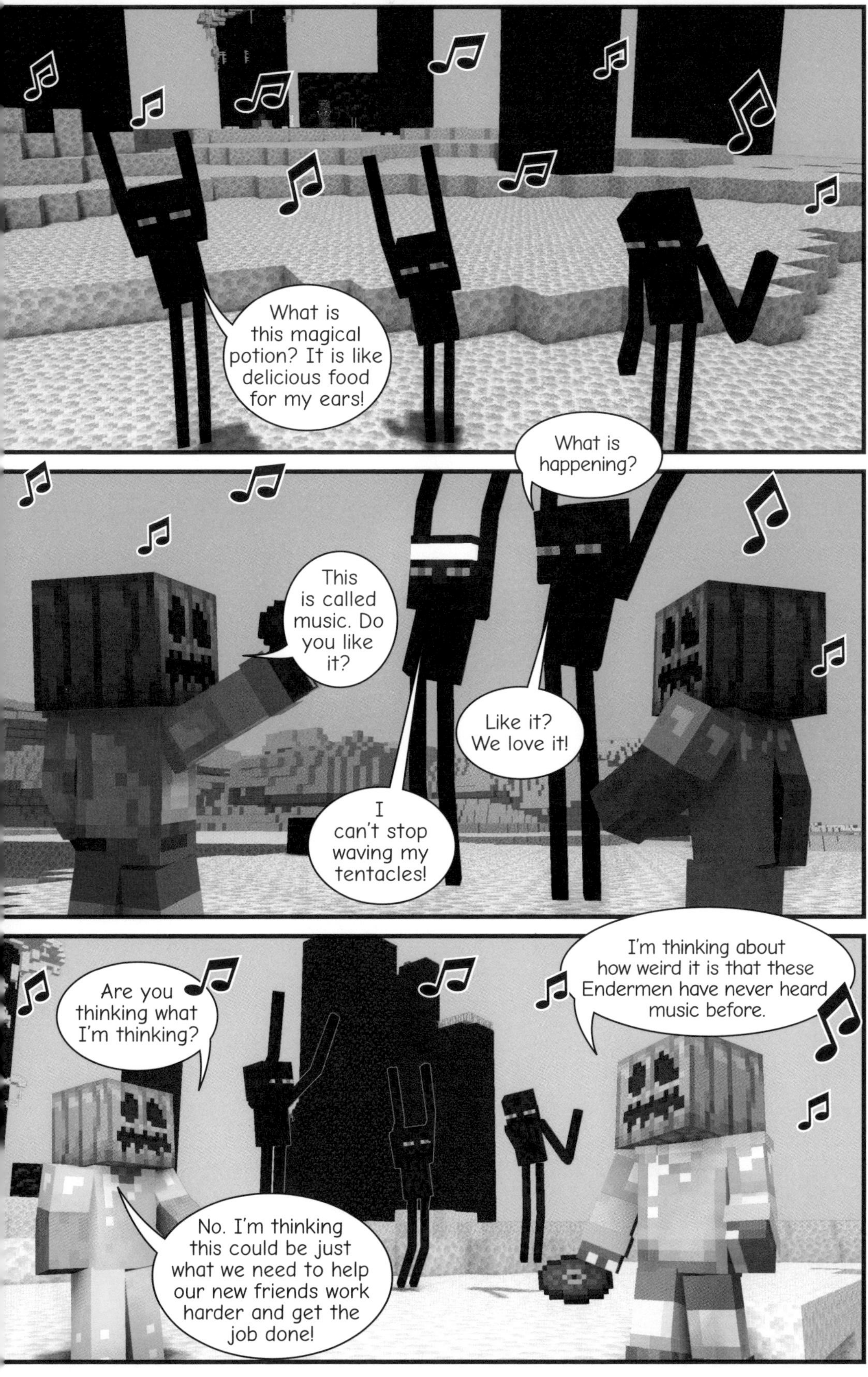
What is this magical potion? It is like delicious food for my ears!
What is happening?
This is called music. Do you like it?
Like it? We love it!
I can't stop waving my tentacles!
Are you thinking what I'm thinking?
I'm thinking about how weird it is that these Endermen have never heard music before.
No. I'm thinking this could be just what we need to help our new friends work harder and get the job done!

CHAPTER 7
SPEED
RUNNING

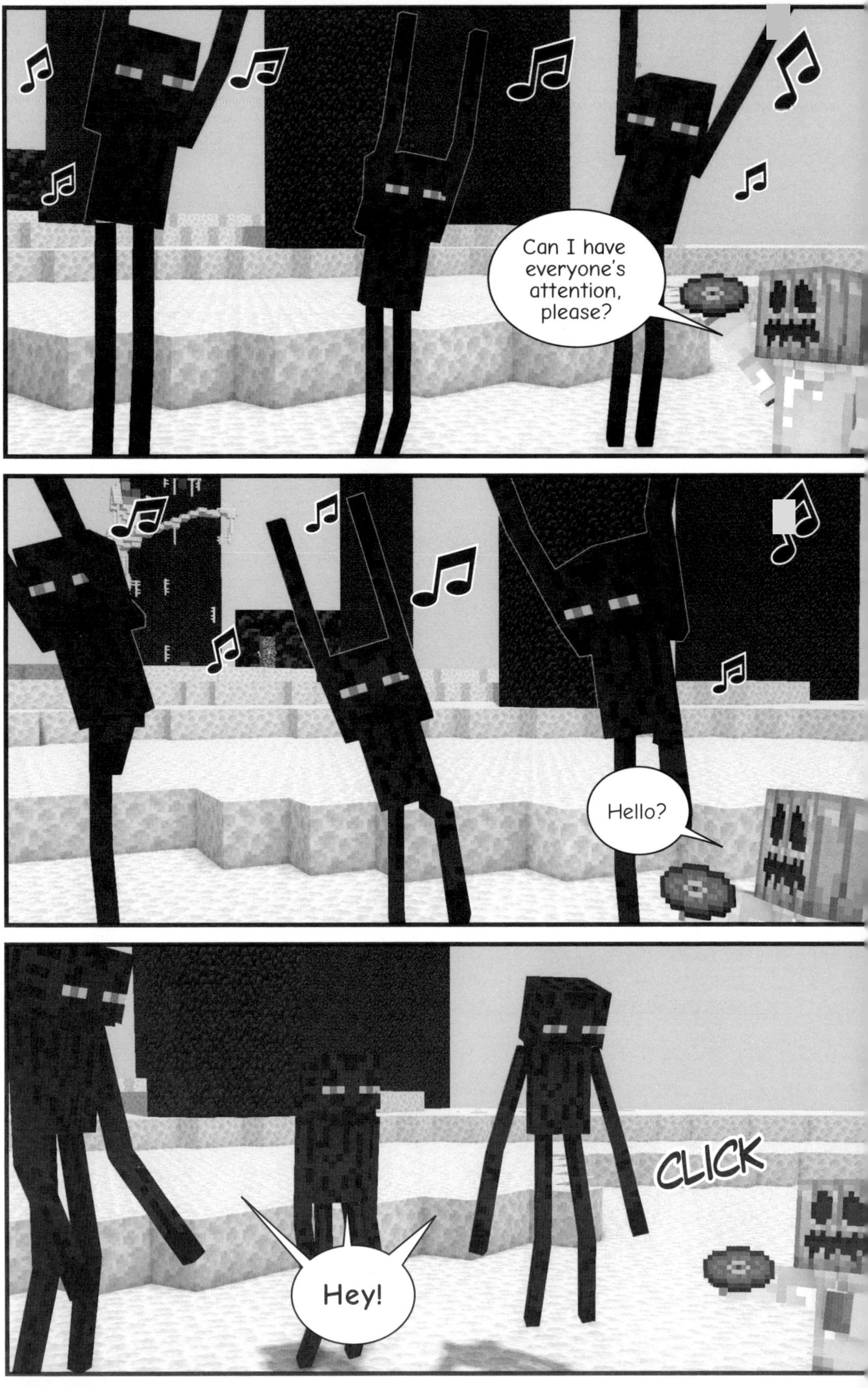
Can I have everyone's attention, please?
Hello?
CLICK
Hey!

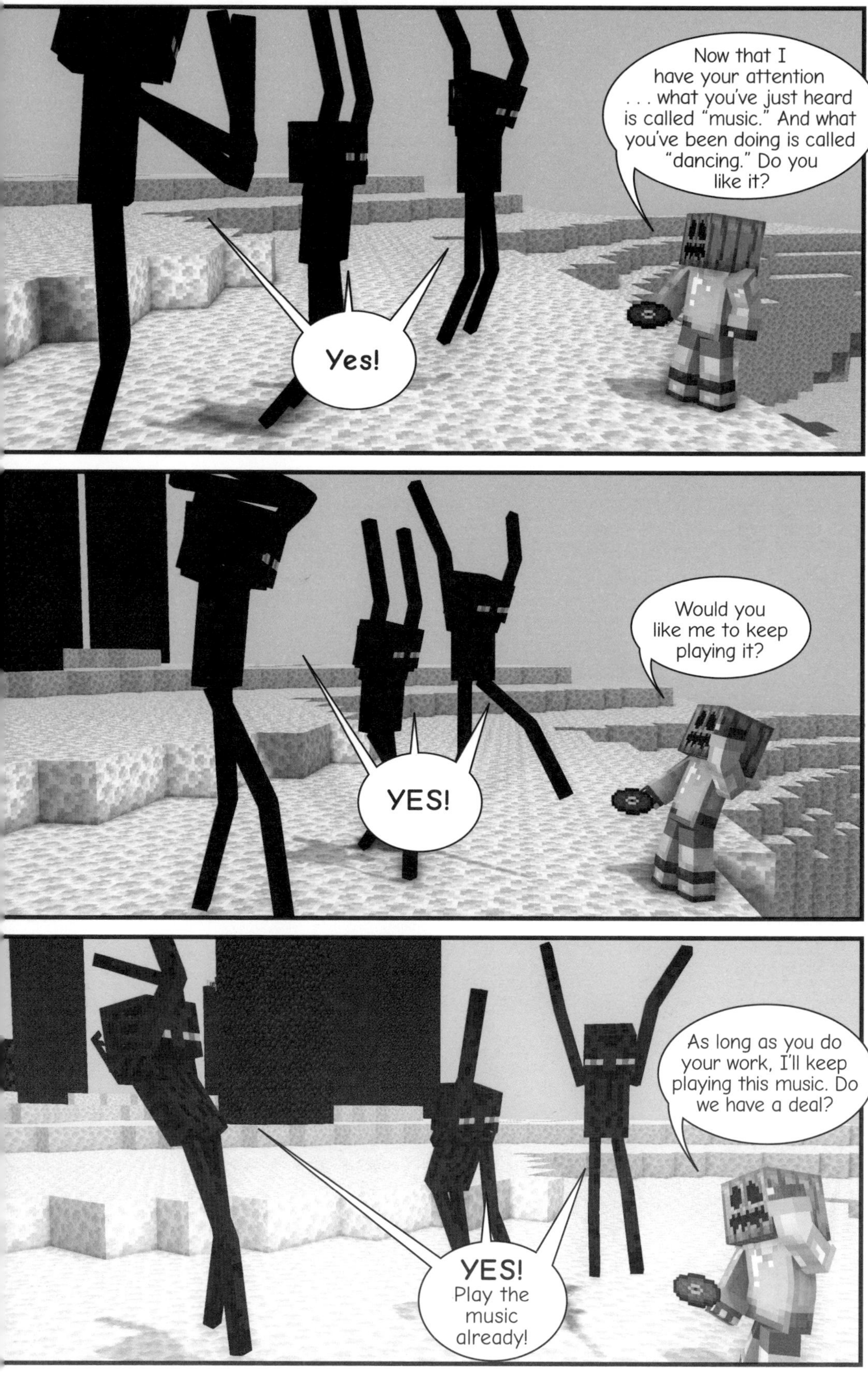
Now that I have your attention . . . what you've just heard is called "music." And what you've been doing is called "dancing." Do you like it?
Yes!
Would you like me to keep playing it?
YES!
As long as you do your work, I'll keep playing this music. Do we have a deal?
YES! Play the music already!

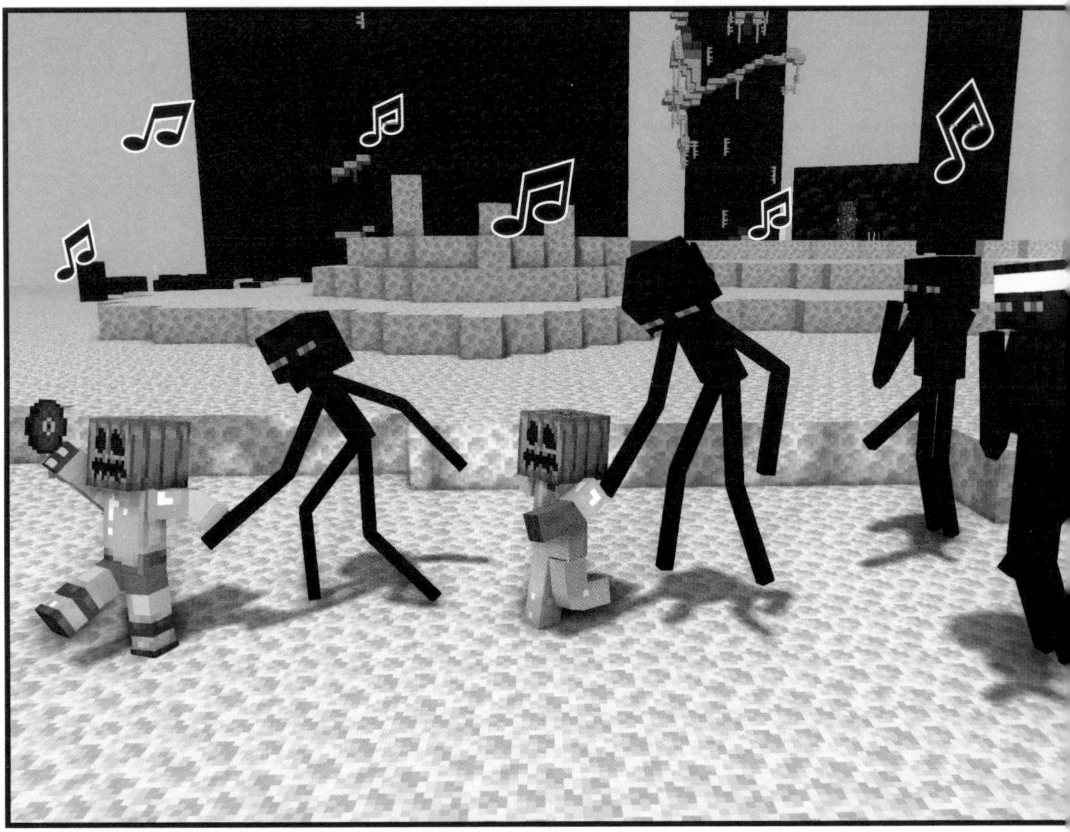

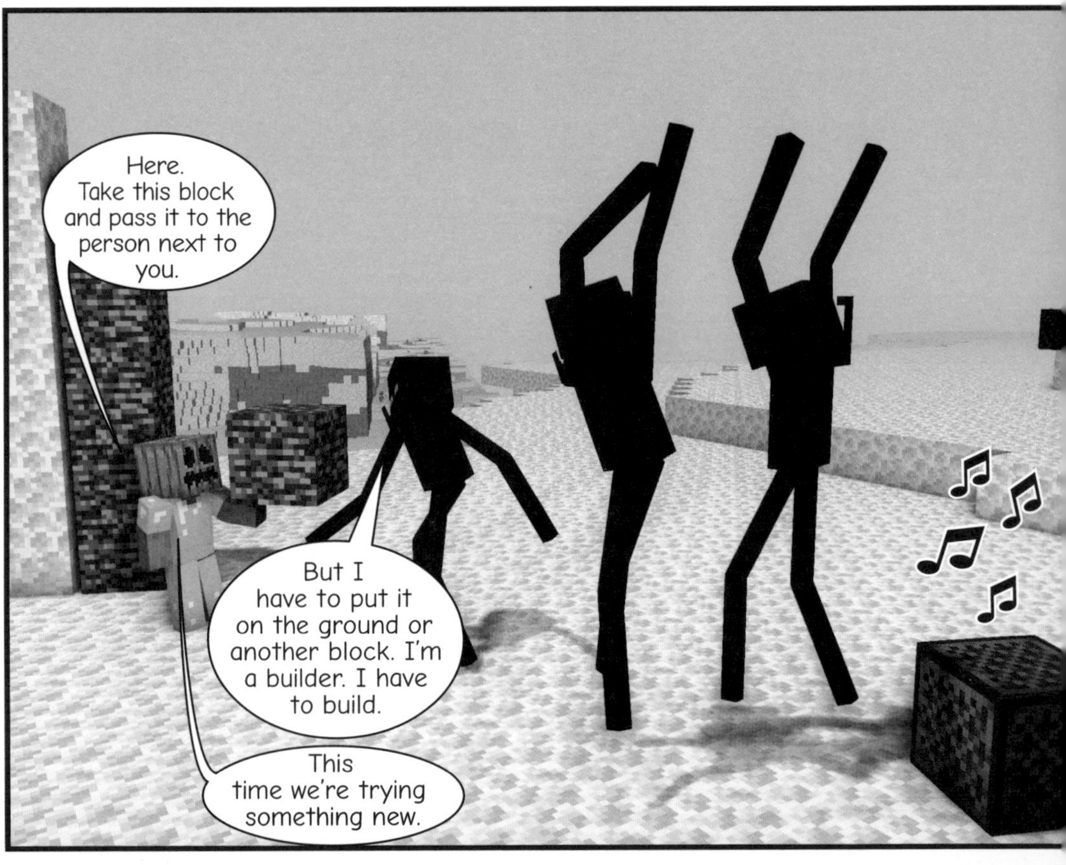

Here. Take this block and pass it to the person next to you.
But I have to put it on the ground or another block. I'm a builder. I have to build.
This time we're trying something new.

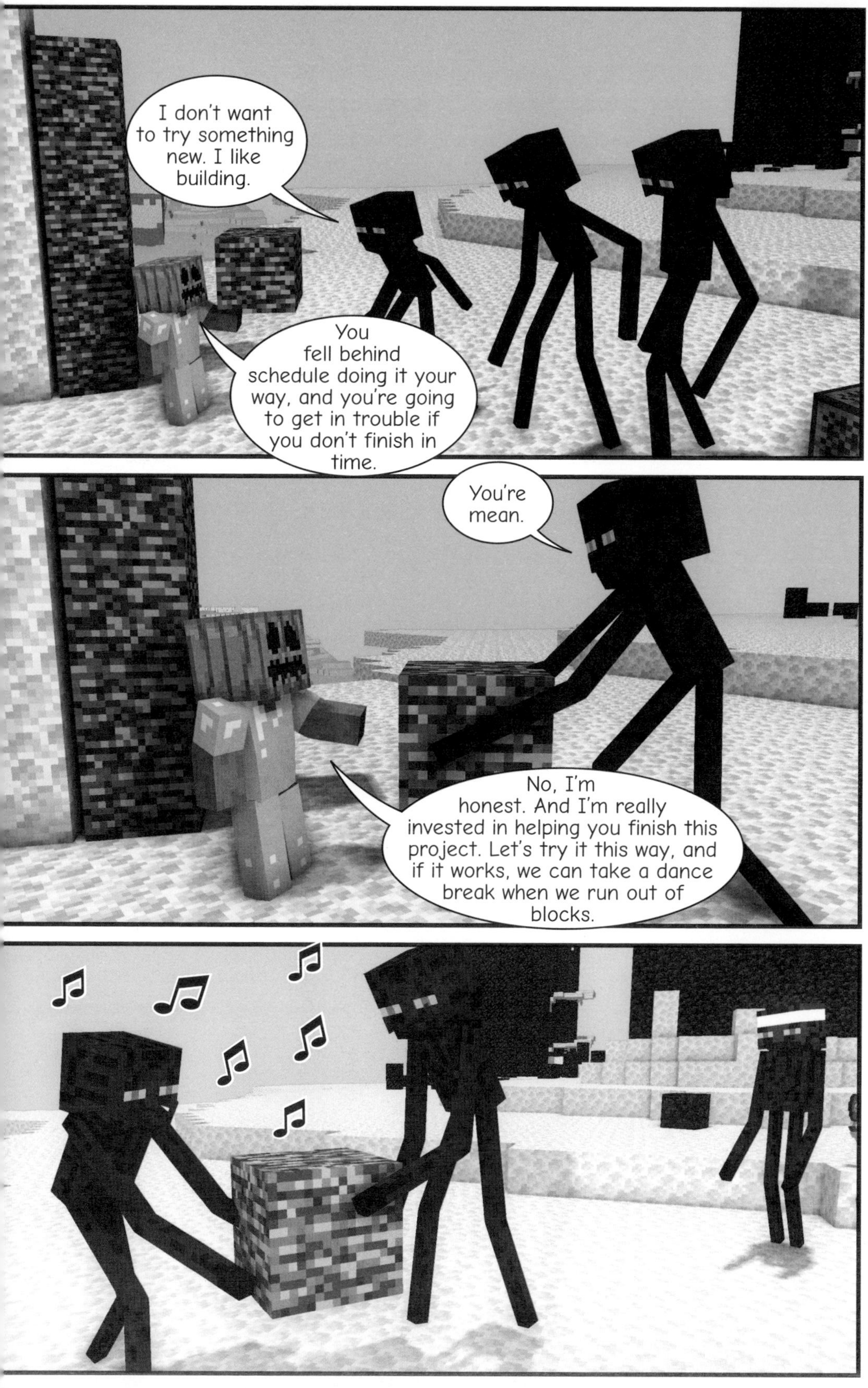
I don't want to try something new. I like building.
You fell behind schedule doing it your way, and you're going to get in trouble if you don't finish in time.
You're mean.
No, I'm honest. And I'm really invested in helping you finish this project. Let's try it this way, and if it works, we can take a dance break when we run out of blocks.

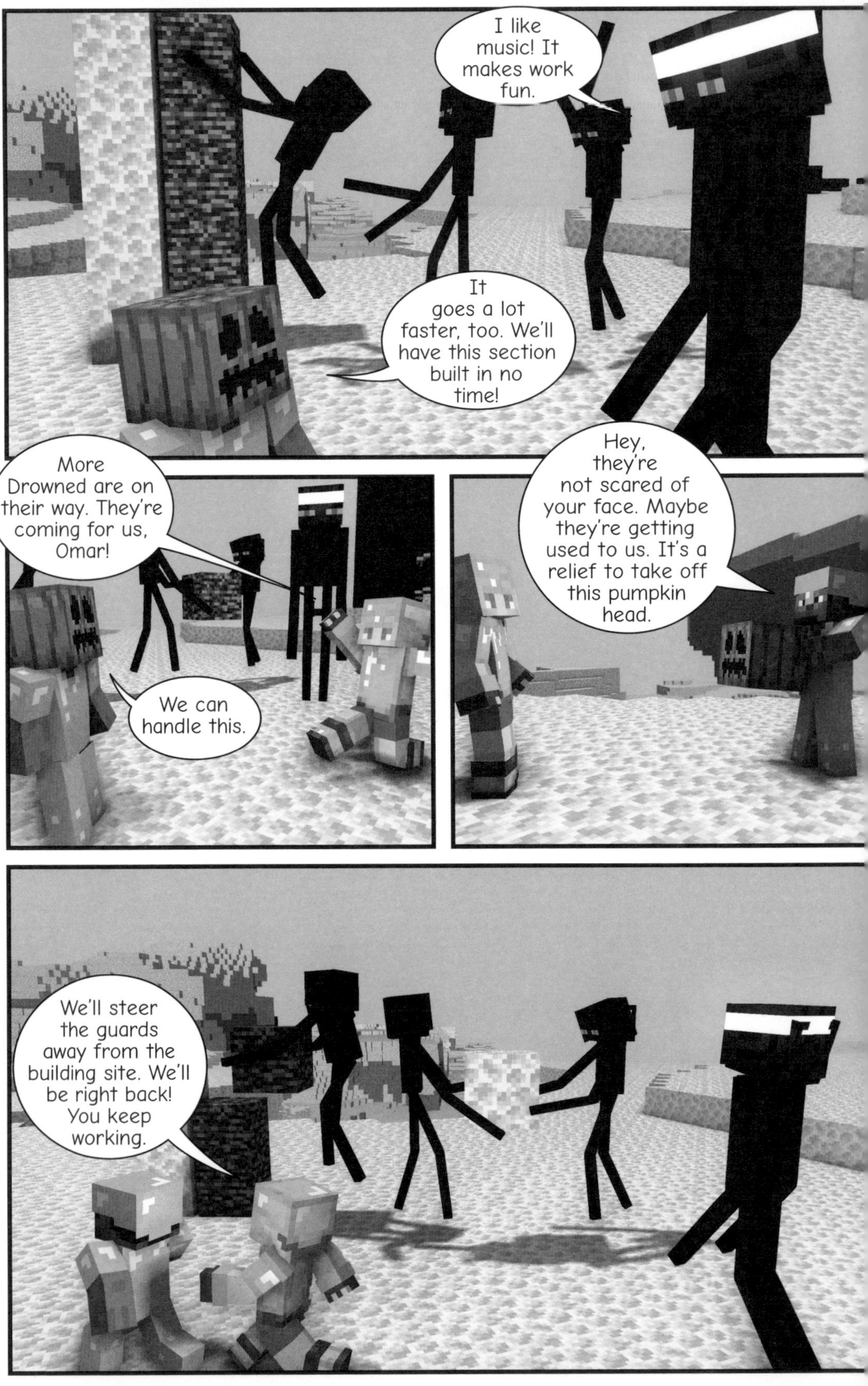
I like music! It makes work fun.
It goes a lot faster, too. We'll have this section built in no time!
More Drowned are on their way. They're coming for us, Omar!
We can handle this.
Hey, they're not scared of your face. Maybe they're getting used to us. It's a relief to take off this pumpkin head.
We'll steer the guards away from the building site. We'll be right back! You keep working.

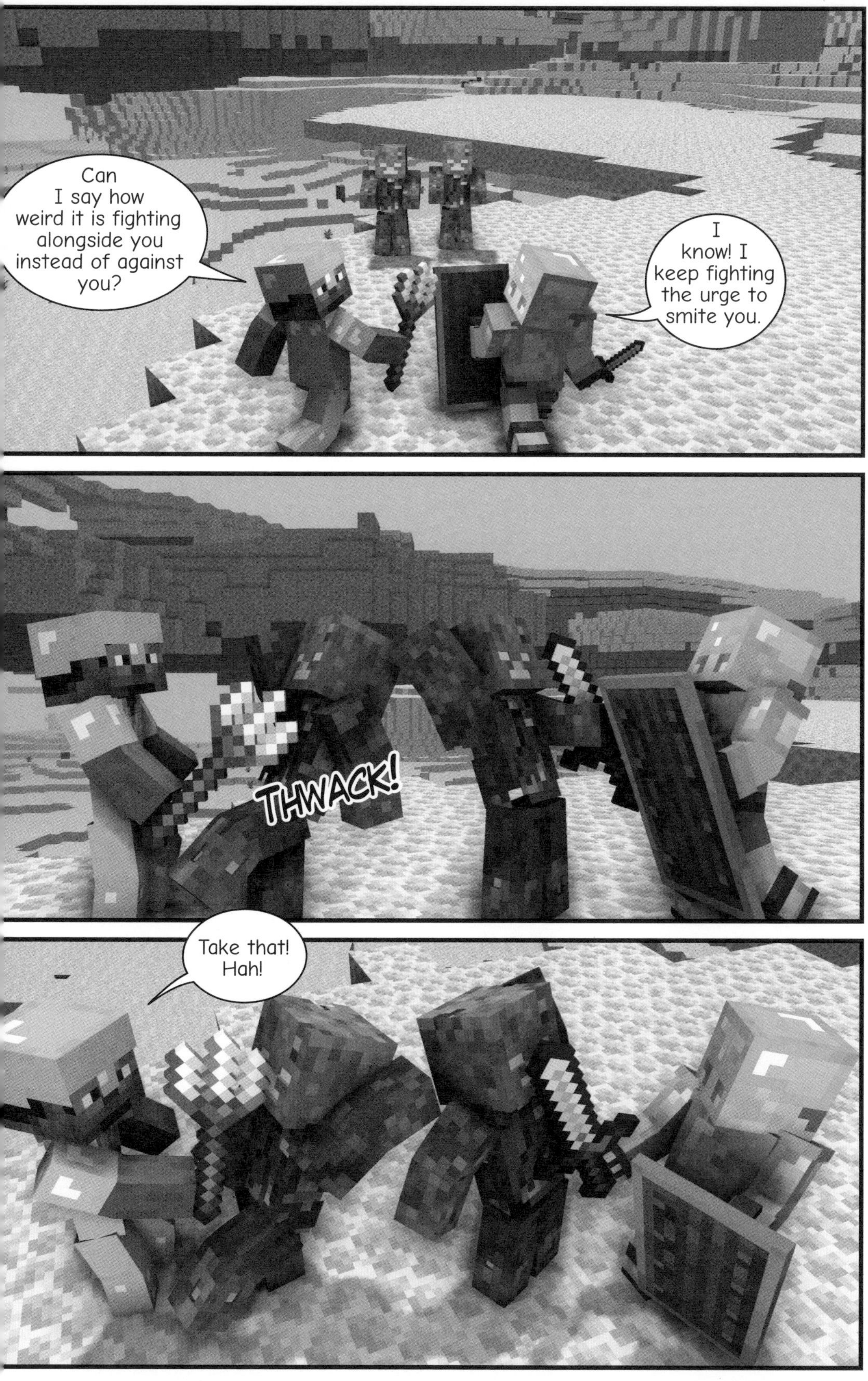

Can I say how weird it is fighting alongside you instead of against you?
I know! I keep fighting the urge to smite you.
THWACK!
Take that! Hah!

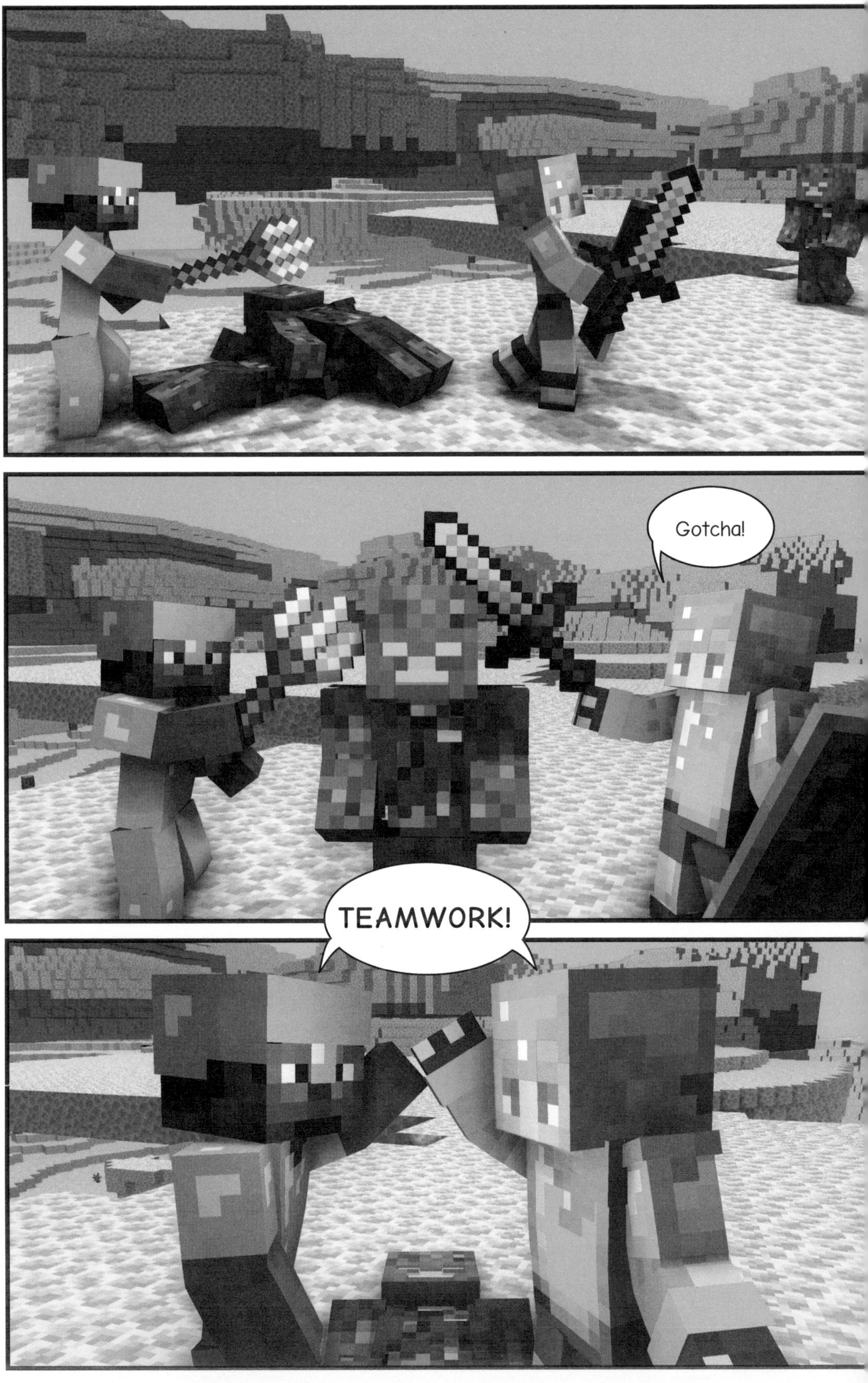
Gotcha!
TEAMWORK!

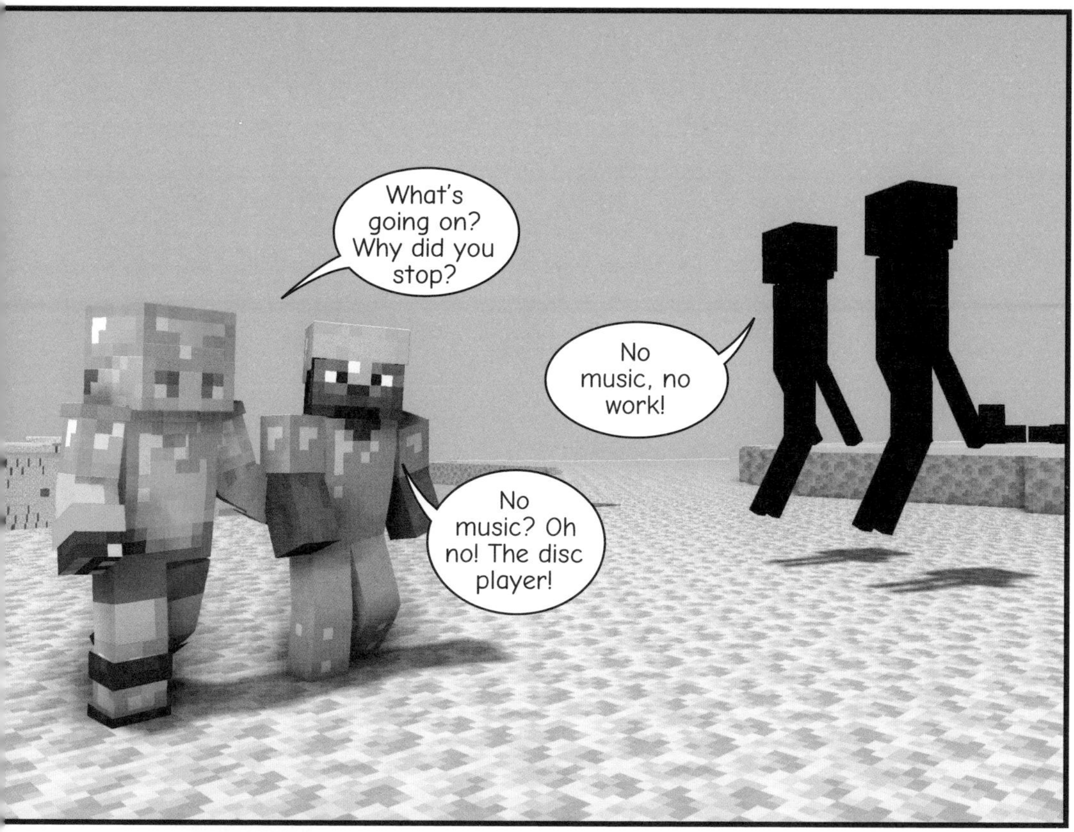
What's going on? Why did you stop?
No music, no work!
No music? Oh no! The disc player!

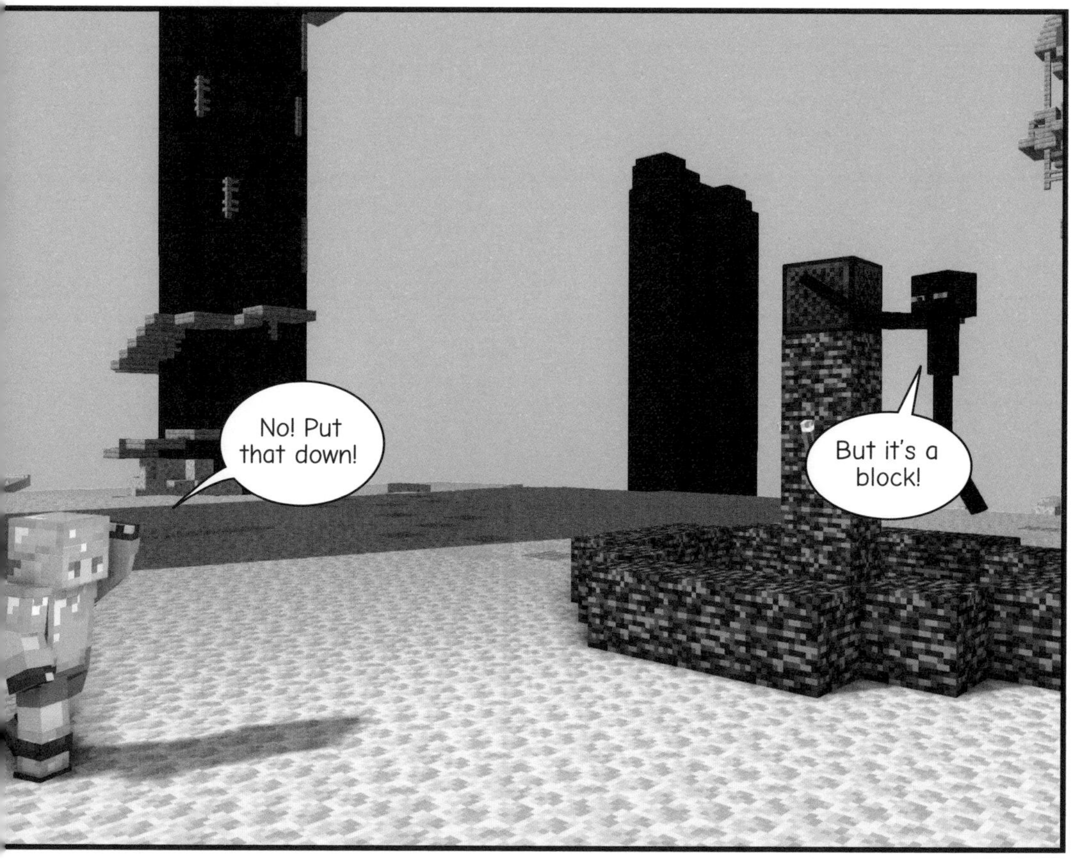
No! Put that down!
But it's a block!

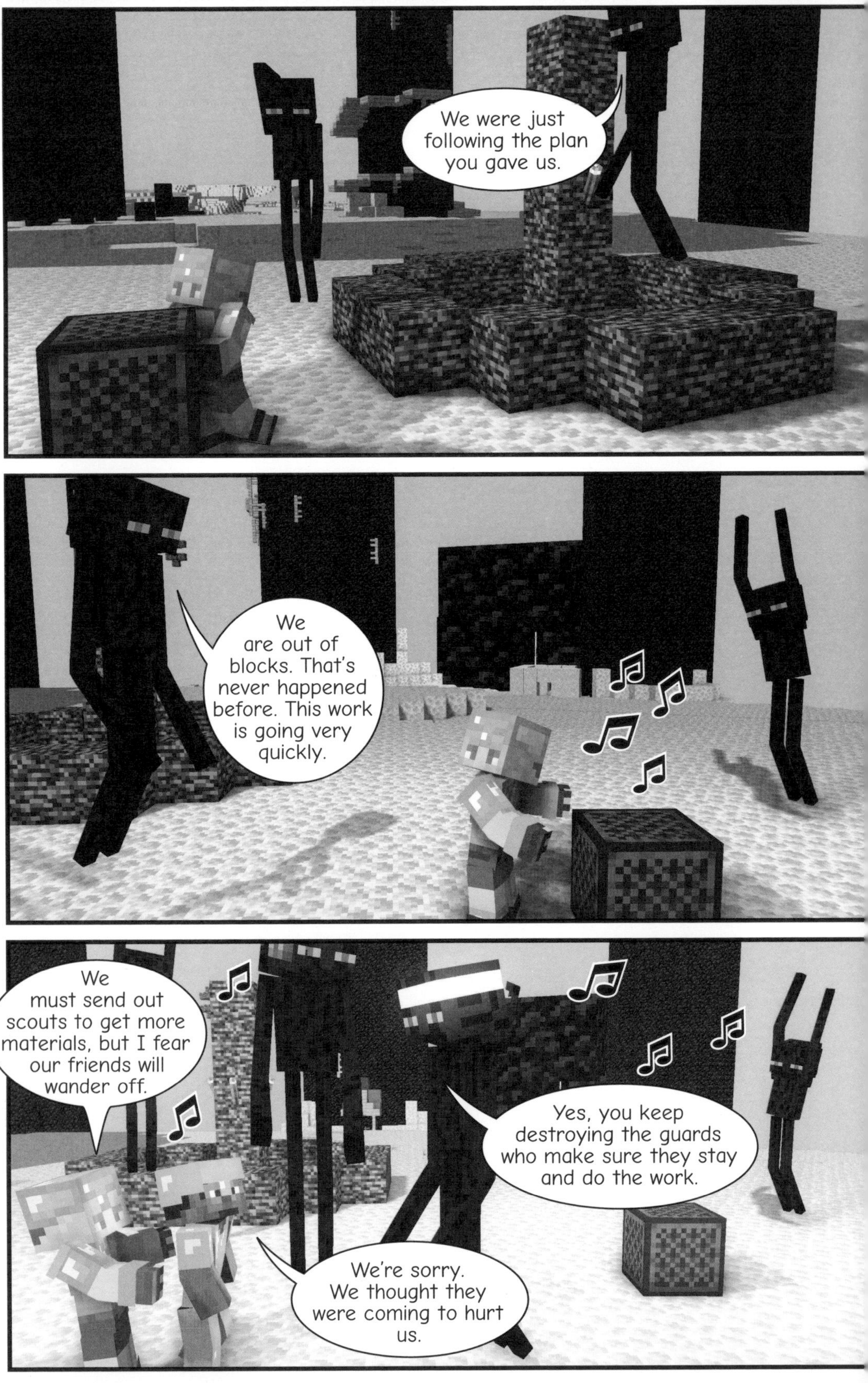
We were just following the plan you gave us.
We are out of blocks. That's never happened before. This work is going very quickly.
We must send out scouts to get more materials, but I fear our friends will wander off.
Yes, you keep destroying the guards who make sure they stay and do the work.
We're sorry. We thought they were coming to hurt us.

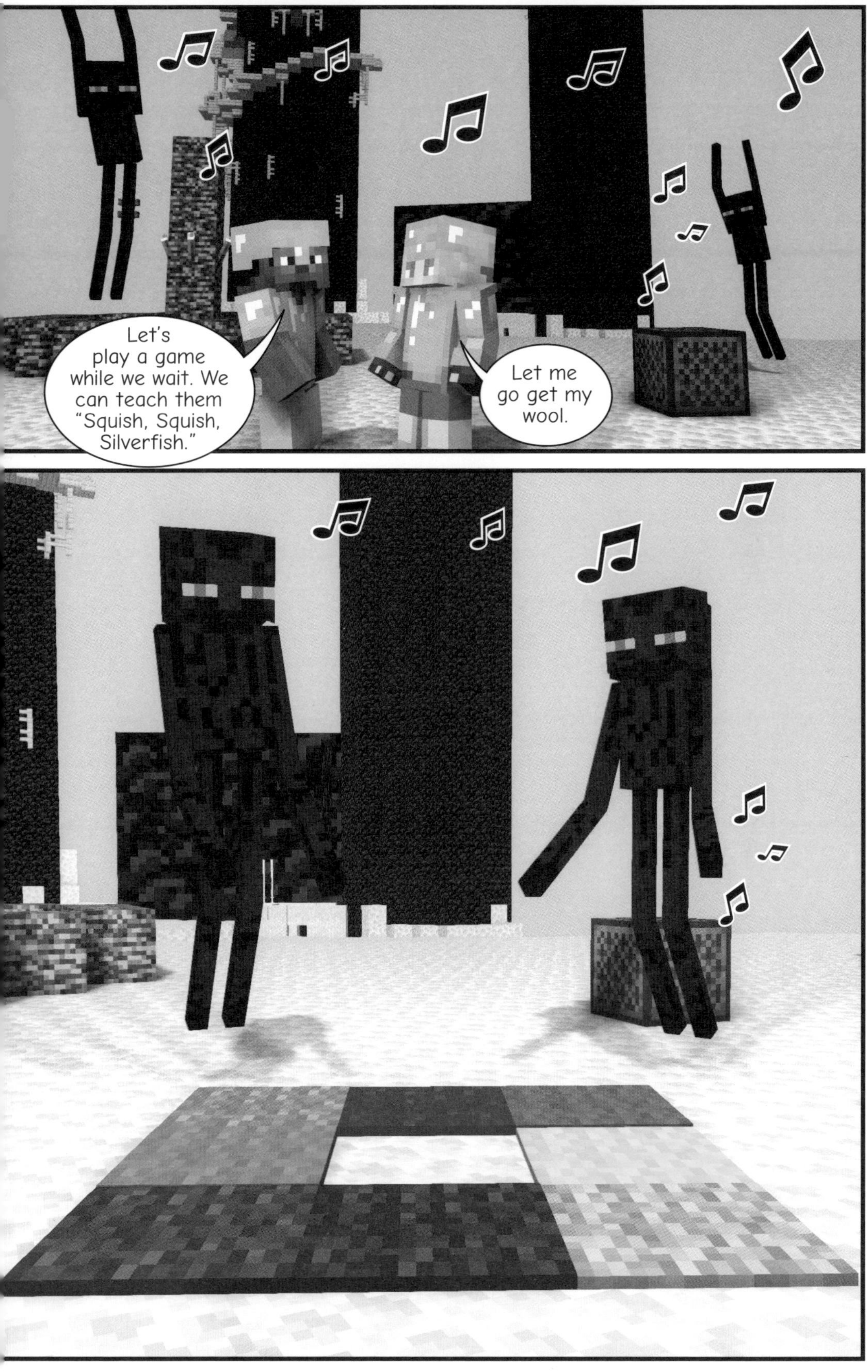
Let's play a game while we wait. We can teach them "Squish, Squish, Silverfish."
Let me go get my wool.

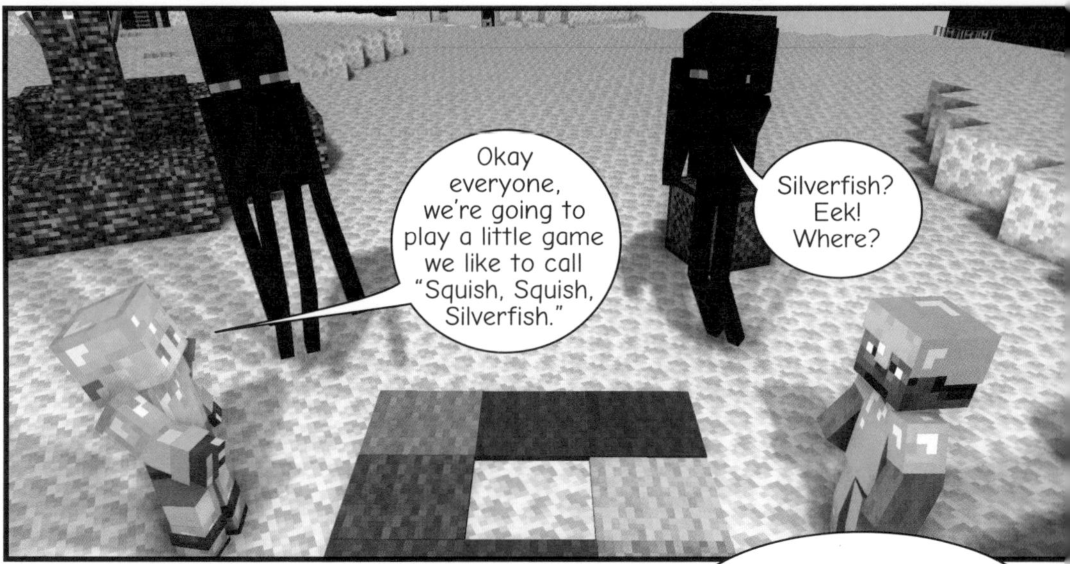
Okay everyone, we're going to play a little game we like to call "Squish, Squish, Silverfish."
Silverfish? Eek! Where?

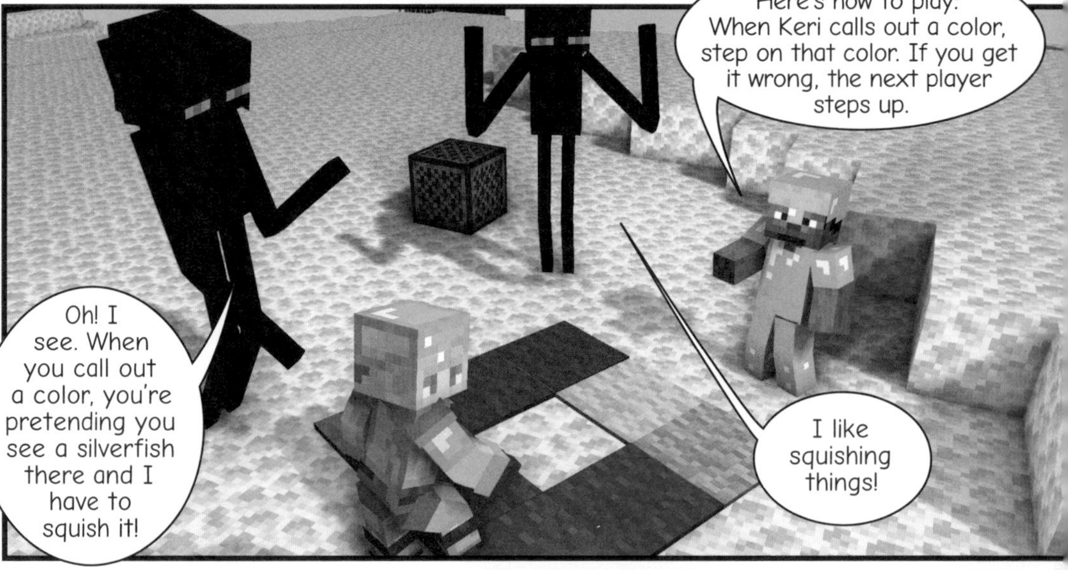
Here's how to play: When Keri calls out a color, step on that color. If you get it wrong, the next player steps up.
Oh! I see. When you call out a color, you're pretending you see a silverfish there and I have to squish it!
I like squishing things!

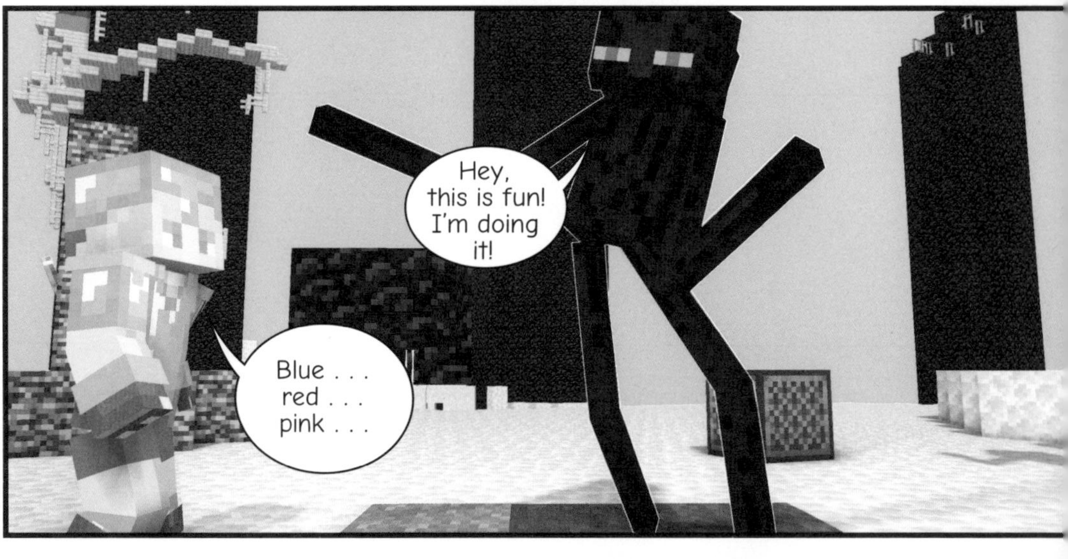
Hey, this is fun! I'm doing it!
Blue . . . red . . . pink . . .

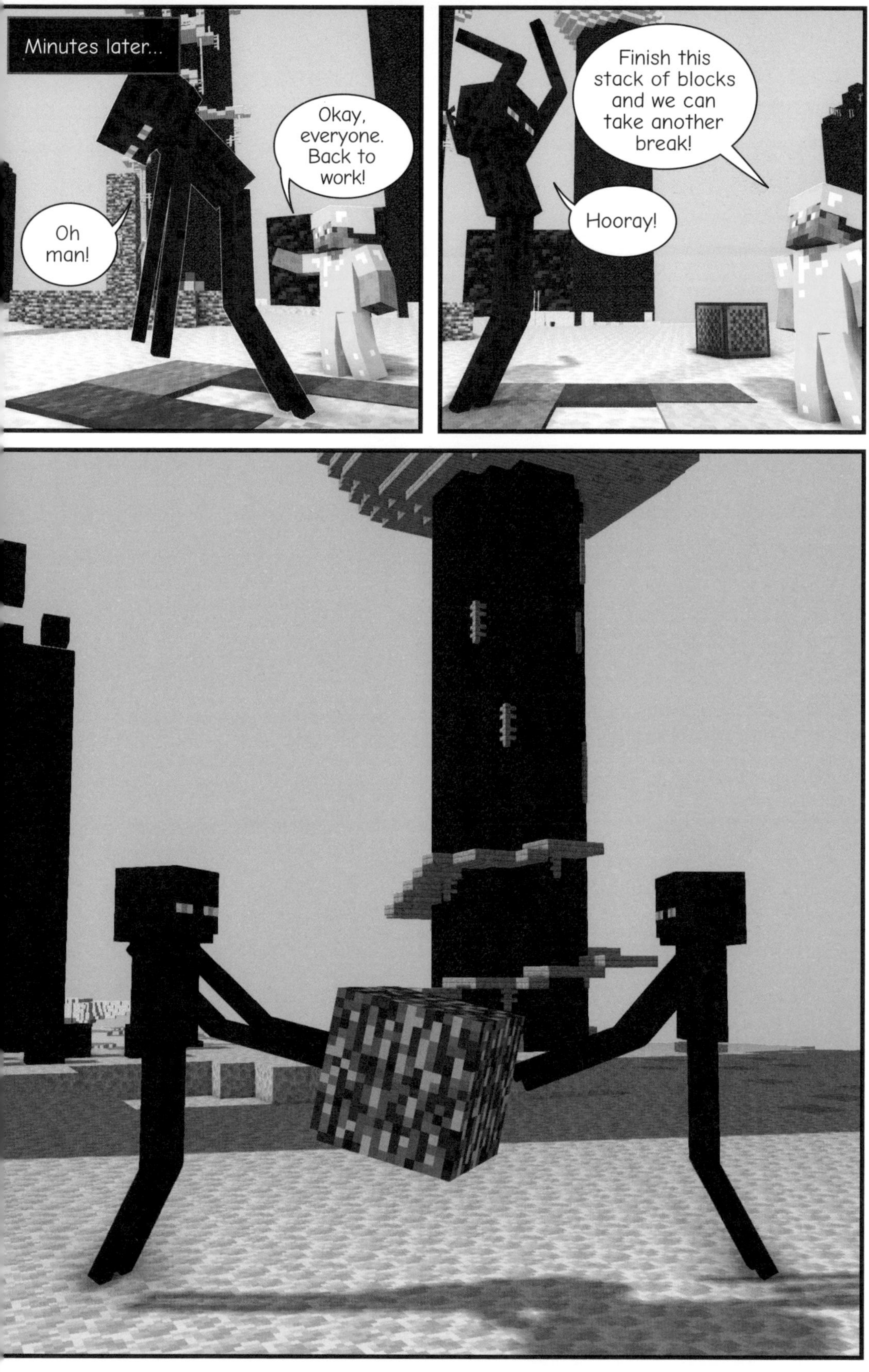
Minutes later...
Okay, everyone. Back to work!
Oh man!
Finish this stack of blocks and we can take another break!
Hooray!

CHAPTER 8
SHIP OF FOOLS

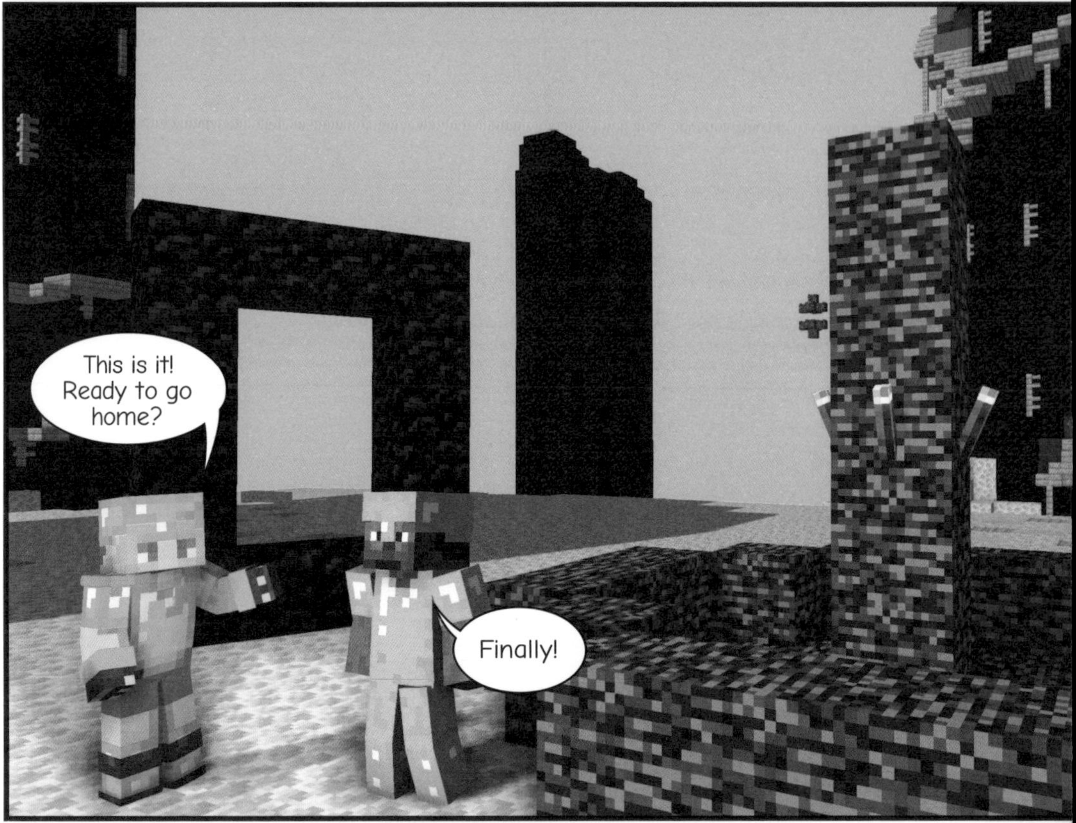
This is it! Ready to go home?
Finally!

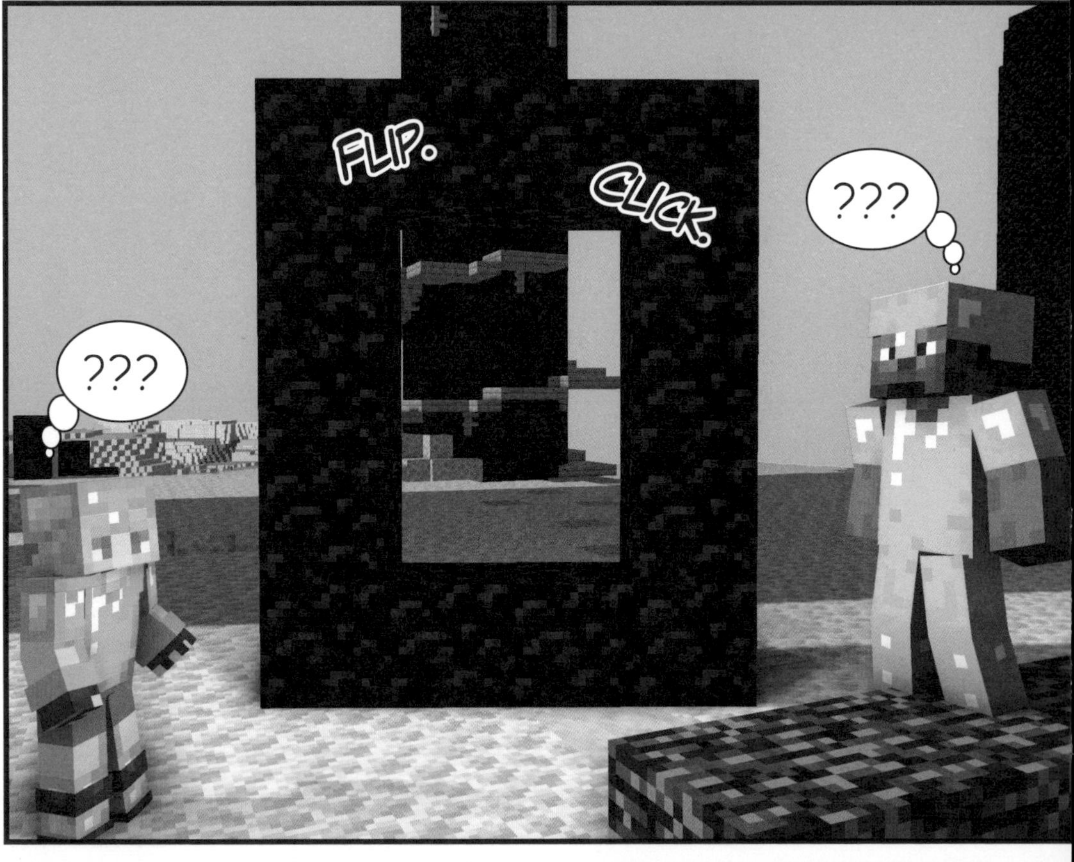
FLIP.
CLICK.
???
???

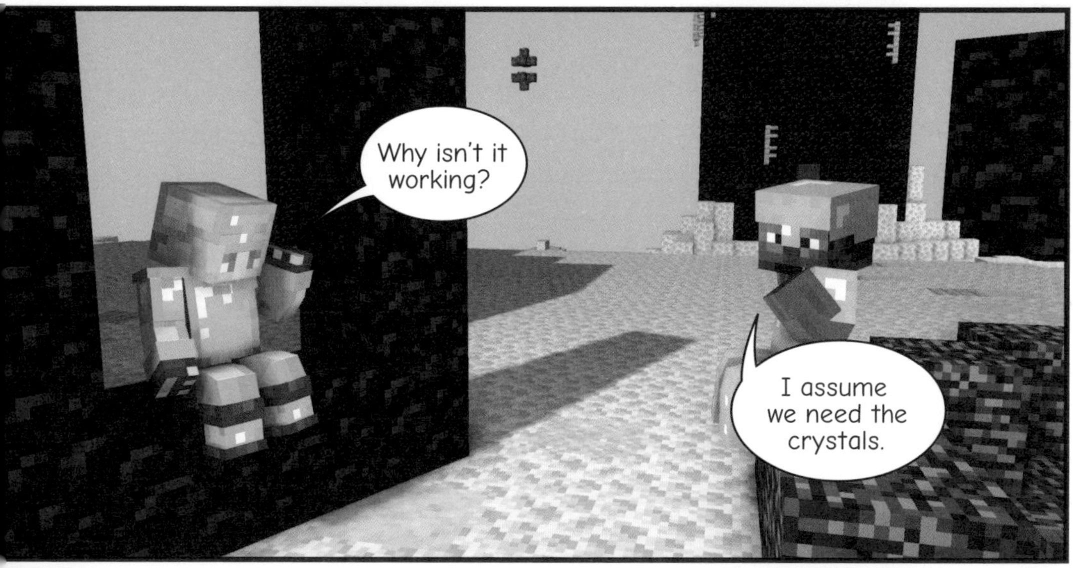
Why isn't it working?
I assume we need the crystals.

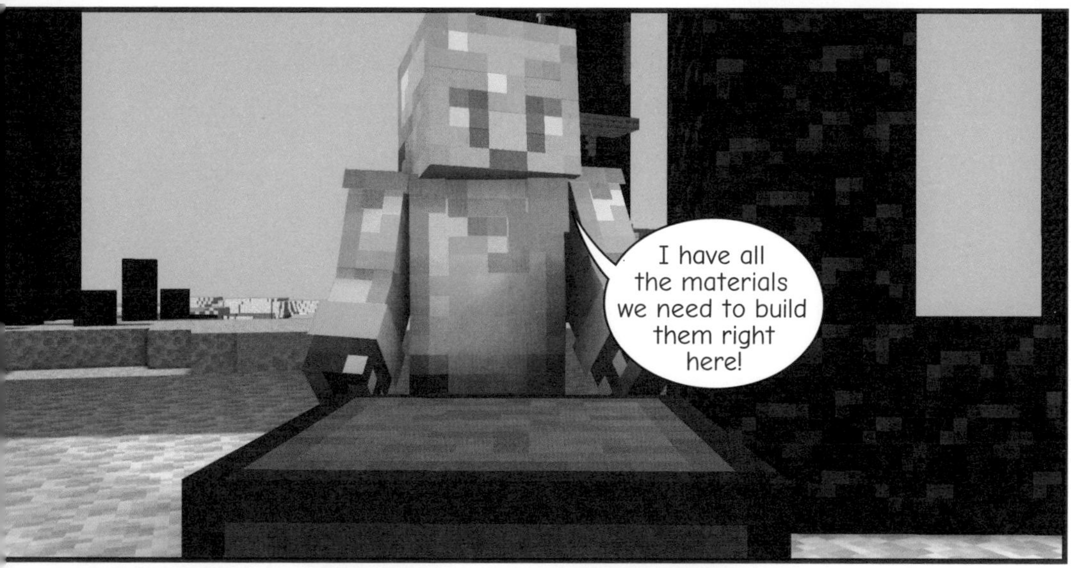
I have all the materials we need to build them right here!

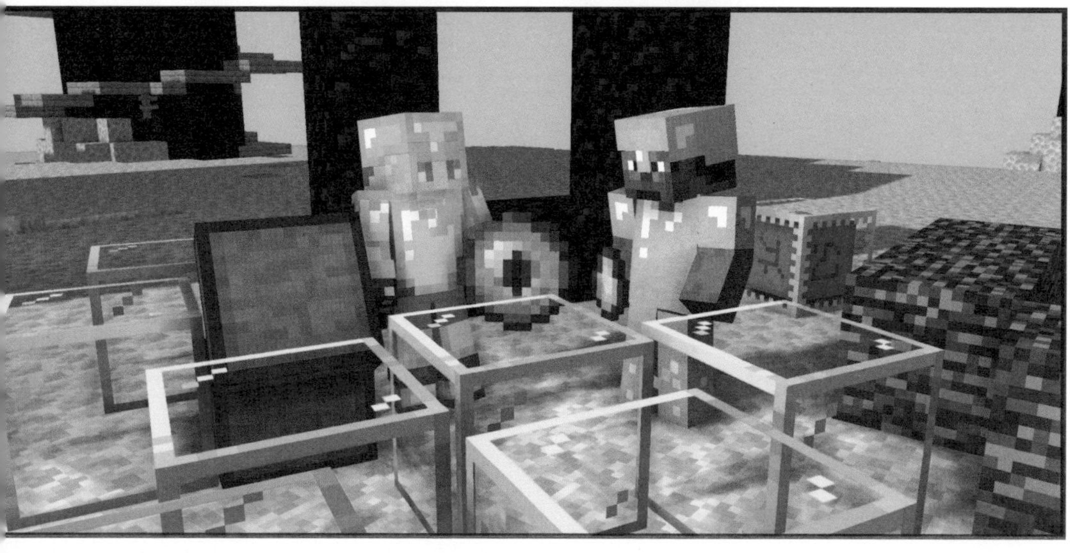

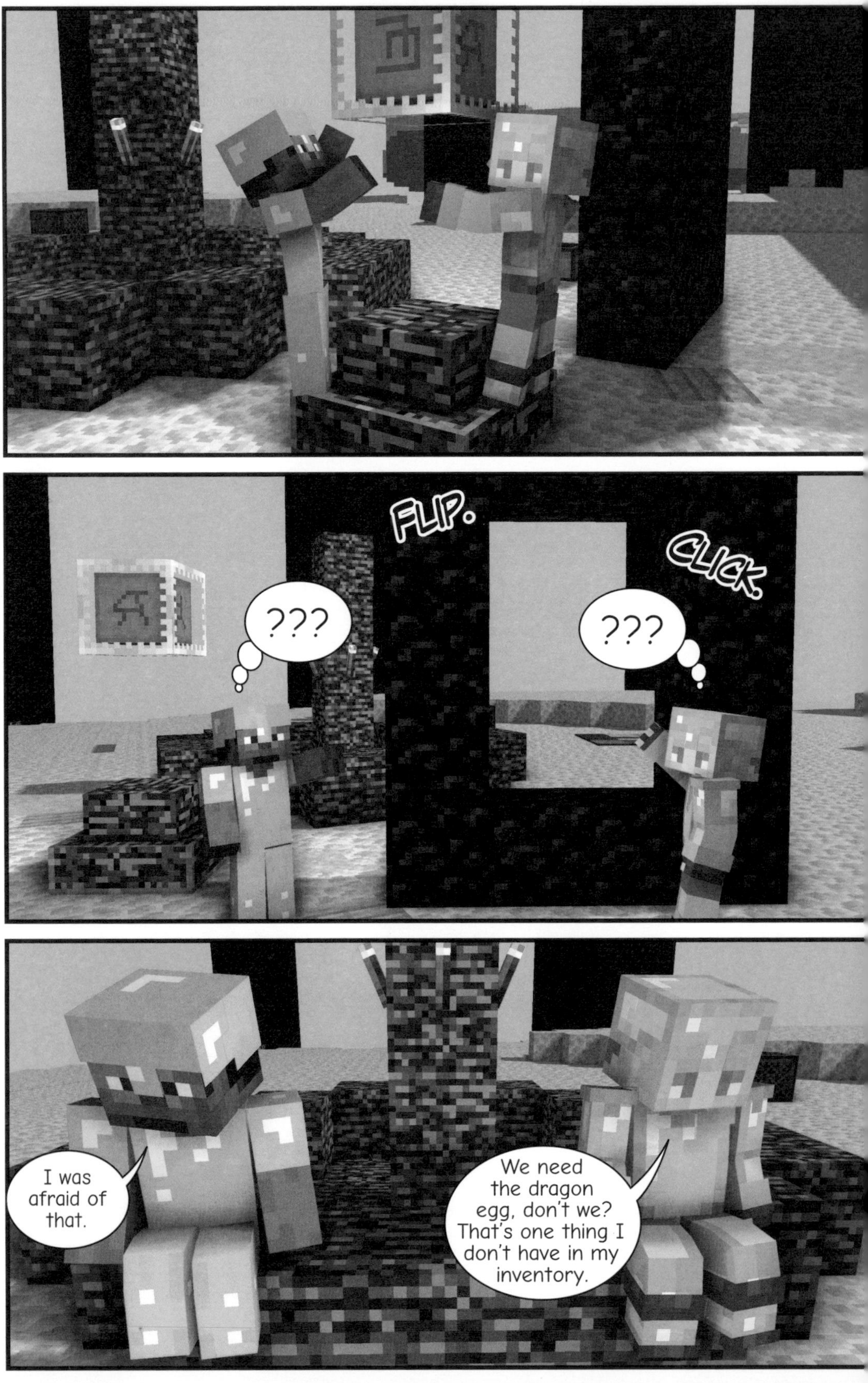
FLIP.
???
???
CLICK.
I was afraid of that.
We need the dragon egg, don't we? That's one thing I don't have in my inventory.

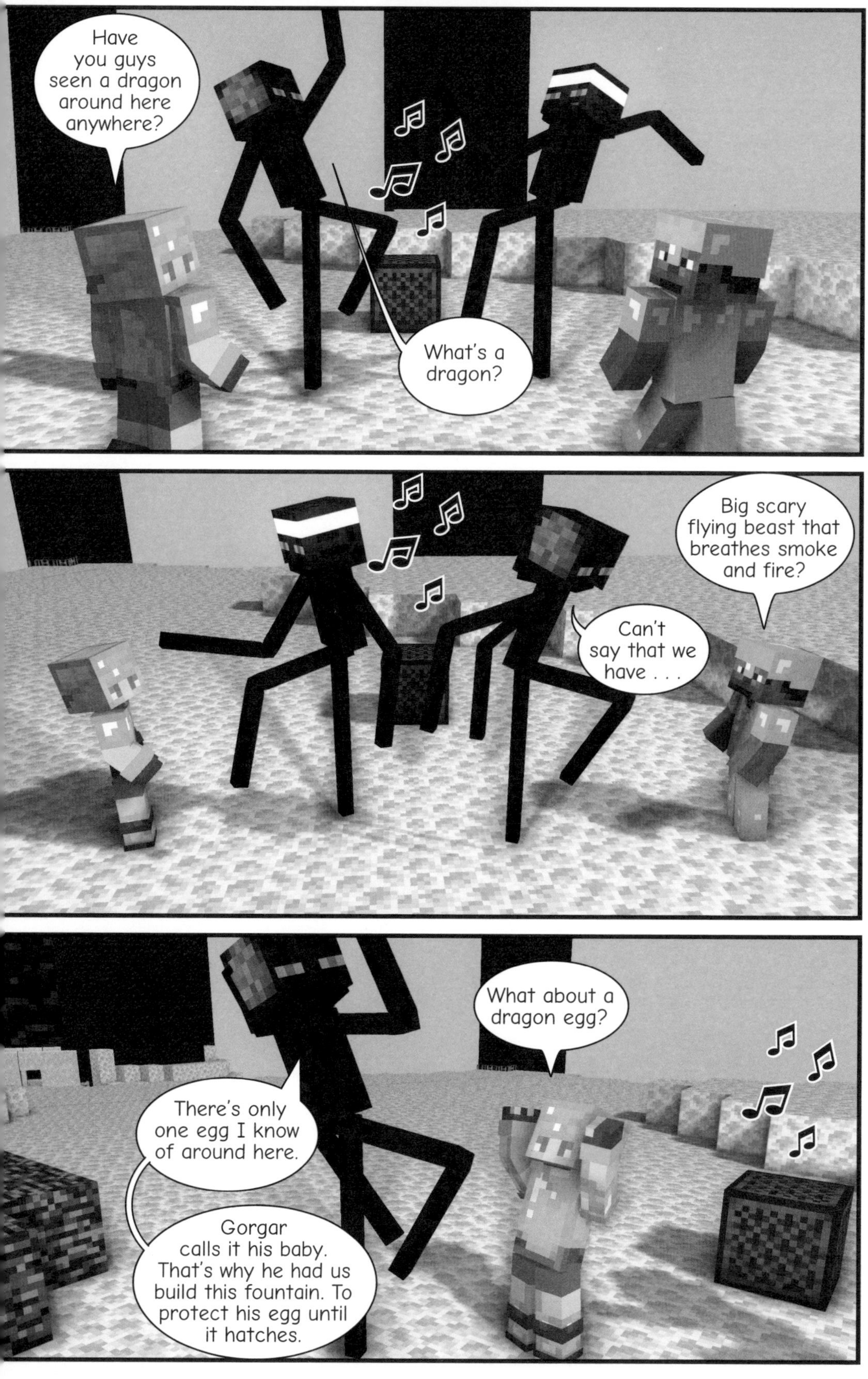
Have you guys seen a dragon around here anywhere?
What's a dragon?
Big scary flying beast that breathes smoke and fire?
Can't say that we have . . .
What about a dragon egg?
There's only one egg I know of around here.
Gorgar calls it his baby. That's why he had us build this fountain. To protect his egg until it hatches.

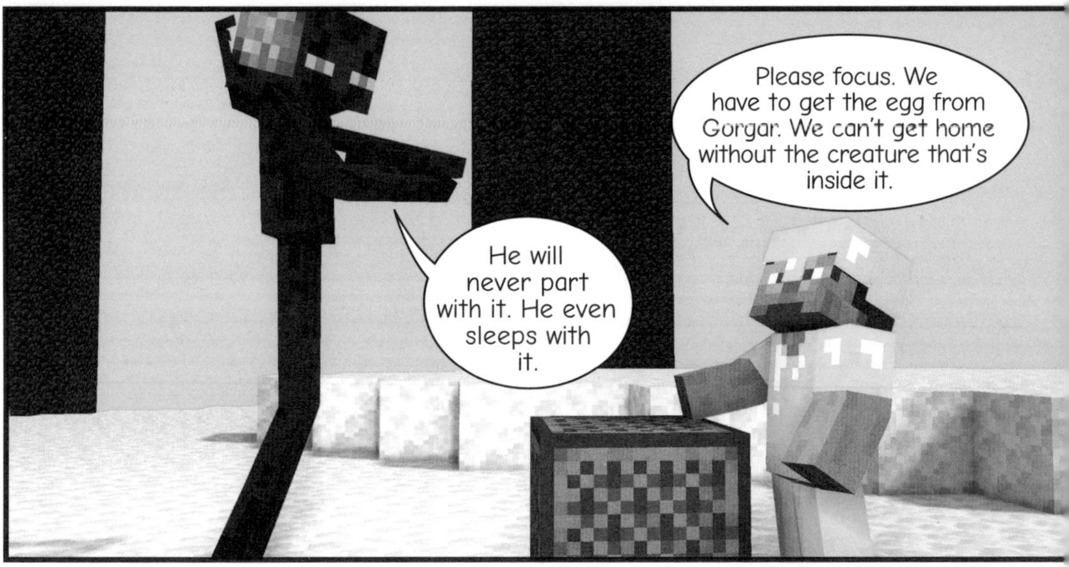
Please focus. We have to get the egg from Gorgar. We can't get home without the creature that's inside it.
He will never part with it. He even sleeps with it.

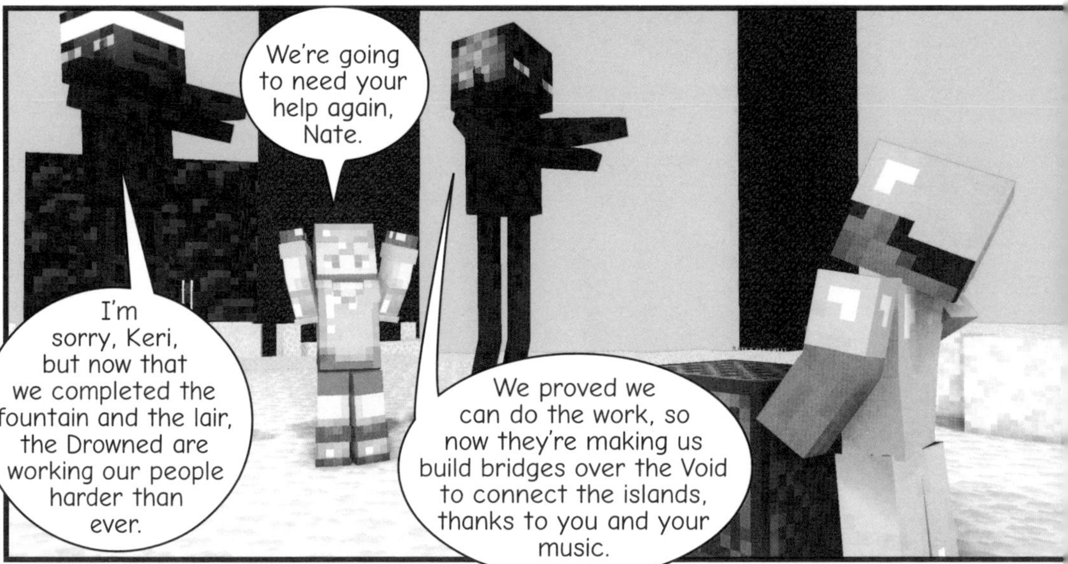
We're going to need your help again, Nate.
I'm sorry, Keri, but now that we completed the fountain and the lair, the Drowned are working our people harder than ever.
We proved we can do the work, so now they're making us build bridges over the Void to connect the islands, thanks to you and your music.

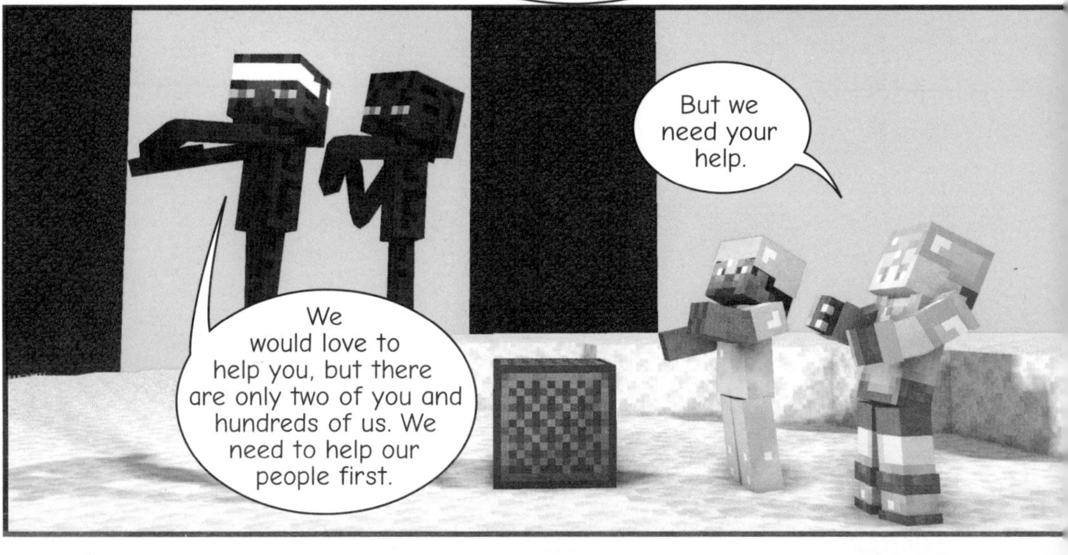
But we need your help.
We would love to help you, but there are only two of you and hundreds of us. We need to help our people first.

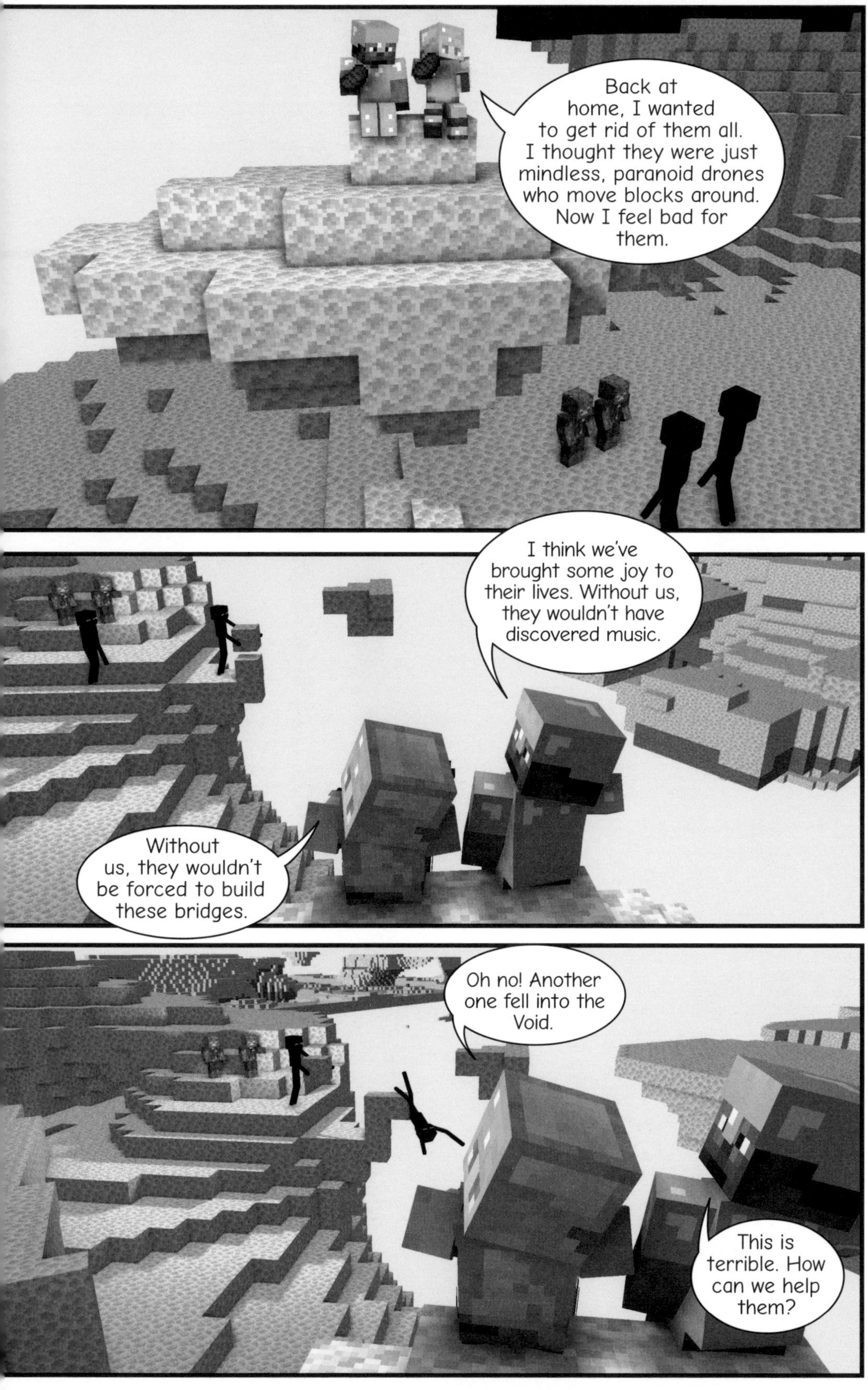
Back at home, I wanted to get rid of them all. I thought they were just mindless, paranoid drones who move blocks around. Now I feel bad for them.
I think we've brought some joy to their lives. Without us, they wouldn't have discovered music.
Without us, they wouldn't be forced to build these bridges.
Oh no! Another one fell into the Void.
This is terrible. How can we help them?

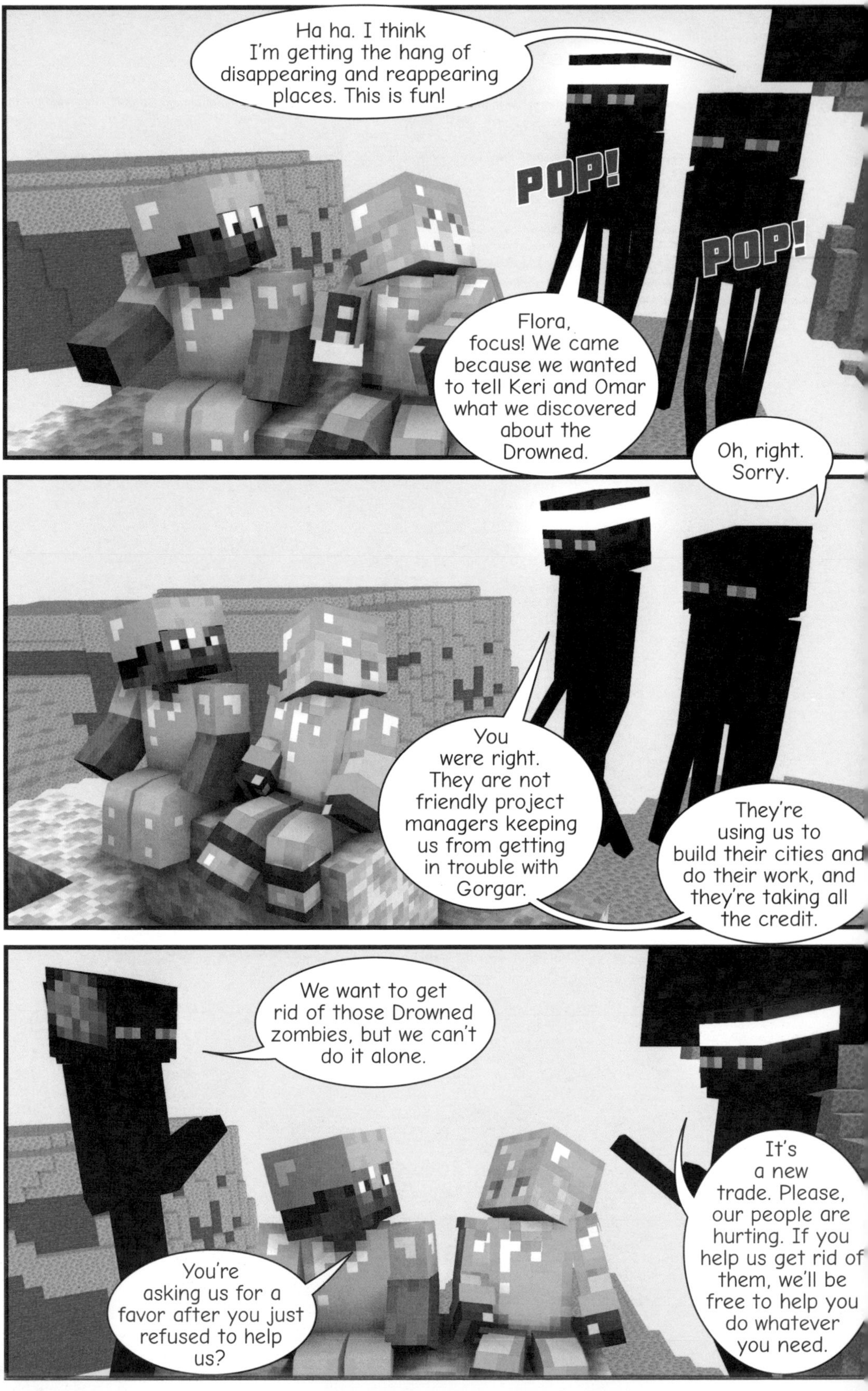
Ha ha. I think I'm getting the hang of disappearing and reappearing places. This is fun!
POP!
POP!
Flora, focus! We came because we wanted to tell Keri and Omar what we discovered about the Drowned.
Oh, right. Sorry.
You were right. They are not friendly project managers keeping us from getting in trouble with Gorgar.
They're using us to build their cities and do their work, and they're taking all the credit.
We want to get rid of those Drowned zombies, but we can't do it alone.
You're asking us for a favor after you just refused to help us?
It's a new trade. Please, our people are hurting. If you help us get rid of them, we'll be free to help you do whatever you need.

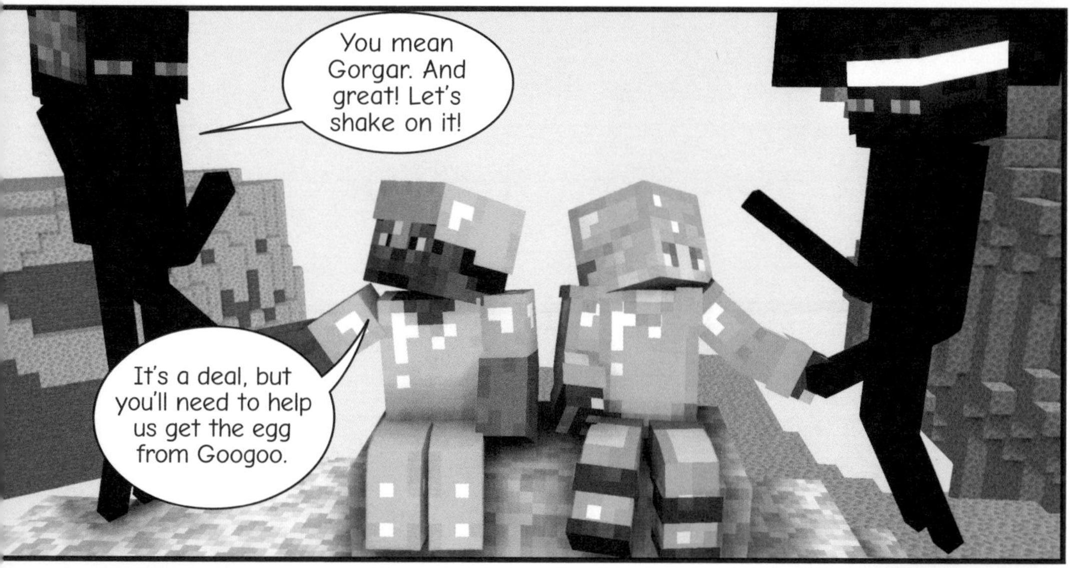
You mean Gorgar. And great! Let's shake on it!
It's a deal, but you'll need to help us get the egg from Googoo.

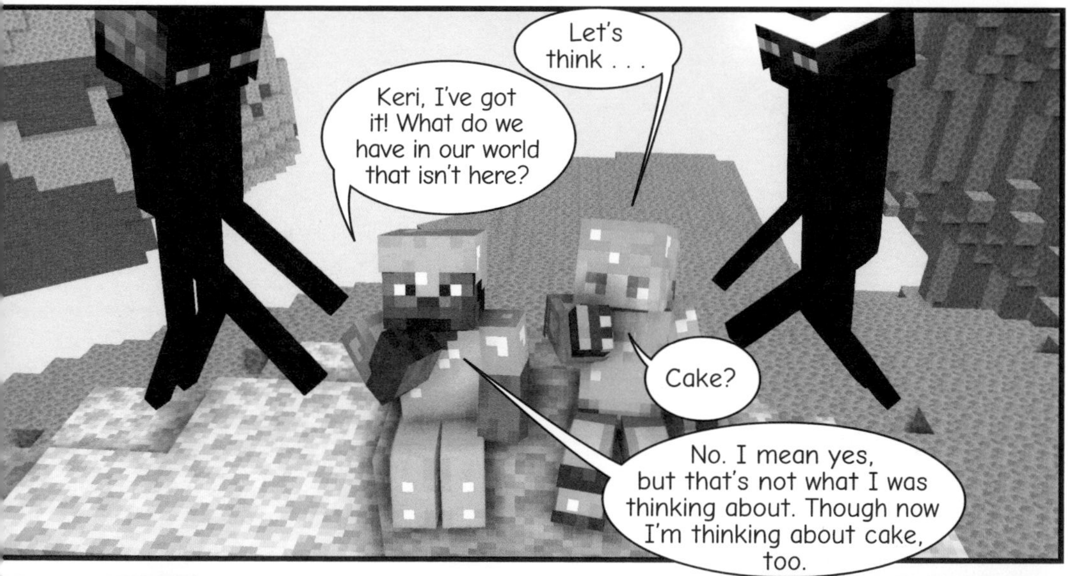
Let's think . . .
Keri, I've got it! What do we have in our world that isn't here?
Cake?
No. I mean yes, but that's not what I was thinking about. Though now I'm thinking about cake, too.

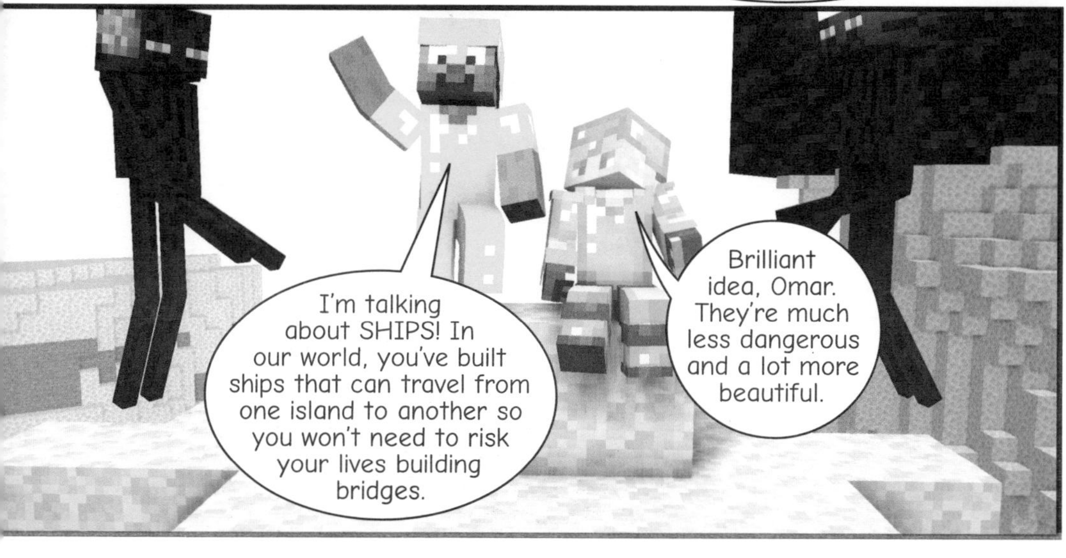
I'm talking about SHIPS! In our world, you've built ships that can travel from one island to another so you won't need to risk your lives building bridges.
Brilliant idea, Omar. They're much less dangerous and a lot more beautiful.

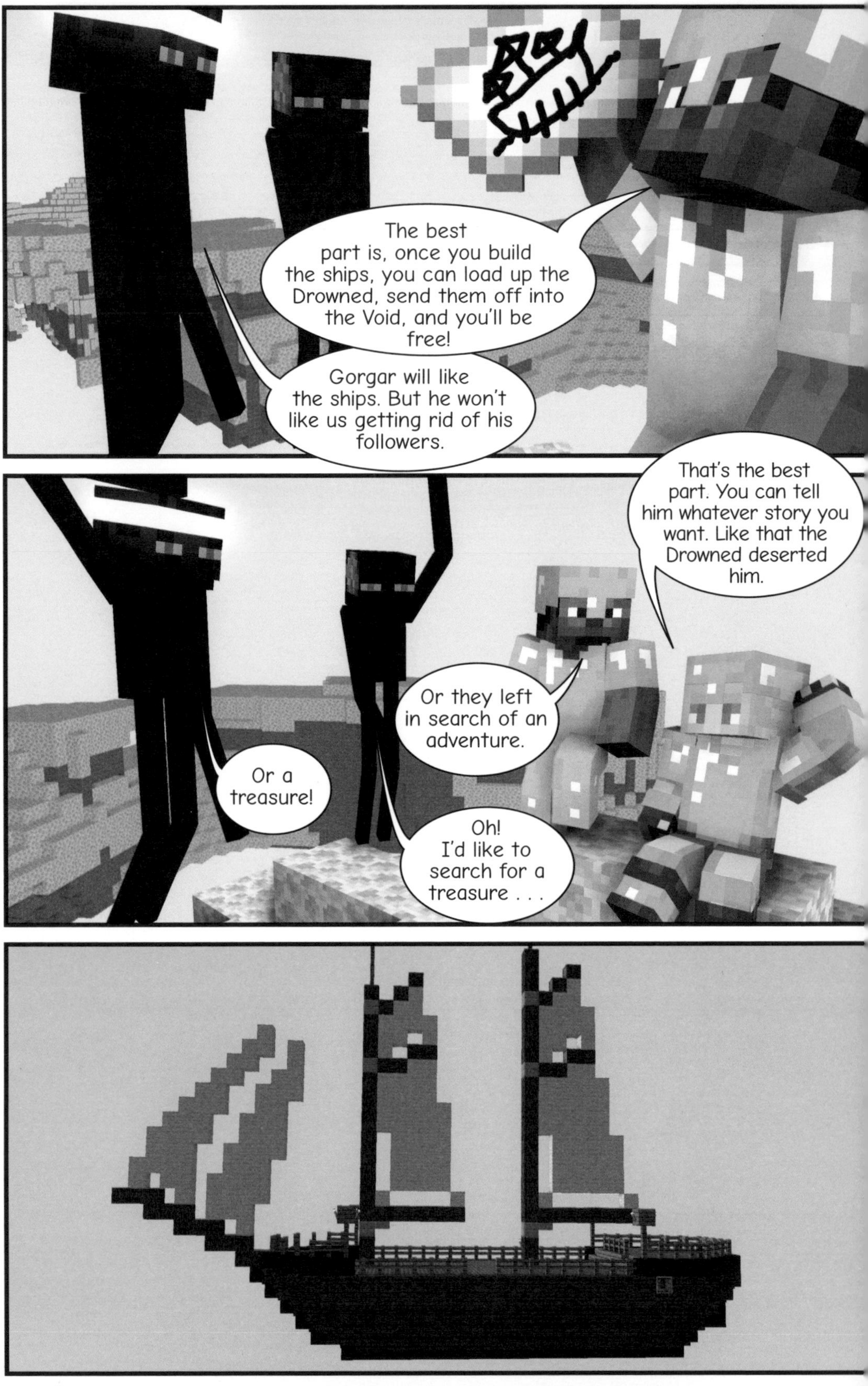
The best part is, once you build the ships, you can load up the Drowned, send them off into the Void, and you'll be free!
Gorgar will like the ships. But he won't like us getting rid of his followers.
That's the best part. You can tell him whatever story you want. Like that the Drowned deserted him.
Or they left in search of an adventure.
Or a treasure!
Oh! I'd like to search for a treasure . . .

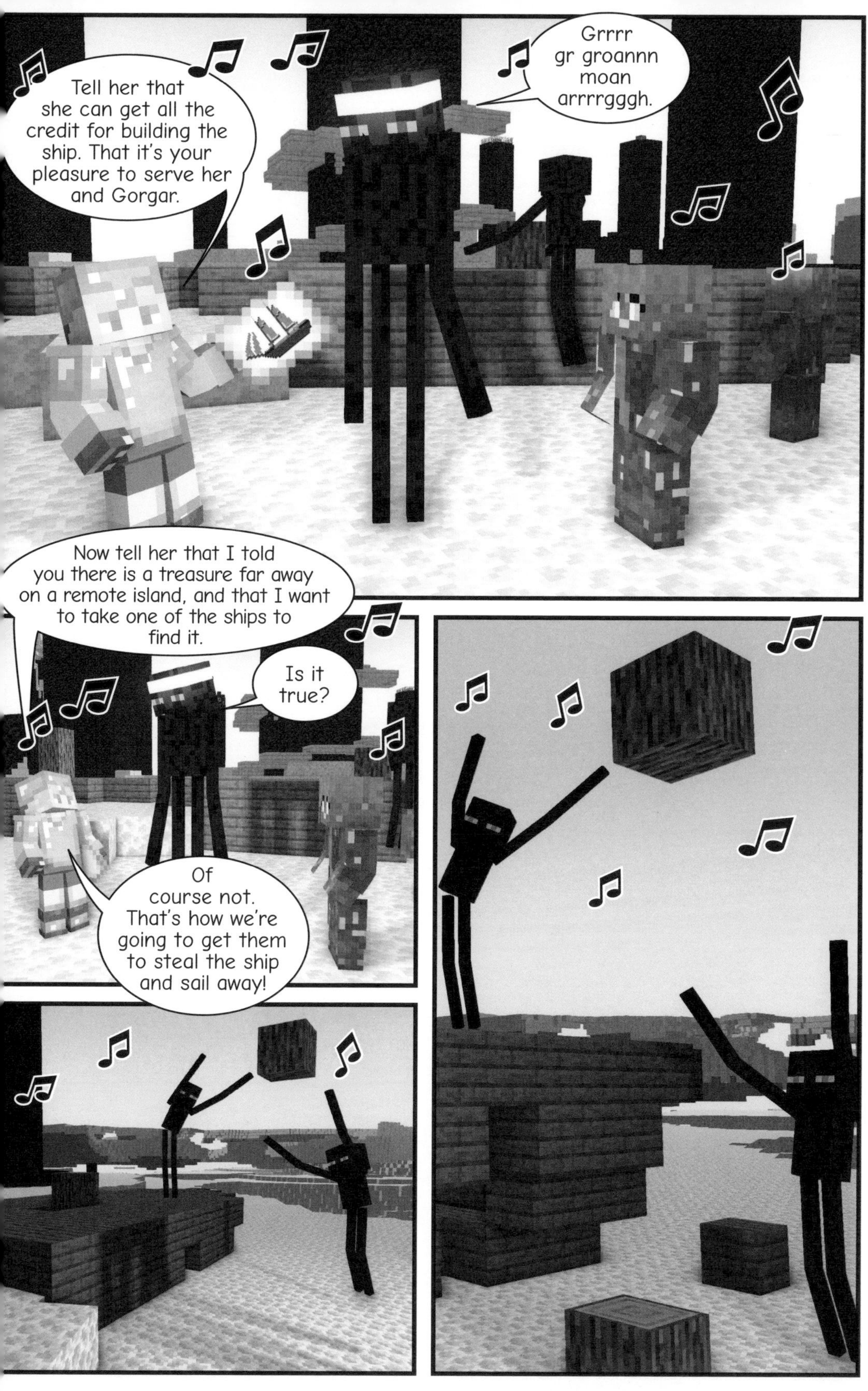

Tell her that she can get all the credit for building the ship. That it's your pleasure to serve her and Gorgar.
Grrrr gr groannn moan arrrrgggh.
Now tell her that I told you there is a treasure far away on a remote island, and that I want to take one of the ships to find it.
Is it true?
Of course not. That's how we're going to get them to steal the ship and sail away!

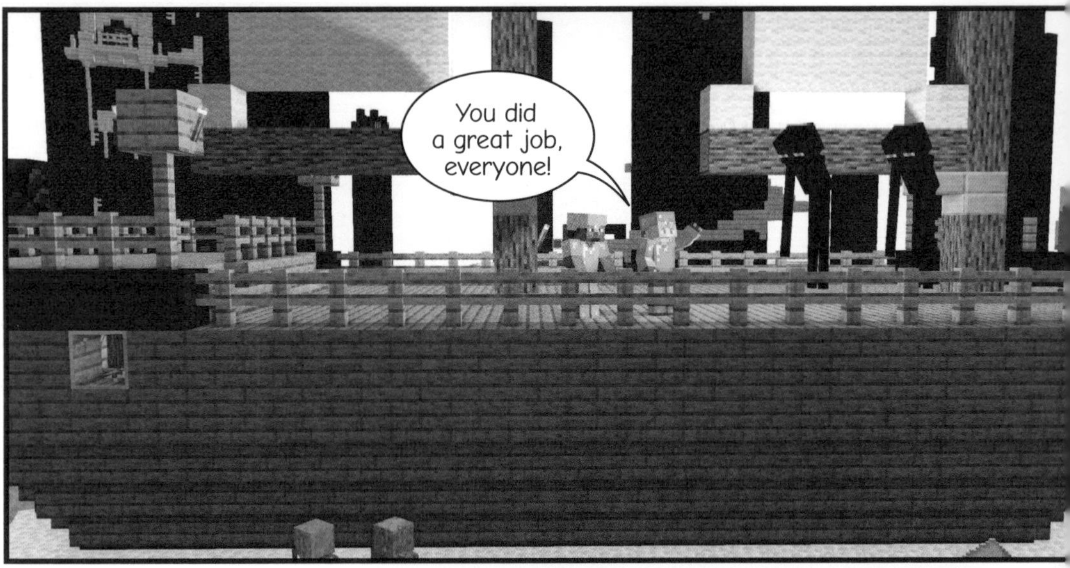
You did a great job, everyone!

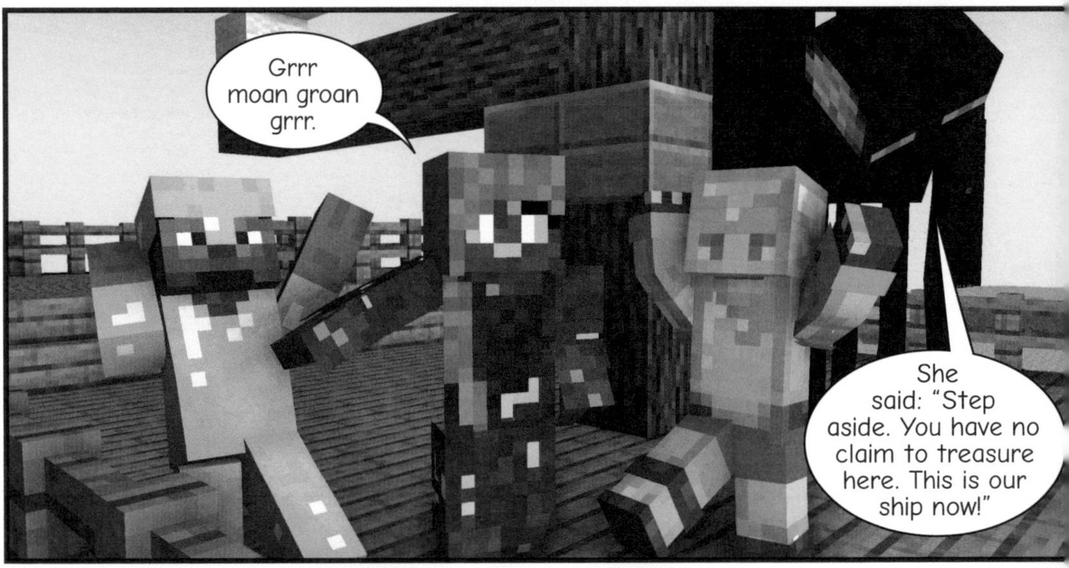
Grrr moan groan grrr.
She said: "Step aside. You have no claim to treasure here. This is our ship now!"

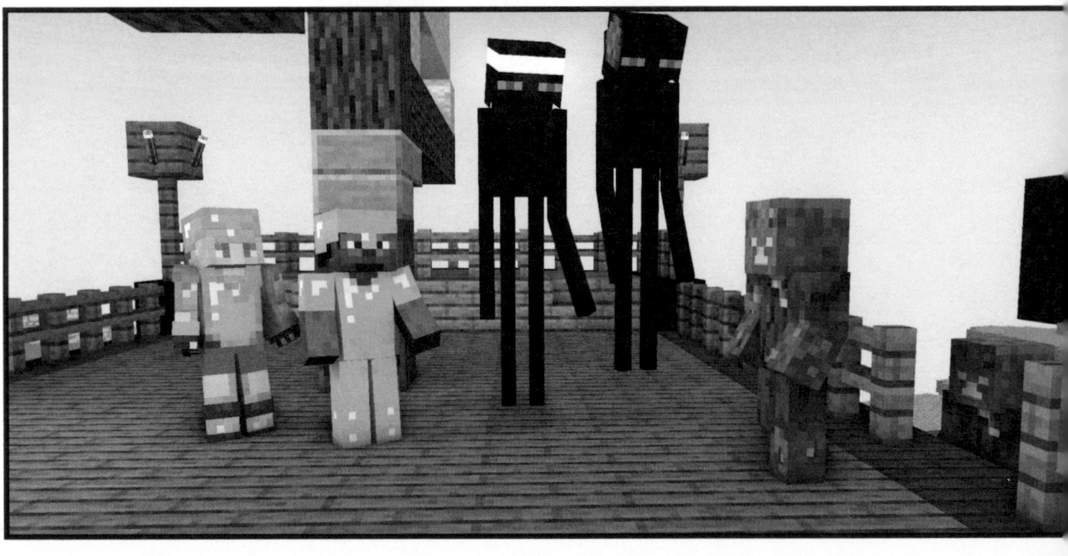

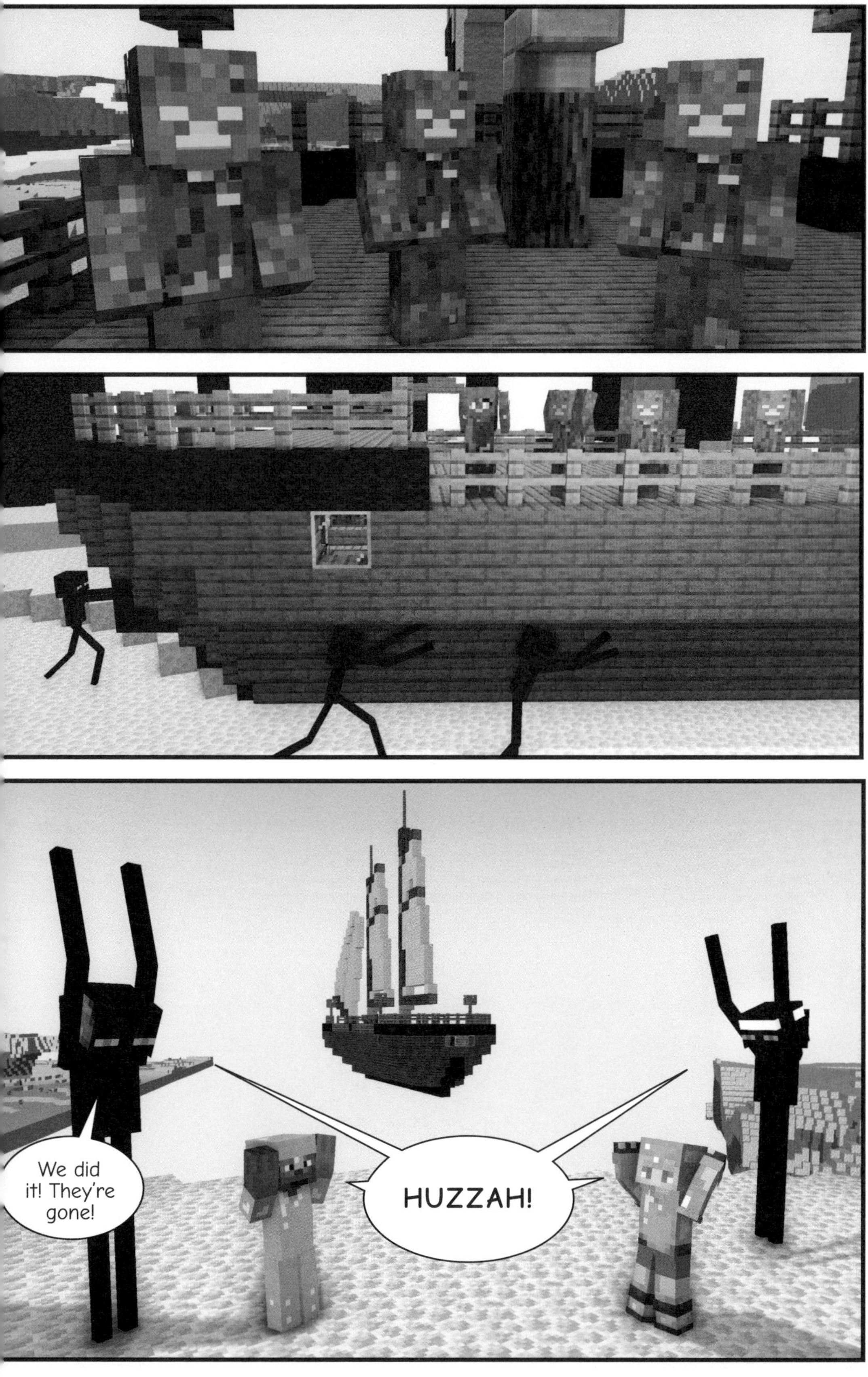
We did it! They're gone!
HUZZAH!

CHAPTER 9
CITY OF LIES

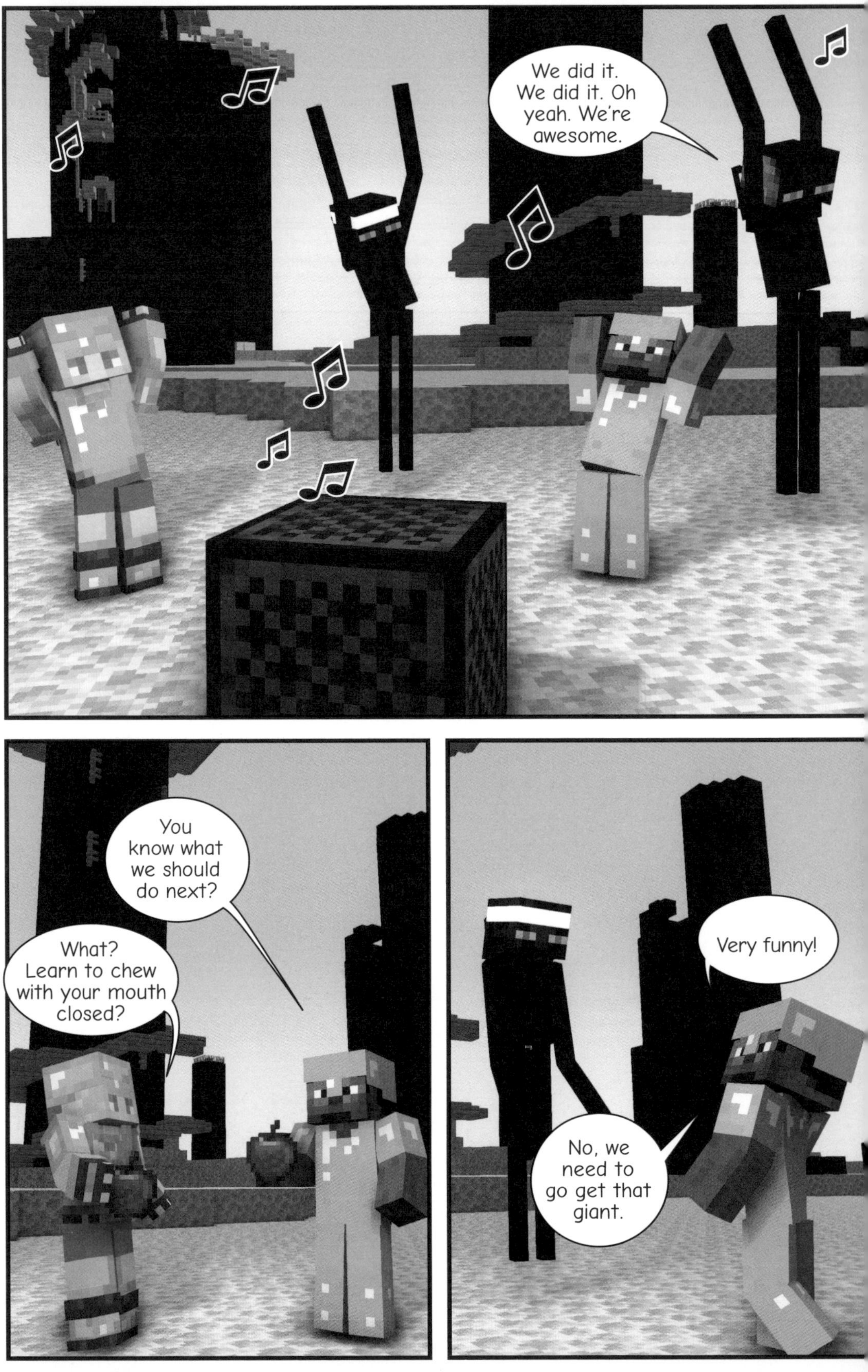
We did it. We did it. Oh yeah. We're awesome.
You know what we should do next?
What? Learn to chew with your mouth closed?
Very funny!
No, we need to go get that giant.

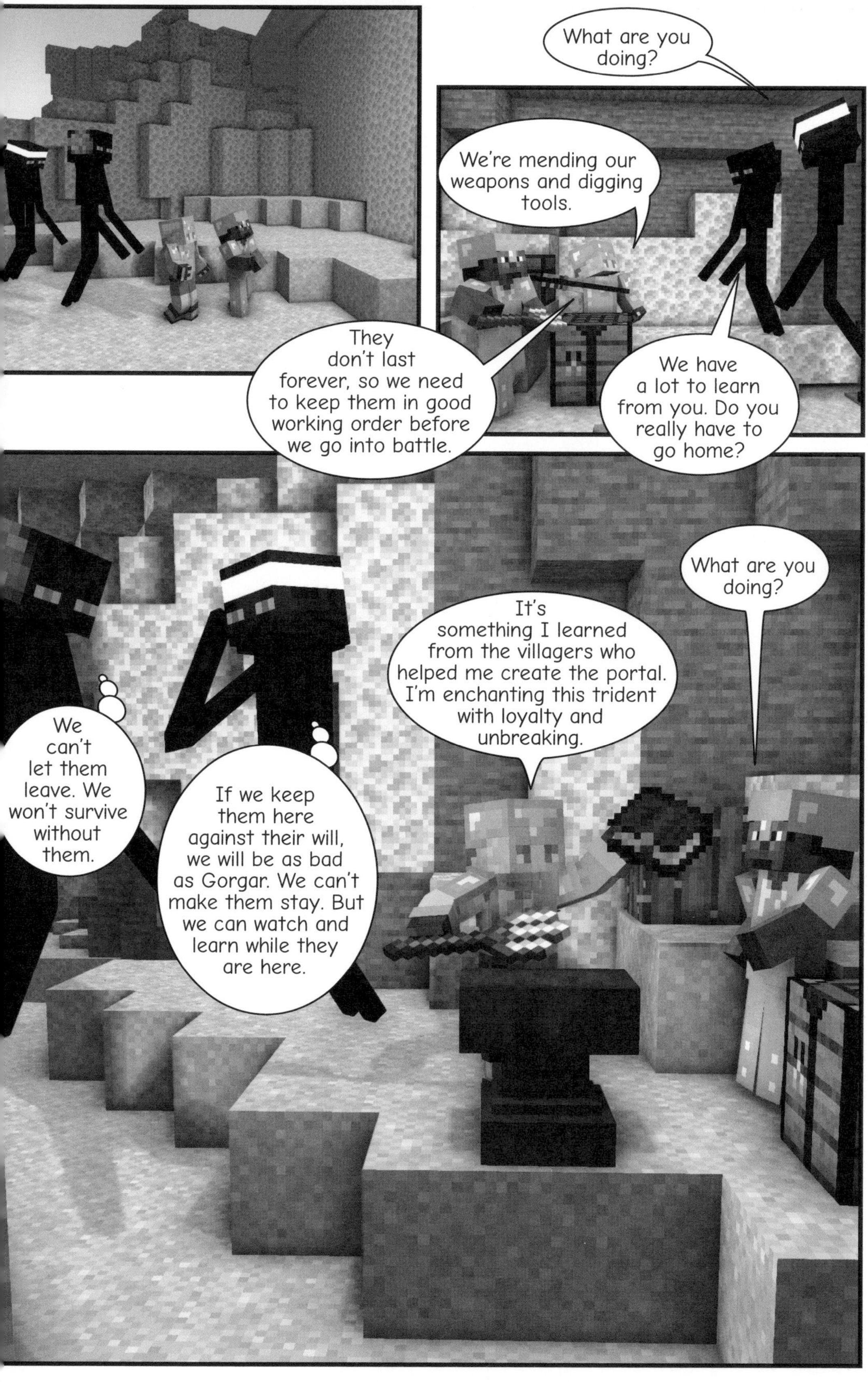
What are you doing?
We're mending our weapons and digging tools.
They don't last forever, so we need to keep them in good working order before we go into battle.
We have a lot to learn from you. Do you really have to go home?
What are you doing?
It's something I learned from the villagers who helped me create the portal. I'm enchanting this trident with loyalty and unbreaking.
We can't let them leave. We won't survive without them.
If we keep them here against their will, we will be as bad as Gorgar. We can't make them stay. But we can watch and learn while they are here.

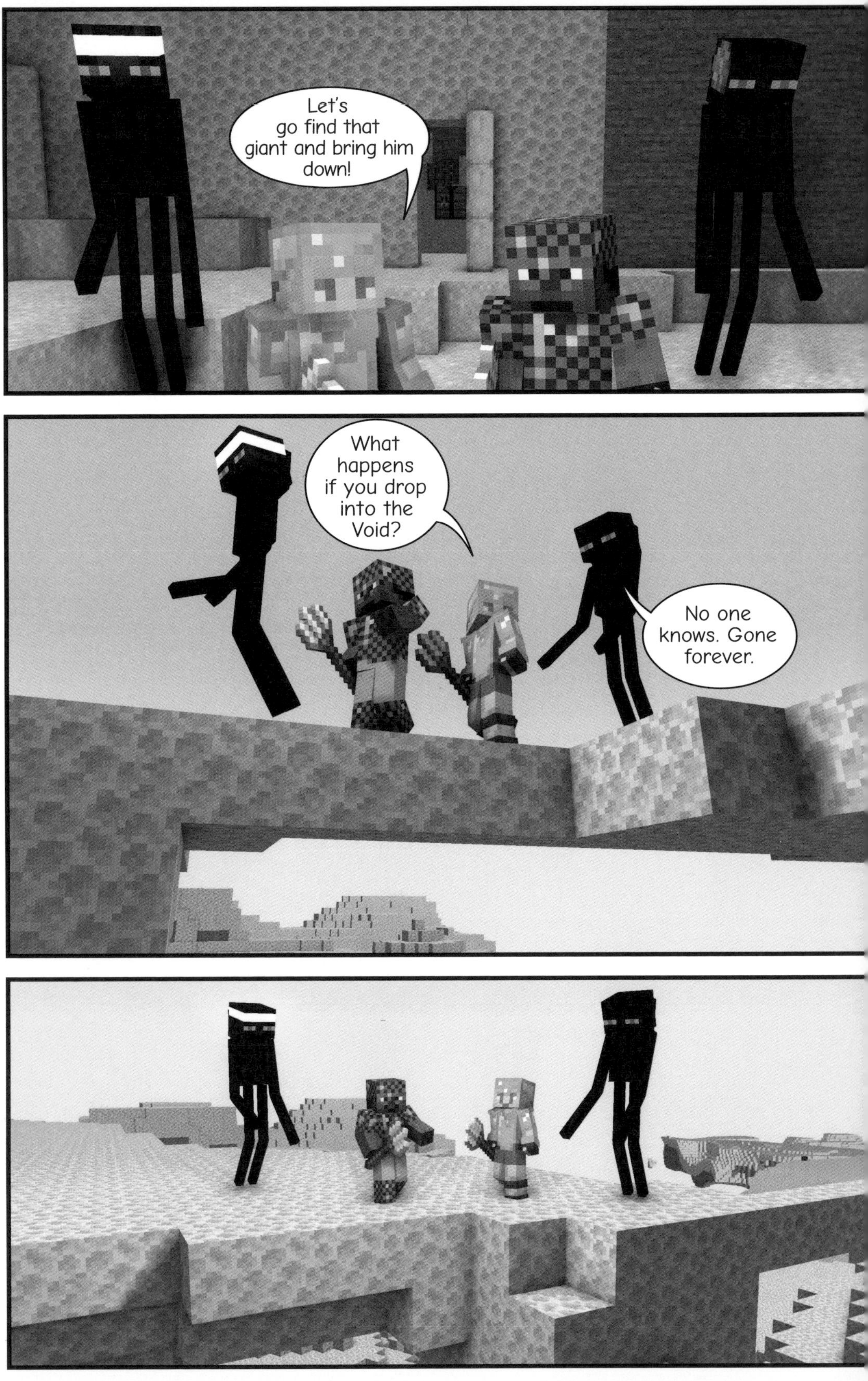
Let's go find that giant and bring him down!
What happens if you drop into the Void?
No one knows. Gone forever.

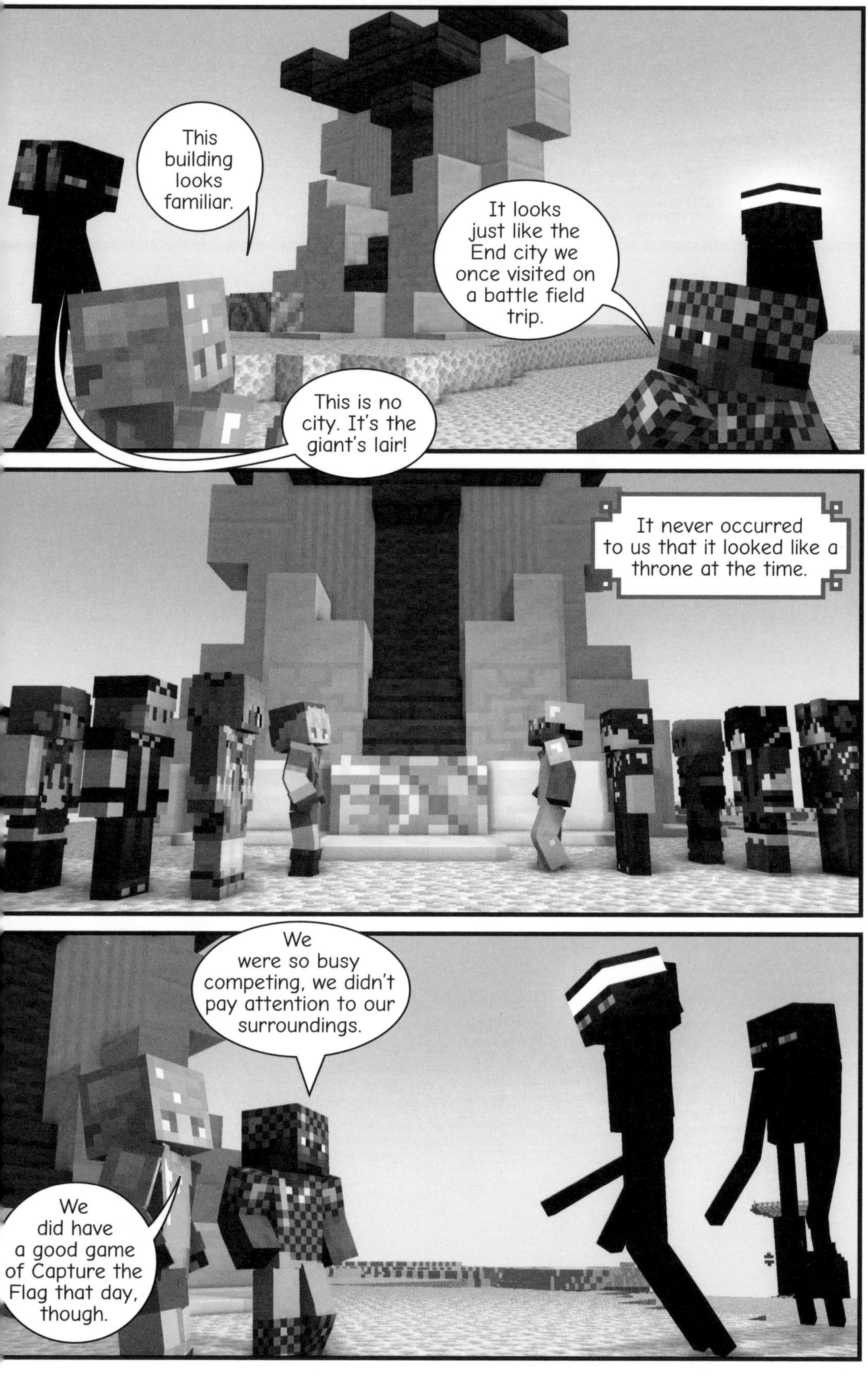
This building looks familiar.
It looks just like the End city we once visited on a battle field trip.
This is no city. It's the giant's lair!
It never occurred to us that it looked like a throne at the time.
We were so busy competing, we didn't pay attention to our surroundings.
We did have a good game of Capture the Flag that day, though.

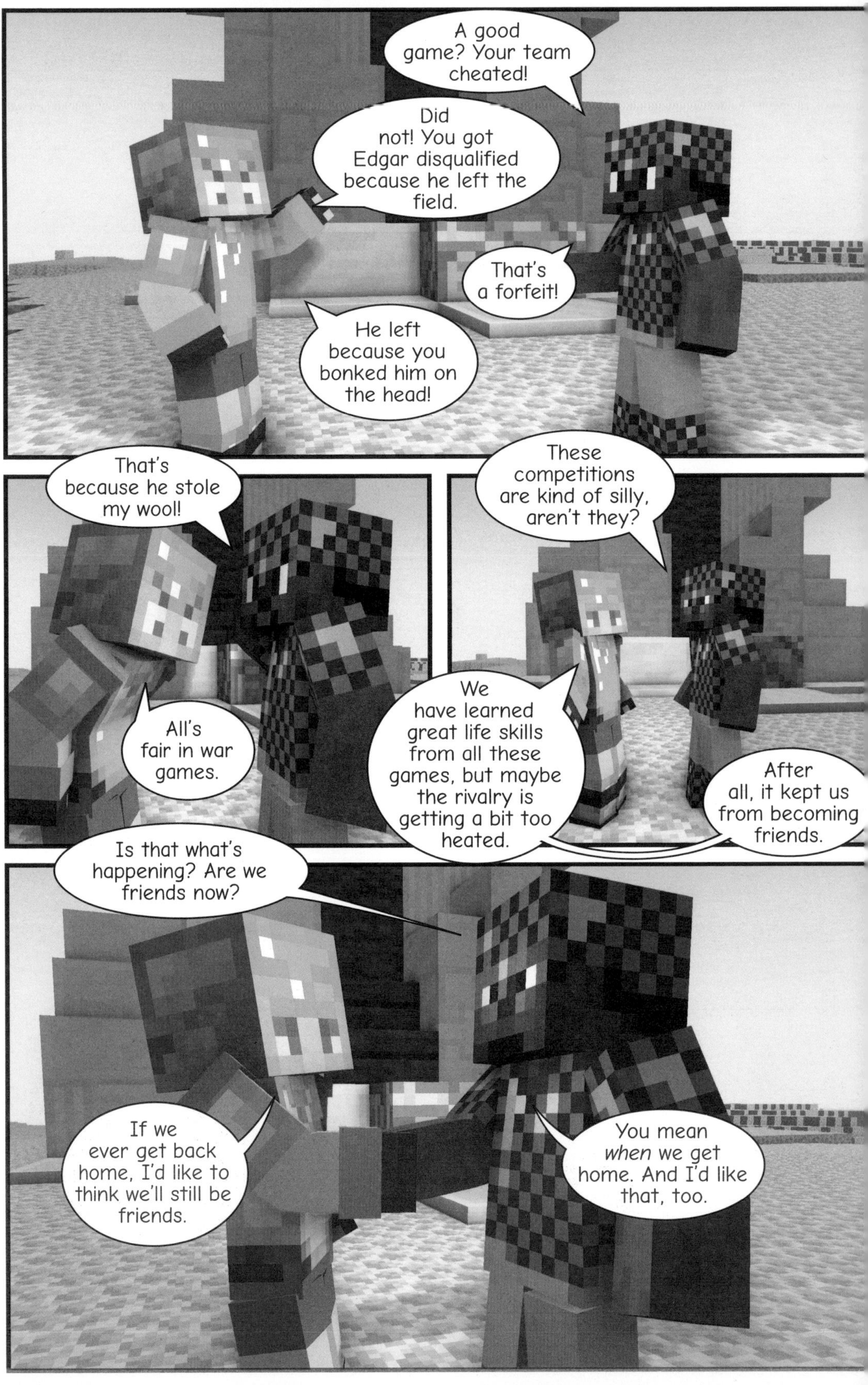
A good game? Your team cheated!
Did not! You got Edgar disqualified because he left the field.
That's a forfeit!
He left because you bonked him on the head!
That's because he stole my wool!
All's fair in war games.
These competitions are kind of silly, aren't they?
We have learned great life skills from all these games, but maybe the rivalry is getting a bit too heated.
After all, it kept us from becoming friends.
Is that what's happening? Are we friends now?
If we ever get back home, I'd like to think we'll still be friends.
You mean *when* we get home. And I'd like that, too.

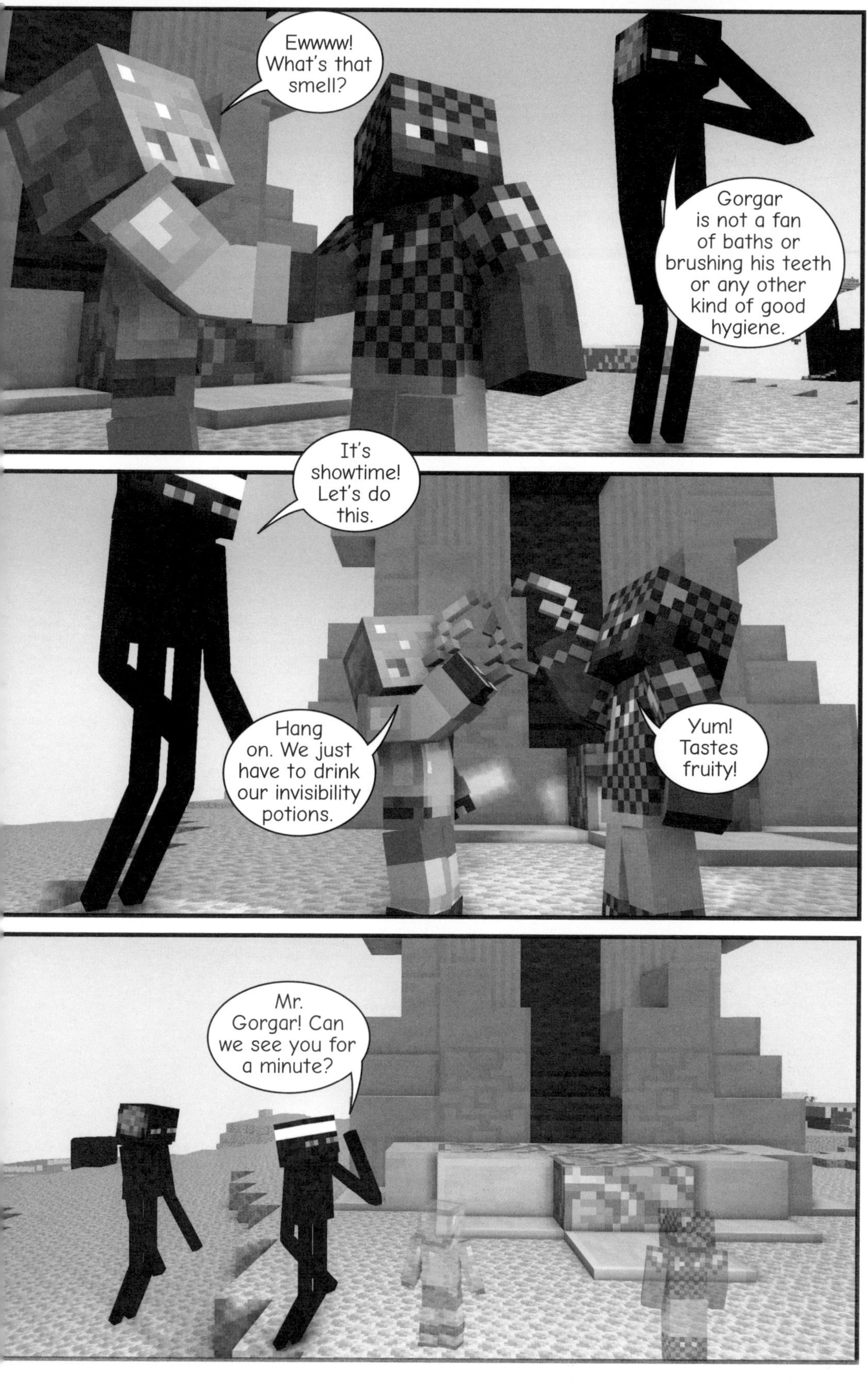
Ewwww! What's that smell?
Gorgar is not a fan of baths or brushing his teeth or any other kind of good hygiene.
It's showtime! Let's do this.
Hang on. We just have to drink our invisibility potions.
Yum! Tastes fruity!
Mr. Gorgar! Can we see you for a minute?

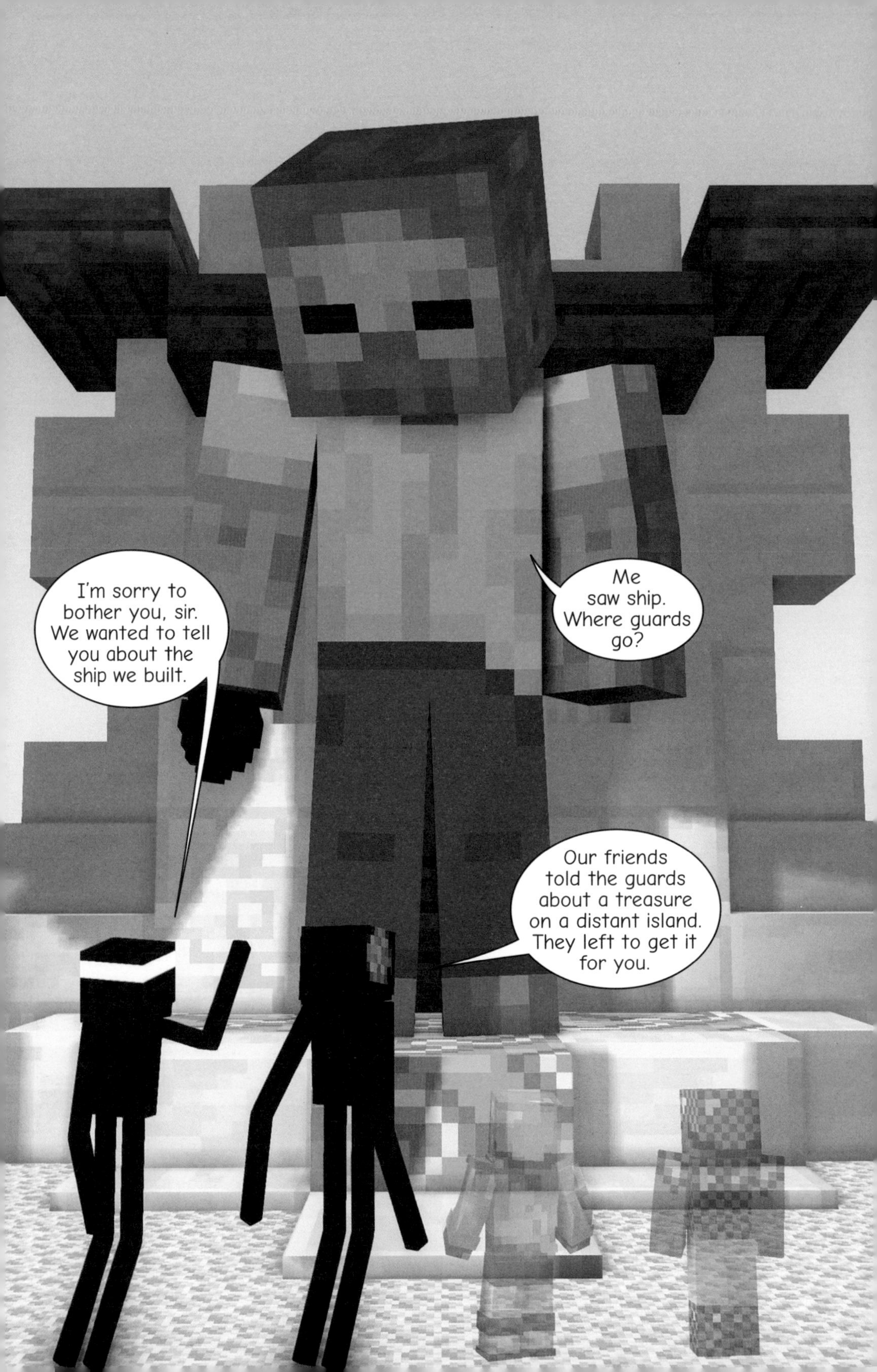
I'm sorry to bother you, sir. We wanted to tell you about the ship we built.
Me saw ship. Where guards go?
Our friends told the guards about a treasure on a distant island. They left to get it for you.

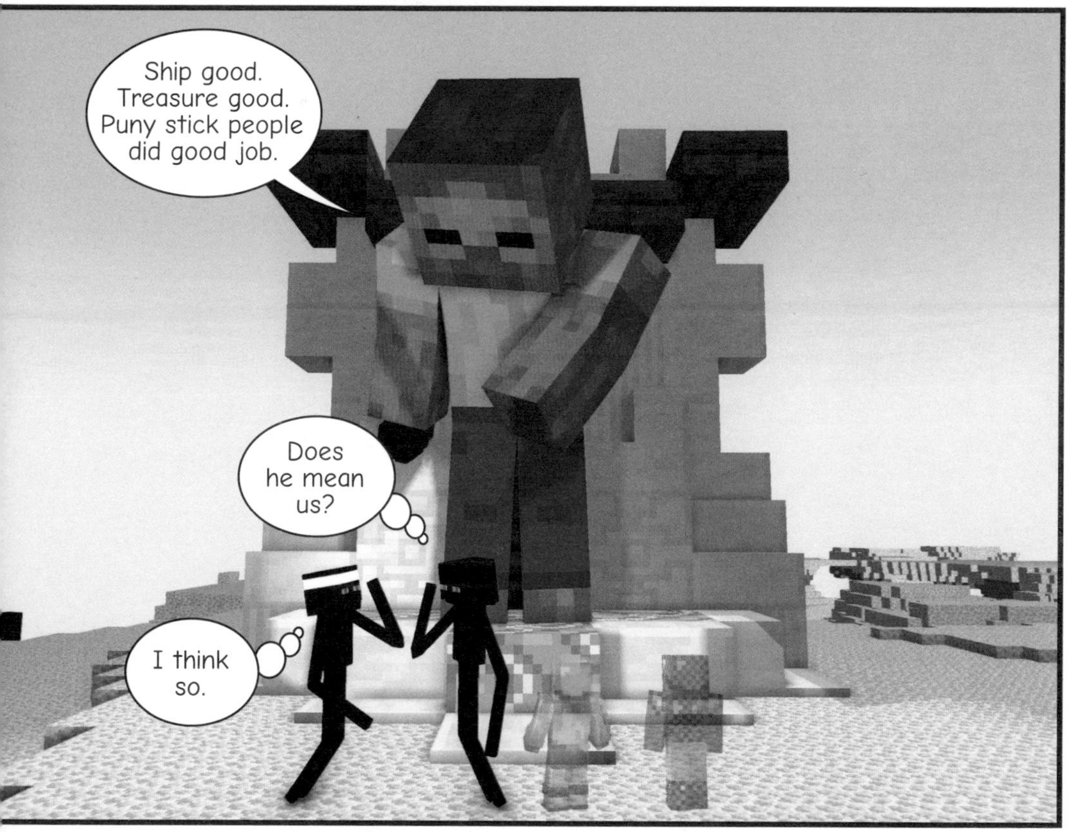
Ship good. Treasure good. Puny stick people did good job.
Does he mean us?
I think so.

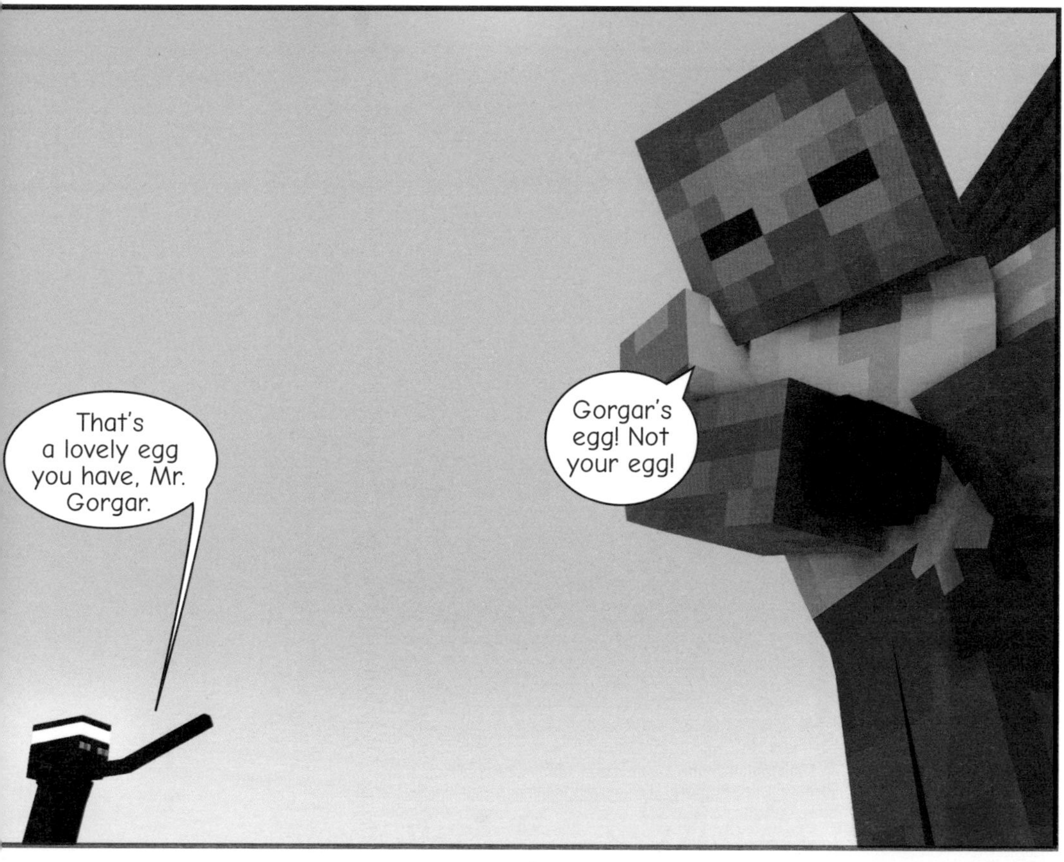
That's a lovely egg you have, Mr. Gorgar.
Gorgar's egg! Not your egg!

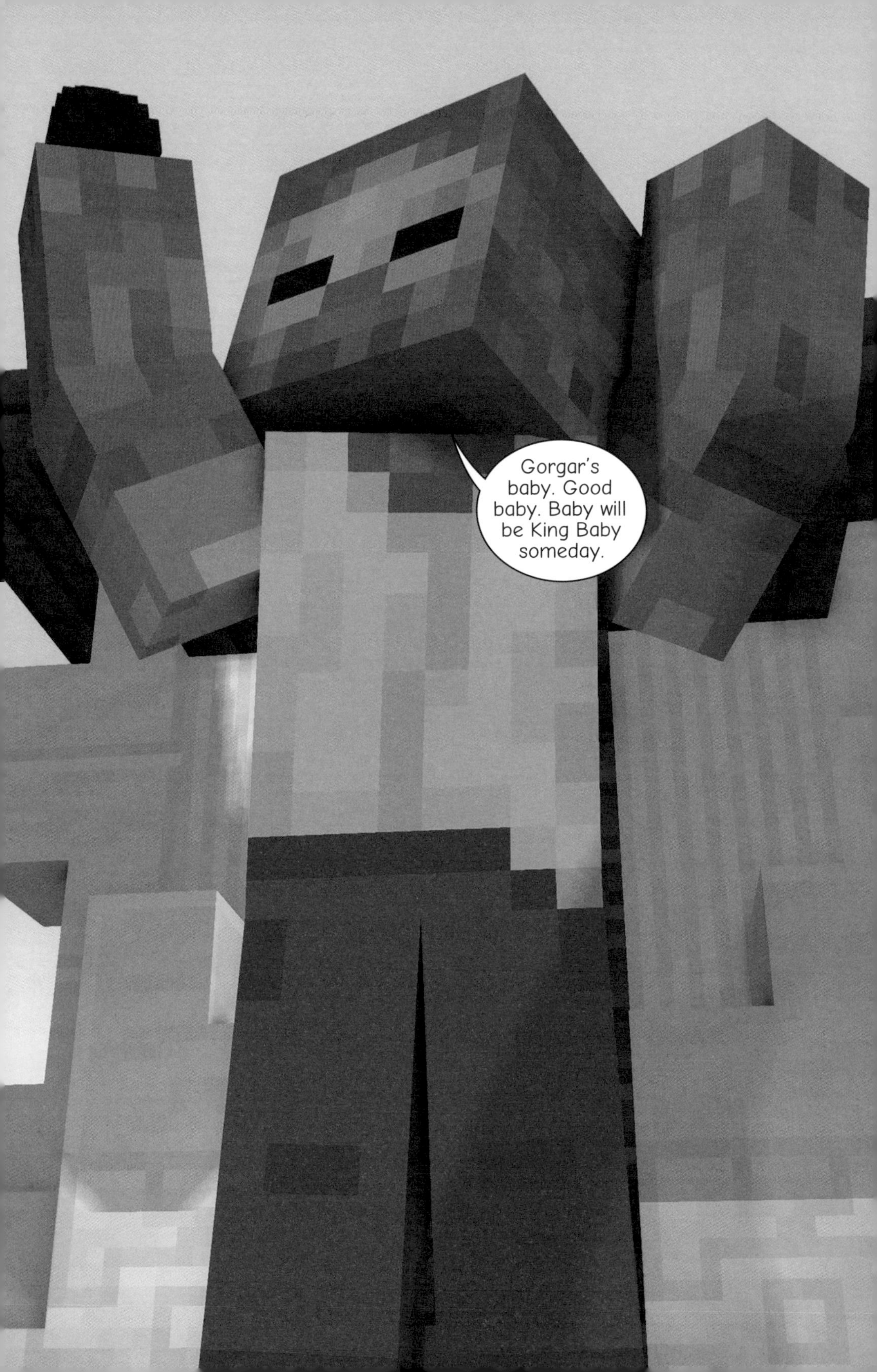
Gorgar's baby. Good baby. Baby will be King Baby someday.

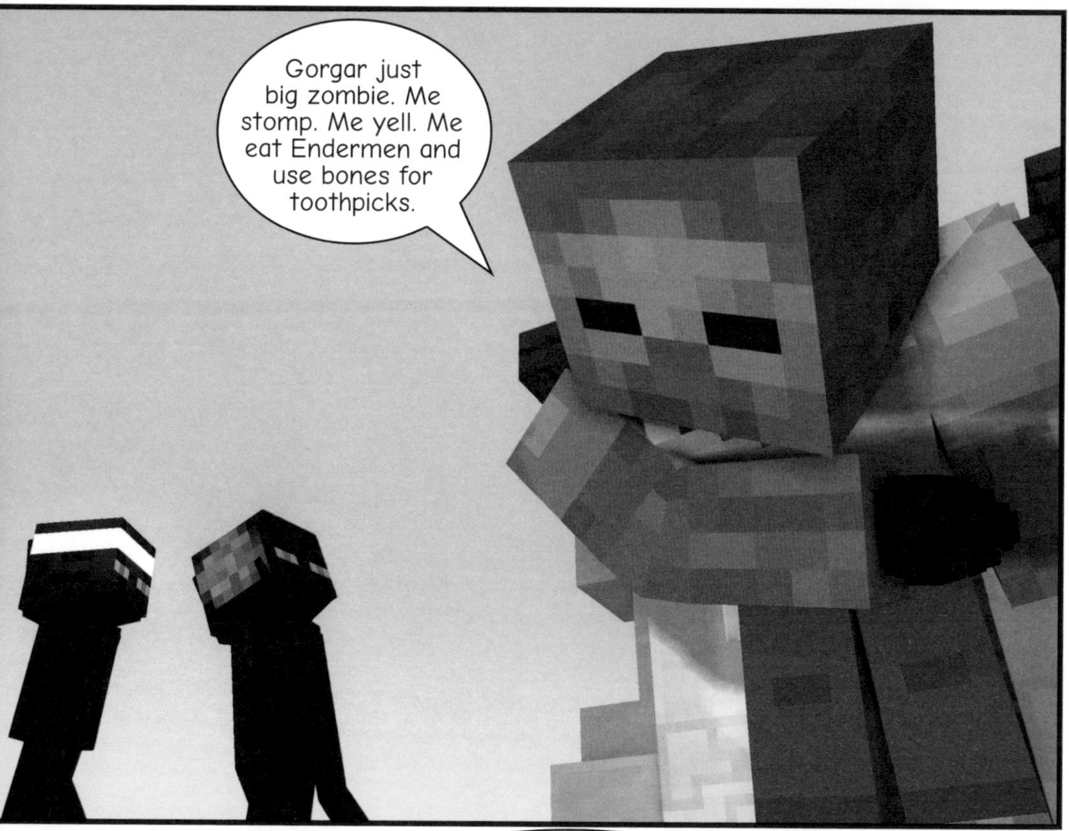
Gorgar just big zombie. Me stomp. Me yell. Me eat Endermen and use bones for toothpicks.

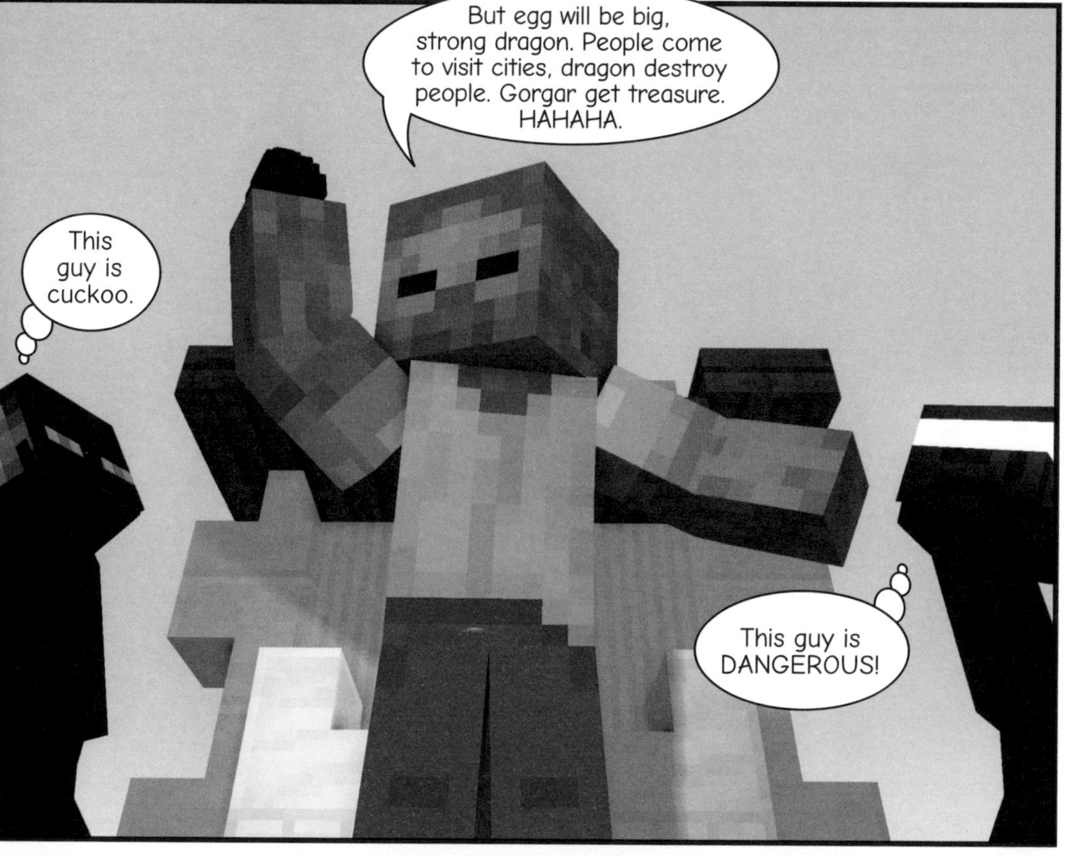
But egg will be big, strong dragon. People come to visit cities, dragon destroy people. Gorgar get treasure. HAHAHA.
This guy is cuckoo.
This guy is DANGEROUS!

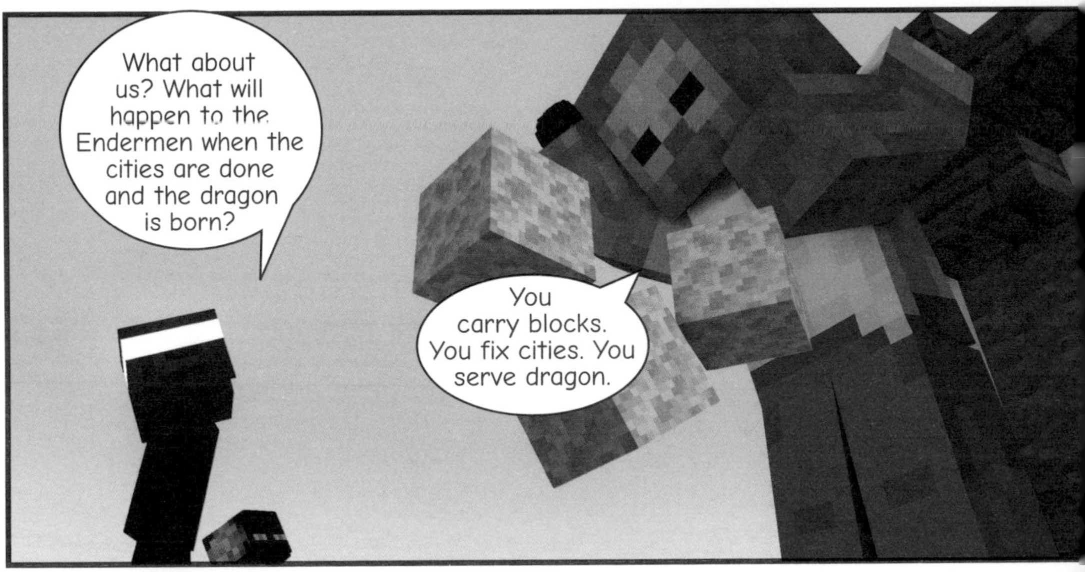
What about us? What will happen to the Endermen when the cities are done and the dragon is born?
You carry blocks. You fix cities. You serve dragon.

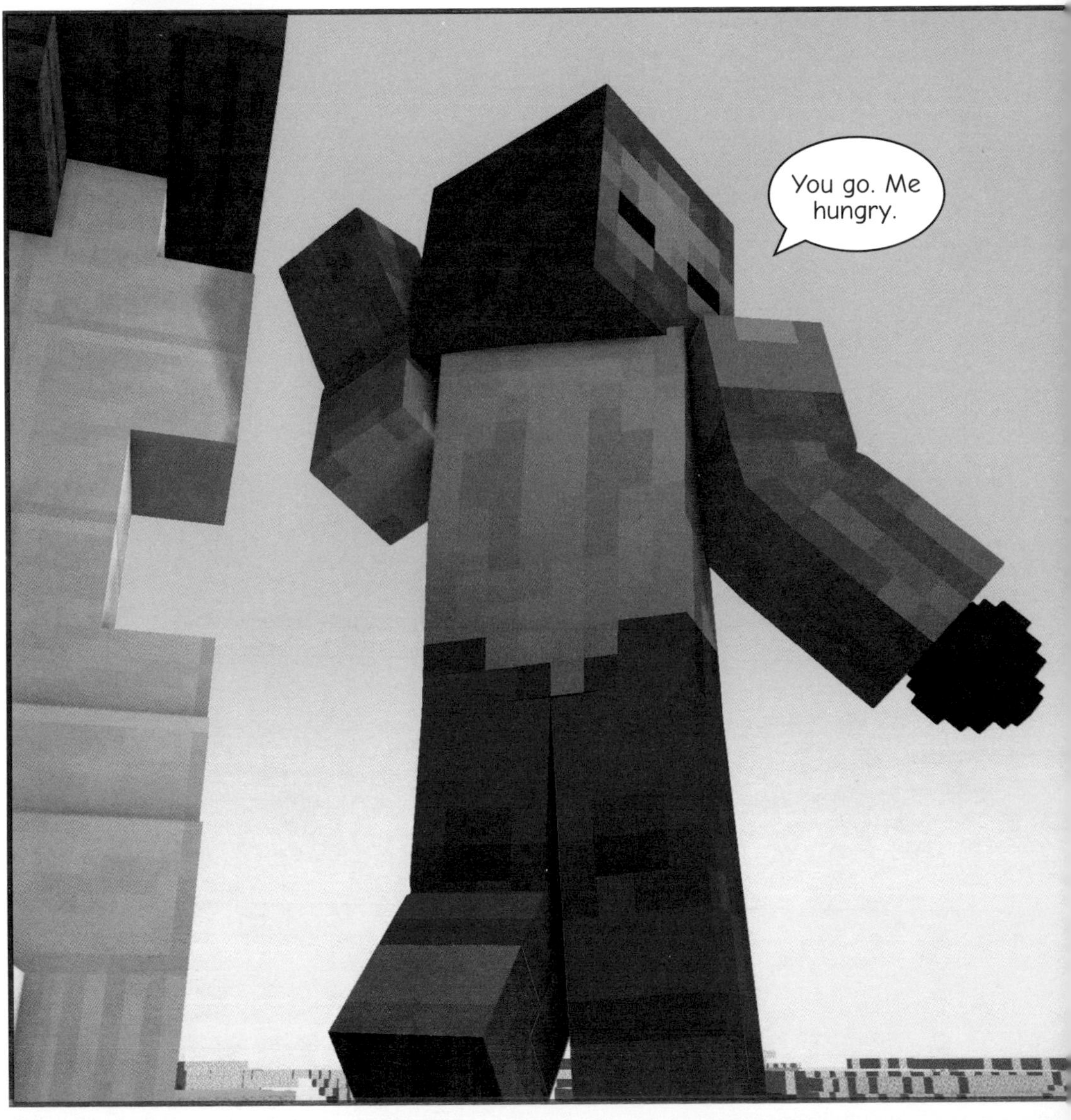
You go. Me hungry.

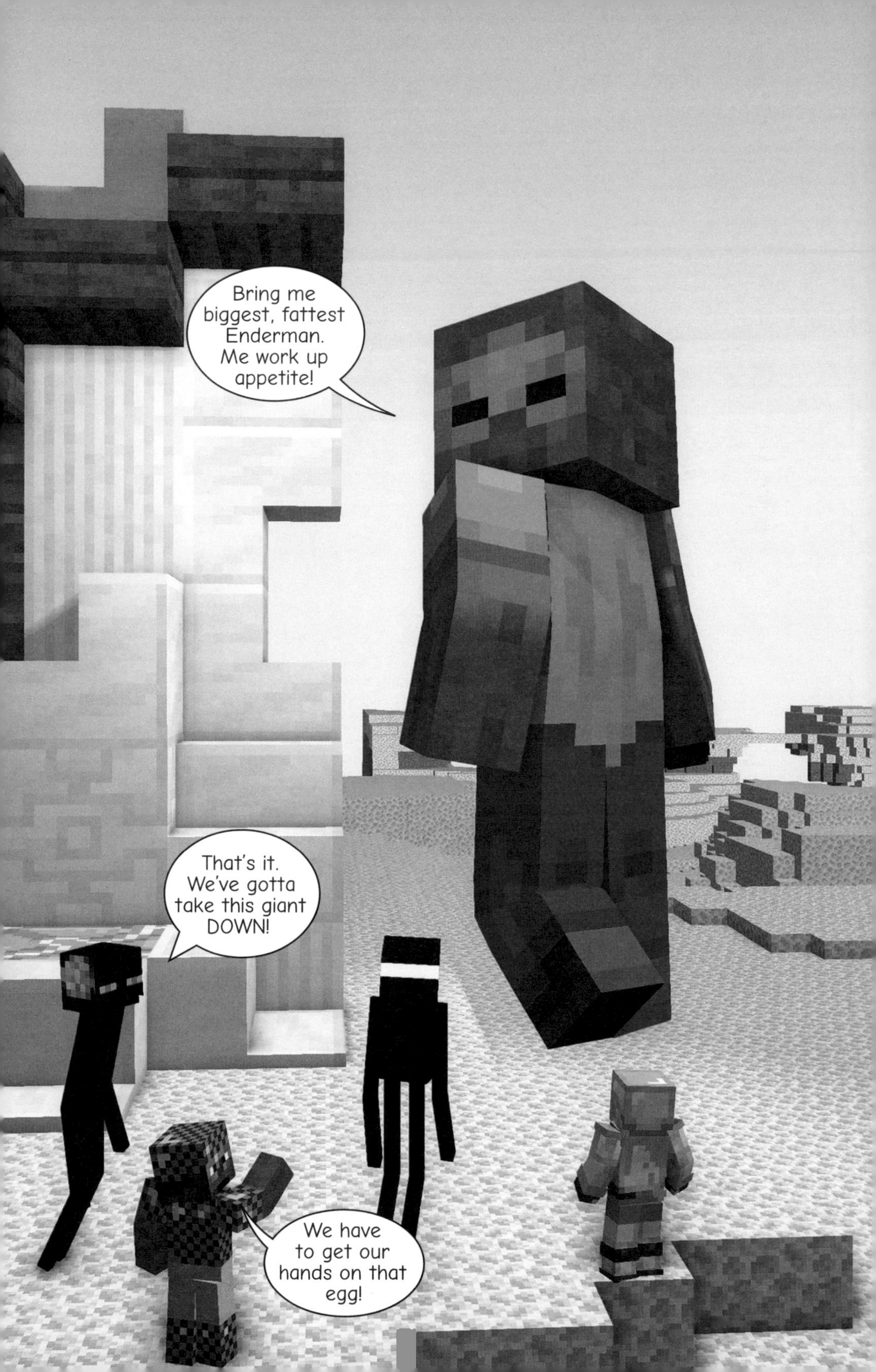
Bring me biggest, fattest Enderman. Me work up appetite!
That's it. We've gotta take this giant DOWN!
We have to get our hands on that egg!

CHAPTER 10
THE HARDER
THEY FALL

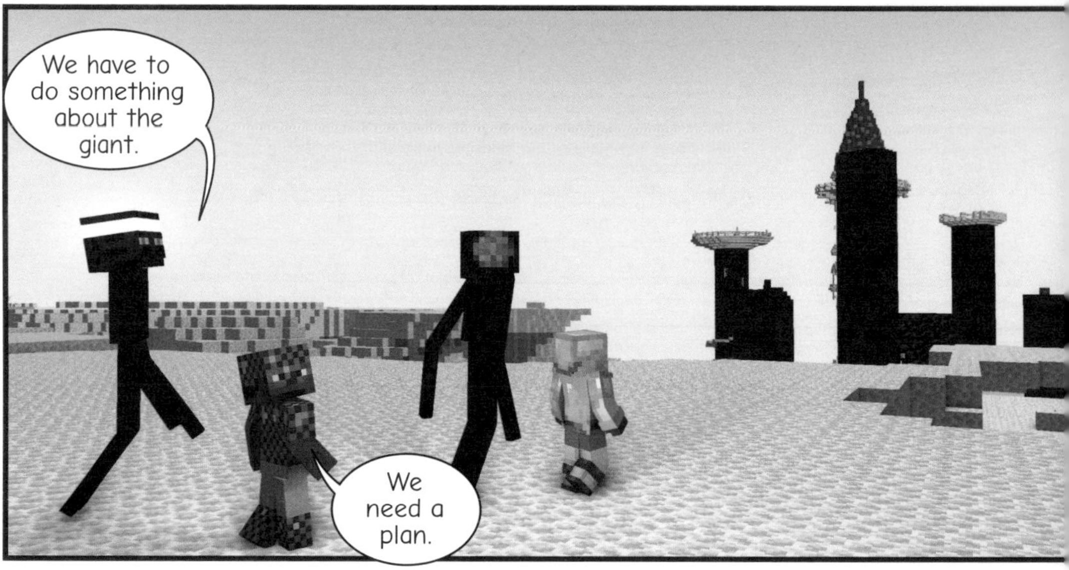
We have to do something about the giant.
We need a plan.

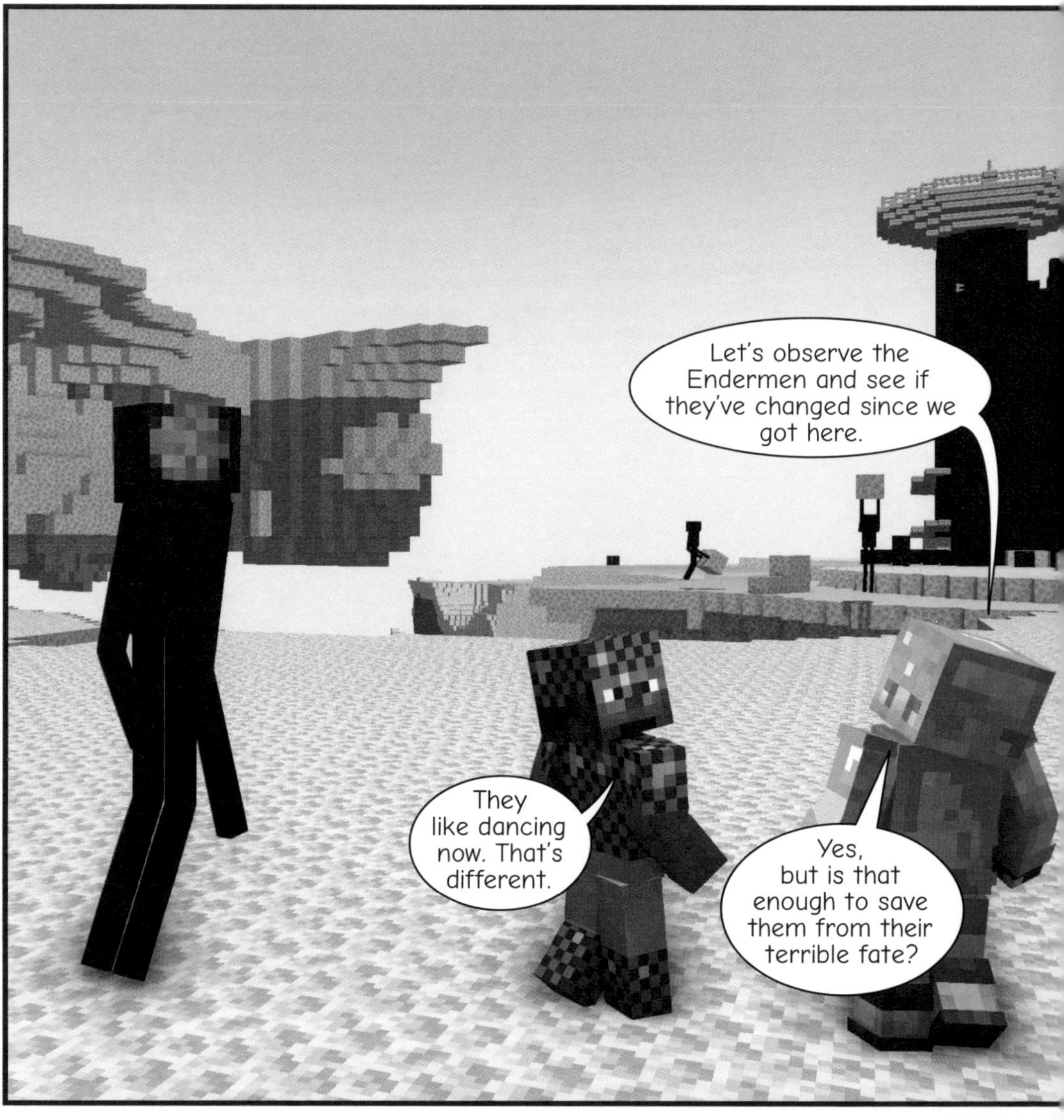
Let's observe the Endermen and see if they've changed since we got here.
They like dancing now. That's different.
Yes, but is that enough to save them from their terrible fate?

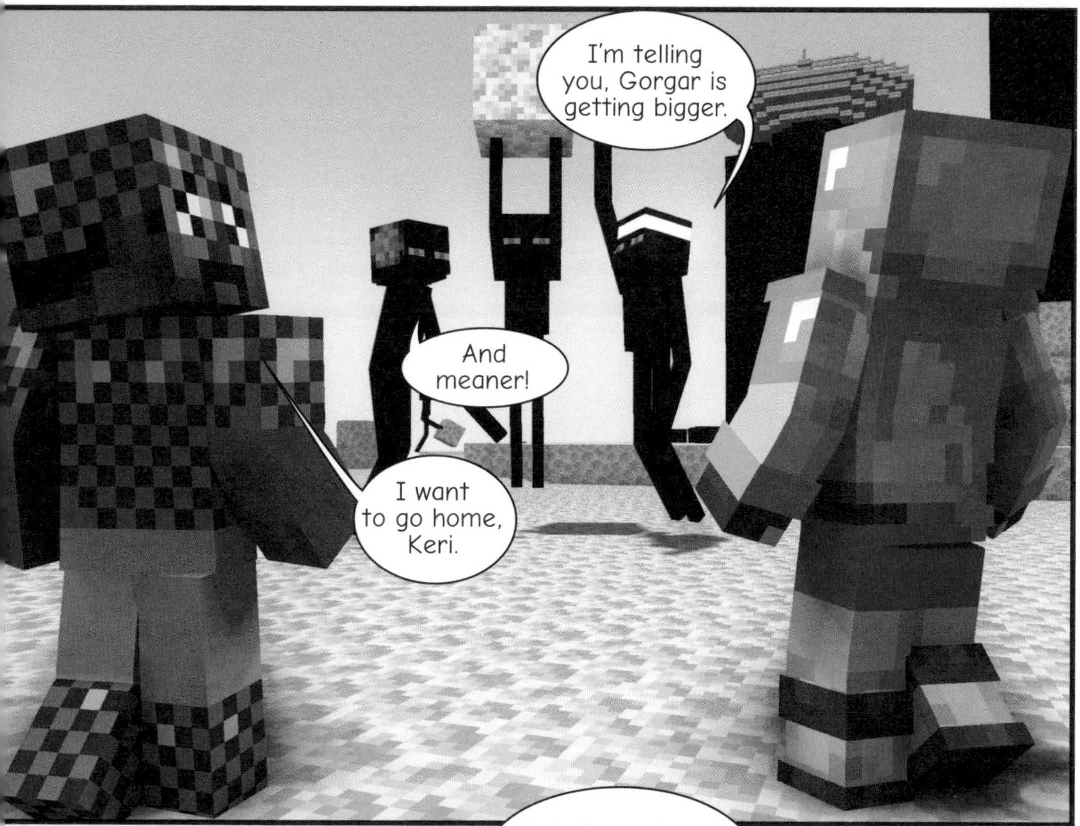
I'm telling you, Gorgar is getting bigger.
And meaner!
I want to go home, Keri.

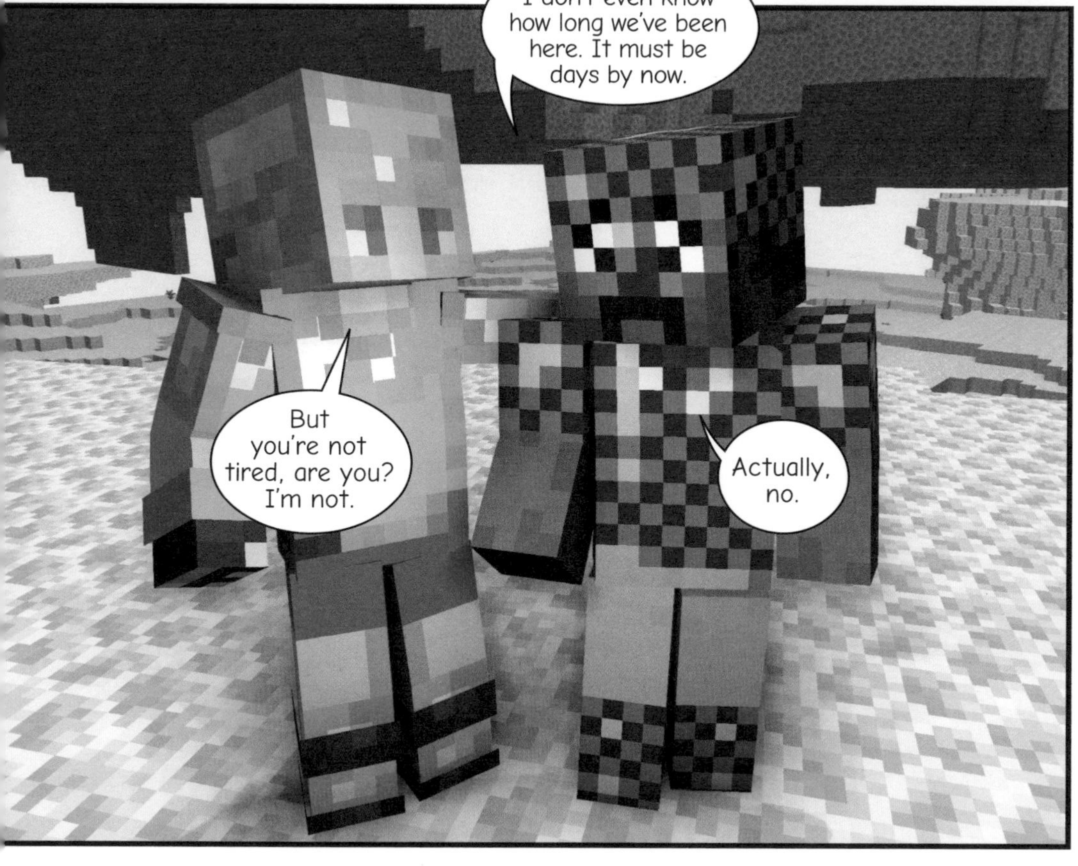
I don't even know how long we've been here. It must be days by now.
But you're not tired, are you? I'm not.
Actually, no.

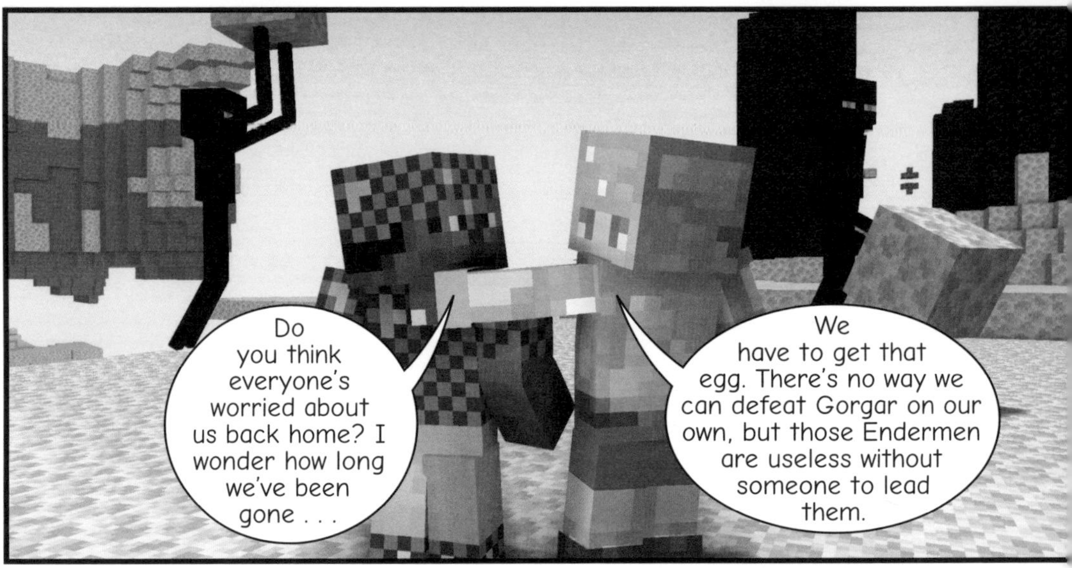
Do you think everyone's worried about us back home? I wonder how long we've been gone . . .
We have to get that egg. There's no way we can defeat Gorgar on our own, but those Endermen are useless without someone to lead them.

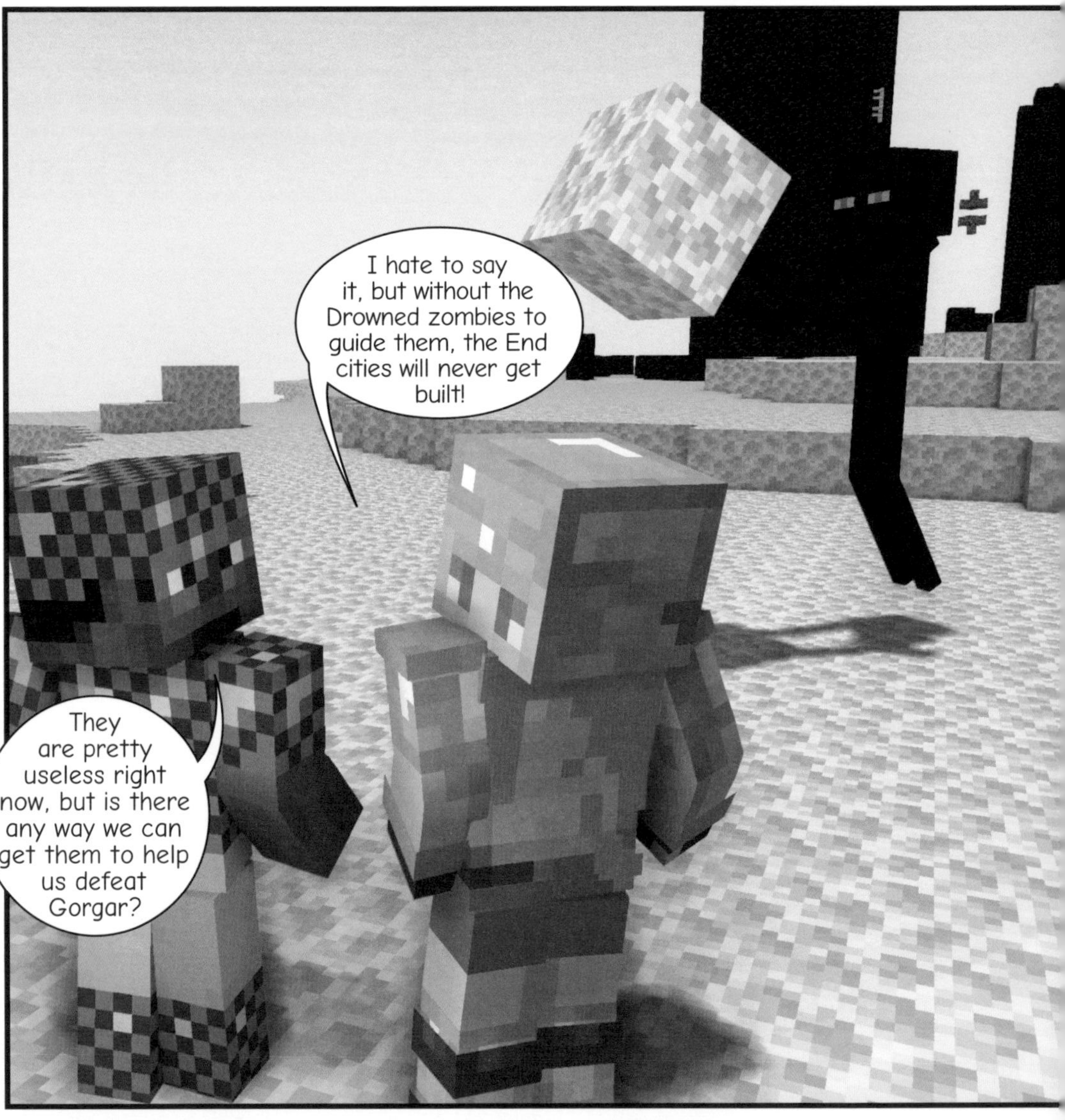
I hate to say it, but without the Drowned zombies to guide them, the End cities will never get built!
They are pretty useless right now, but is there any way we can get them to help us defeat Gorgar?

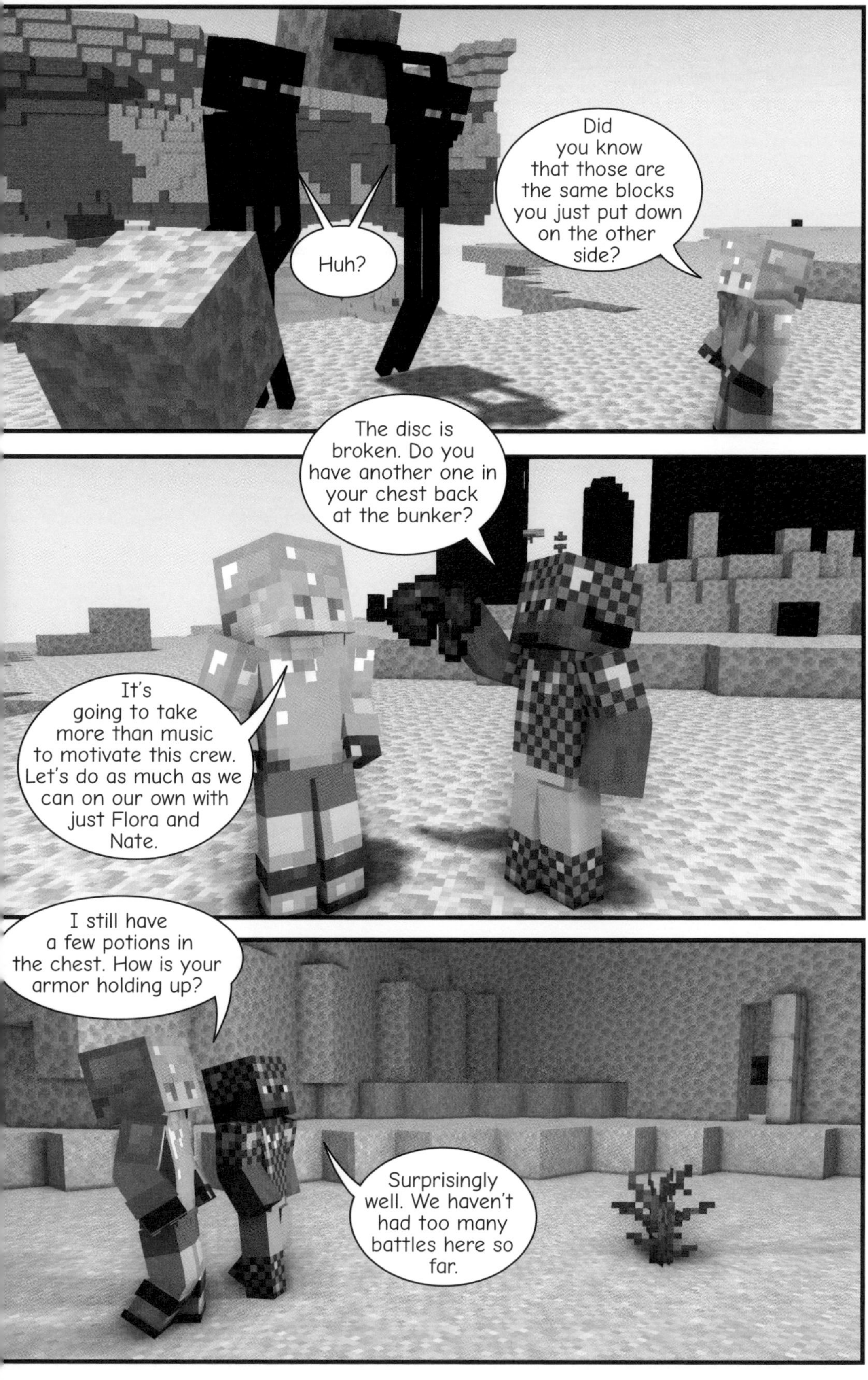
Huh?
Did you know that those are the same blocks you just put down on the other side?
The disc is broken. Do you have another one in your chest back at the bunker?
It's going to take more than music to motivate this crew. Let's do as much as we can on our own with just Flora and Nate.
I still have a few potions in the chest. How is your armor holding up?
Surprisingly well. We haven't had too many battles here so far.

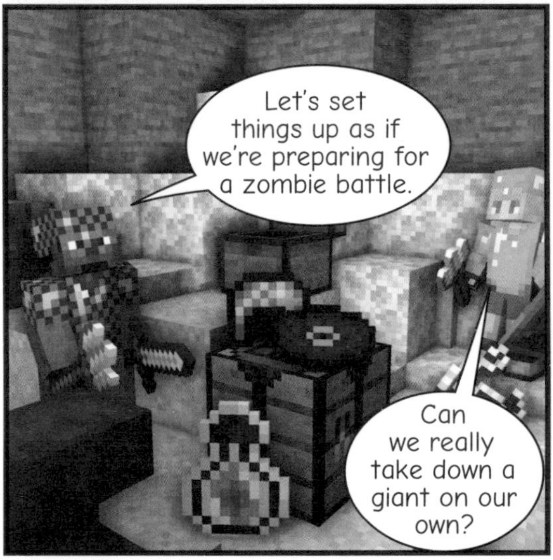
Let's set things up as if we're preparing for a zombie battle.
Can we really take down a giant on our own?

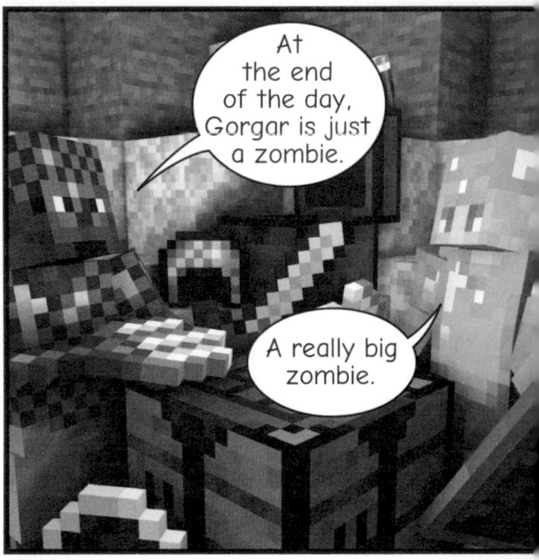
At the end of the day, Gorgar is just a zombie.
A really big zombie.

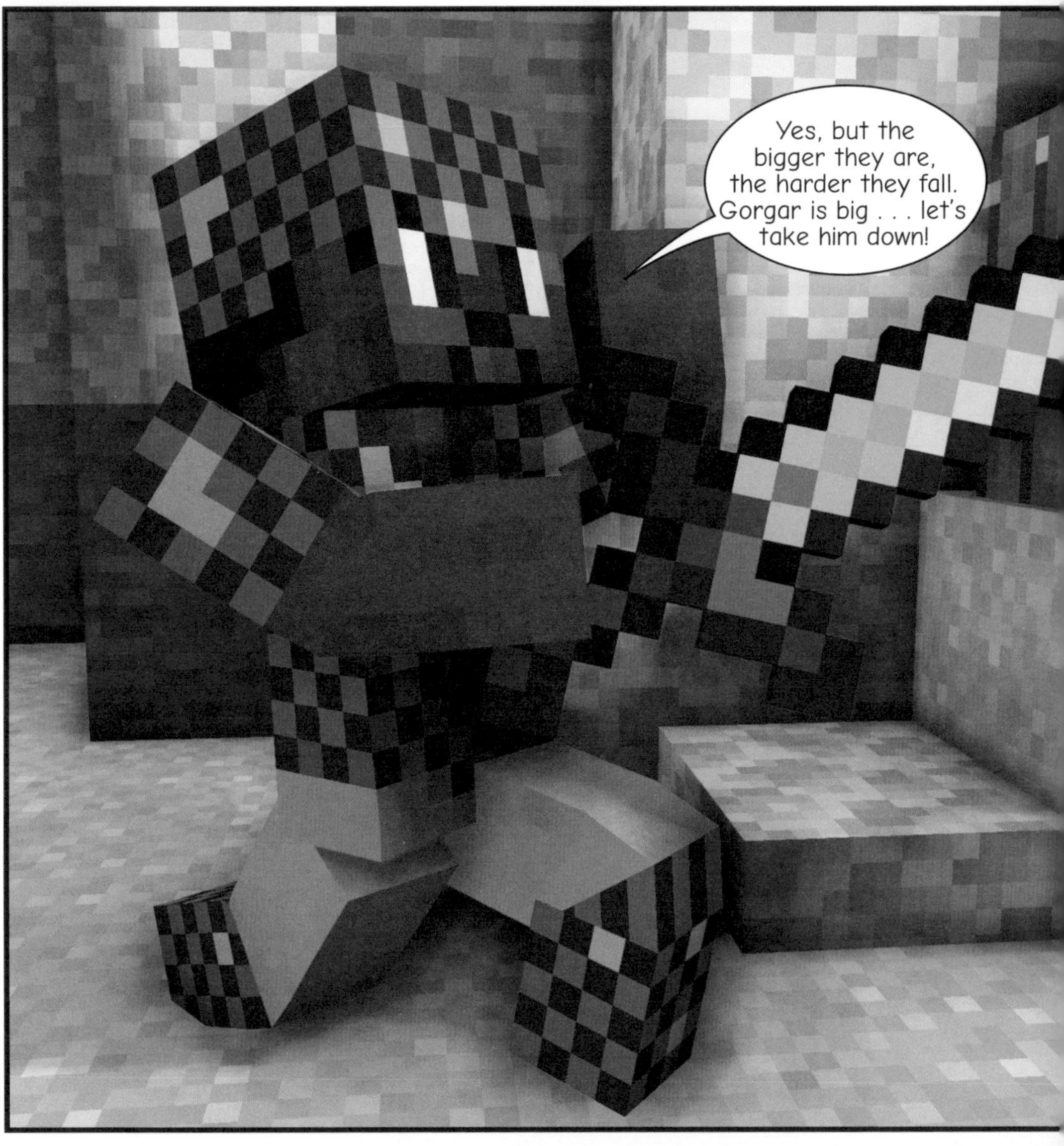
Yes, but the bigger they are, the harder they fall. Gorgar is big . . . let's take him down!

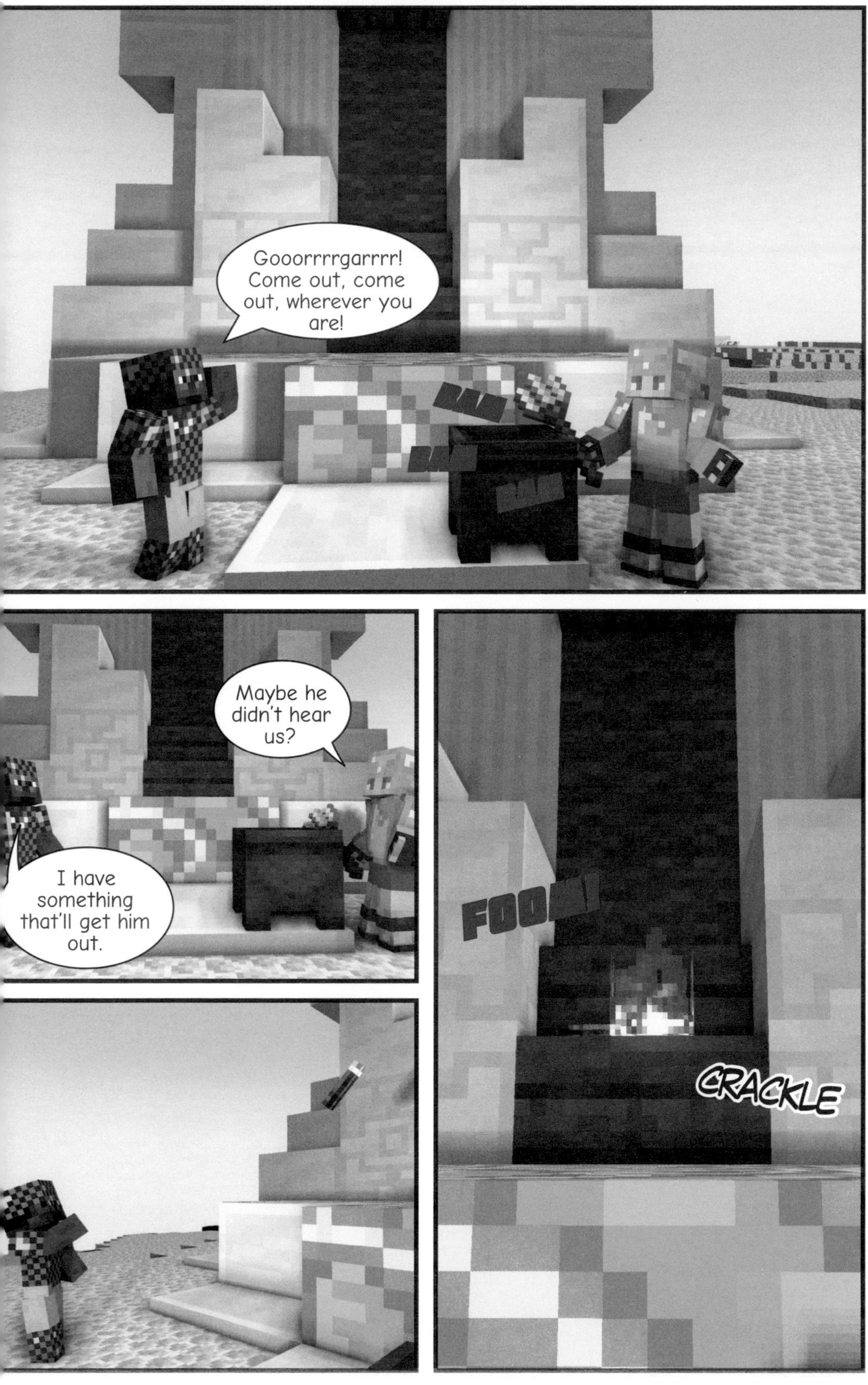
Gooorrrrgarrrr! Come out, come out, wherever you are!
Maybe he didn't hear us?
I have something that'll get him out.
CRACKLE

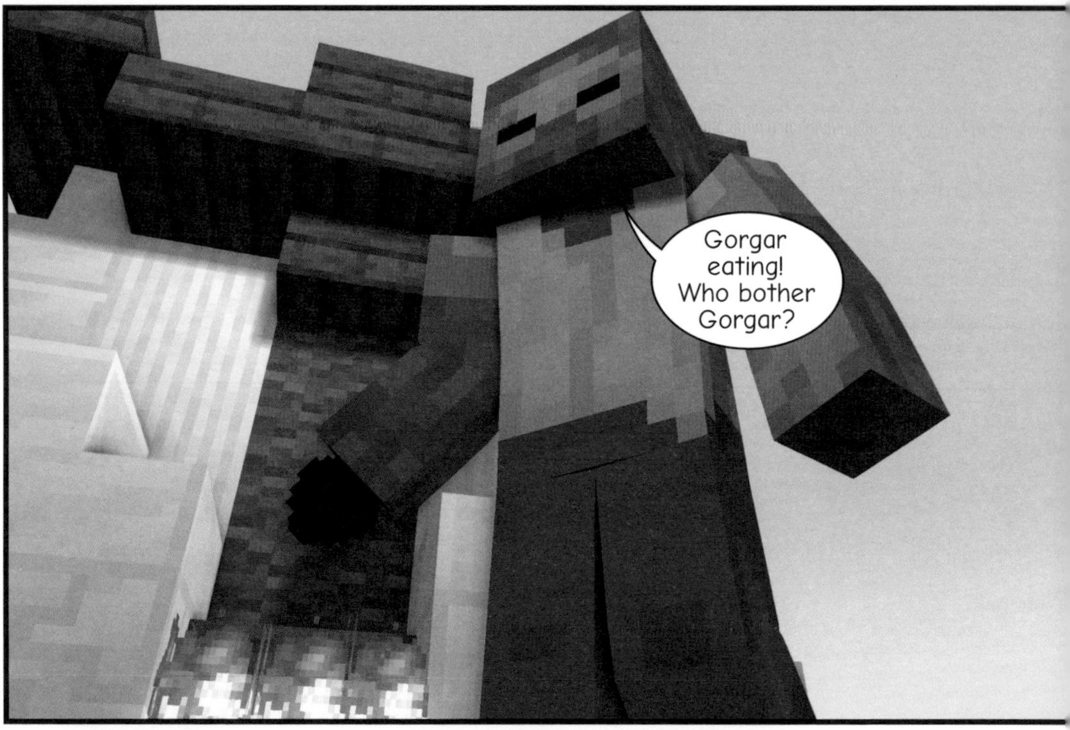
Gorgar eating! Who bother Gorgar?

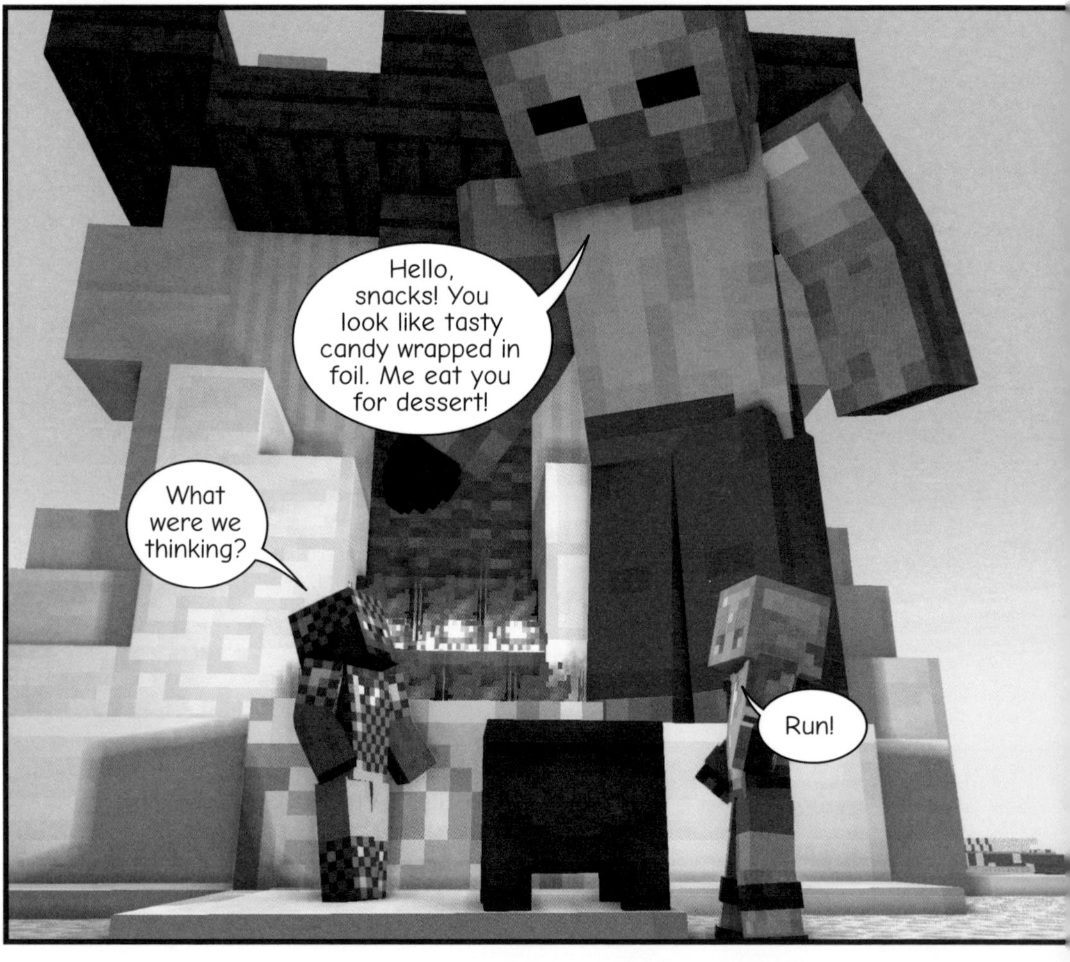
Hello, snacks! You look like tasty candy wrapped in foil. Me eat you for dessert!
What were we thinking?
Run!

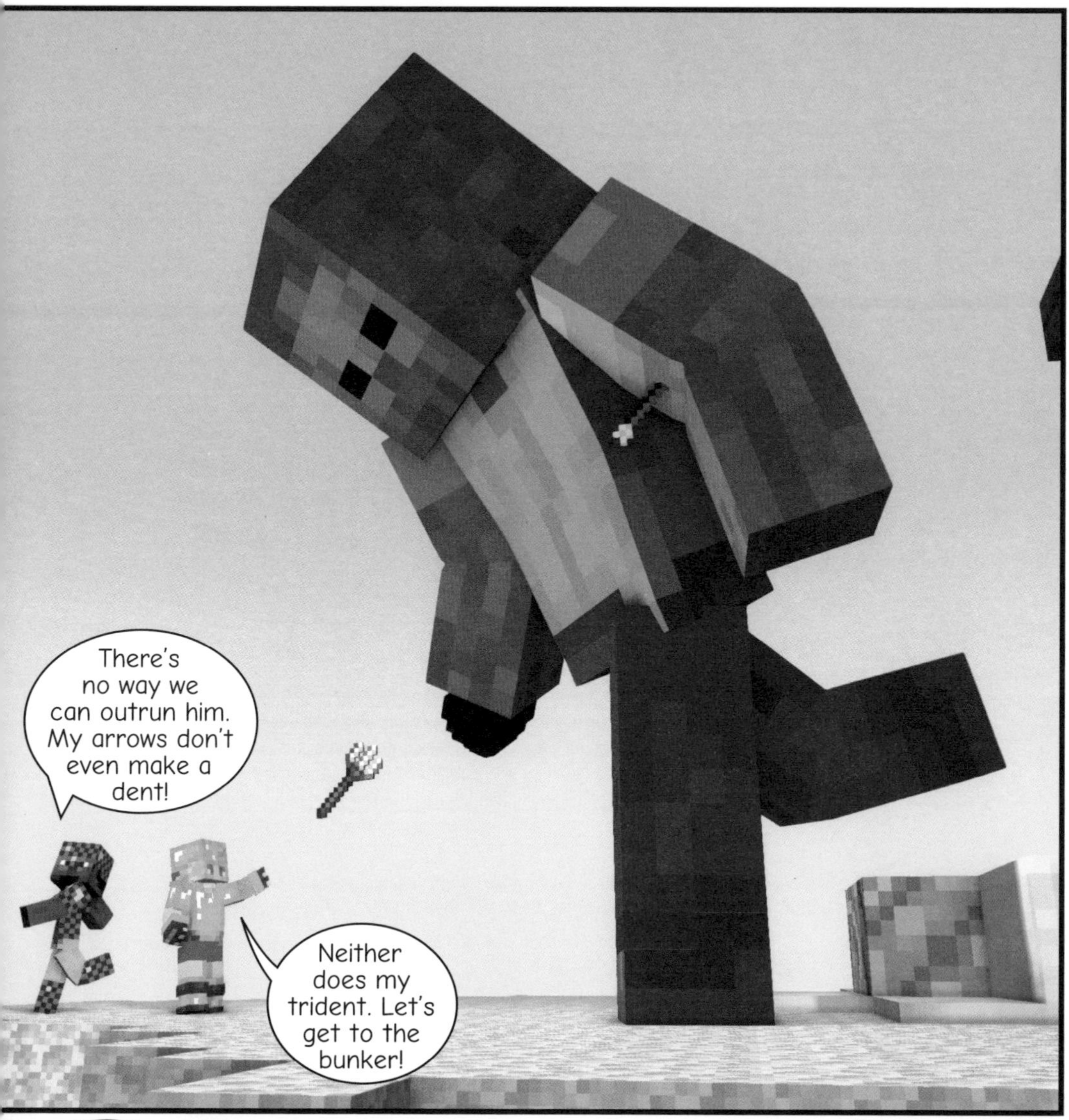
There's no way we can outrun him. My arrows don't even make a dent!
Neither does my trident. Let's get to the bunker!

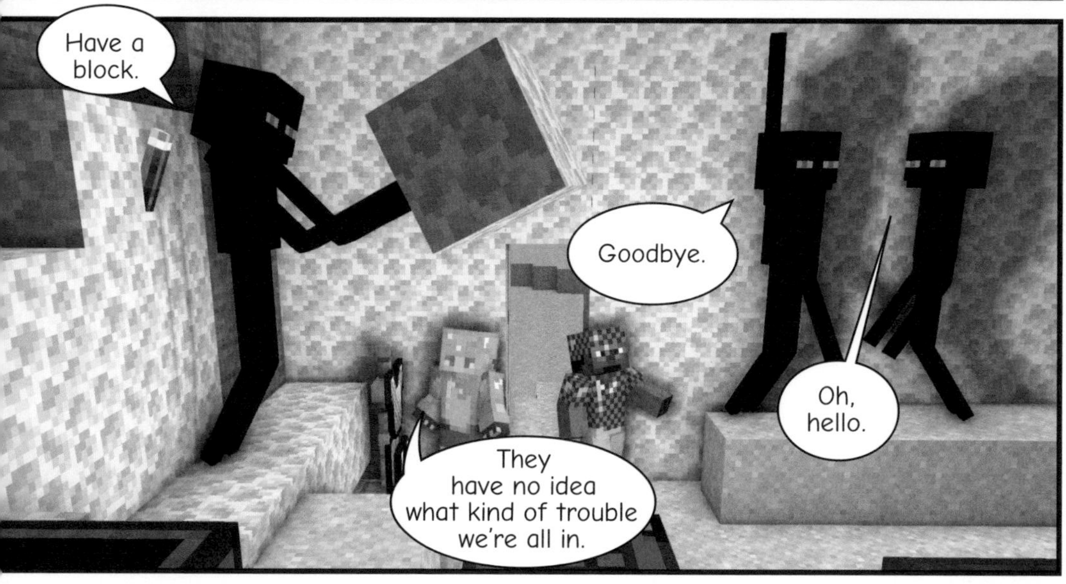
Have a block.
Goodbye.
Oh, hello.
They have no idea what kind of trouble we're all in.

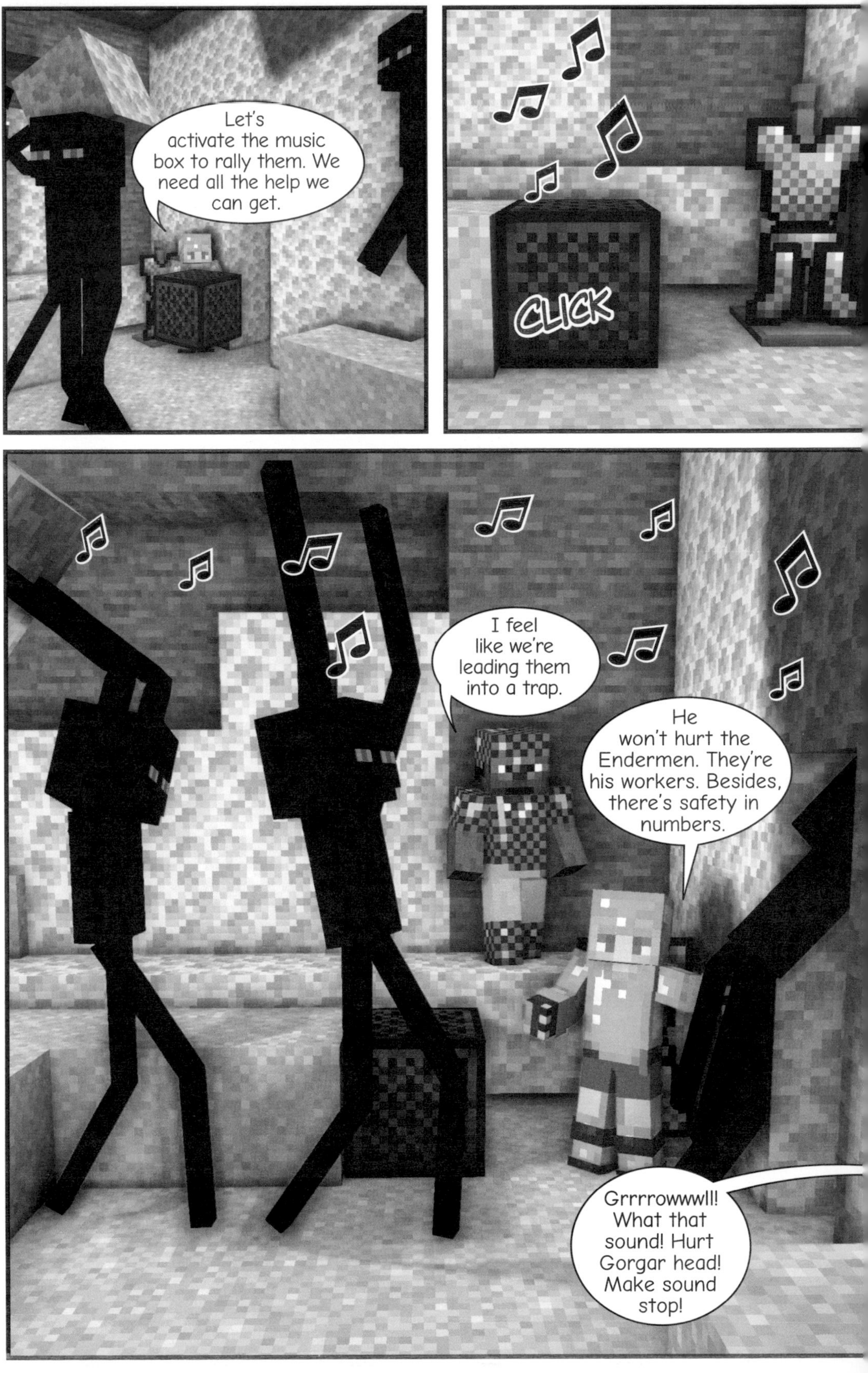
Let's activate the music box to rally them. We need all the help we can get.
CLICK
I feel like we're leading them into a trap.
He won't hurt the Endermen. They're his workers. Besides, there's safety in numbers.
Grrrrowwwll! What that sound! Hurt Gorgar head! Make sound stop!

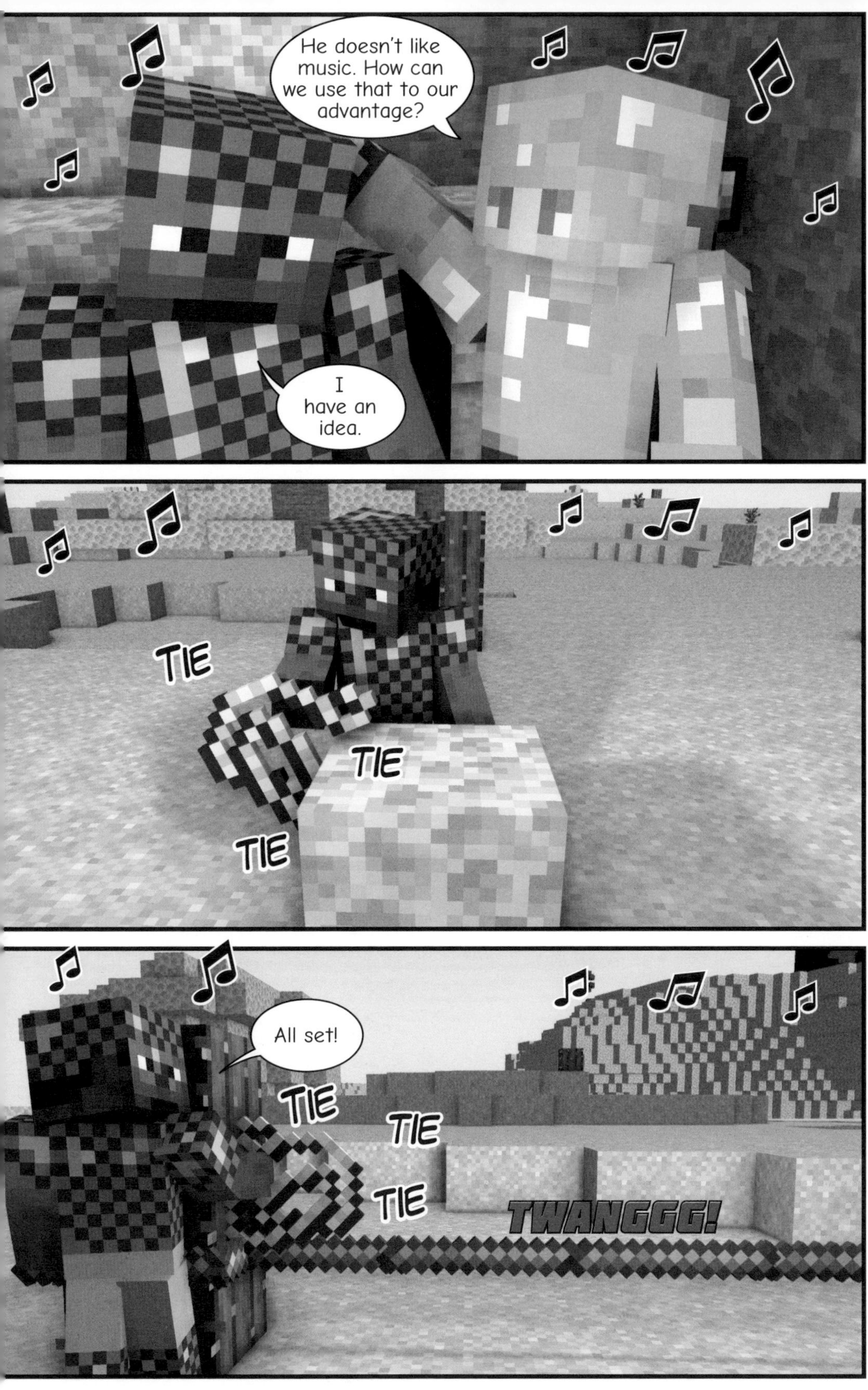
He doesn't like music. How can we use that to our advantage?
I have an idea.
TIE
TIE
TIE
All set!
TIE
TIE
TIE
TWANGGG!

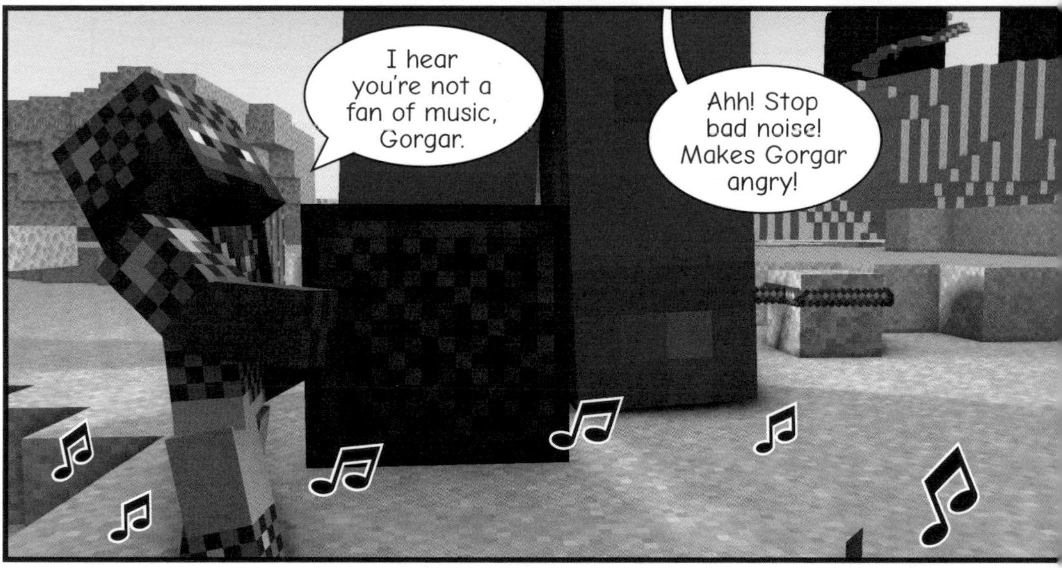
I hear you're not a fan of music, Gorgar.
Ahh! Stop bad noise! Makes Gorgar angry!

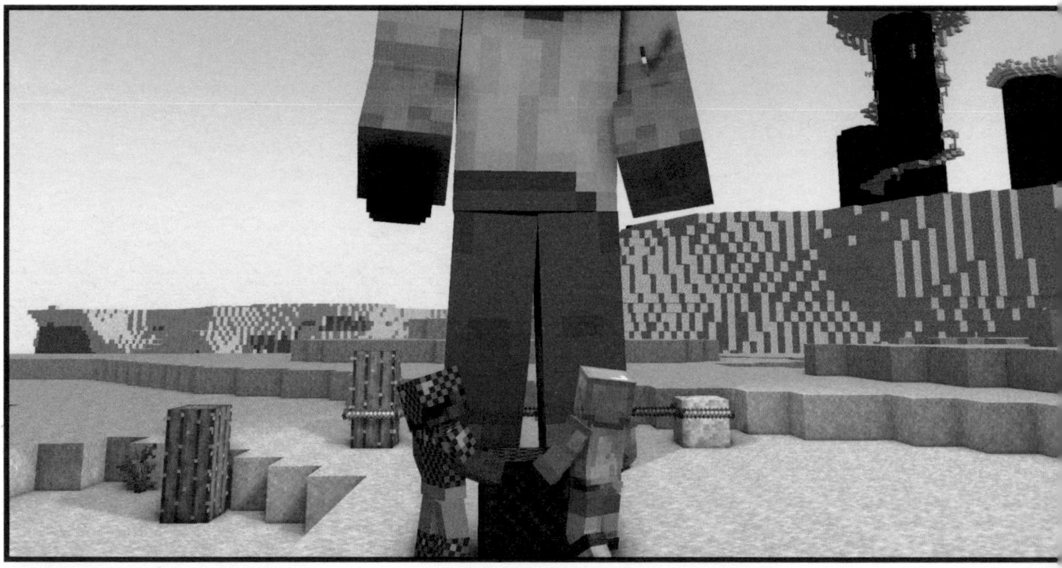

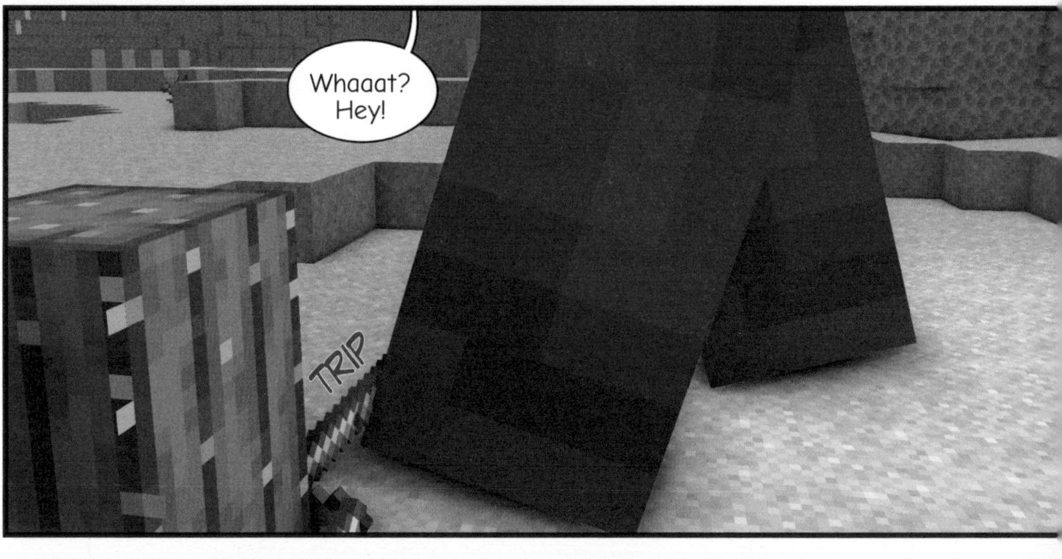
Whaaat? Hey!
TRIP

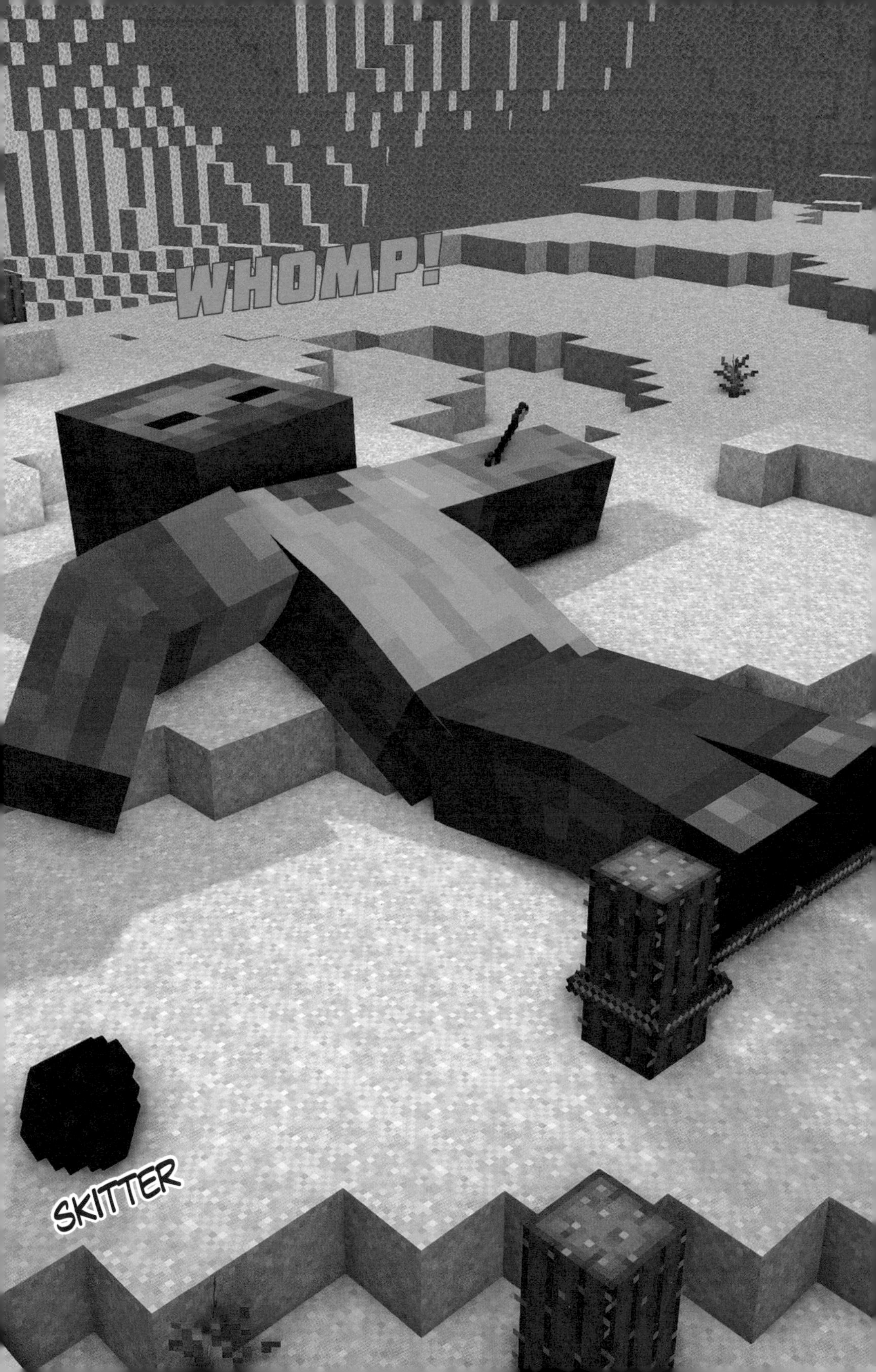
WHOMP!
SKITTER

CHAPTER 11
DRAGON DANCE

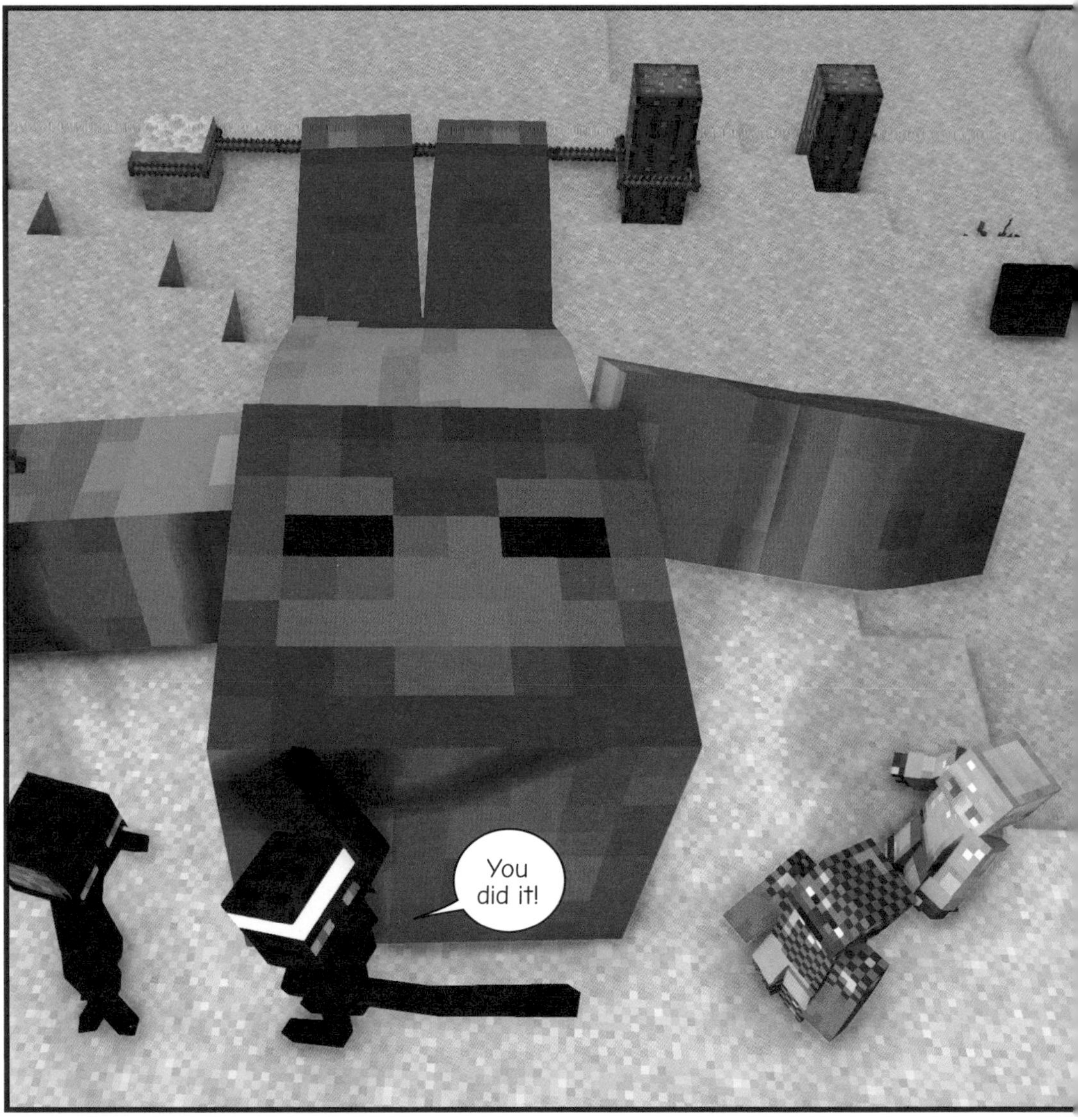
You did it!

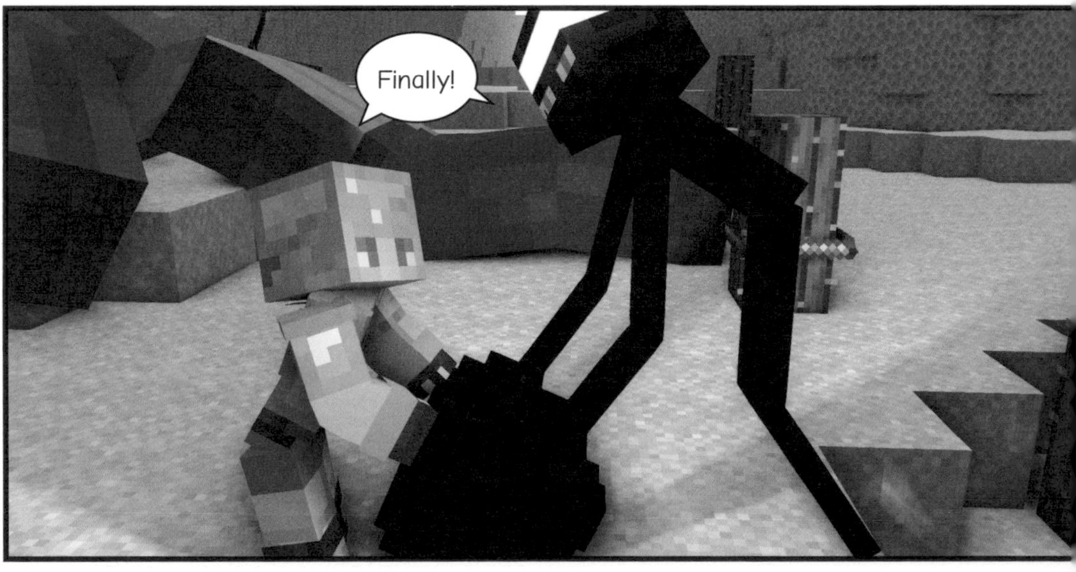
Finally!

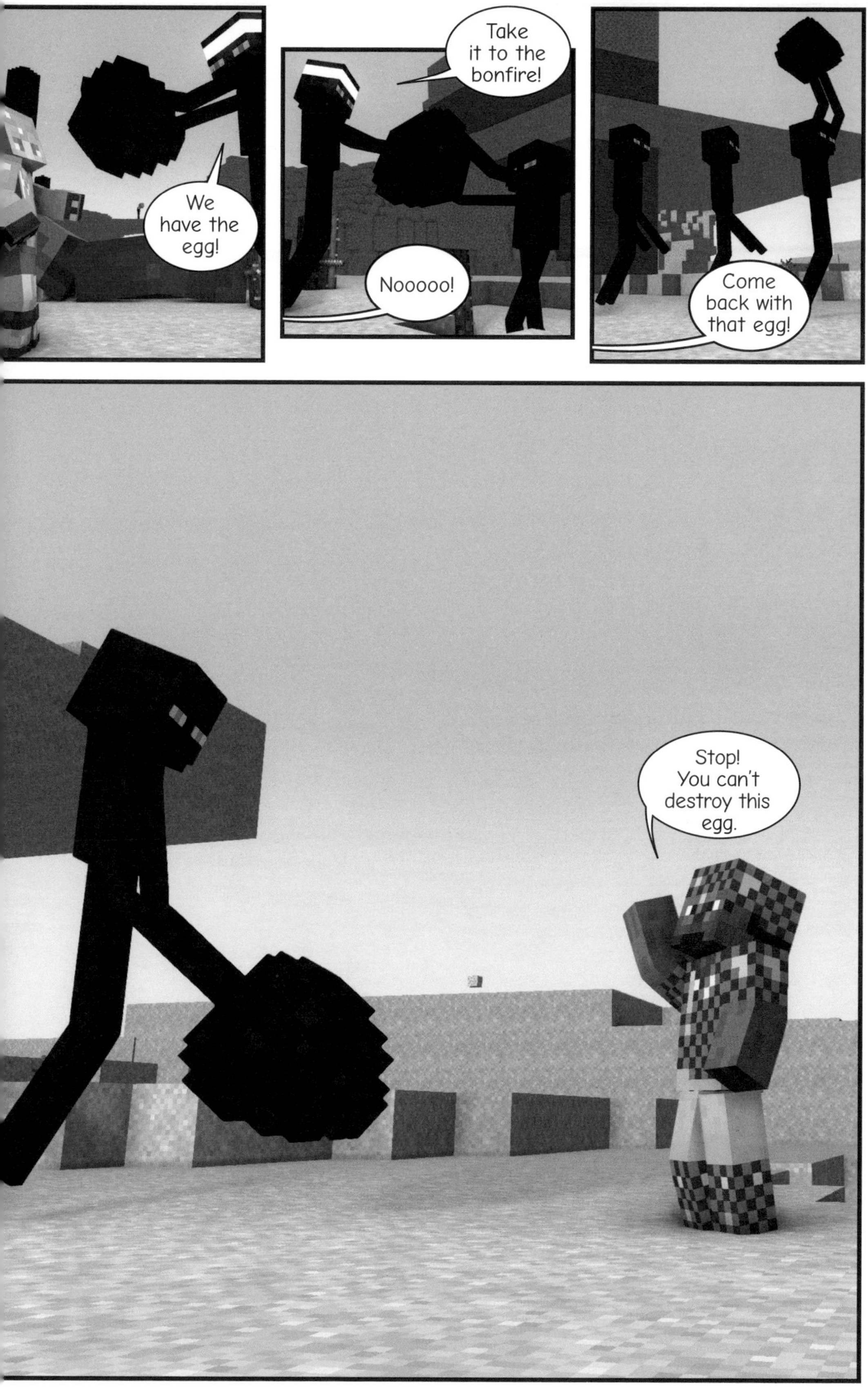
We have the egg!
Take it to the bonfire!
Nooooo!
Come back with that egg!
Stop! You can't destroy this egg.

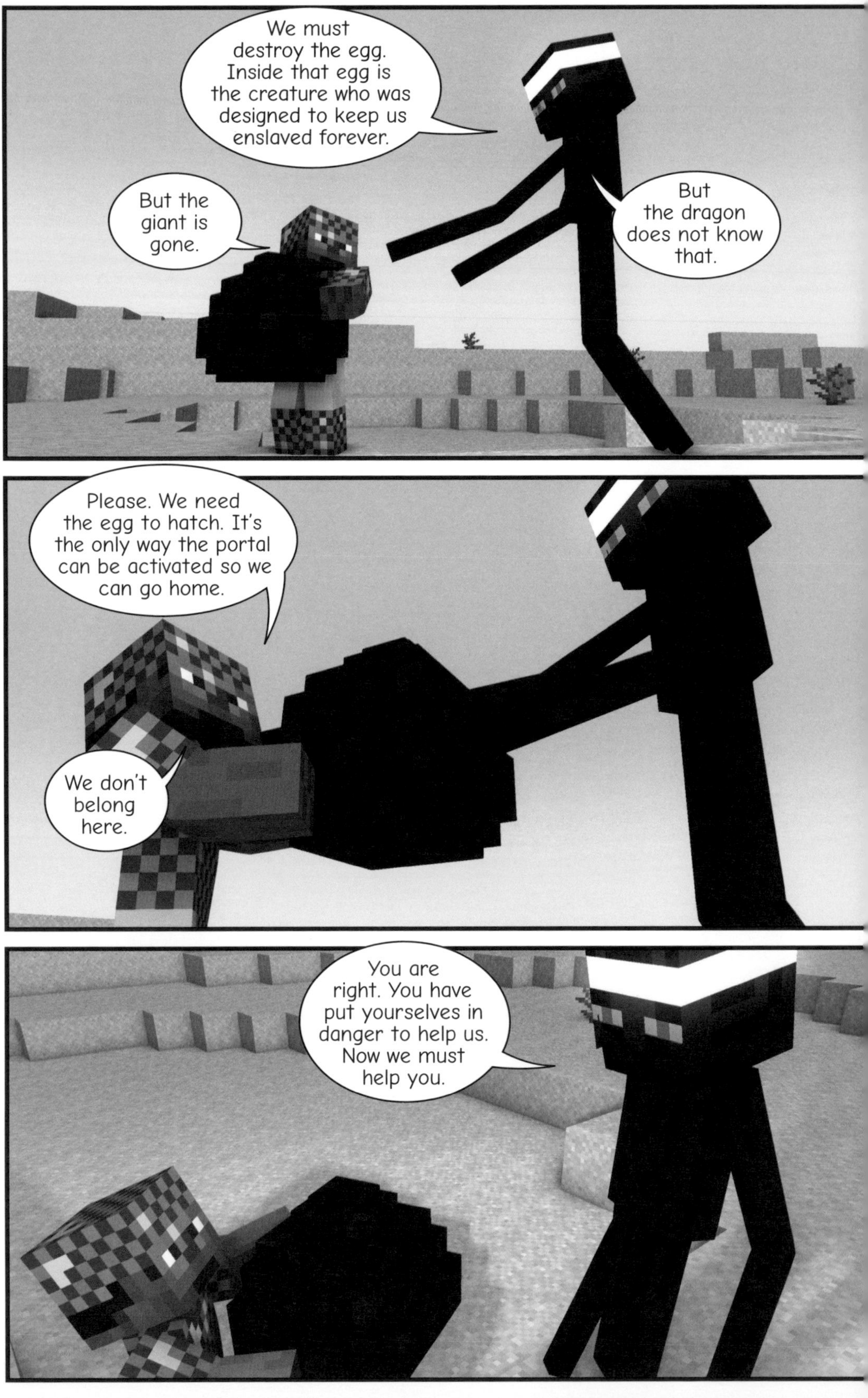
We must destroy the egg. Inside that egg is the creature who was designed to keep us enslaved forever.
But the giant is gone.
But the dragon does not know that.
Please. We need the egg to hatch. It's the only way the portal can be activated so we can go home.
We don't belong here.
You are right. You have put yourselves in danger to help us. Now we must help you.

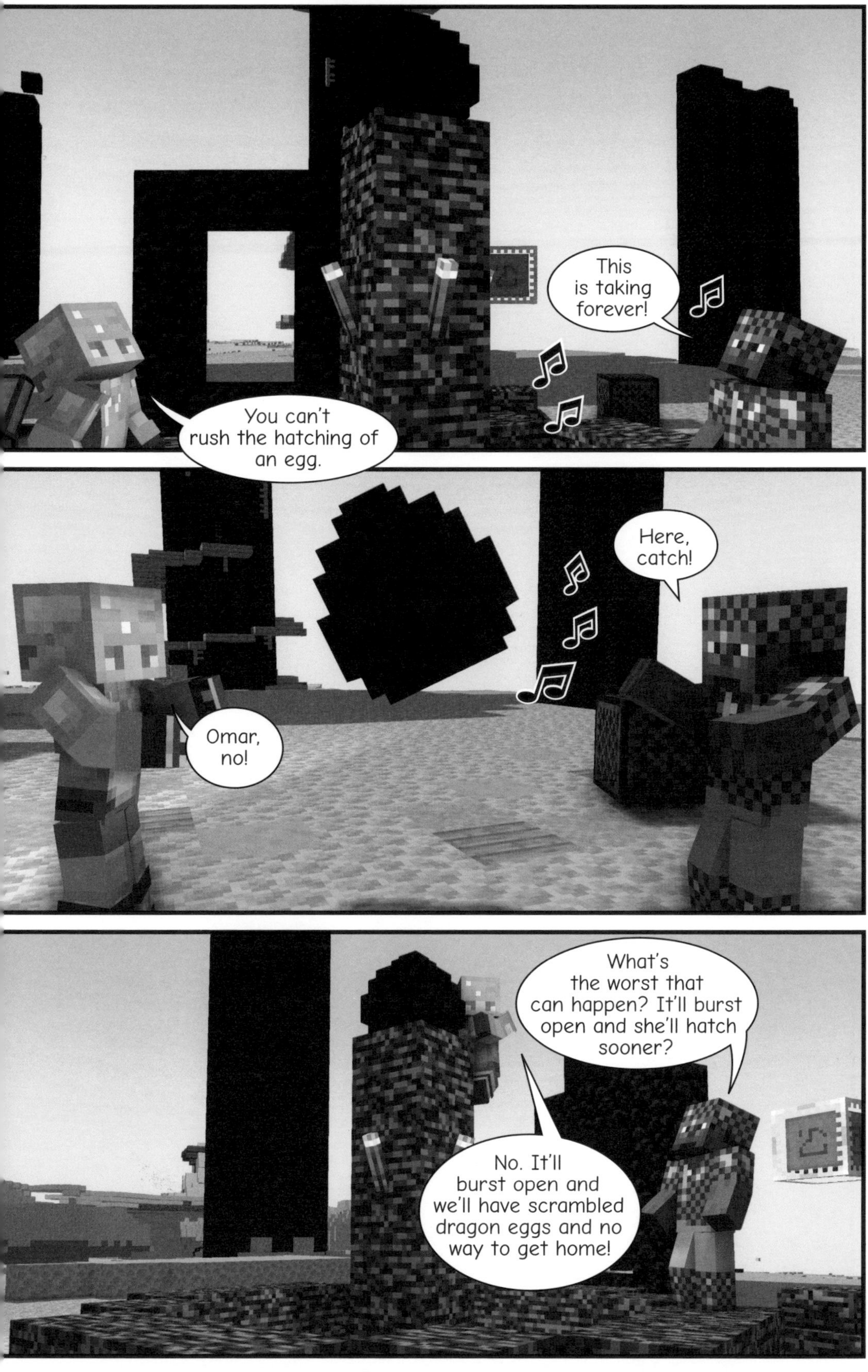
This is taking forever!
You can't rush the hatching of an egg.
Here, catch!
Omar, no!
What's the worst that can happen? It'll burst open and she'll hatch sooner?
No. It'll burst open and we'll have scrambled dragon eggs and no way to get home!

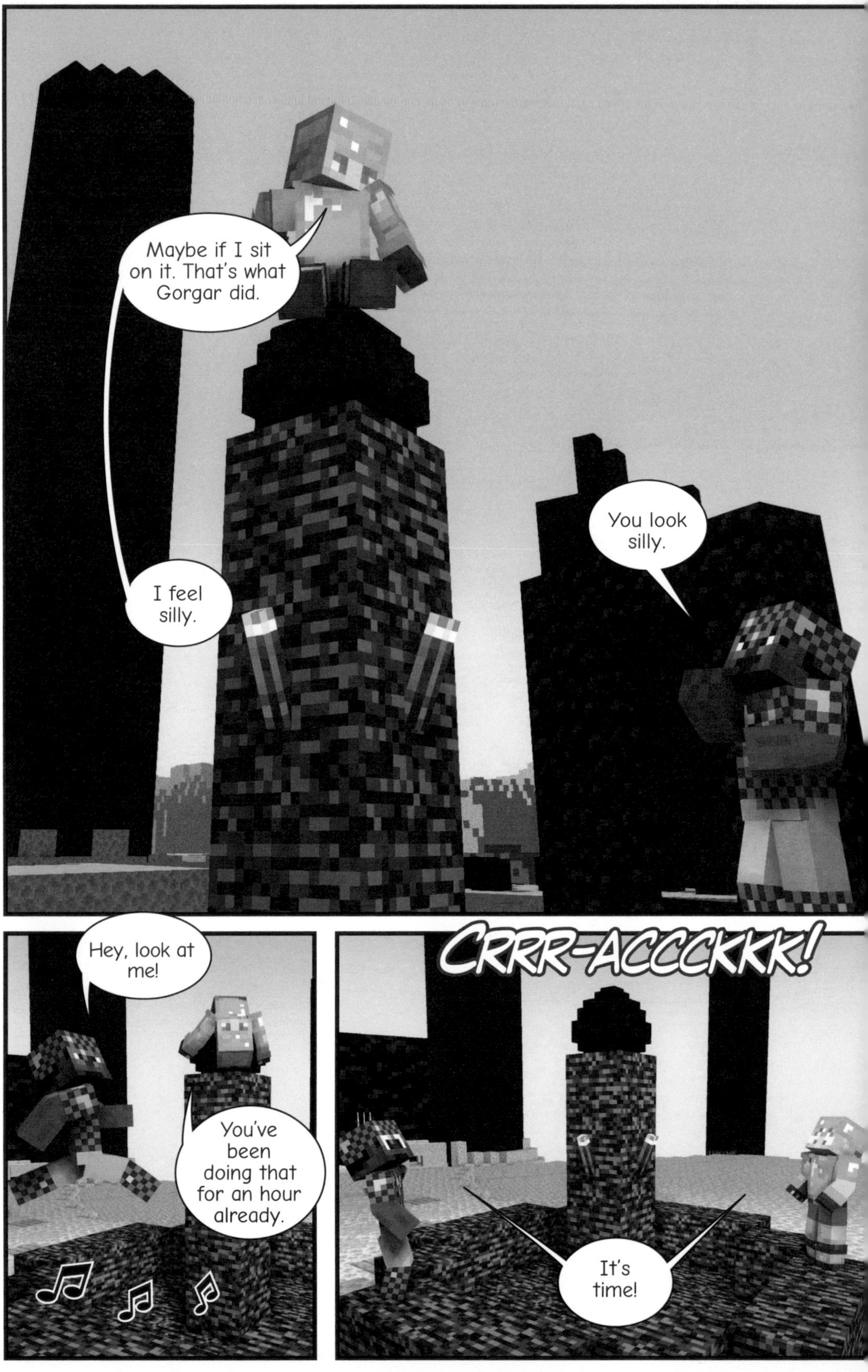

Maybe if I sit on it. That's what Gorgar did.
I feel silly.
You look silly.
Hey, look at me!
You've been doing that for an hour already.
CRRR-ACCCKKK!
It's time!

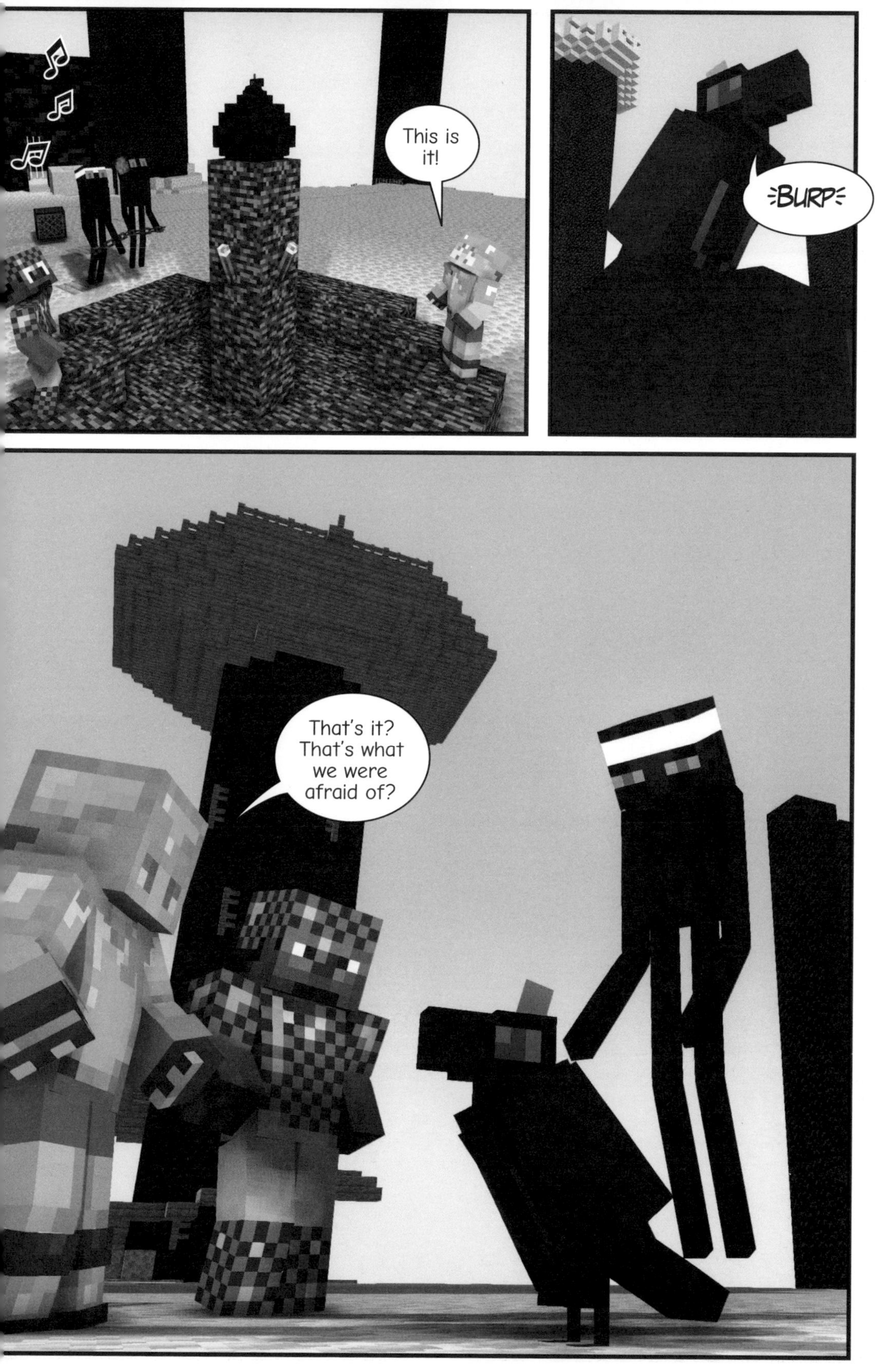

This is it!
BURP
That's it? That's what we were afraid of?

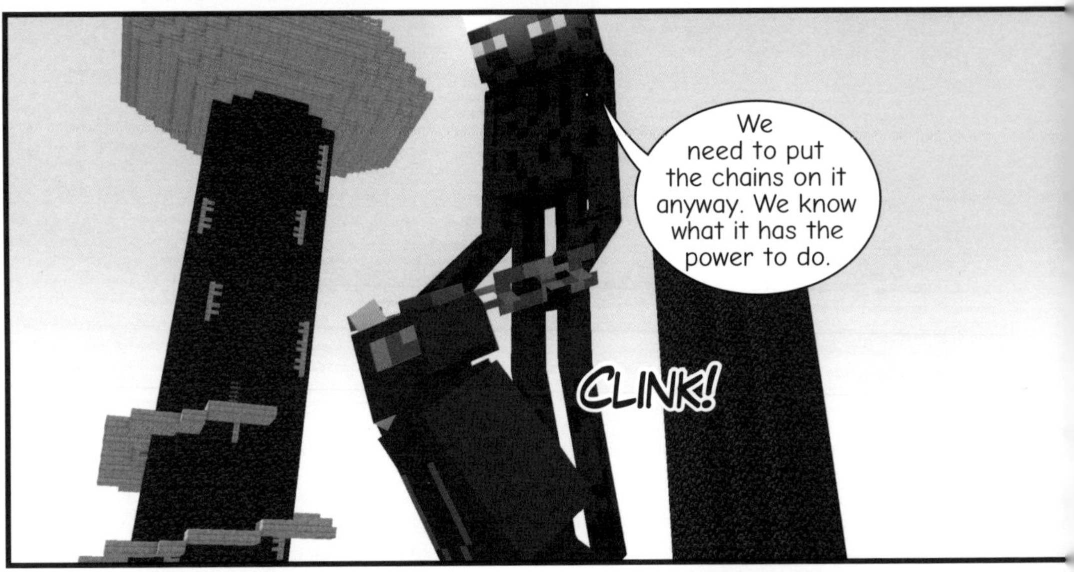
We need to put the chains on it anyway. We know what it has the power to do.
CLINK!

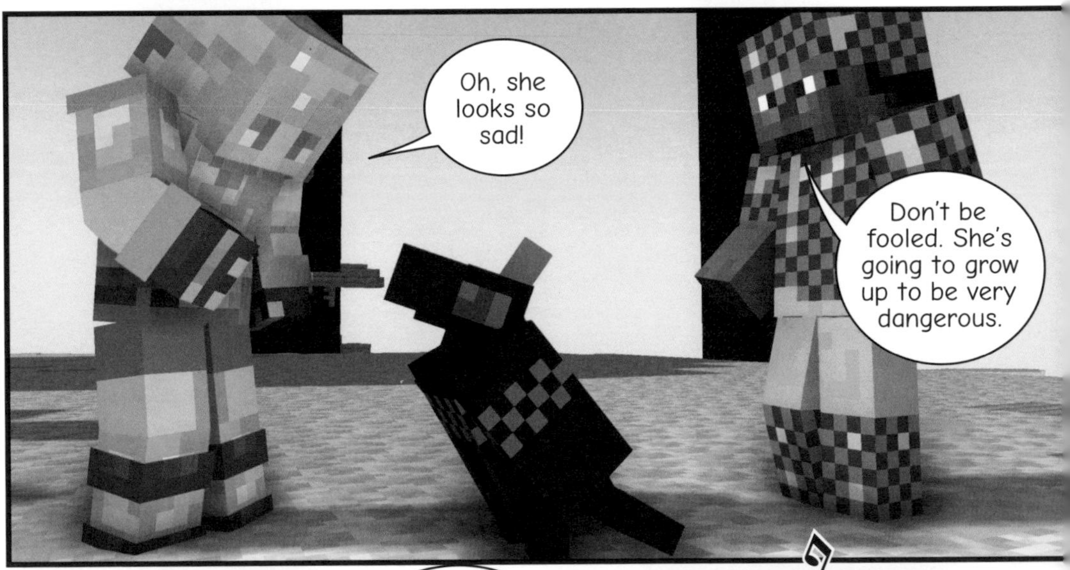
Oh, she looks so sad!
Don't be fooled. She's going to grow up to be very dangerous.

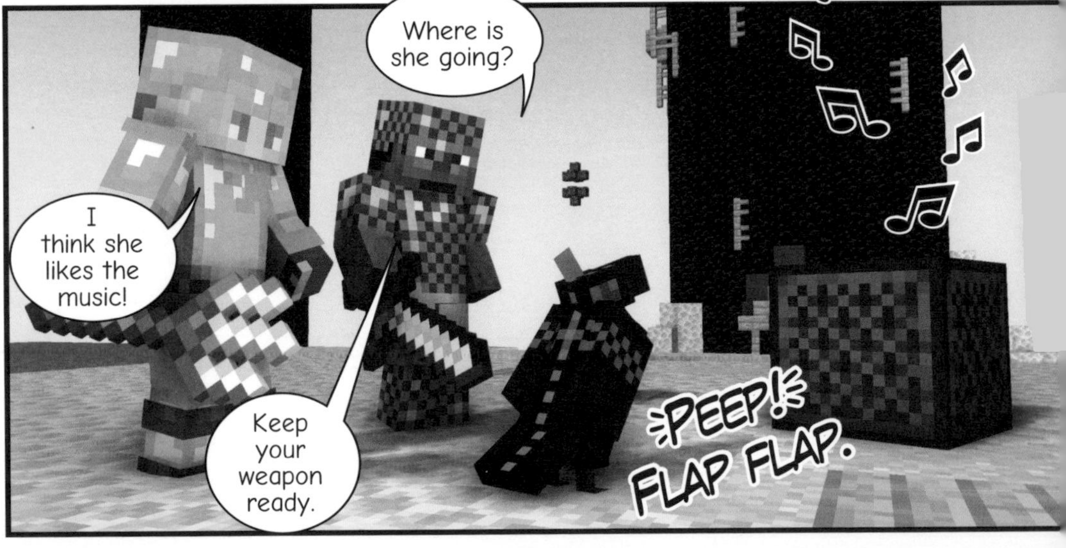
Where is she going?
I think she likes the music!
Keep your weapon ready.
PEEP!
FLAP FLAP.

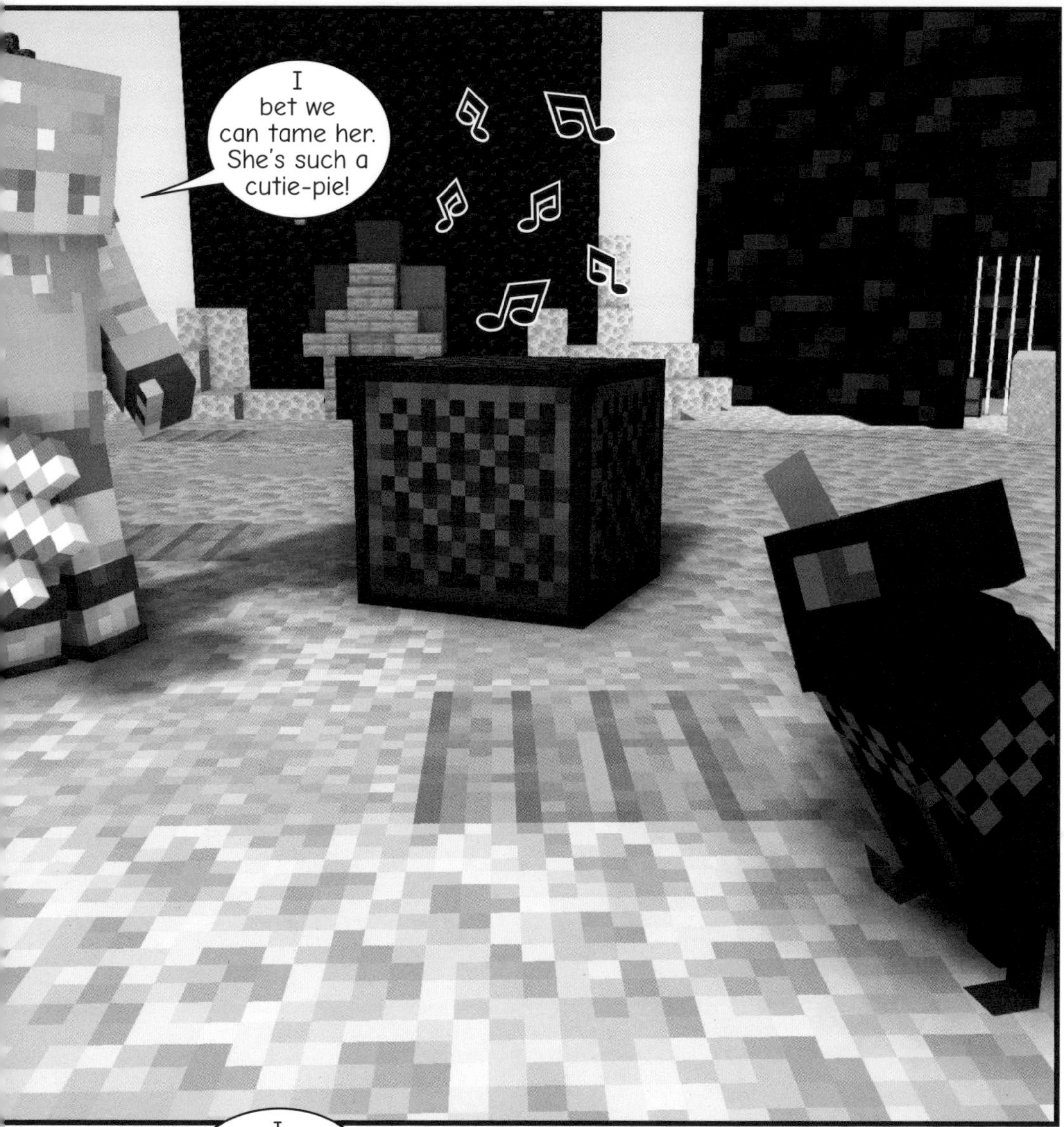
I bet we can tame her. She's such a cutie-pie!

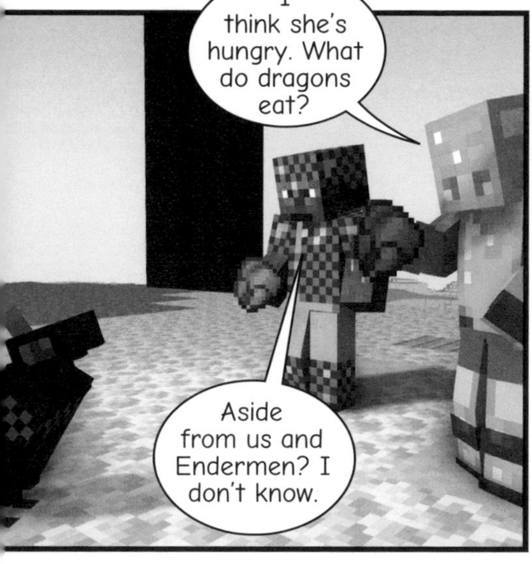
I think she's hungry. What do dragons eat?
Aside from us and Endermen? I don't know.

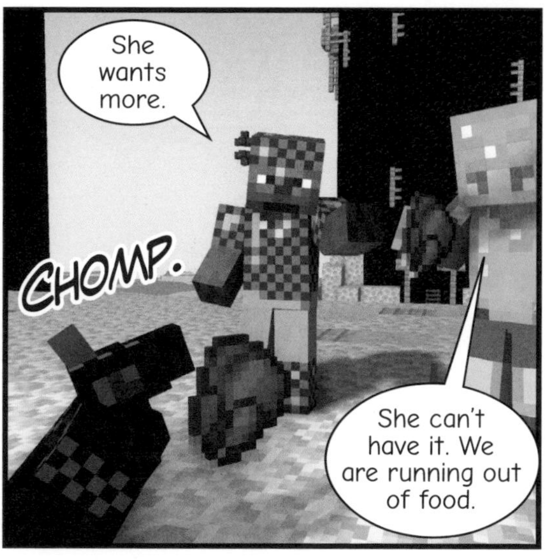
She wants more.
CHOMP.
She can't have it. We are running out of food.

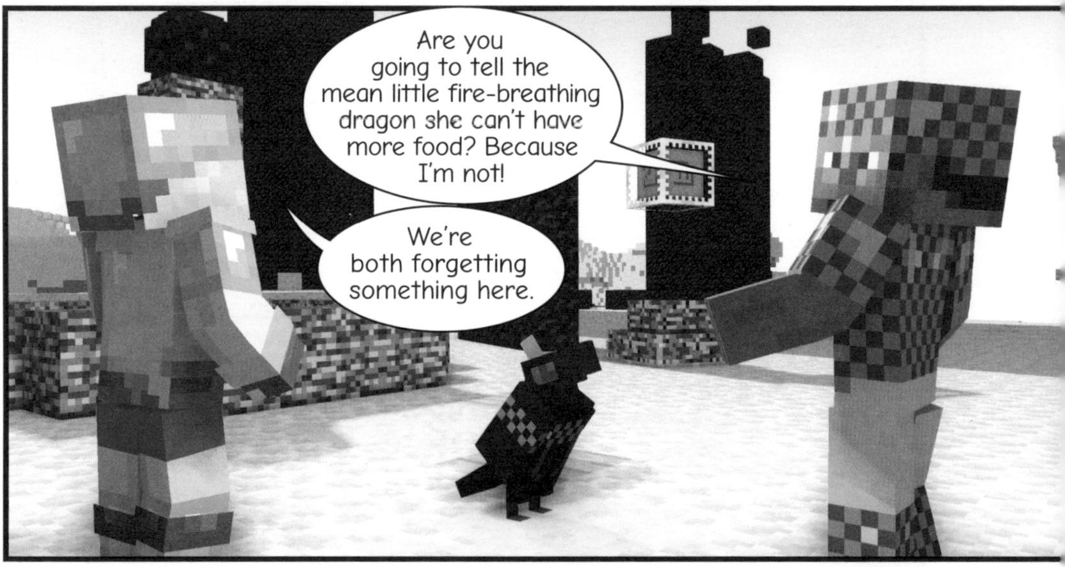
Are you going to tell the mean little fire-breathing dragon she can't have more food? Because I'm not!
We're both forgetting something here.

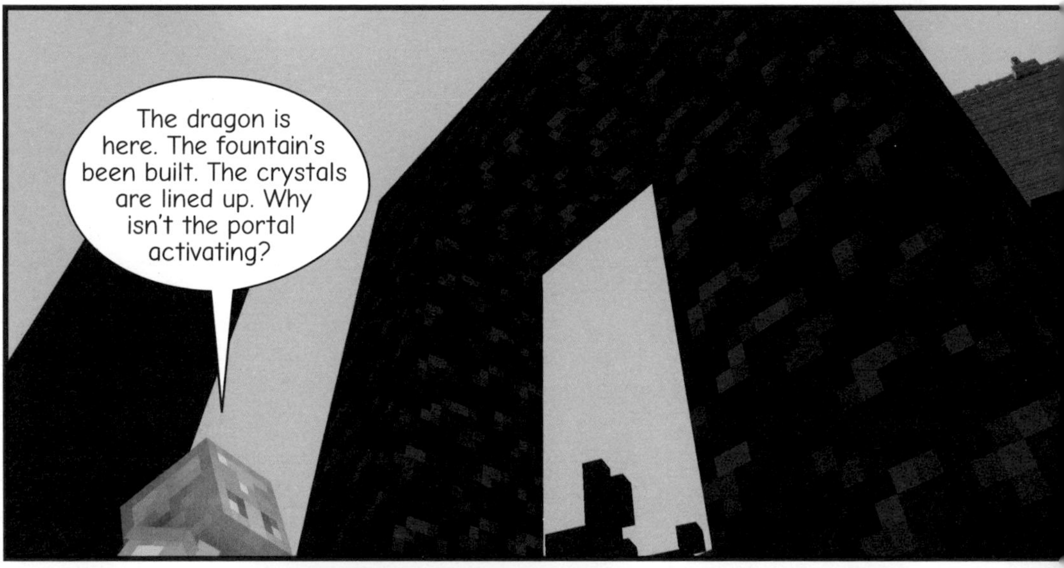
The dragon is here. The fountain's been built. The crystals are lined up. Why isn't the portal activating?

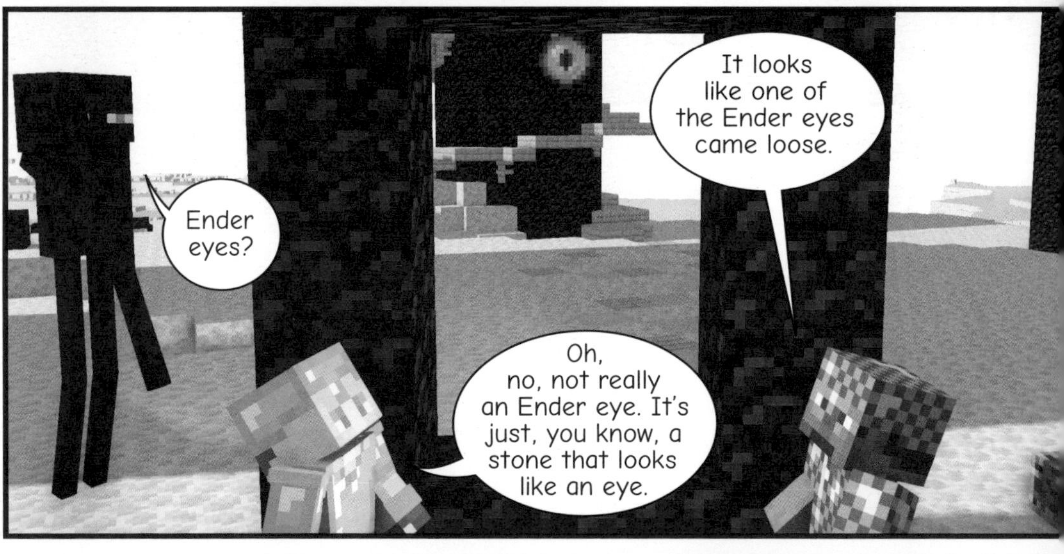
Ender eyes?
It looks like one of the Ender eyes came loose.
Oh, no, not really an Ender eye. It's just, you know, a stone that looks like an eye.

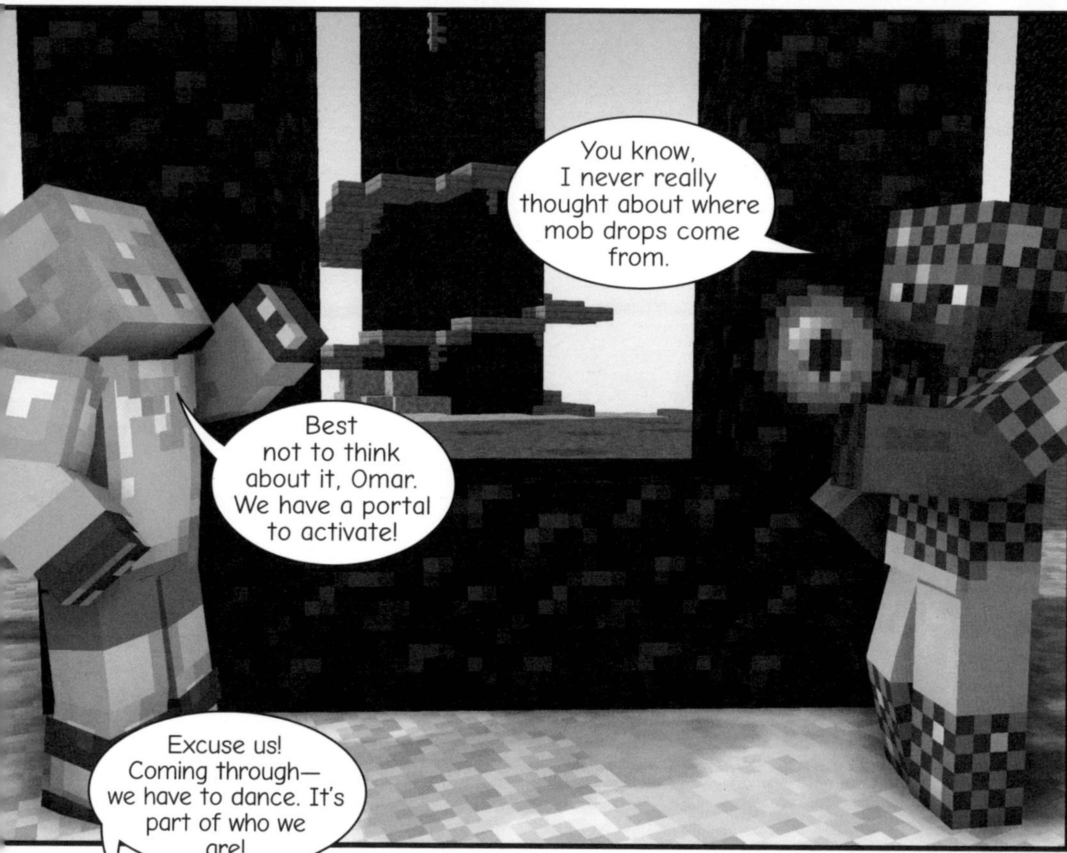
You know, I never really thought about where mob drops come from.
Best not to think about it, Omar. We have a portal to activate!
Excuse us! Coming through— we have to dance. It's part of who we are!

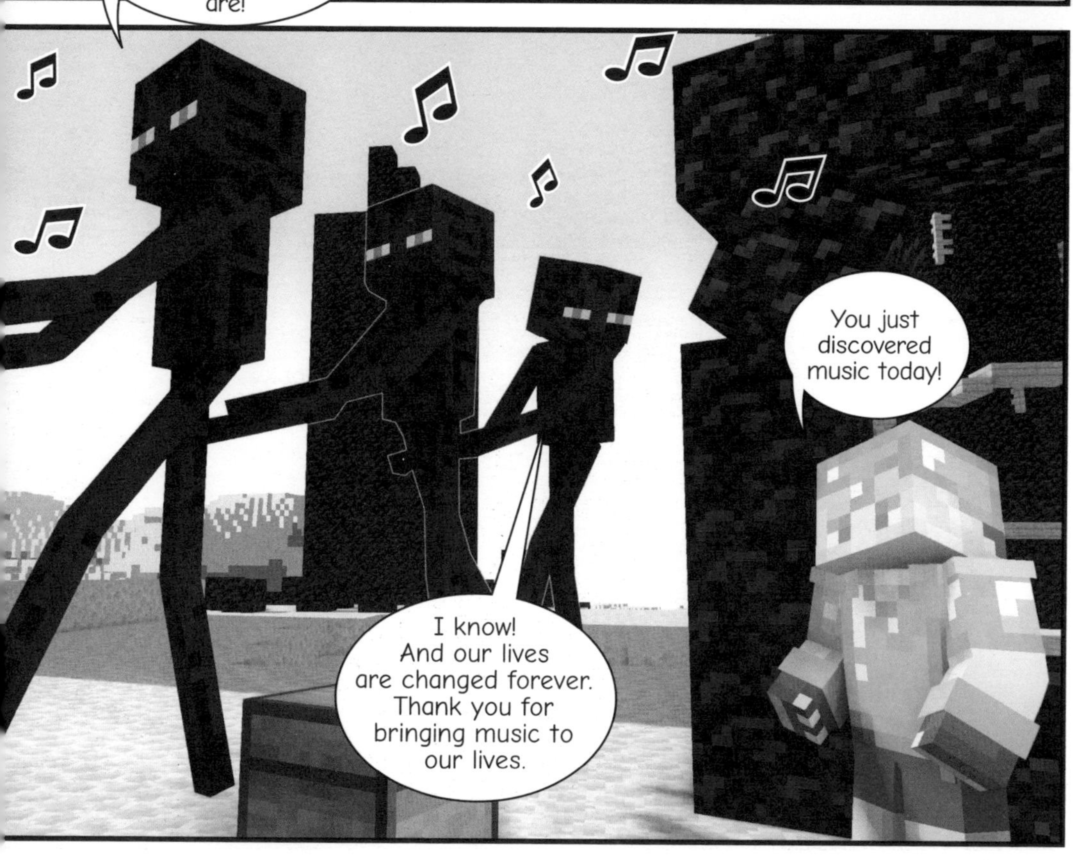
You just discovered music today!
I know! And our lives are changed forever. Thank you for bringing music to our lives.

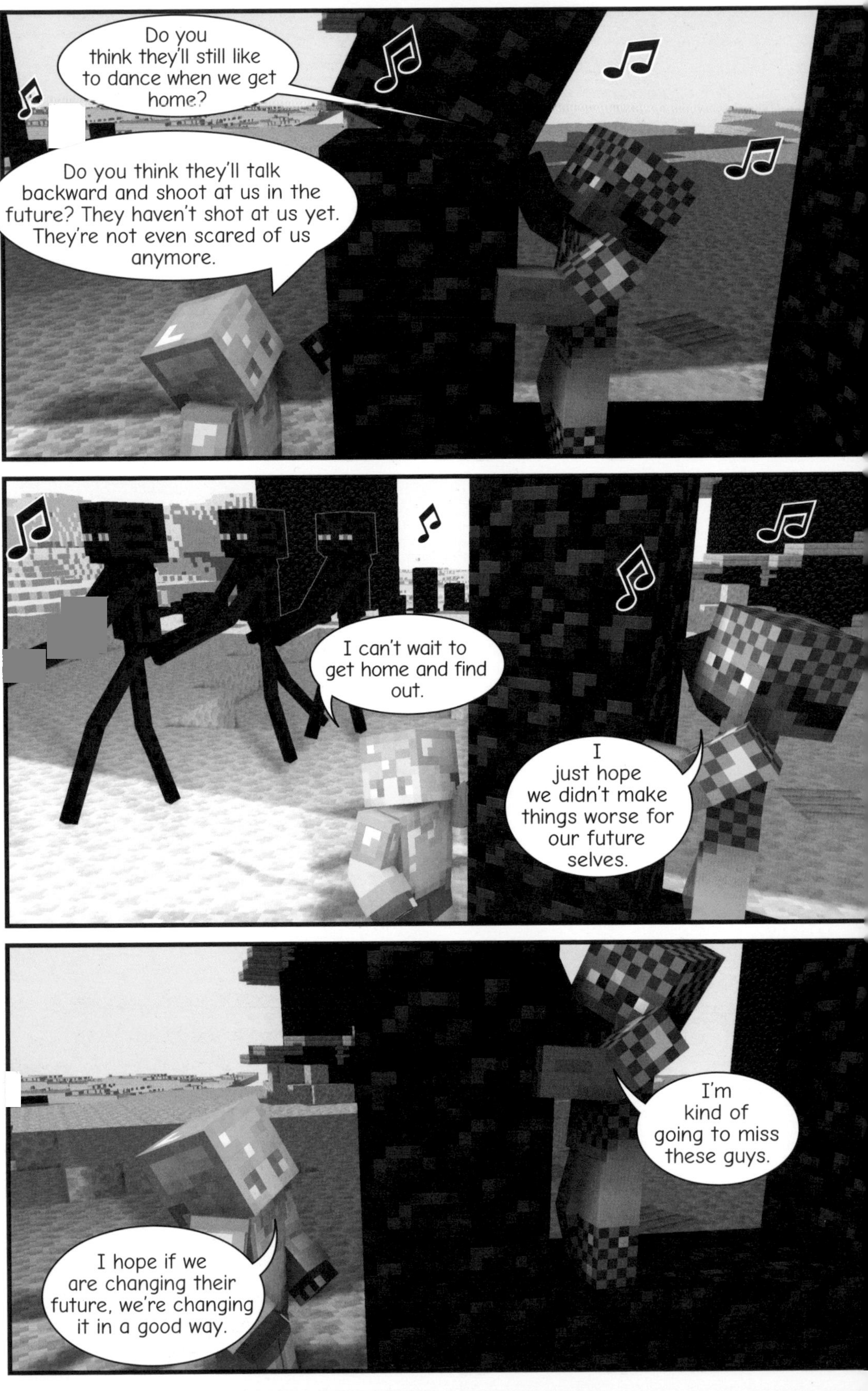
Do you think they'll still like to dance when we get home?
Do you think they'll talk backward and shoot at us in the future? They haven't shot at us yet. They're not even scared of us anymore.
I can't wait to get home and find out.
I just hope we didn't make things worse for our future selves.
I'm kind of going to miss these guys.
I hope if we are changing their future, we're changing it in a good way.

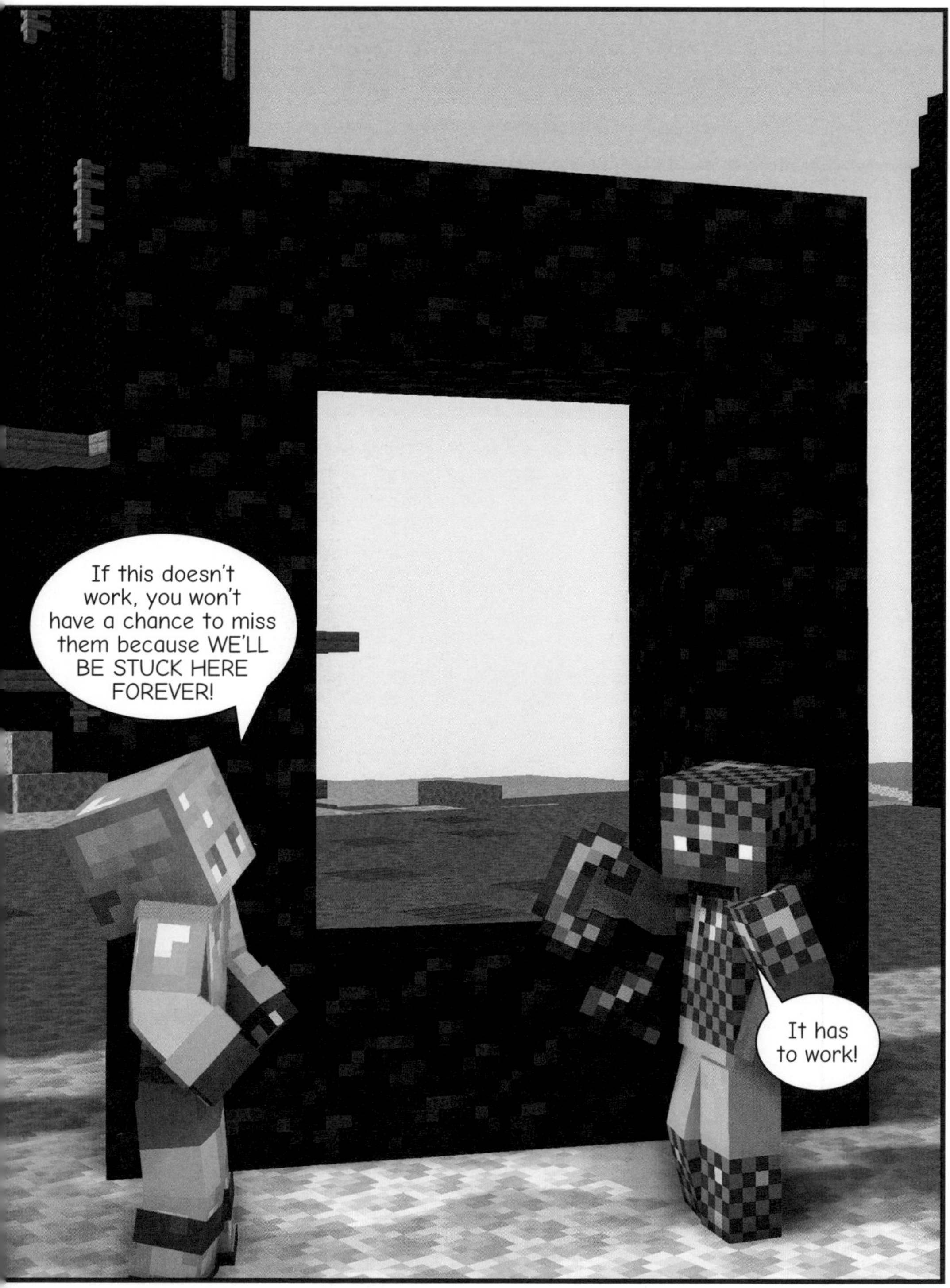
If this doesn't work, you won't have a chance to miss them because WE'LL BE STUCK HERE FOREVER!
It has to work!

CHAPTER 12
ACTIVATE!

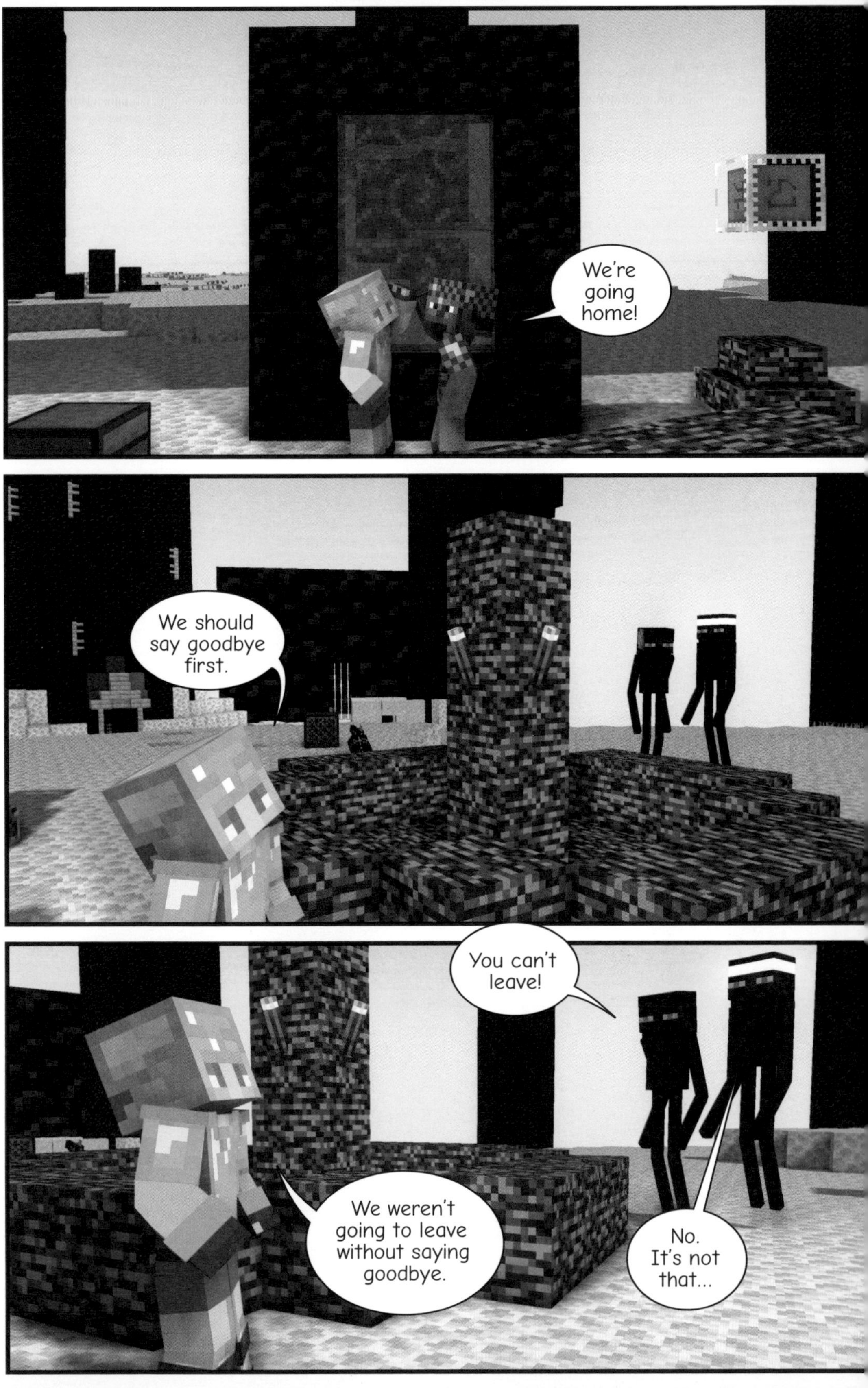
We're going home!
We should say goodbye first.
You can't leave!
We weren't going to leave without saying goodbye.
No. It's not that...

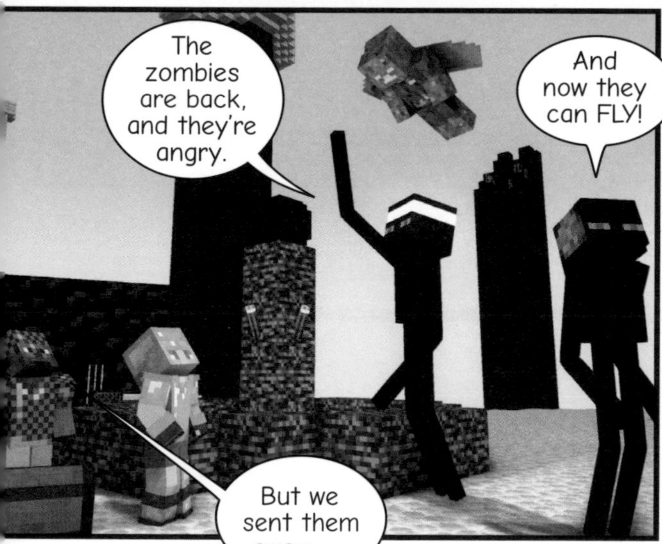
The zombies are back, and they're angry.
And now they can FLY!
But we sent them away . . .

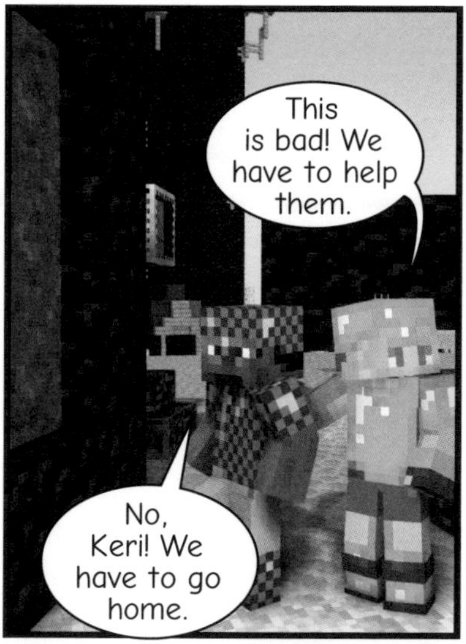
This is bad! We have to help them.
No, Keri! We have to go home.

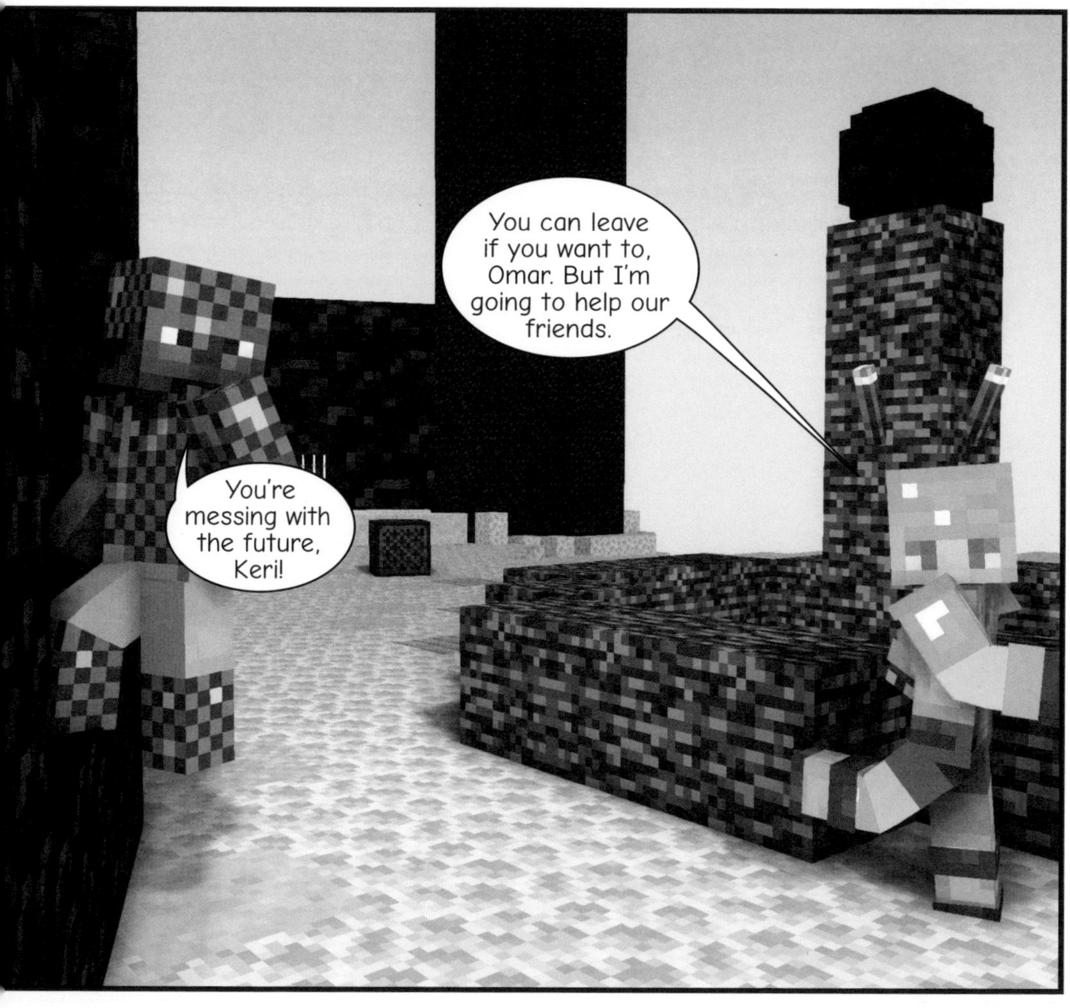
You can leave if you want to, Omar. But I'm going to help our friends.
You're messing with the future, Keri!

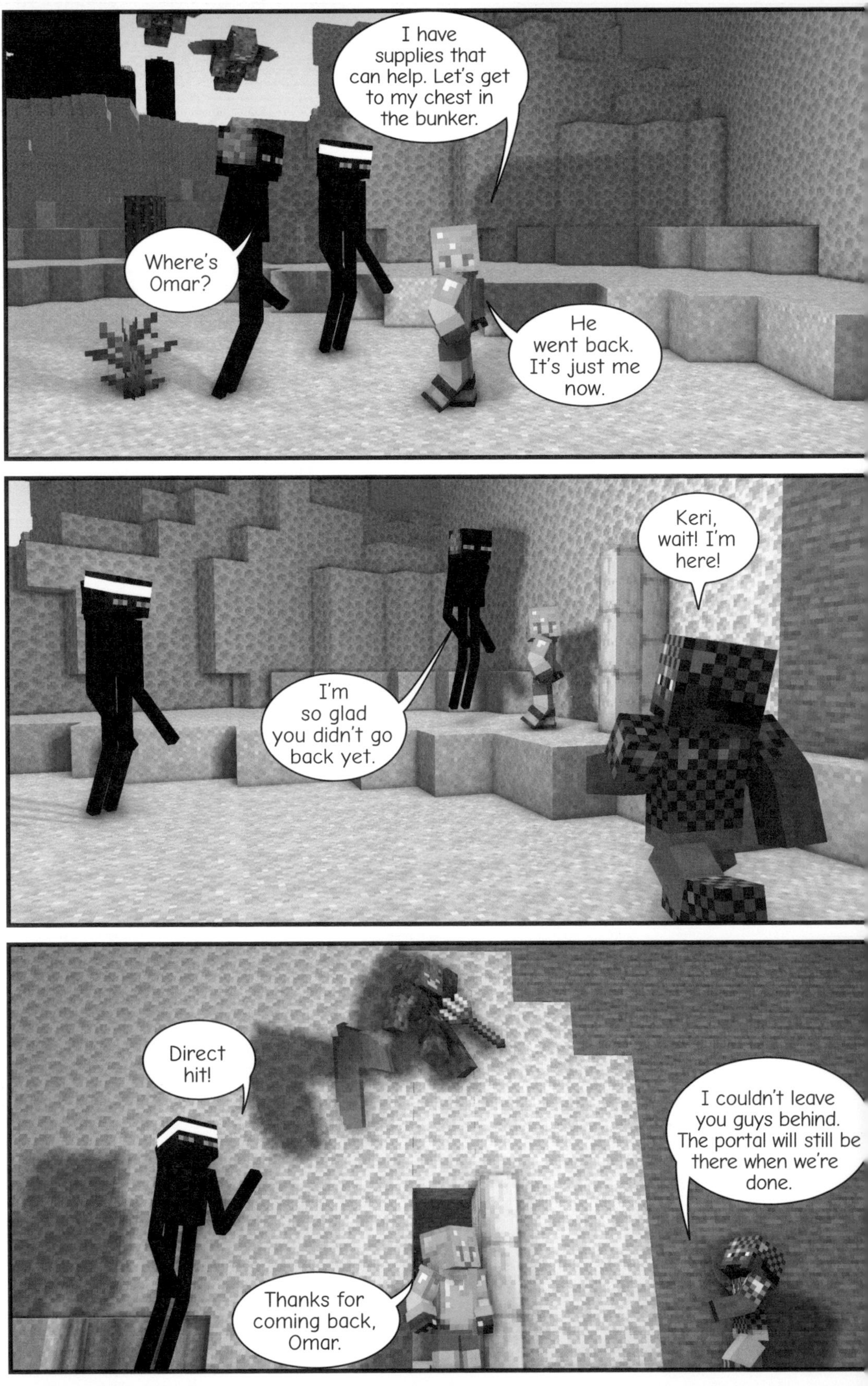
I have supplies that can help. Let's get to my chest in the bunker.
Where's Omar?
He went back. It's just me now.
Keri, wait! I'm here!
I'm so glad you didn't go back yet.
Direct hit!
I couldn't leave you guys behind. The portal will still be there when we're done.
Thanks for coming back, Omar.

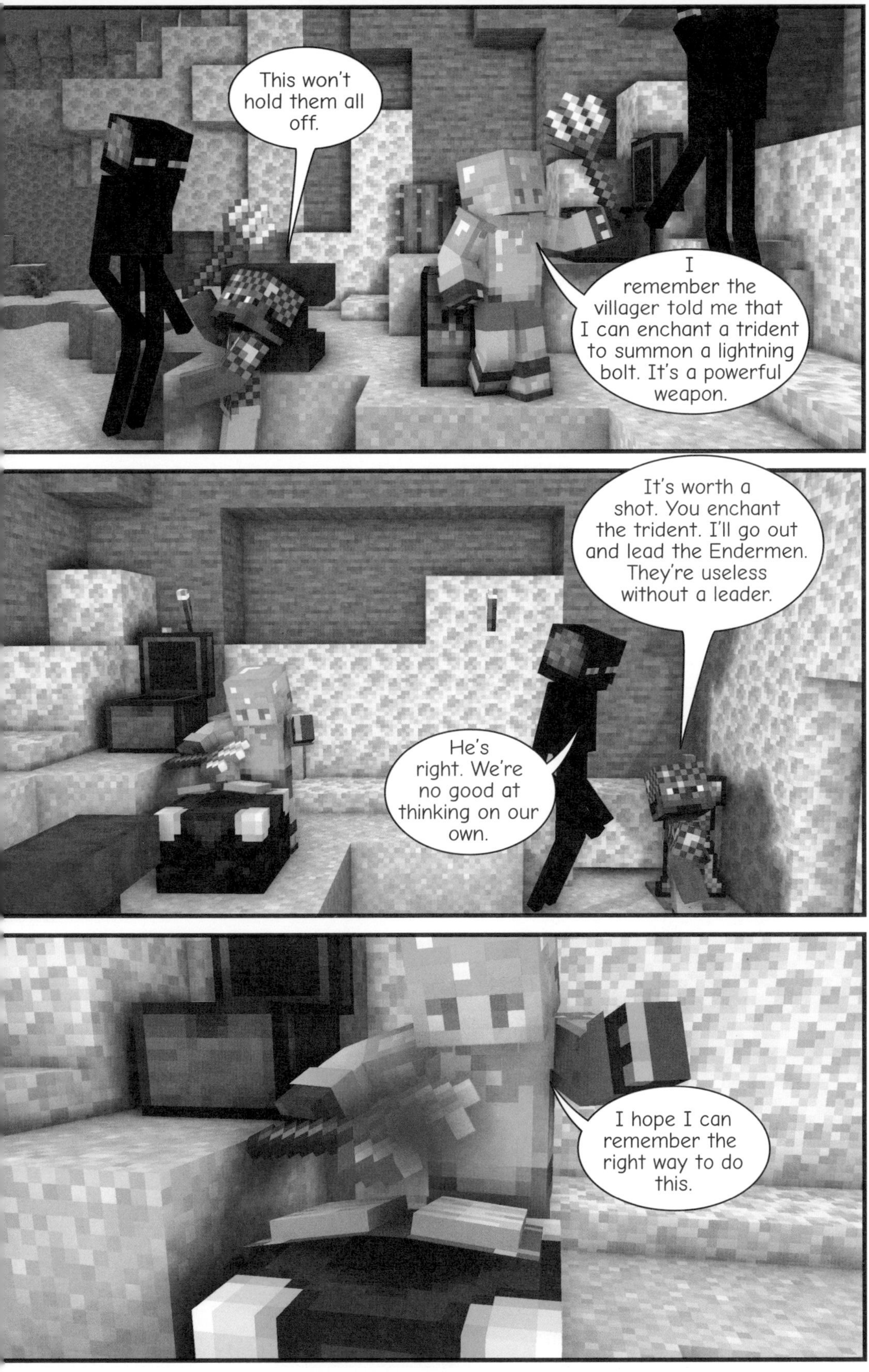
This won't hold them all off.
I remember the villager told me that I can enchant a trident to summon a lightning bolt. It's a powerful weapon.
It's worth a shot. You enchant the trident. I'll go out and lead the Endermen. They're useless without a leader.
He's right. We're no good at thinking on our own.
I hope I can remember the right way to do this.

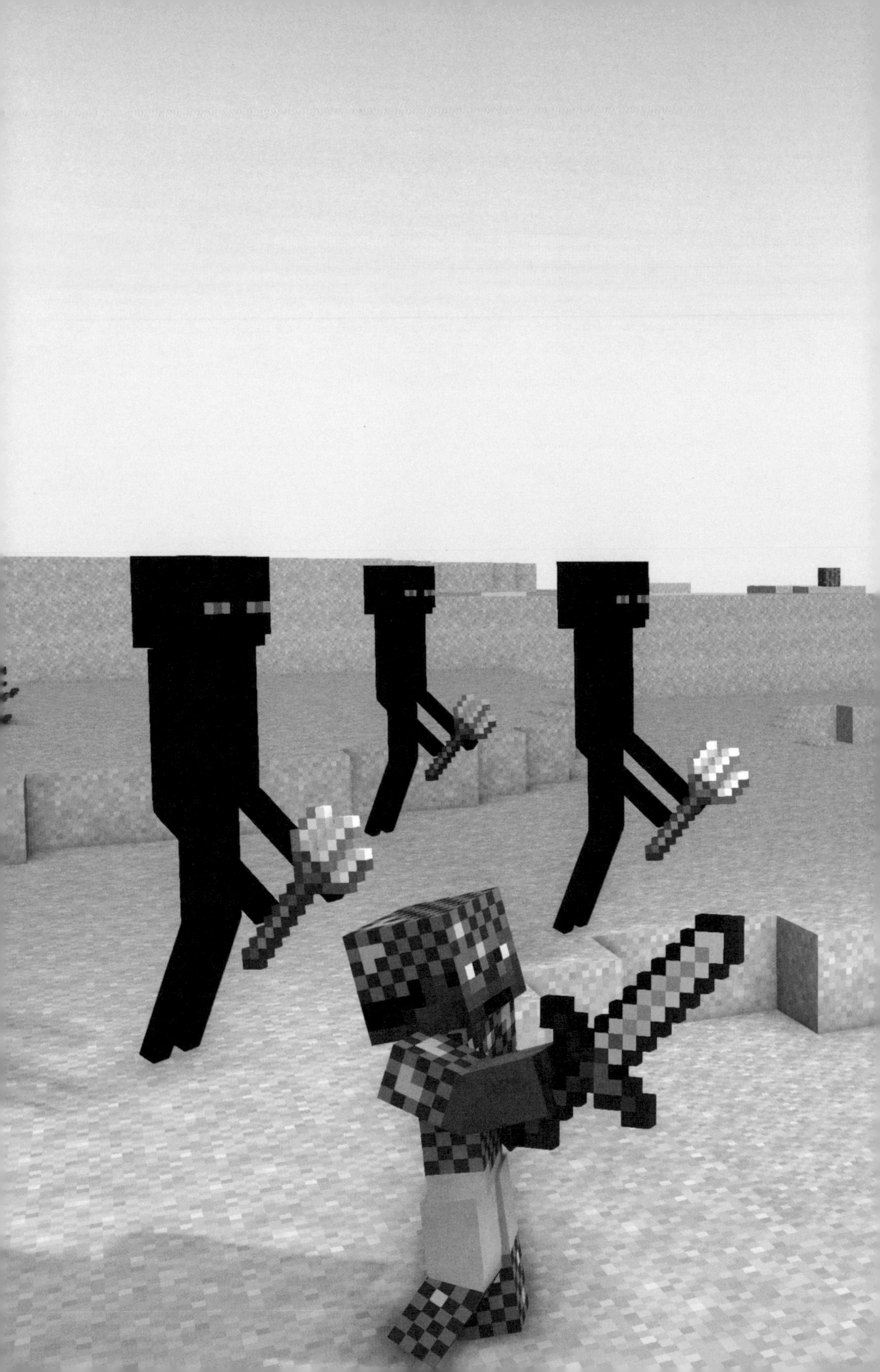

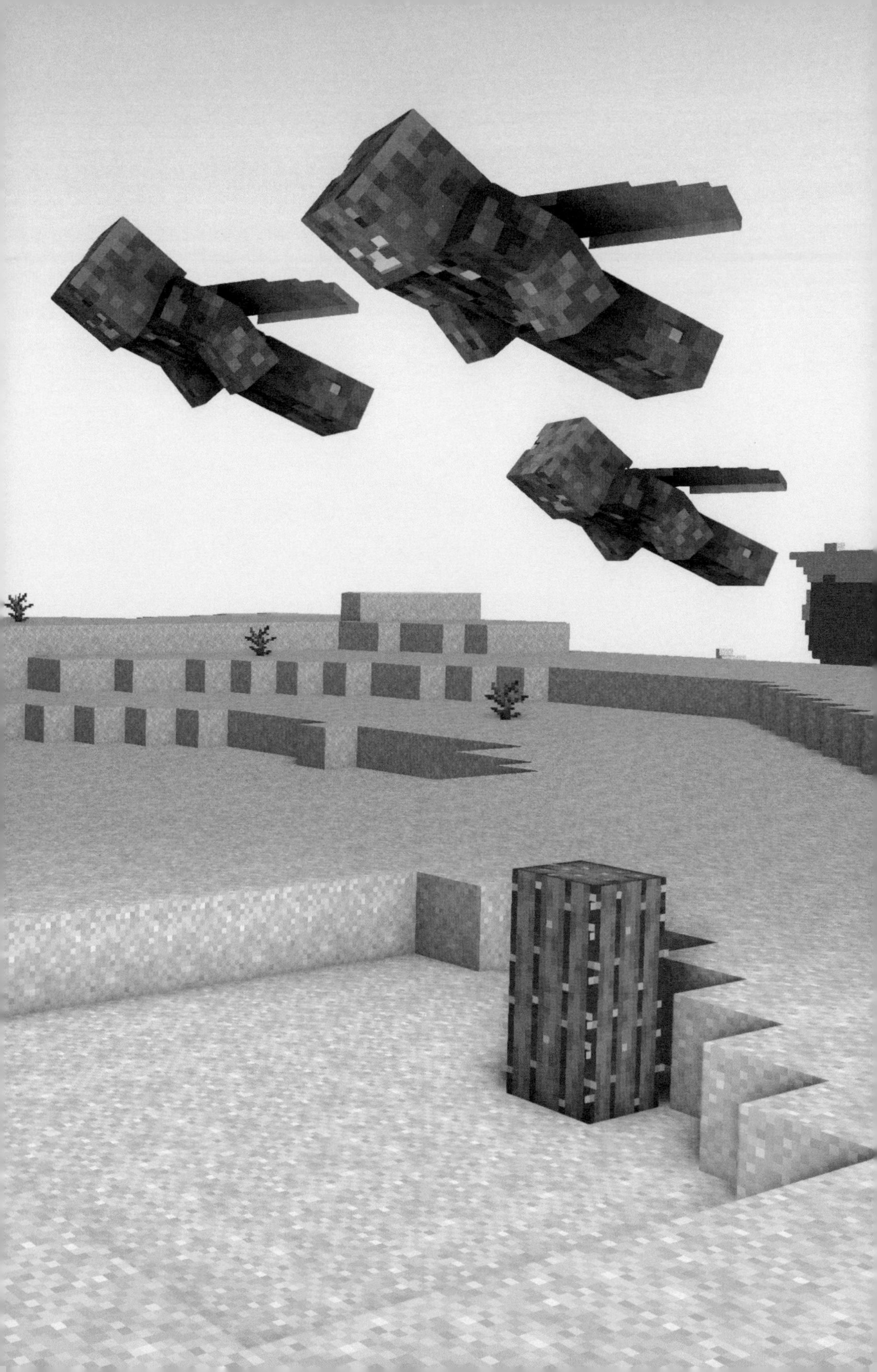

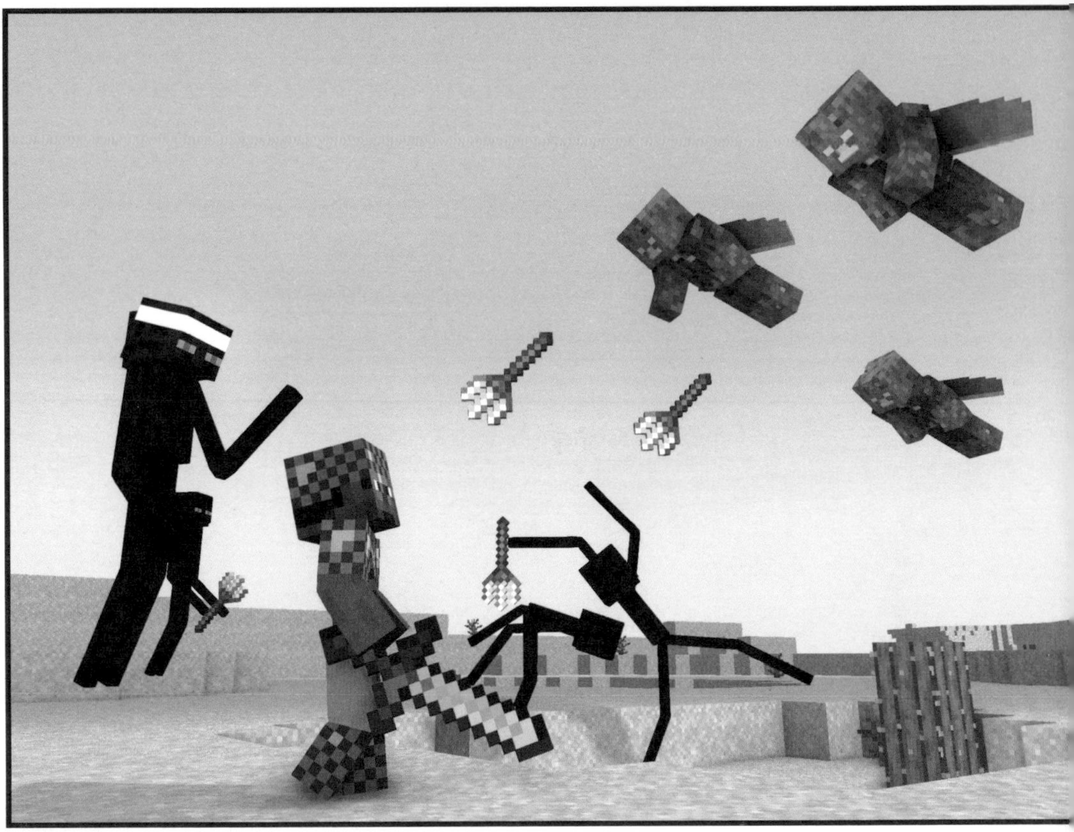

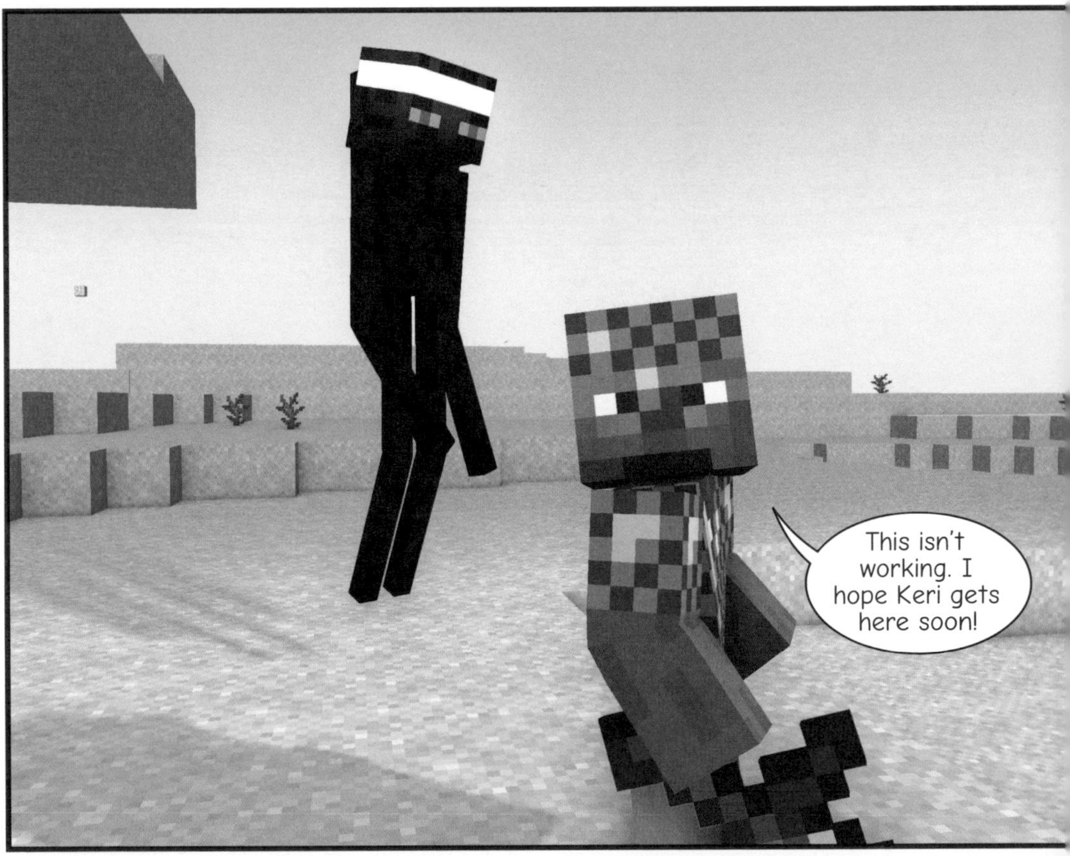
This isn't working. I hope Keri gets here soon!

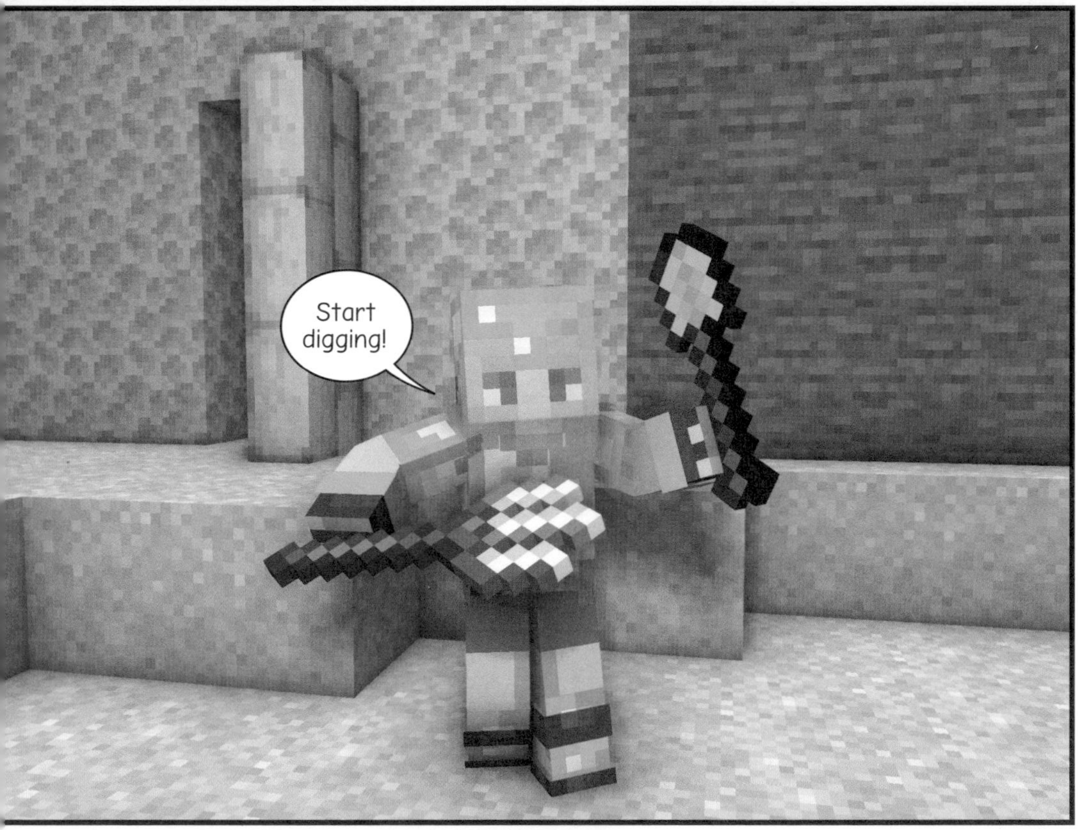
Start digging!

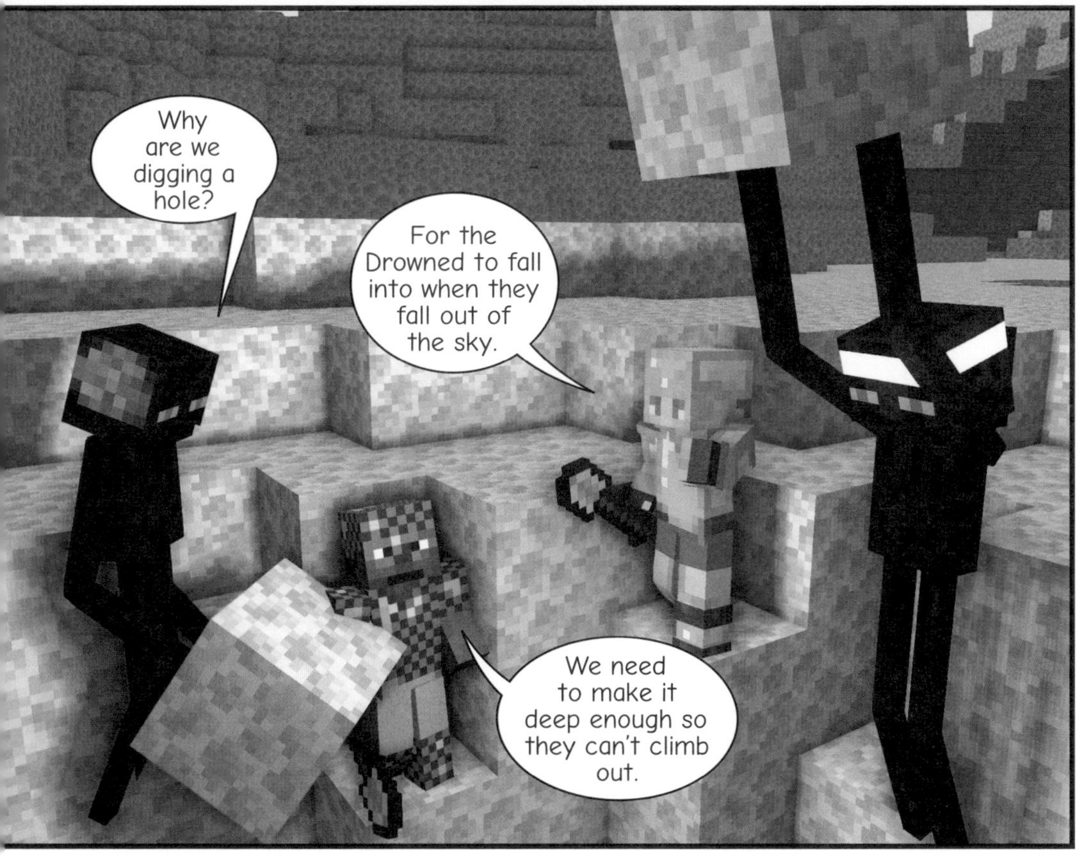
Why are we digging a hole?
For the Drowned to fall into when they fall out of the sky.
We need to make it deep enough so they can't climb out.

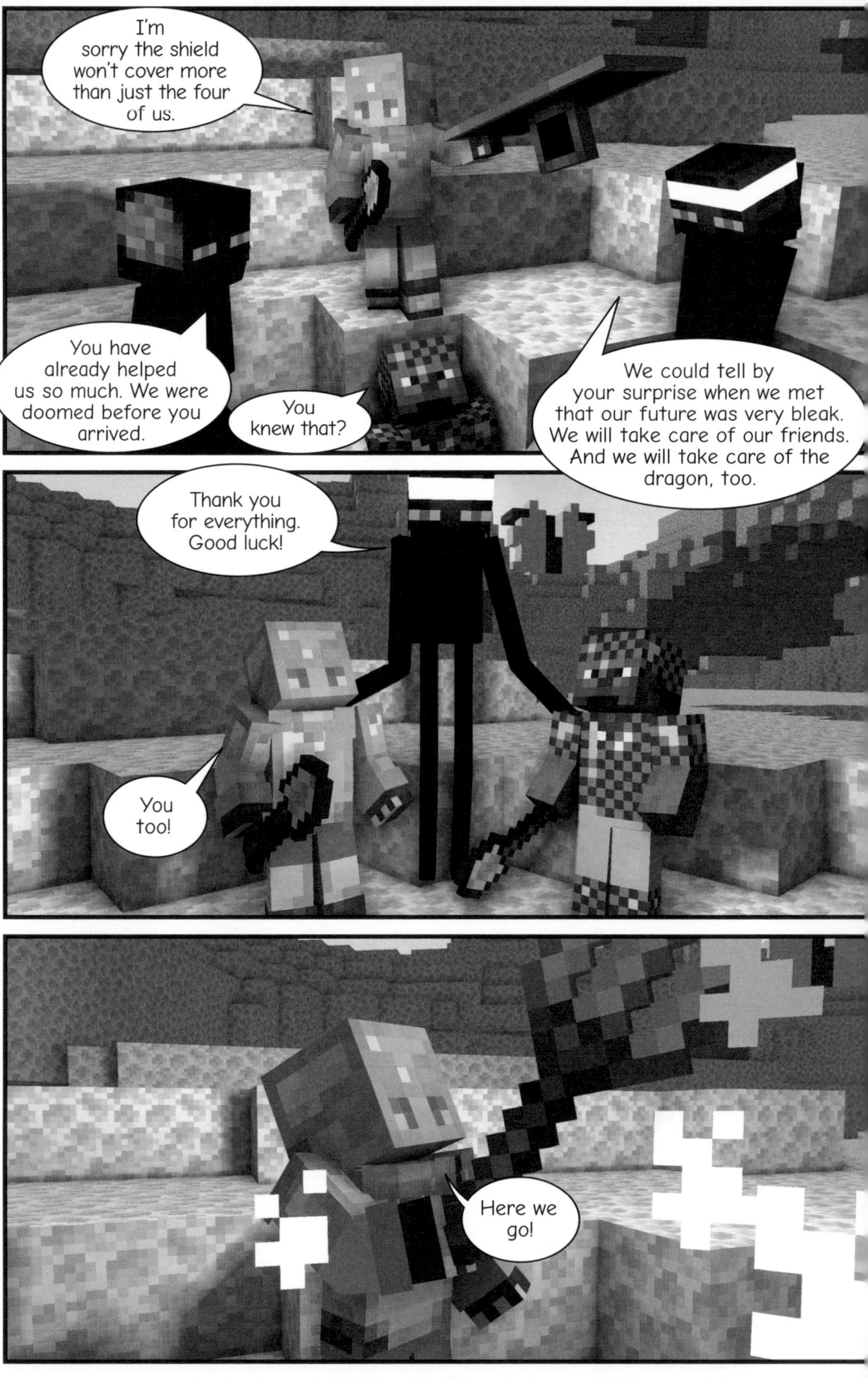
I'm sorry the shield won't cover more than just the four of us.
You have already helped us so much. We were doomed before you arrived.
You knew that?
We could tell by your surprise when we met that our future was very bleak. We will take care of our friends. And we will take care of the dragon, too.
Thank you for everything. Good luck!
You too!
Here we go!

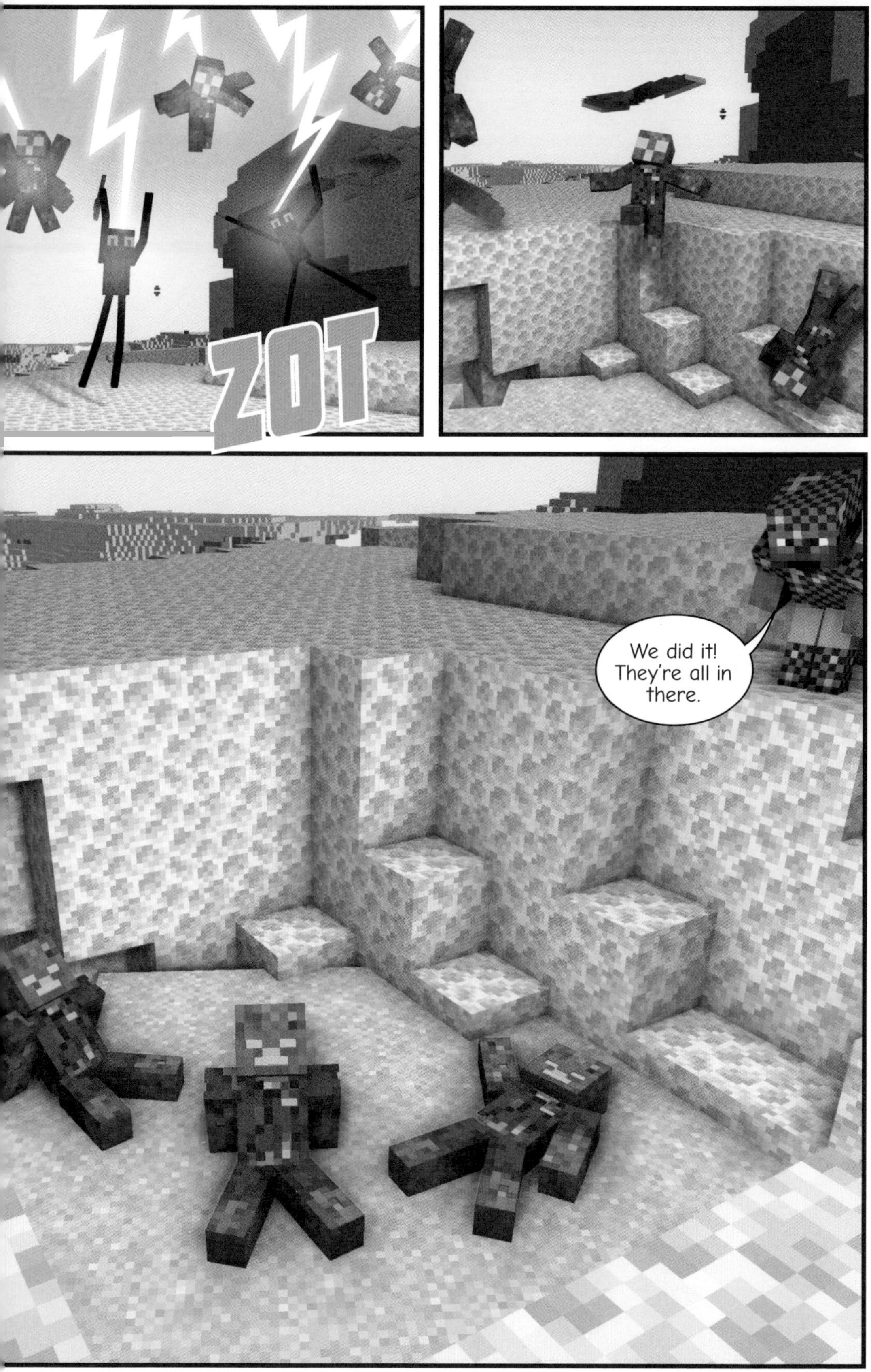
ZOT
We did it! They're all in there.

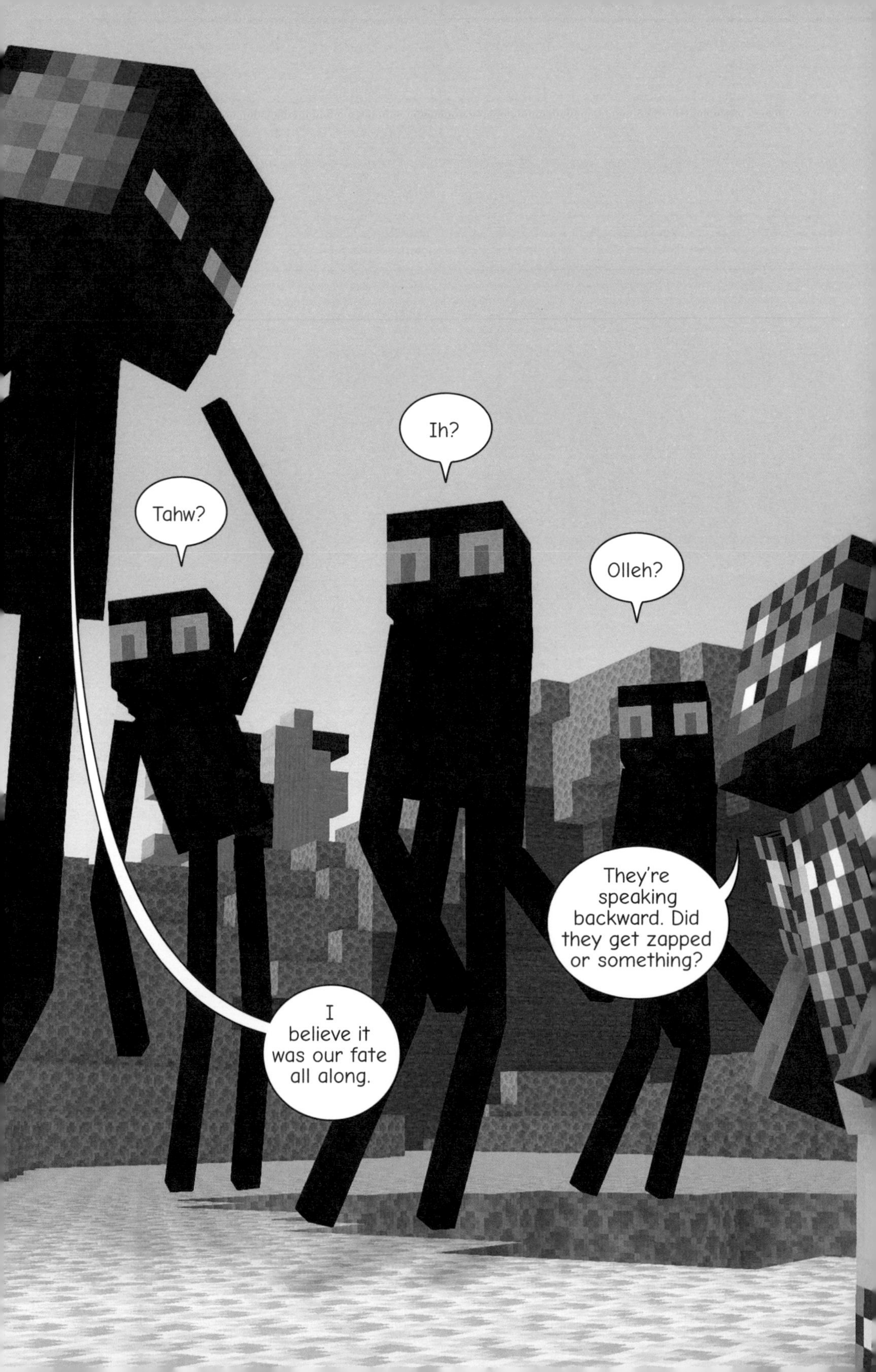
Tahw?
Ih?
Olleh?
They're speaking backward. Did they get zapped or something?
I believe it was our fate all along.

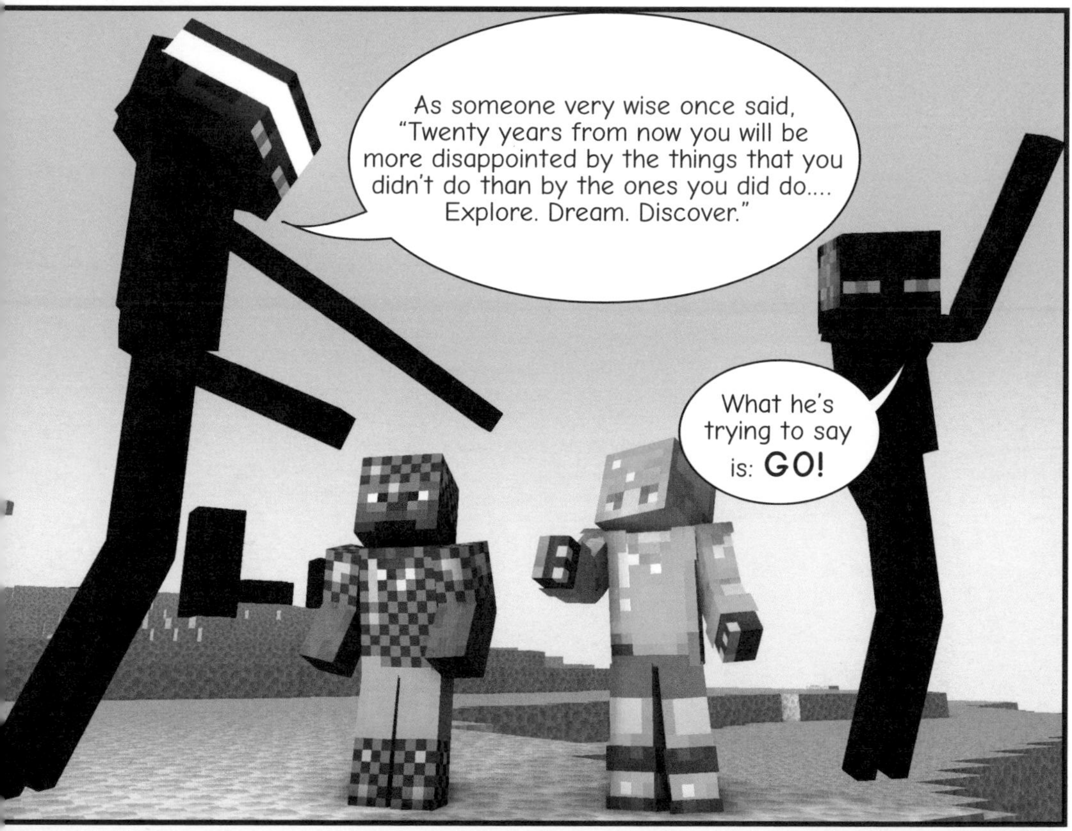
As someone very wise once said, "Twenty years from now you will be more disappointed by the things that you didn't do than by the ones you did do.... Explore. Dream. Discover."
What he's trying to say is: **GO!**

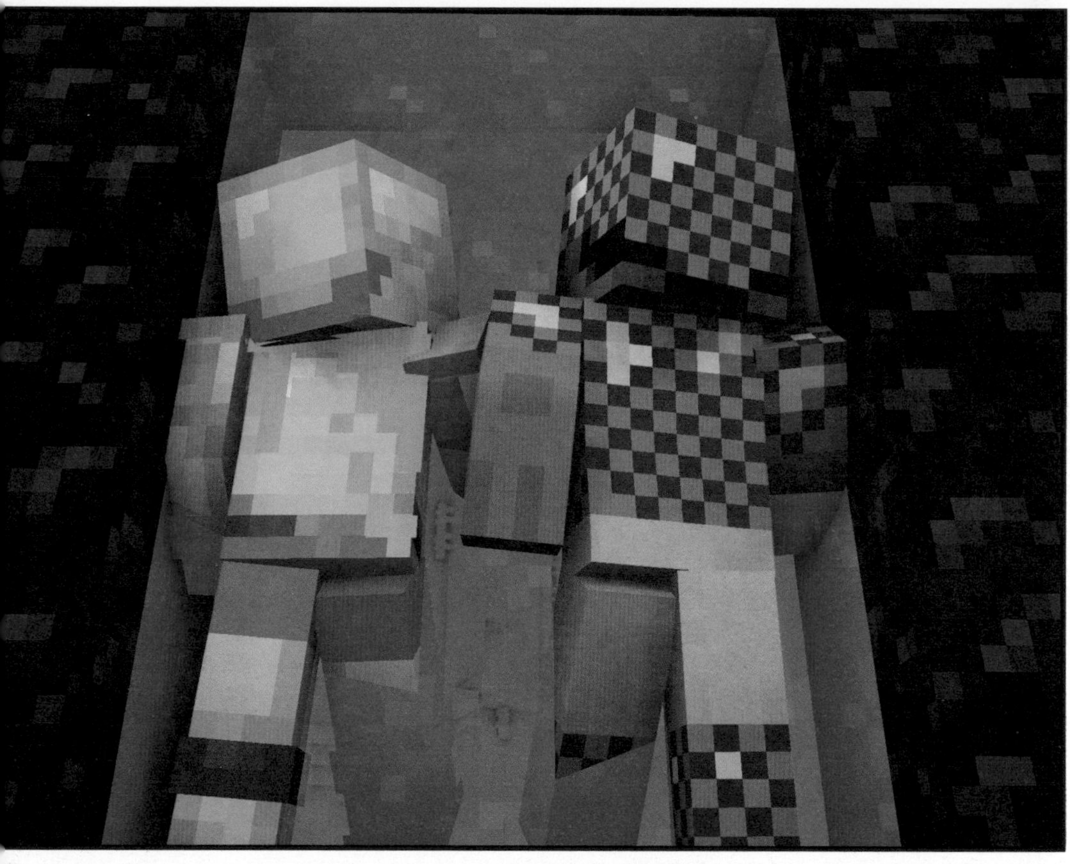

CHAPTER 13
HOME AT LAST

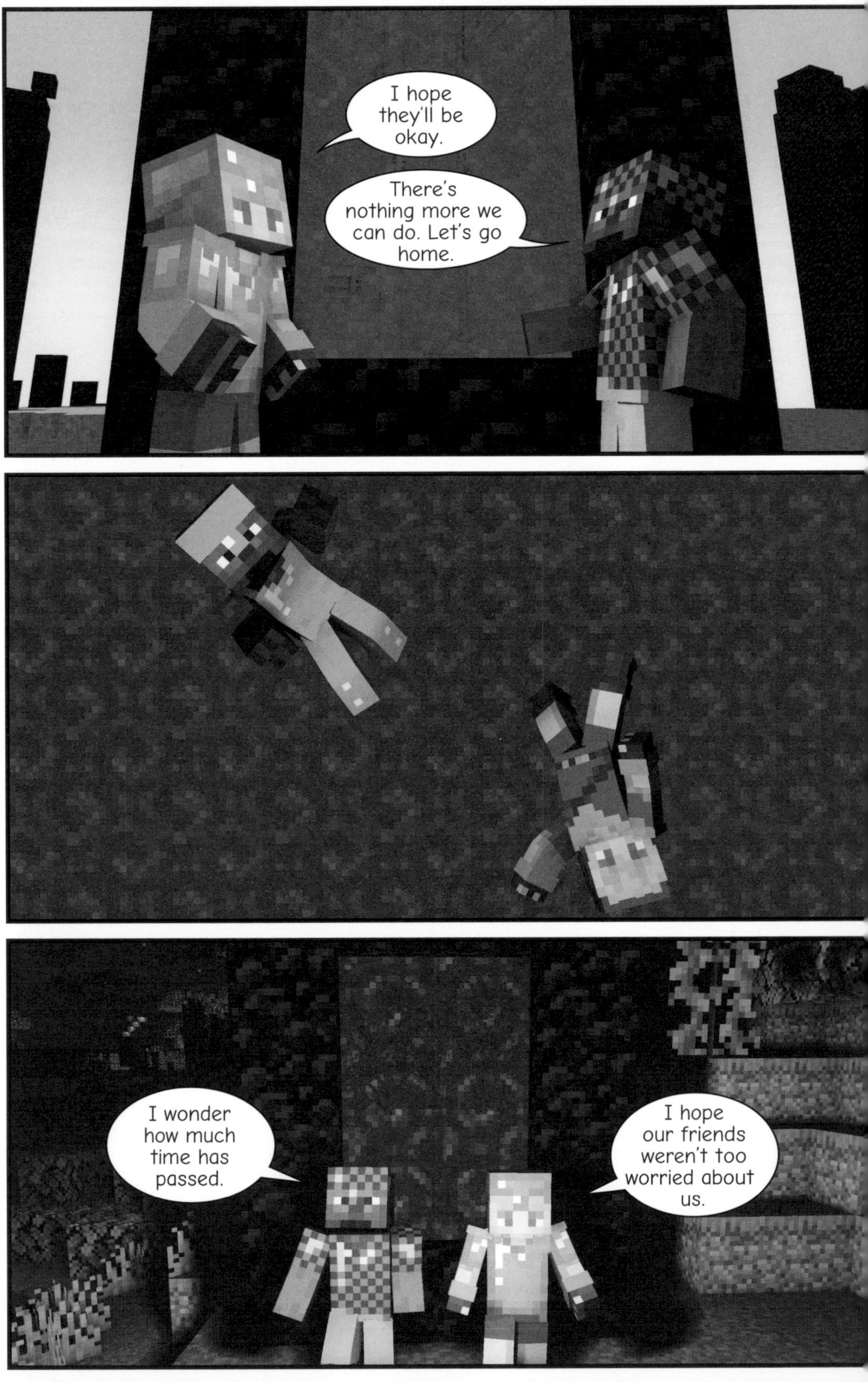
I hope they'll be okay.
There's nothing more we can do. Let's go home.
I wonder how much time has passed.
I hope our friends weren't too worried about us.

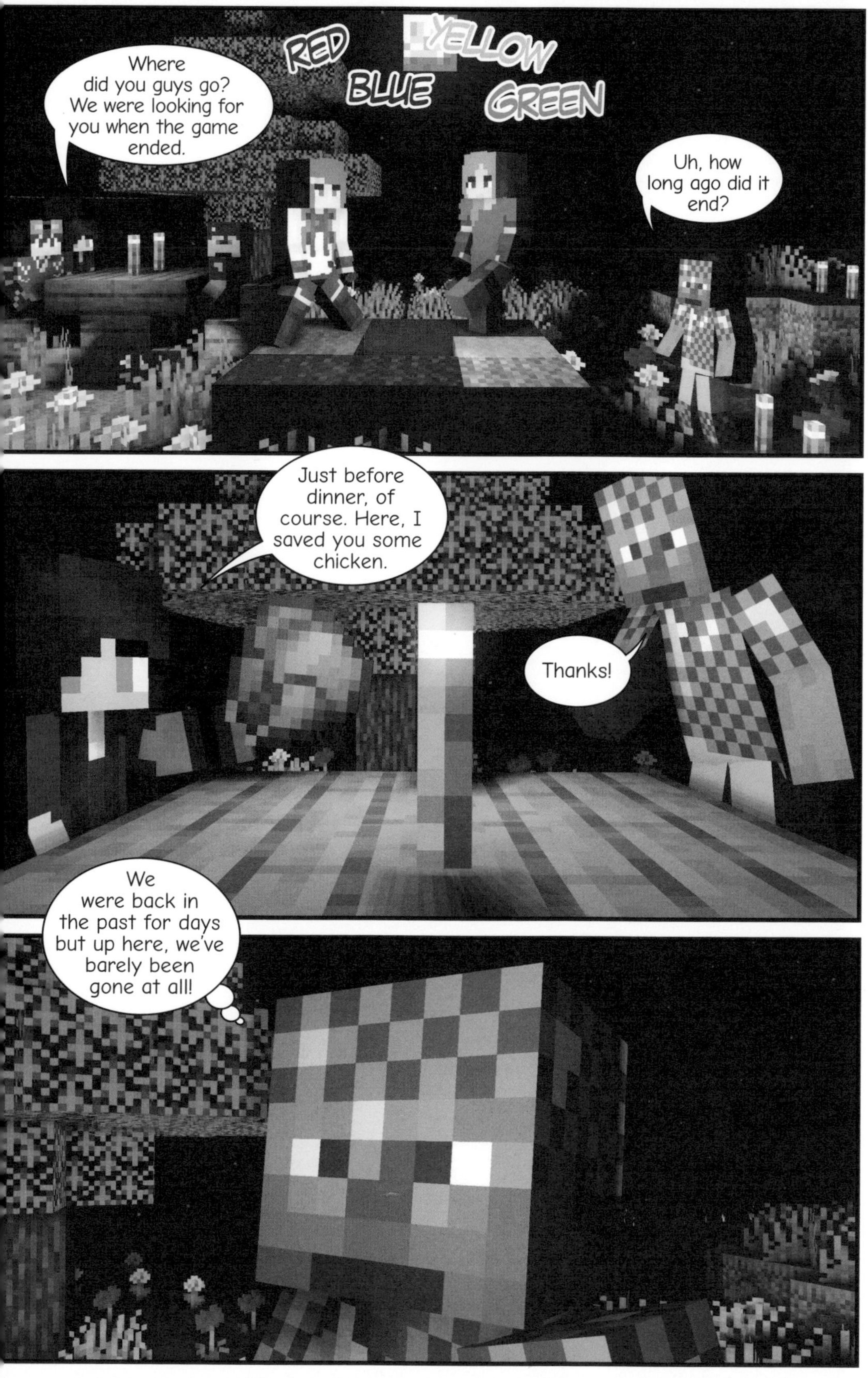
RED
YELLOW
BLUE
GREEN
Where did you guys go? We were looking for you when the game ended.
Uh, how long ago did it end?
Just before dinner, of course. Here, I saved you some chicken.
Thanks!
We were back in the past for days but up here, we've barely been gone at all!

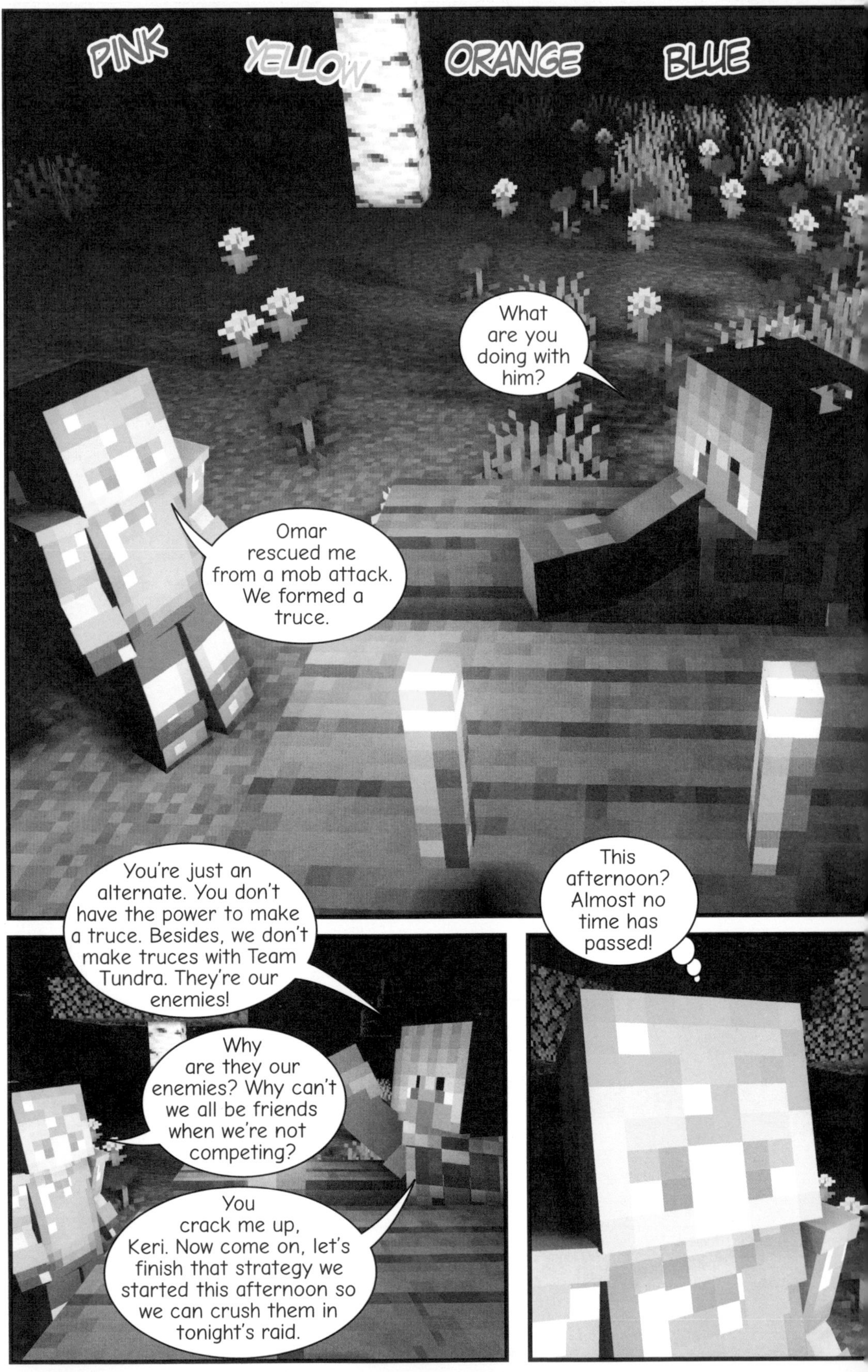
PINK
YELLOW
ORANGE
BLUE
What are you doing with him?
Omar rescued me from a mob attack. We formed a truce.
You're just an alternate. You don't have the power to make a truce. Besides, we don't make truces with Team Tundra. They're our enemies!
Why are they our enemies? Why can't we all be friends when we're not competing?
You crack me up, Keri. Now come on, let's finish that strategy we started this afternoon so we can crush them in tonight's raid.
This afternoon? Almost no time has passed!

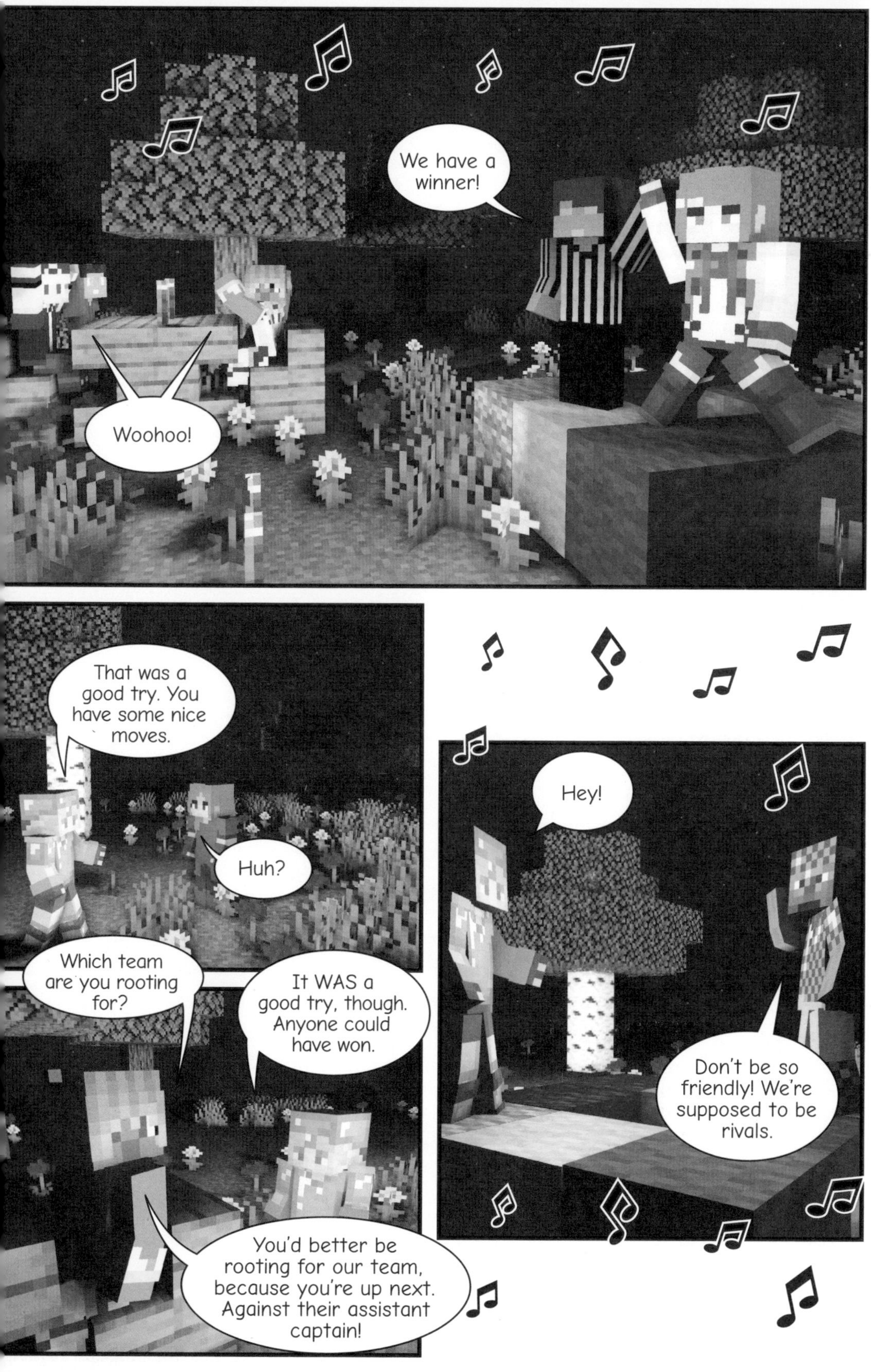
We have a winner!
Woohoo!
That was a good try. You have some nice moves.
Huh?
Which team are you rooting for?
It WAS a good try, though. Anyone could have won.
You'd better be rooting for our team, because you're up next. Against their assistant captain!
Hey!
Don't be so friendly! We're supposed to be rivals.

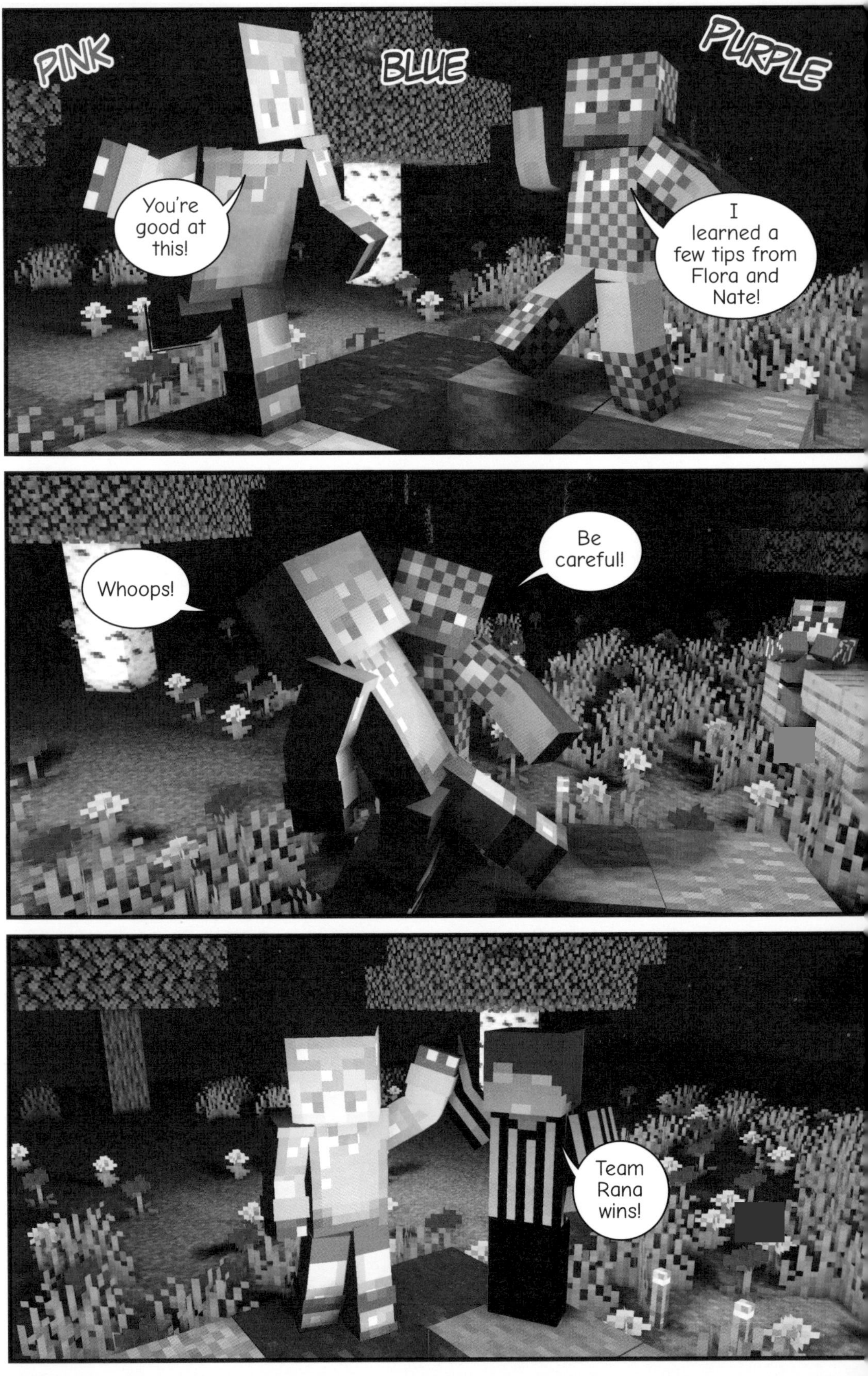
PINK
BLUE
PURPLE
You're good at this!
I learned a few tips from Flora and Nate!
Whoops!
Be careful!
Team Rana wins!

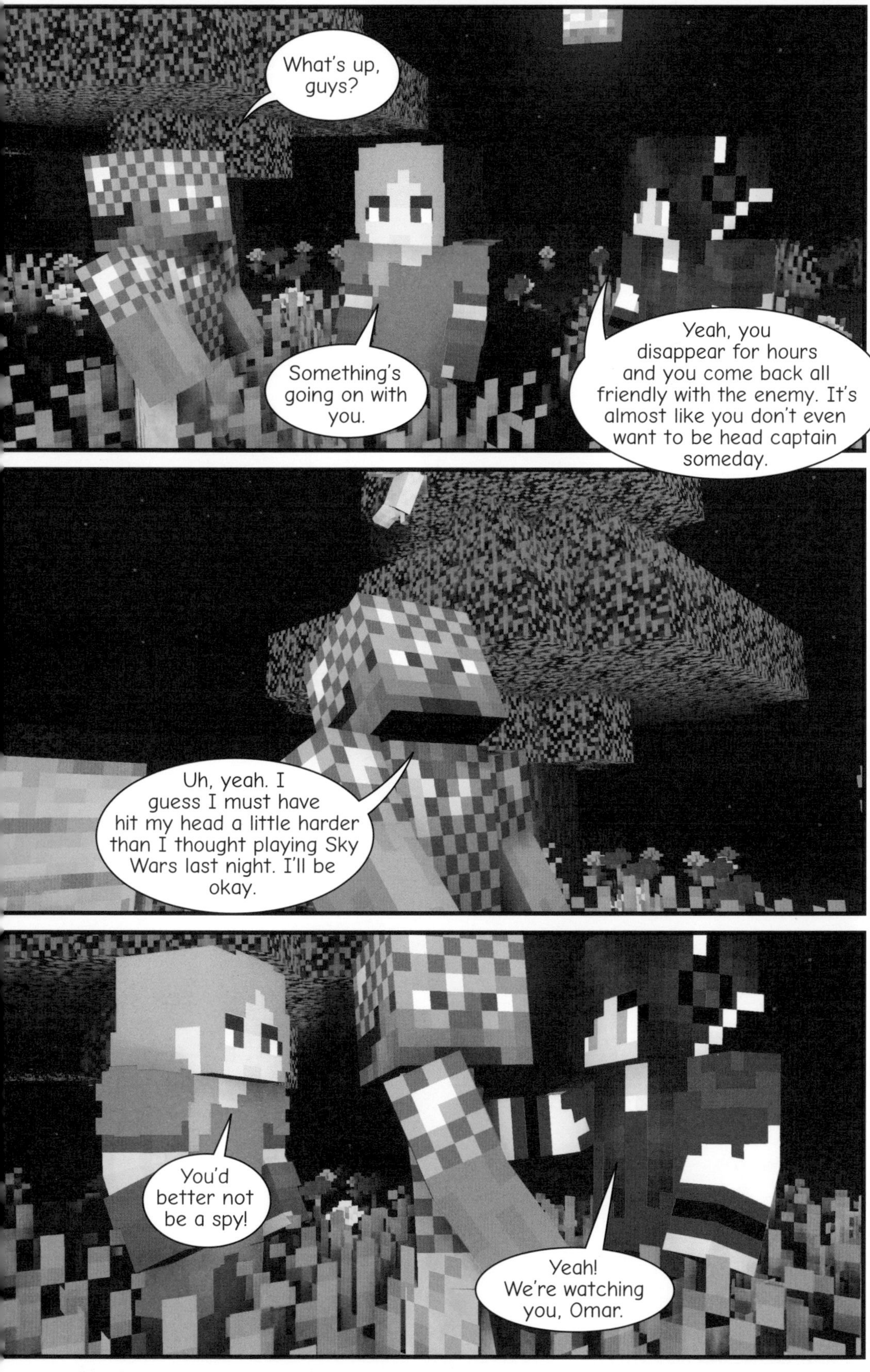
What's up, guys?
Something's going on with you.
Yeah, you disappear for hours and you come back all friendly with the enemy. It's almost like you don't even want to be head captain someday.
Uh, yeah. I guess I must have hit my head a little harder than I thought playing Sky Wars last night. I'll be okay.
You'd better not be a spy!
Yeah! We're watching you, Omar.

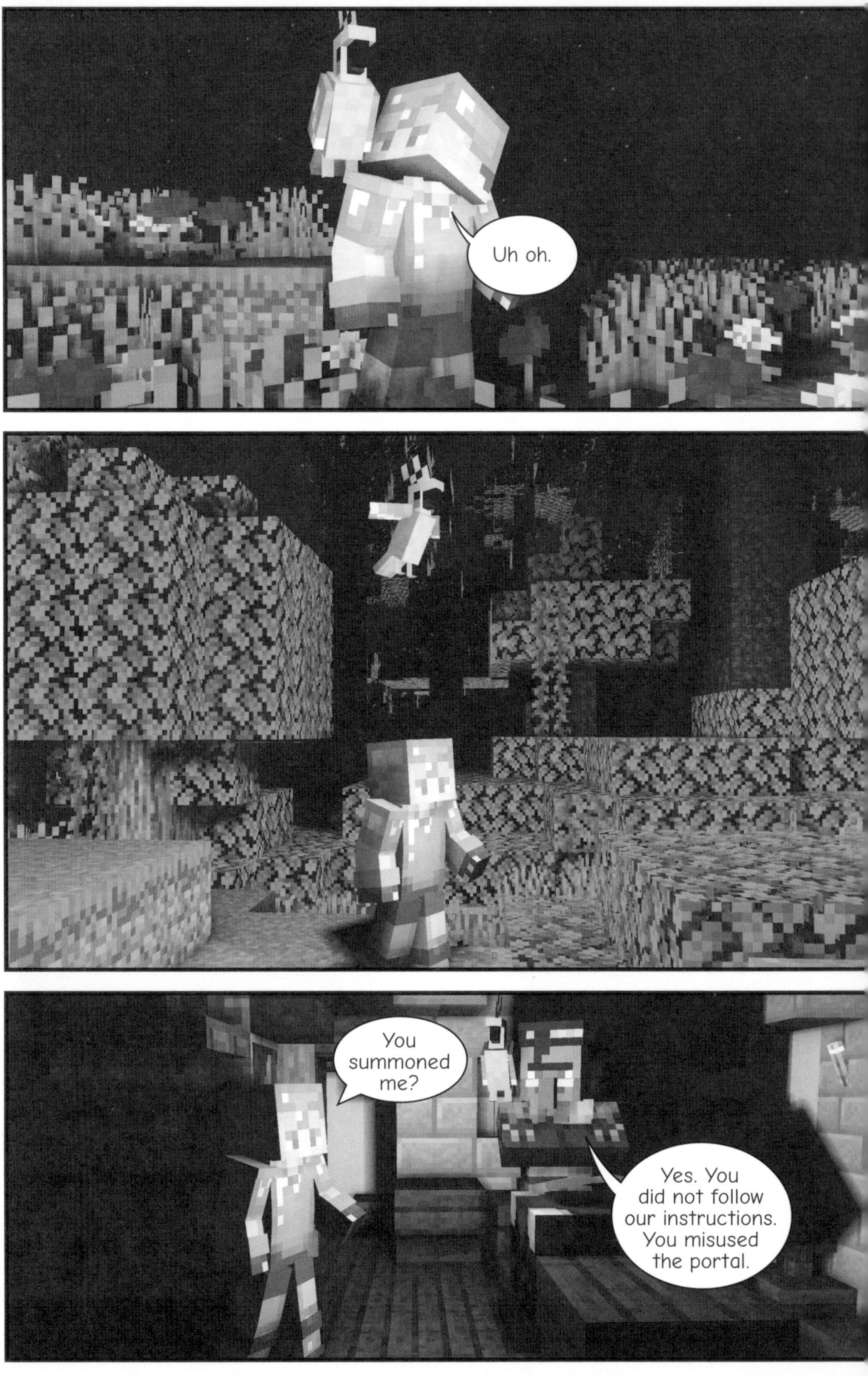
Uh oh.
You summoned me?
Yes. You did not follow our instructions. You misused the portal.

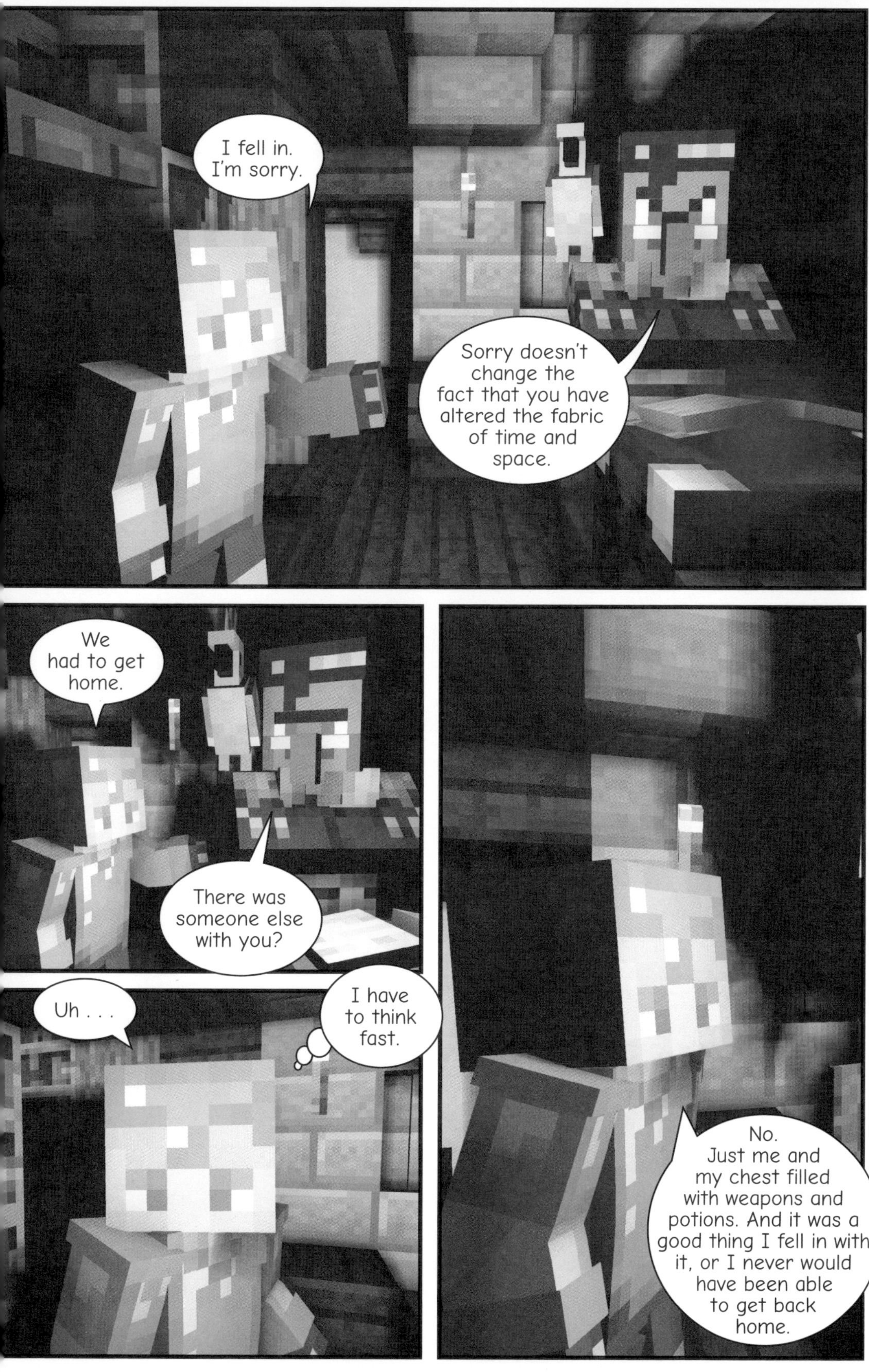

I fell in. I'm sorry.
Sorry doesn't change the fact that you have altered the fabric of time and space.
We had to get home.
There was someone else with you?
Uh . . .
I have to think fast.
No. Just me and my chest filled with weapons and potions. And it was a good thing I fell in with it, or I never would have been able to get back home.

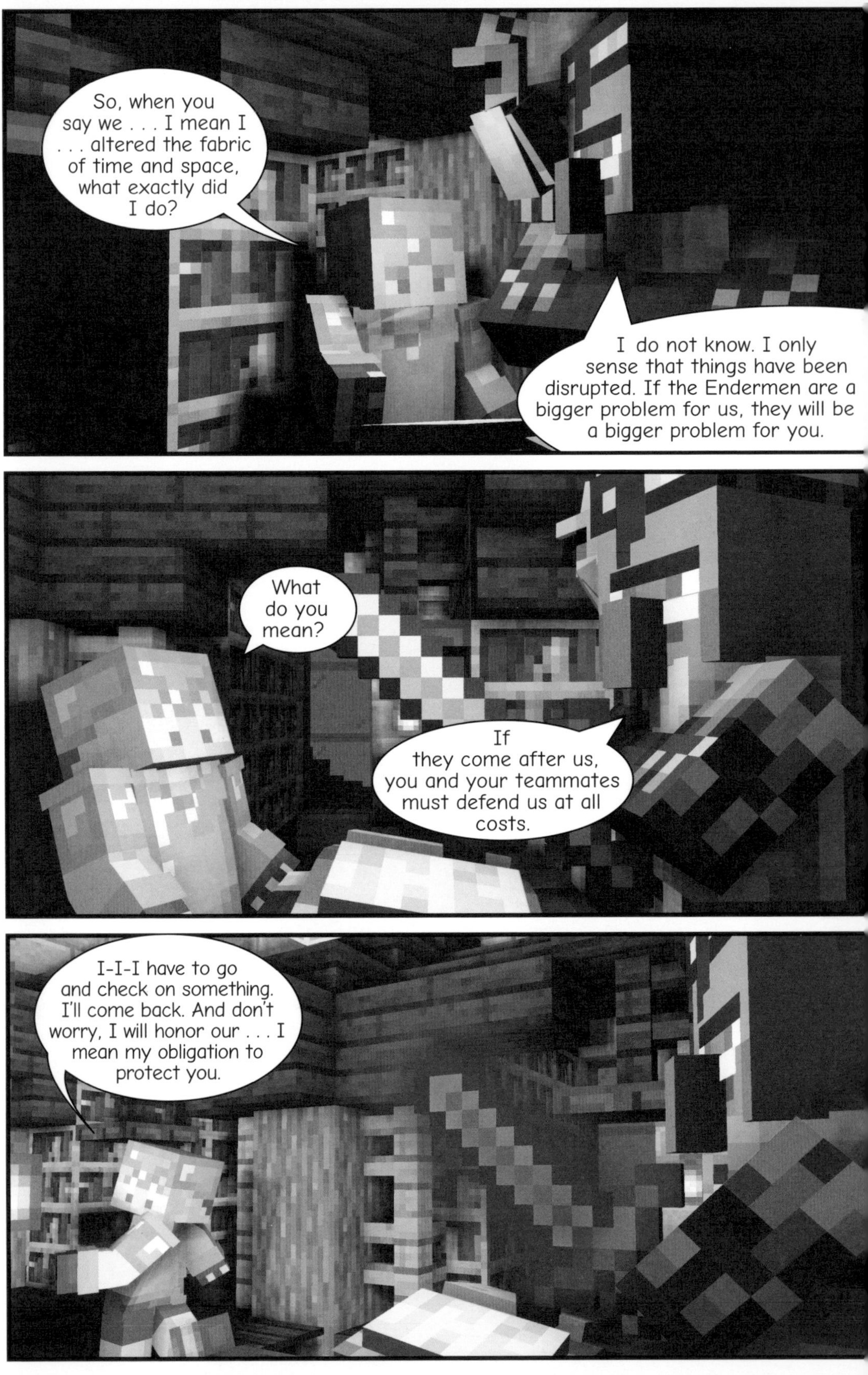
So, when you say we . . . I mean I . . . altered the fabric of time and space, what exactly did I do?
I do not know. I only sense that things have been disrupted. If the Endermen are a bigger problem for us, they will be a bigger problem for you.
What do you mean?
If they come after us, you and your teammates must defend us at all costs.
I-I-I have to go and check on something. I'll come back. And don't worry, I will honor our . . . I mean my obligation to protect you.

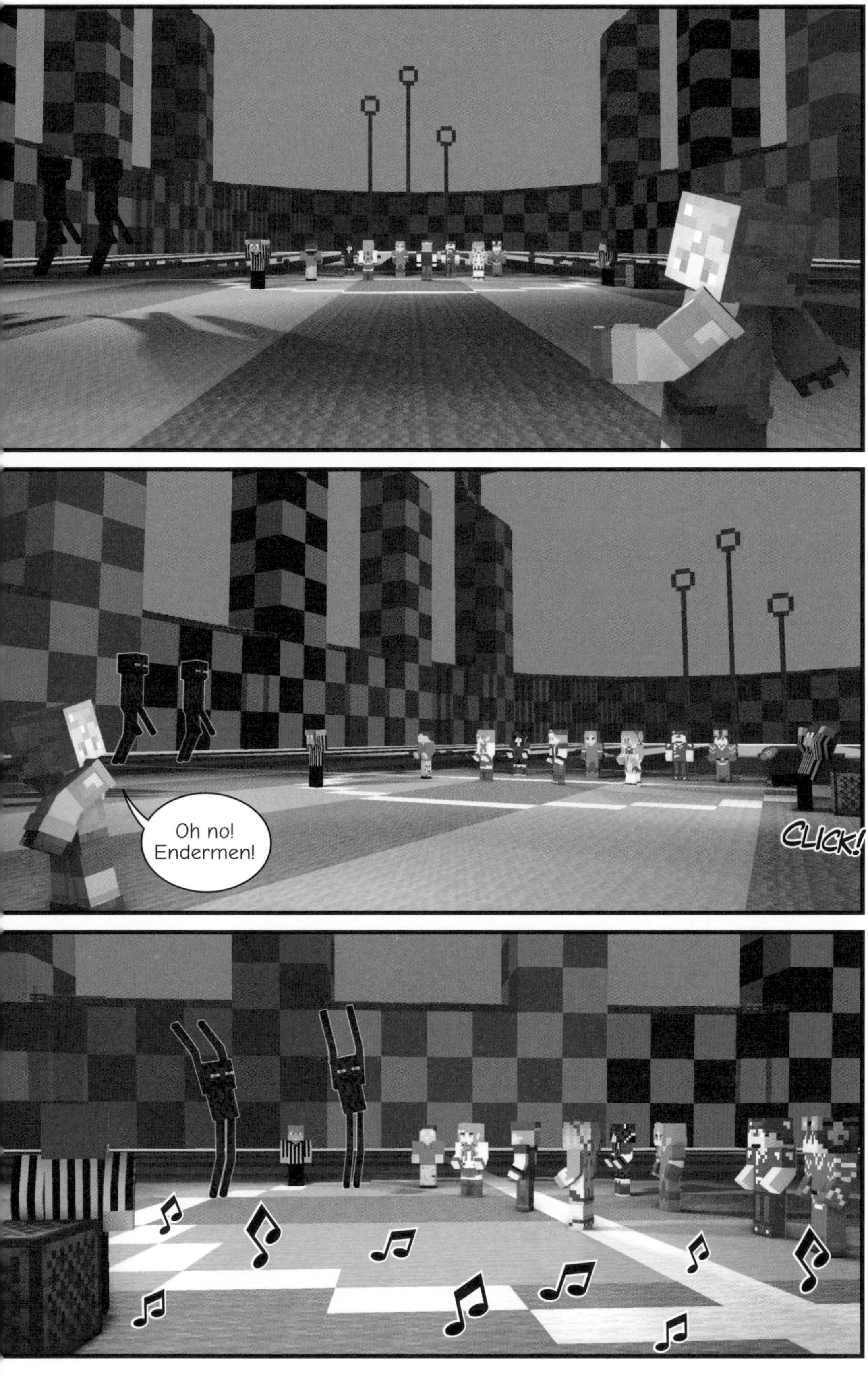
Oh no! Endermen!
CLICK!

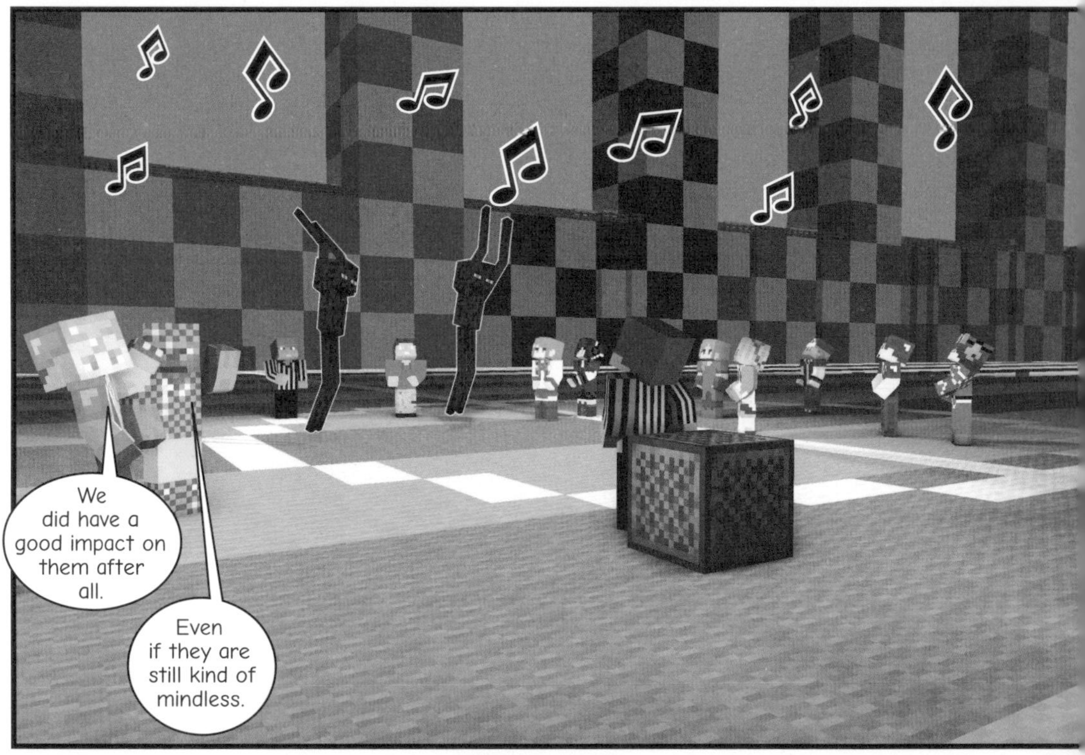
We did have a good impact on them after all.
Even if they are still kind of mindless.

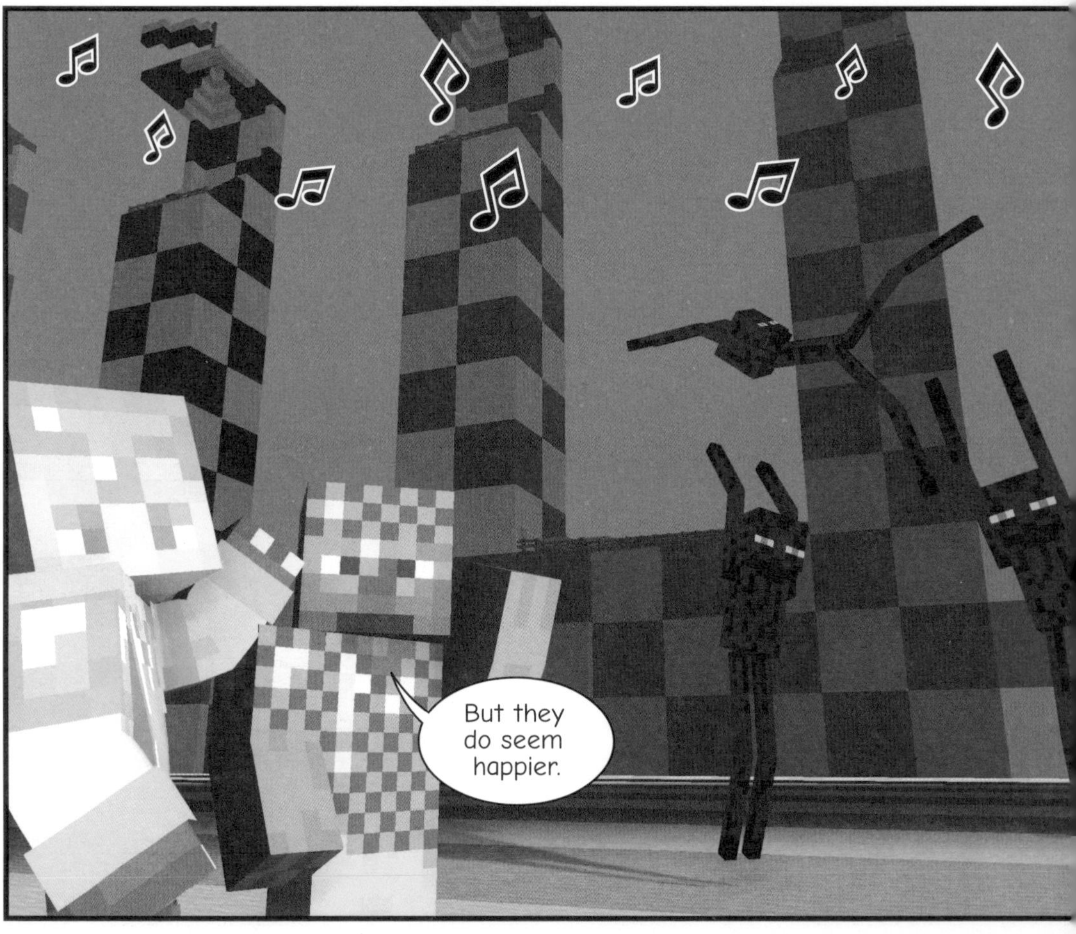
But they do seem happier.

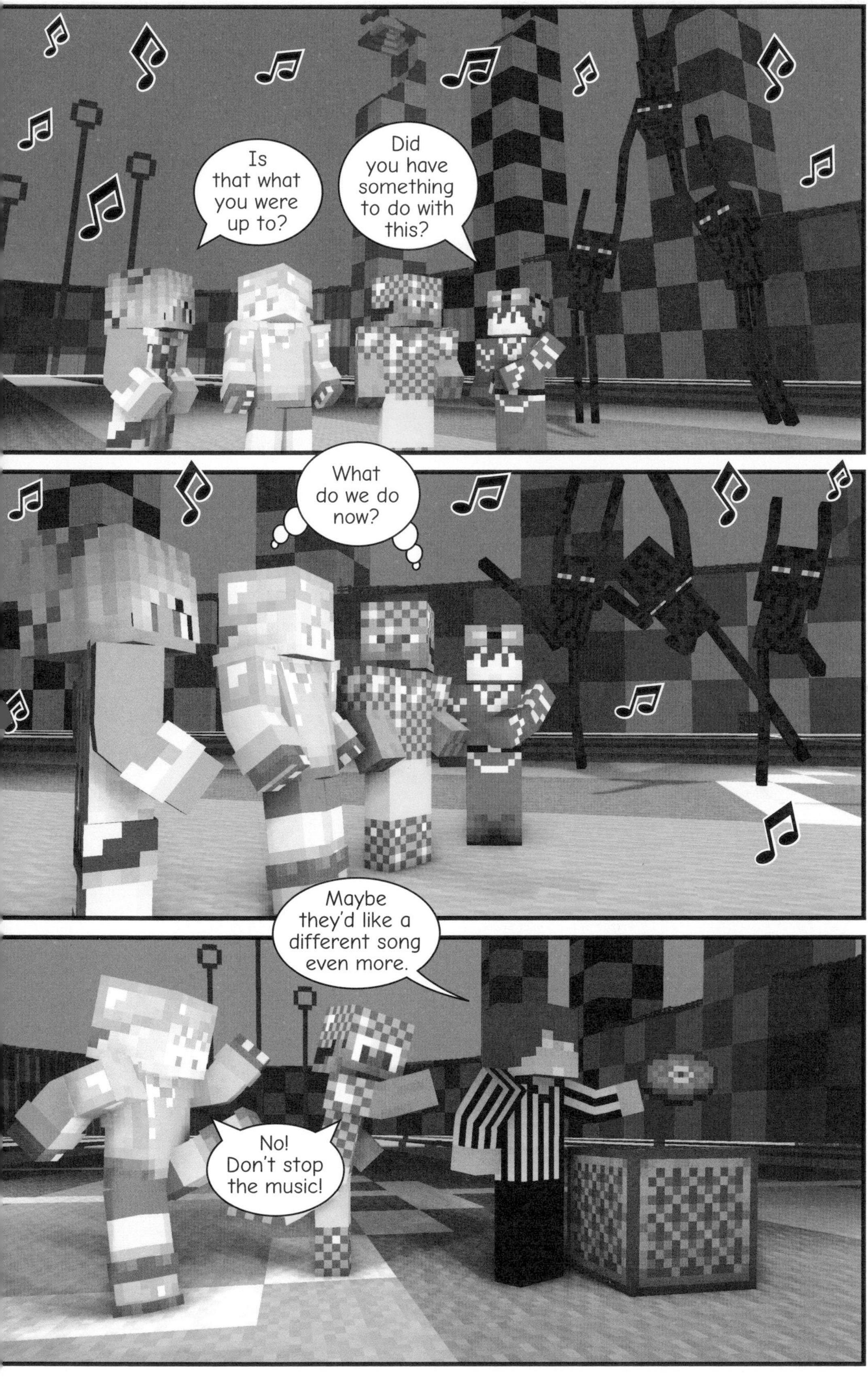
Is that what you were up to?
Did you have something to do with this?
What do we do now?
Maybe they'd like a different song even more.
No! Don't stop the music!

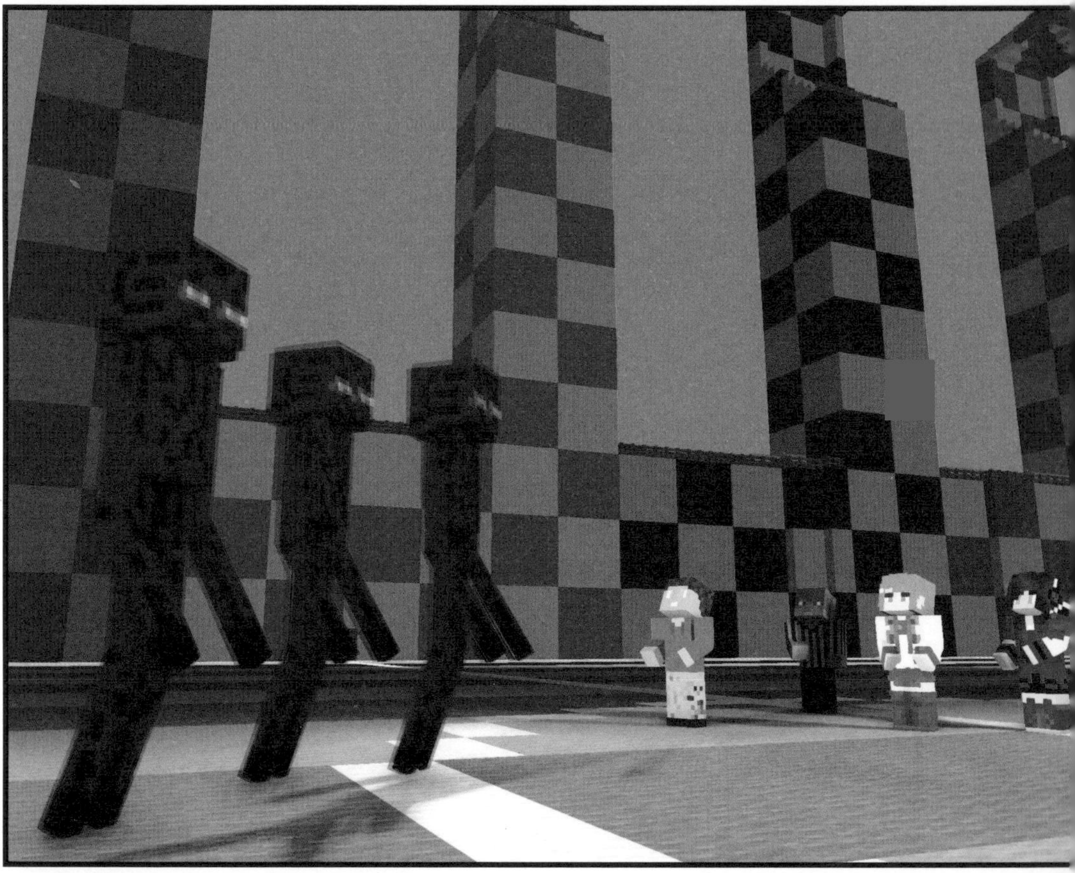

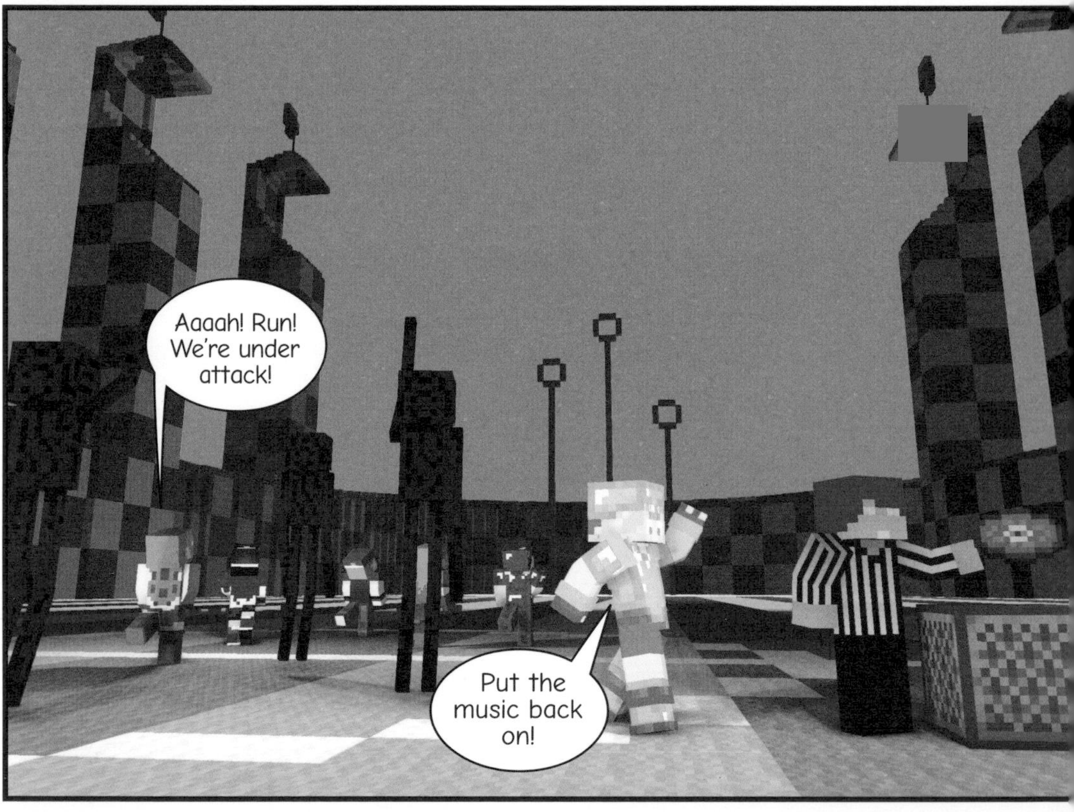
Aaaah! Run! We're under attack!
Put the music back on!

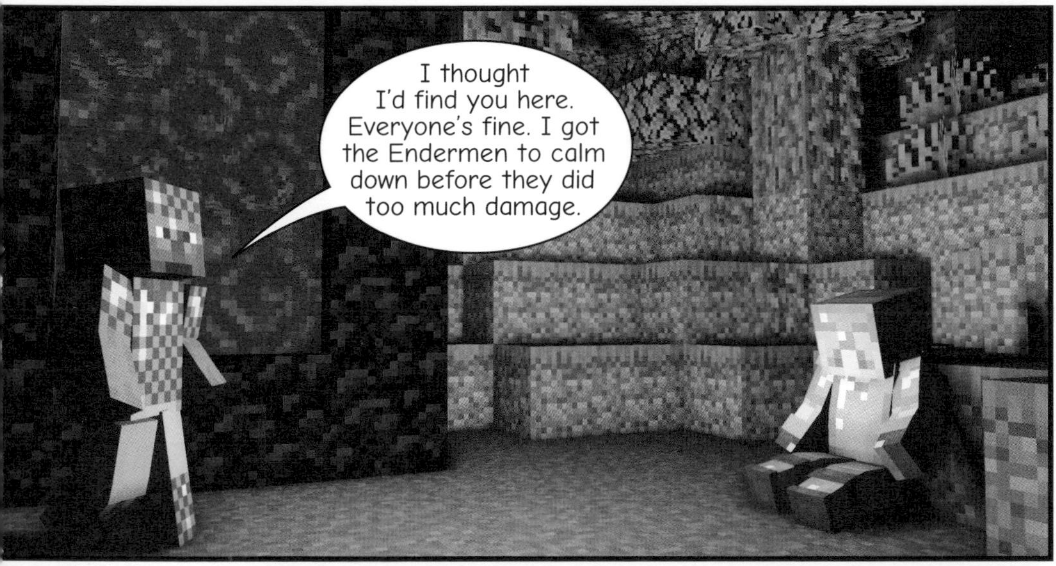
I thought I'd find you here. Everyone's fine. I got the Endermen to calm down before they did too much damage.

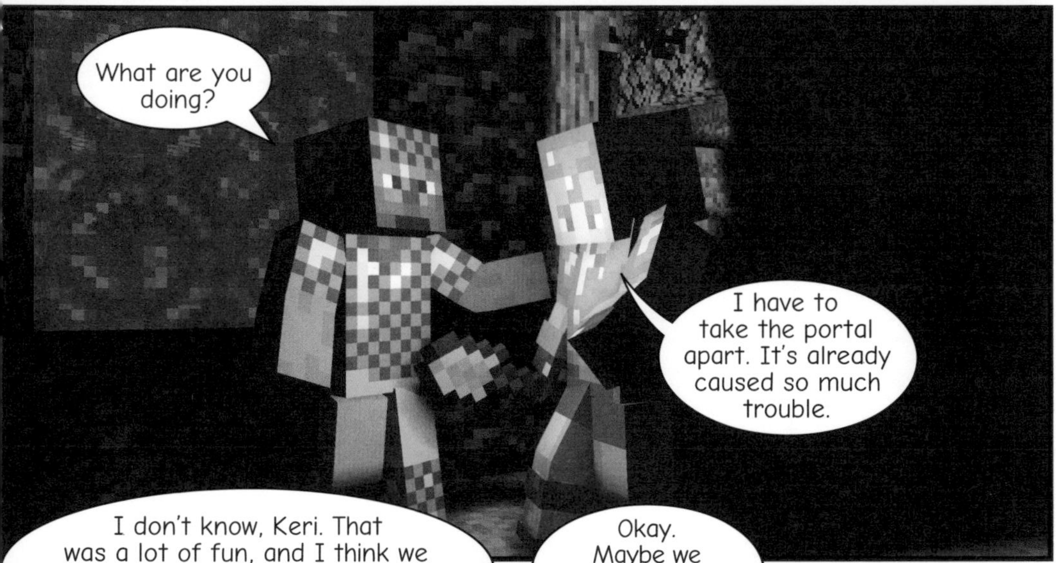
What are you doing?
I have to take the portal apart. It's already caused so much trouble.

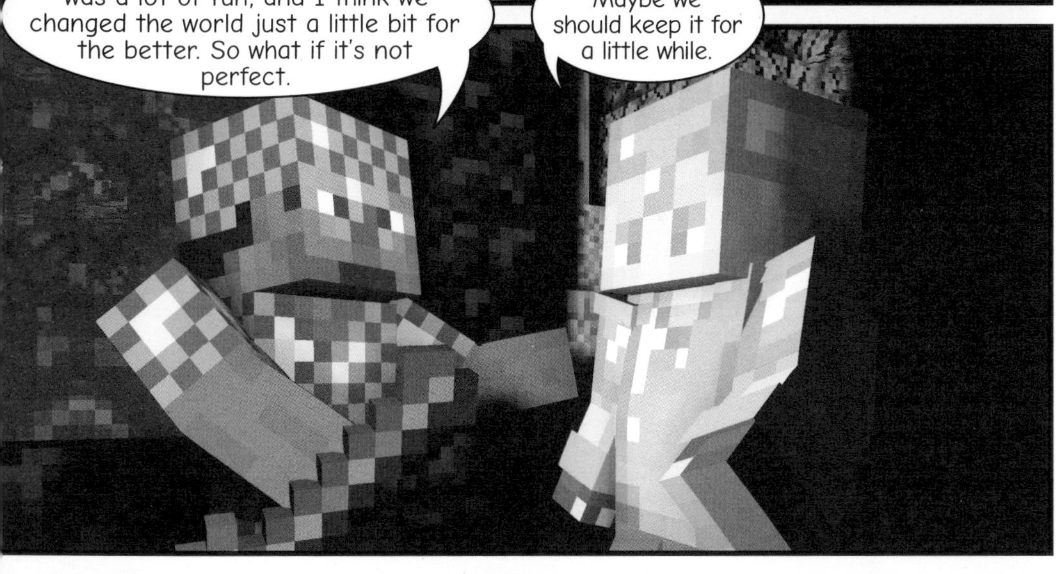
I don't know, Keri. That was a lot of fun, and I think we changed the world just a little bit for the better. So what if it's not perfect.
Okay. Maybe we should keep it for a little while.

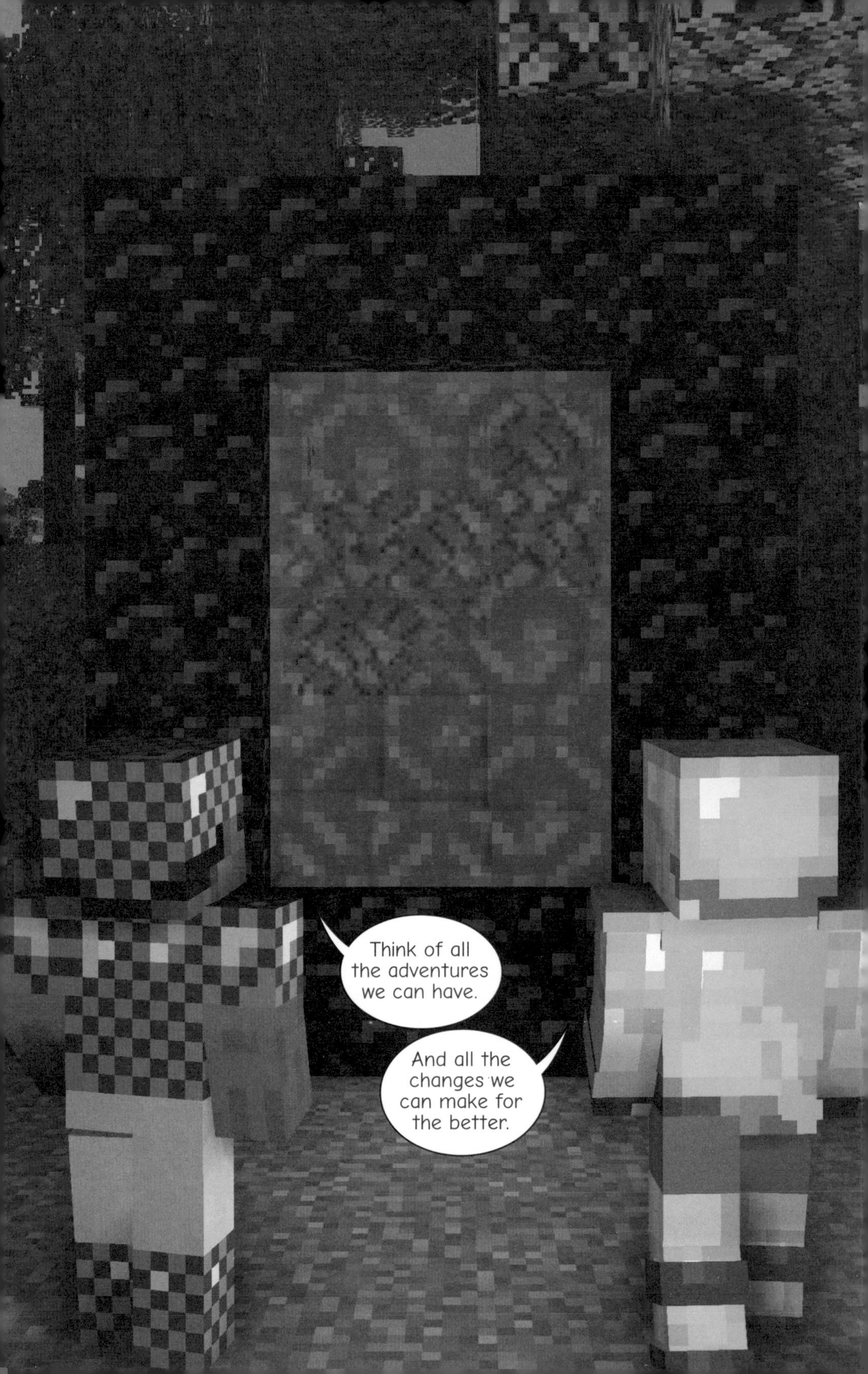
Think of all the adventures we can have.
And all the changes we can make for the better.